Murder in Two Parts

By

Patrick Finneran

ISBN: 1-4033-8330-8 (e-book)
ISBN: 1-4033-8331-6 (Paperback)
ISBN: 1-4033-8332-4 (Dust Jacket)

This book is printed on acid free paper.

1stBooks – rev. 11/20/02

For Dorothy

Acknowledgements

Many good people have played a large part in the creation of this effort. My special thanks to Captain Dennis Hawkins former head of the Indianapolis Police Department's Homicide & Robbery Branch, Doctor Dennis Nichols former Marion County (Indiana) County Coroner, Narcotics detectives whom I am not at liberty to name—they will know who they are, Wilson W. Wright, Executive Director, Chris-Craft Antique Boat Club, Tallahassee, Florida. A very special acknowledgment for the invaluable assistance of my long time friend, and sharp eyed proofreader, Ed Eckstein. To these very special people and others, my deepest gratitude.

Friday, 3:45 p.m.

The Windom Towers

He held the blood soaked towels away from his naked body as he walked quickly from the master bedroom to the bath just down the hall. Brushing the shower curtain aside with his forearm, he reached inside the tub and dropped the pile just in front of the drain. From the bathroom closet, he selected a clean wash cloth and returned to the master bedroom to retrieve the tools of his trade, wrapping them in the cloth and returning to the bathroom, he laid the cloth with its bloody contents in the ornate marble sink and returned to the tub where he turned on the single, water mixer control, carefully adjusting the water temperature–not too hot, not too cold. When he was satisfied, he swiveled the water selector from the bath spigot to the shower head. Taking care not to touch any part of the tub or walls, he stepped in and stood beneath the running water, both feet carefully placed on the pile of bloody bath towels. He let the pounding water wash his body clean of all traces of blood. No soap, no rubbing–eliminating the chances of leaving behind any traces of his skin. He'd pretty much solved the problem of body hair by using a highly effective depilatory cream he purchased in a Hollywood department store. He smiled to himself as he fantasized police evidence technicians' frustration at finding nothing. He'd employed this clean up technique several times in recent years, and it had proven a success–leaving him beyond detection.

When he could see no more traces of blood on his body, he shut off the water and stepped from the tub onto a clean towel. When the soles of his feet were dry, he tossed the towel into the tub with the rest of the bloody towels and went into the living room to retrieve a large dopp kit from his airline, carry-on bag. Returning to the bathroom, he removed a can of Drano crystals from the kit. He unscrewed the cap, and leaning over the edge of the tub, he carefully poured about half the can's content into the drain. As the acrid smell rose and the foaming action began, he smiled with satisfaction. "Let them trace that!" Removing several sheets of toilet paper from the roll next to the stool, he began to carefully blot the water remaining on his skin. As each wad became soaked, he dropped it into the toilet. It took about half the roll to get his body nearly dry. He flushed the toilet, eliminating that link to his DNA.

Still damp, he searched the bath closet for something with which to complete the job–and leave no trace of his DNA. Catching sight of a hair dryer on the shelf, he'd found the answer. To further confuse any diligent police technician, he plugged the dryer in a hallway outlet and stood in the hall to dry himself. After several minutes of playing the warm air over his body–a sensation he found surprisingly pleasant–he was satisfied. In fact, it had proven so successful and sensuous he made a mental note to include a hair dryer as a permanent addition to his "tool kit".

Still naked, he carried the dopp kit and wash cloth that contained the surgical knives, which he'd used, to the kitchen, set them on the drain board next to the deep, stainless steel sink, and removed a velveteen, roll-up case with individual sleeves for each knife and surgical tool. He untied the binding ribbon, unrolled the case, and folded back the flap covering the sleeves. Taking great care not to cut or nick himself on the razor sharp blades, he unrolled the wash cloth and placed the knives and instruments he'd employed over the past several hours, in the bottom of the sink. He then washed each knife clean of all traces of blood. Using a tooth brush he carried for the task, he diligently brushed every nook and crevice clean. He then dried each instrument using the kitchen paper towels. Finally, he reached into his kit and withdrew a can of number 10 sewing machine oil, squeezed a few drops on a clean paper towel, and anointed each blade with the preserving oil. His clean up chores accomplished, he inserted each instrument into its designated sleeve, folded the flap over the tips of the instruments, and rolled the case into a tight package. As he tied the ribbon, he recalled how much this case with its instruments reminded him of his mother's fine sterling silver. She kept it in just such cases between her Sunday family dinners. It was time to get dressed and take his leave. The remainder of the can of Drano went into the kitchen drain. The empty can went into his dopp kit. He walked to the living room and dressed.

Now, fully dressed, with credentials identifying him as a salesman for a major, California, surgical supply house resting nicely in his wallet, he attended to one final detail as he departed. Withdrawing a Nice N' Clean packet from his kit, he carefully wiped his fingerprints from every surface and knob he might have touched. He paused in the living room giving the scene a final review in his mind, and with his experienced eye, he decided everything had been covered. He opened the apartment door and silently checked the hallway for any other occupants. Seeing none, he stepped into the hall and used the wipe to pull apartment 33C's door closed. He dropped the wipe together with its foil container into the kit. He removed the latex gloves he'd worn since entering the apartment several hours earlier and placed them in the kit. He'd dispose of everything later. The disposable elements of his kit would, as was his habit, be dropped in a trash container located far from the scene of his work in a highly trafficked area. He closed the zipper on the dopp kit and then his flight bag and walked at a normal pace toward the elevators at the center of the hall.

Taking her leave of the firm's aging clients, Monica Flynn quietly closed the apartment door and consulted her wrist watch. Yes, there'd be just enough time to get back downtown in time to get Norma's car back before the office closed. She made a mental note to thank Norma again for the use of her car on this cold, windy, November day. Her paralegal work accomplished–the clients happy with their revised will–Monica tucked the thin leather case containing the precious legal paperwork under her arm and pulled her warm winter coat tightly around her throat.

Moving quickly, the deep pile carpet hushing her footsteps, she set off for the elevator at the center of the hall, her shoulder-length, honey-blond hair bouncing with every step. As she walked, her thoughts turned to her fiancée, Mike, and the weekend they'd planned. Arriving at the alcove housing the elevators, she pushed the call button and waited. Erotic thoughts of Mike filled her imagination as she waited. She rather enjoyed the fact her five-foot-eight height was short next to his six-foot-two. In her imaginings, she saw his blue-green eyes smiling down at her as his face came close. She fantasized about stroking his lean, hard body.

Her warm thoughts were abruptly wrenched back to reality as the bell sounded, announcing the arrival of the elevator. The polished brass doors slid open, revealing a single passenger already in the car. Unconsciously, as women do, Monica made a quick mental assessment of the occupant. He was tall, maybe six feet, with moderately long, light brown hair. Intense brown eyes stared ahead from beneath heavy, darker eyebrows. Just beside his left nostril a dark brown freckle stood out against his white skin. There was a hard look about those eyes. Monica's initial reaction was one of mild alarm, and for a moment, she hesitated to enter the elevator. But as her glance took in the rest of the man, she saw he was dressed in an expensive-looking, two-piece, dark blue, pinstripe suit, white, oxford-cloth shirt with button-down collar, a silver gray tie, gleaming, black shoes, a black, cashmere top coat was across one arm, and at his feet, an expensive-looking, leather, airline carry-on bag with shoulder strap.

This had to be a tenant off to the airport. Relieved, she smiled and stepped into the elevator. He nodded an acknowledgment. Turning her back toward the stranger, she pushed the button marked garage. Uninterrupted by other stops, they rode to the garage level in silence. The doors slid open, and Monica stepped off the elevator first, quickly making her way to the red, Mustang convertible parked a good sixty feet away in the "visitors' " area.

She was unaware the man had stayed back, concealing himself behind one of the huge, concrete columns supporting the tall building. He watched as she unlocked the car, got in, started it, and carefully backed out of the parking slot. As the rear of the car came into view, he quickly copied the license number on the back of a Continental Airlines boarding pass he'd pulled from his suit coat breast pocket. The flight was to depart Indianapolis for Los Angeles at seven o'clock the following morning.

He waited until the car had pulled up the exit ramp and turned out of his view on the main street in front of the building. Replacing the boarding pass in his breast pocket, he put on his top coat, slung the travel bag's strap over his shoulder, and walked up the ramp and out onto Meridian Street. Turning to his right, he walked about two blocks and hailed a Yellow Cab from the front entrance of another high-rise, apartment building. He directed the driver to take him to the downtown Hyatt Regency Hotel.

As the cab headed south toward the hotel, he began to consider this unexpected development. The woman posed a definite threat. He'd caught that momentary look of alarm on her face when she saw him in the elevator. He pulled the boarding pass from his pocket and considered the license number written there. There had to be a way; however, it would mean delaying leaving town for a few days while he located the girl in the red, Mustang convertible.

11:00 p.m.

The distant California phone rang four times before it was answered. "Yes?"

"I'm calling to let you know the contract has been filled. Took him at his place, The Windom Towers."

"The Windom Towers!?" The voice reflected surprise. "What's the apartment number?"

"Thirty-three something. Thirty-three C, I think."

"Jesus Christ! That's *our* place!"

"*What the hell!* I didn't know you had a place. You shoulda told me. What the hell was he doing in your place?"

"We gave him a key card last year. He needed an out-of-the-way place to do business and get his ashes hauled. Up 'till now the guy moved a lot of product. It was a reward for his work."

"How the hell was I supposed to know?"

"Hey! We're *both* surprised! How much damage did you do?"

"Trashed the place. Had to make it look like a robbery gone bad."

There was a long pause before the California voice spoke again. "Did you at least get the information?"

"No. He wouldn't give it up."

"Where else have you looked?"

"Just the apartment."

"God-damnit! He didn't live there! You've got to check *his* place!"

"Hey! Look–I followed the guy when he left his office at noon on Friday. He picked up this girl, took her to lunch and then to the apartment. How was I supposed to know he didn't live there? All you gave me was his picture and an address for this City-County Building. You've been working with this guy for a few years. How come you don't know where he lives?"

"I never met him in Indianapolis. We did business only when he came to Miami. I never had a reason to contact him at his place. He's got to have his own place. Find it! You still in Indianapolis?"

"Yes. But before I go looking for his place, I've got a loose end to tie up."

"What kind of loose end?"

"A possible witness. Girl saw me when I was leaving the building. Can't chance it."

"Well, that's *your* problem. Find his records. And remember, there's to be *nothing* which could even remotely connect you to me. Any more problems and you can kiss the remainder of your fee good-bye."

"Yes, it's *my* problem. With any luck at all I'll handle it and be back in L.A. by the middle of the week–Thursday at the latest. Have my money ready then."

"Anything in the local news yet?"

"No, nothing. It's too soon. Unless you've got a maid service for that layout, I'd say it'll be the first of the week before anybody finds the bodies."

"Don't know about a maid. The lease is handled by the Los Angeles investment office. Maybe you've got some time then. Tell me, is this girl going to pose any special problems?"

"Don't think so. I got the license number on her car as she drove out of the basement. Didn't look to me like she lived in the building. She was parked in the visitors' spaces. Come Monday, I'll trace it and have her found in a day or two at the outside."

"Good. Now, find Blakemore's place and search it. Find those files. Look for anything with my name on it. Even if it is only a scrap of paper. Did you take all his belongings?"

"Certainly. That's my style."

"Is there one of those bar-code key cards among his stuff?"

"Yeah."

"That's the key to the apartment door and security card for the building.   I want you to mail that card, his wallet– everything you took off him– to me."

"Yes, I already told you."

"Good. Send it all to my mail drop box. Do it tonight. Remember, it's your ass hanging out. If you get picked up with that card, they can link you to the scene. So, get it in the mail tonight!"

"Shit. This is Indianapolis. The cops here are country bumpkins. Couldn't find their asses with both hands at high noon in a phone booth!"

"That may be, but if I've learned anything in my years of practicing criminal law, it only *seems* that way. I've learned to never underestimate a dedicated policeman. You'd be well- advised to keep that in mind. You're on your own. Don't call me here again until you get back." The distant voice broke the connection before the killer could reply.

The killer replaced the receiver and began to pace his hotel room. Laid out on one of the two beds was the soft-side, fold- over, carry on bag. The killer unzipped one of the outside pockets and withdrew a woman's handbag. He dumped the contents on the bed and made an inventory. He started with the contents of Blakemore's wallet. There was three hundred fifty dollars in cash, a gold American Express Card issued to John Blakemore, an Indiana Operator's License, and several City of Indianapolis business cards, identifying Blakemore as a deputy mayor for economic development. There was also a note paper with several phone numbers and a photo of Blakemore with two other young men. He separated out Blakemore's key ring and the Windom Tower, bar coded, reader card. He pocketed the cash and put everything back in the wallet.

He examined the girl's personal effects. Her Indiana Operator's License with picture identified her as Jennifer Wick, age twenty. Her small wallet contained only fifty dollars which the killer also pocketed. There was a lipstick, a compact with face powder, several pictures of the girl with other men and women, a small, black, telephone and address book, and a key ring, which appeared to hold a house key and car keys for something made by General Motors. The killer scooped up her keys and other effects and dropped them back into the girl's purse. He unzipped the center compartment of his bag and removed a partially filled, large, heavy-duty, black-plastic, trash bag. He untied the top, dropped in the girl's hand bag, and retied the bag.

Pacing the room, he reviewed his situation, considering the problem of the witness. It didn't take long to hit upon a plan. He let his mind drift back to his days in the Special Forces. He'd show them yet! How could they have given him the so called Section Eight Discharge– mental problems! He'd show them yet. What was it he heard somebody say? Something about the best revenge is living well. Well, he was living high on the hog as they said back home. He turned his thoughts back to the girl.

As he was leaving the apartment building, she had gotten on the elevator. He recalled her image to mind. Tall, about five-foot-nine or ten in her high heels, light brown hair, sunbleached to streaked blonde, bright-violet-blue eyes, and she had been wearing a tan, trench-style, winter coat. She had a beautiful figure–the coat didn't hide the fact. In fact, the cinched, belted waist emphasized her figure. He'd registered with the girl. Her swift look of surprise when she saw him–she'd gotten a good look at him, of that there was no doubt. He knew that he would know the girl the next time that he saw her. He also knew that he couldn't run the risk she'd remember him when the news of Blakemore's death broke. Eventually, she would tell the police about the man in the elevator. That defined his problem. The girl had to be eliminated.

Monday, 3:45 p.m.
The Windom Towers

Sergeant Julie Crooks took the phone call from Patrolman Gardner about a robbery at The Towers, the far Northside's extremely exclusive and posh high-rise, just minutes earlier. She passed the call to her boss, Captain Flynn. The day shift was due to end shortly, so Robbery-Homicide Branch Commander, Captain Dennis Flynn decided he'd take the call. The Towers was on his way home anyway. He asked Sergeant Gaffney to join him. Mike Gaffney was just six months away from becoming his son-in-law, something Flynn was looking forward to with considerable relief. At twenty-one years of age, his daughter, Monica, had become very much her own woman and no longer much inclined to defer to her father.

Mike, at twenty-seven, had a great many things to recommend him. Flynn truly liked the young man, and early on, when Mike had come calling on Monica, he'd decided the young officer would make a great husband for his daughter.

The two men, accompanied by the building manager, were standing at the apartment door, where about an hour or so earlier, according to the manager, a private maid had discovered the apartment had been vandalized. She said there was a terrible odor too. Flynn took the manager's key card and inserted it in the reader slot. He heard the door bolt retract. Using the toe of his shoe, Flynn carefully pushed on the bottom of the door. Slowly, the apartment door swung open. Darkness. The overpowering, unmistakable odor of death wafted past the three men gathered in the doorway. As his eyes adjusted to the dark of the apartment, Flynn was able to make out dark shadows of objects in the room. Ahead, a thin sliver of daylight showed through drawn draperies. The heating system was on, the furnace fan forcing the overwhelming coppery-sweet odor of blood and body waste everywhere. Eleven years a homicide detective and he was still affected by the smells and sight of violent human death. Flynn took a pocket handkerchief from a baggy he always carried in his hip pocket for just such moments and covered his nose and mouth. It was a "survival trick" he'd been taught by a long retired captain who'd taken him under his wing when Flynn was a rookie detective. The handkerchief was saturated with a chemical which masked most of the revolting odor.

Taking a ball point pen from his inside coat pocket, he located a nearby wall switch. He used the pen to raise the toggle. The once elegant, large, living room was lit by three overturned but still working table lamps. Standing in the doorway, Flynn surveyed the room. It appeared to be a good thirty feet square. Walnut bookshelves surrounded a fireplace on the wall to the right. The wall to the left was covered in a very expensive-looking covering, Flynn guessed it was a watered silk of some kind. Two hallways ran off the small reception vestibule, one to the left and one to the right. Flynn looked again at the room. Once elegant, expensive sofas faced each other across a glass-topped coffee table. The seat cushions and backs had been savagely cut open. The foam and cotton insides strewn about the room. Three upholstered arm chairs had suffered a similar fate. Books had been pulled from the bookshelves. Magazines, ripped to shreds, covered the expensive, deep pile, white carpet. Pictures had been torn from their frames, and the frames smashed. Someone had made a very thorough search for something. Flynn wondered if they'd found it. Turning to his right, he spoke to the short, obsequious building manager, politely ordering the man to remain in the hall. Then facing Sergeant Gaffney, he instructed the young detective to stand guard in the doorway and let nobody enter until he had completed an initial inspection of the apartment.

Cautiously, careful of each step, Flynn entered the apartment. He couldn't help but make a mental comparison between the mortgage he paid on his modest, Northside two-story and the probable monthly lease on this huge layout. He took it all in; the wall coverings were costly, the extra plush carpet probably cost more than fifty dollars a square yard. He'd become more aware of such things in the twelve years since his beloved wife, Mary, passed away leaving him alone to raise their daughter, Monica, and handle the family finances, a task Mary had done with such ease.

According to the building manager, the hallway to the left led to the bedrooms and bath. The hall to the right led to the kitchen and beyond that, a large, formal dining room. Flynn turned to his left and started down the hall toward the bedrooms. Locating the wall switch for the hall lighting, he repeated the trick with his ball point pen. In the now well-lit hall, halfway toward the door at the far end, he could see large stains of what appeared to be dried blood– large patches of rusty brown. The stains appeared to come from the door at the far end of the hall. Moving slowly, unconsciously holding his breath, he approached the door on the right into which the trail of blood led. The door was just slightly ajar. Again, using the toe of his shoe, he carefully pushed the door open and looked inside.

The large bath was spattered with blood and strewn with at least a dozen blood-soaked towels. The white tile floor was streaked with dried blood. An oversized, green marble tub held several bloody towels.

Tearing his eyes away, he backed out of the bath and continued down the hall toward the darkened doorway at the end, dreading what he might find. Instinct and years of experience came together as a small voice somewhere in his mind told him he was nearing the end of his search. The room was dark. He turned on the lights.

"Jesus, Mary, and Joseph! Oh God! Oh, God-damn–!" burst from his lips. His stomach convulsed. Quickly, he ran from the room and into the bath where he unceremoniously emptied the contents of his stomach into the toilet. Even with his stomach now empty, he had to breathe deeply several times before he could get on with it. His duty required him to look at the situation as dispassionately and analytically as he could. Walking a bit further into the large bedroom, he stood in front of the chair in which what had once been a very pretty girl, probably around his Monica's age, had died a horrible death. Her hair was of the same shoulder length, honey-blonde as his daughter's. The killer had used duct tape to fix this hapless girl to an upright, ladder back, formal dining chair–undoubtedly taken from the dining room. He'd have to check that. The girl's nude, blood-spattered body, chalky bluish-white in death, sat firmly fixed to the chair. The chair itself was glued to the carpet in a pool of her dried blood.

Taking a breath, he shifted his eyes back up to her face. It was a very pretty face–or had been. Around the girl's forehead and mouth, tape had firmly fixed her head against the top cross piece of the high backed chair. Flynn's eyes traveled slowly down the corpse. The girl's wrists were taped to the chair arms; her ankles to the legs. He returned to her face. Sightless, blue eyes stared ahead, the muscles about her eyes still registered pain, shock, and terror.

Flynn wrenched his eyes away and willed himself to regain his composure. He began by taking careful mental notes– the written and videotaped versions would follow soon. He concentrated once more on the girl's body. Both the girl's aureole had been excised from her breasts. Approaching the body, he squatted down to get a closer look at the torso. He could see several incisions beneath each breast, each with a dried trail of blood. His eyes slowly traced the blood toward her crotch–or more properly what had once been her crotch. Real anger began to replace all other emotions as he beheld yet another unspeakable violation! Her vagina had been viciously cut, laid open. The girl had literally been repeatedly and deliberately slashed.

Flynn crossed to the bedroom window, reached behind the draperies, located the pull cord, and opened the drapes. The room flooded with cold, November light. He cranked open the casement window. Cold as it was, he badly needed some fresh air! He was about to call for Sergeant Gaffney, when his mind registered something about the bed. He turned back to look. Almost hidden from sight beneath the pile of pillows and sheets on the side of the bed was a wrist. Quickly, he crossed to the bed and lifted the pile of sheets, revealing the body of a man! Flynn began to take more mental notes. The body looked to be about six feet in length and was lying face down. He too was naked and lay in his own pool of dried blood. Flynn estimated the man to be about twenty-eight to thirty years of age judging from the good musculature and generally youthful appearance of the body.

Instead of calling out for Gaffney, he returned to the apartment door and quietly took the sergeant aside and a few steps down the hall, away from the building manager and out of the man's hearing. Speaking quietly and directly into Sergeant Gaffney's ear, he said, "Mike, we're gonna need a lid on this. Understand me? A very tight lid. I don't want any newsies getting wind of this until we're damn good and ready. Now, I want you to take the manager down to his office. Don't tell him anything. Let him go on thinking this is a burglary case. Interview the maid if she's still here. Find out what she knows— what she saw. Find out if she actually entered the apartment when she came to clean it, or did she go directly to the building manager after she looked in."

Gaffney's eyes widened. His face showed puzzlement. "How bad is it in there anyway?"

"This was no God damn burglary!" Flynn hissed through clenched teeth. "Smell the blood? This is the worst, most violent double murder I've ever seen in my life! A pretty young girl and some guy. You'll see it soon enough. Somebody tossed the hell out of the place. That much is obvious. As for the why, look where we are for Christ's sake! This is one of the most fashionable addresses in town, rich people— *connected* people live here. We don't need a media circus. I don't need reporters up my ass! Understand?"

"Yes. I get it. So, what, exactly, do you want me to do?"

"Use your cell phone to call in the Forensics team and the coroner. Get them over here on the double. Try to get Chuck and his team in Forensics if you can. You got Chuck's direct number?"

"Yes. Got it on the speed-dialer."

"Good. Now tell everybody no lights or sirens and to stay the hell off their radios. Better yet, instruct them to pull into the basement garage. You meet them down there. I'm sure this place has a service elevator of some kind. Use it. Have everybody use it. I'll wait for you to bring them up here. Also, get ahold of Sam Elberger and have him get over here. Have him start a door-to-door in the entire building. Tell him to use burglary as a cover story. As exclusive as this place is, I think we stand a good chance everybody knows who belongs here and who doesn't. Somebody just might have seen a stranger or two in the building in the last day or so. Better have Sam call in a couple of our off-duty homicide people, some uniforms and start a search of all the dumpsters and trash cans in the public areas of the building, and then continue it for say a two block radius around the building. Tell them they're looking for bloody clothing and a very sharp knife—or maybe a scalpel—might or might not have blood on it. If we're lucky, the killer dumped the knife. Question the manager. Find out about visitors. How they handle them—closed circuit security video—whatever. Find out who owns this apartment. Hell, he's right here. I'll ask him that one myself before you go."

"You got it, Boss. Sam will have to call in the off-duty people himself. Any more with the manager?" Mike asked.

"Find out if the building has a doorman or any kind of security, that sort of thing. If they do, are the comings and goings recorded? If they have a doorman, find out who it is and where we can find him. Like I said, security cameras? Video tapes? You know the drill."

"Sure, Denny. No sweat. Think we'll be tied up here long?"

"On a double homicide—are you *kidding* me? Why? You and Monica got plans for tonight?"

"Well, yes. Sort of a six-month anniversary of our engagement. Her idea."

"In that case, your second phone call had better be to her. You can tell my daughter her dad is keeping you late tonight.

And tell her I'm sorry. Now, I want to know who pays for this apartment."

It didn't take much to convince the building manager to tell all he knew. The lease was held by a Los Angeles corporation, an investment firm. The apartment was infrequently used by several different people. Executives of the company, he assumed, both men and women who came and went without fuss or announcement, and no, he didn't have any idea who had occupied the apartment over the weekend.

Flynn watched as Mike took the building manager by the elbow and steered him down the long hall toward the elevator. Flynn reentered the apartment and carefully closed the door. Letting go of the questions swirling in his mind, his thoughts turned to his daughter. He felt sorry for Mike. He knew there'd be pure hell to pay when Mike called Monica with the bad news. She'd get her Irish up!

Monica was all he had left of his marriage to Mary. Flynn offered a silent prayer the murdered, disfigured girl wouldn't turn out to be the daughter of some local bigwig. Flynn was immediately ashamed of himself! What of this poor girl's own parents? Bigwigs or not, their lives would be scarred forever. They'd lost their beautiful little girl.

The Towers was one of the *best* addresses in the city, boasting bank presidents, retired GM, Ford, and Daimler-Chrysler executives, and active and retired politicians, one of them a former governor of the state. There were wealthy, blue-haired widows and very well-heeled yuppies among its residents. He needed time to organize the investigation and to get everybody headed in the same direction before the publicity seekers and headline hunters began their self serving posing and speech making, especially, if these two victims turned out to be important people!

After inspecting the kitchen, Flynn walked into the large, formal dining room. He fumbled about for a light switch and eventually located a knob of some sort on a switch plate. He twisted it. Nothing. He pushed it, and suddenly, the room was lit by a very large, elaborate, crystal chandelier. In the sudden brightness, he noted a chair missing from the near end of a long refectory table. He took a minute to view the room. The huge table occupied the middle of the room. The wall opposite was floor-to-ceiling mirrors. Flynn focused on his image in the mirrors. He beheld a man whose face wore a worried and haggard look–a definite five o'clock shadow showed. It took him by surprise. He saw a man he knew was forty-one, going on forty-two, yet who looked much younger–perhaps thirty-five. He stood erect, stretching himself to his full five-foot-ten inches. Examining his image, he decided he was still in damn good physical shape; thirty-three inch waist and no flab at all. A full head of dark brown, wavy, slightly too long hair, beneath that, a strong face–which, after two generations, still advertised the map of Ireland. Kindly hazel eyes gazed back from the mirror. All-in-all, not bad, Flynn thought.

Flynn remembered how not long after he'd made it to Homicide and Robbery, all the violent death was getting to him. A fairly devout Catholic, Flynn knew he was questioning God– even His very existence! How could a loving God allow the death and mutilation he saw almost daily? What was the point of it all anyway? Mary advised him to go see her cousin at his apartment. Taking her advice, he'd gone to visit with the relative, a Catholic priest, Tom Carey. Father Carey had only recently retired from active parish work and was living in retirement at The Hermitage in Beech Grove. The two had shared a beer as Flynn poured out his soul, his doubts. It was Tom Carey, who'd pointed out the true meaning, as he saw it, of a policeman's life, particularly, the work of those who investigate death. Toward the end of their visit, Father Tom had asked quite simply, "Who speaks for the dead?" Flynn remembered how he'd felt flummoxed by the question. Taking pity, Father Tom answered his own question. "You do!" he'd said. From that day forward Flynn had, indeed, looked upon his job as a vocation. A calling from God. He and others like him worked to bring murderers to justice. Still, without Mary to confide in each evening, it was a lonely life.

A knock at the apartment door broke his reverie. Four men from Forensics stood at the door, tall, blond-haired Lieutenant Chuck Holland in the lead. Holland flashed a winning smile at his old friend. "Hi, Denny. Whadya got?" he asked as Flynn opened the apartment door.

Flynn stuck his head out into the hall, checked the hallway, and seeing only Department people, he ordered everybody but Holland to stay in the hall for a minute. Inside, he answered, "We've got two bodies, cut up and slashed like I've never seen before. Girl and a guy. The girl is taped to a chair, carved up– well, you won't believe it even when you see it! The guy is off the side of the bed on the floor, laying on his face, one arm taped to a bed post. I'm worried about possible connections downtown and at the State House. In any event, it's going to be bad when the word gets out."

Observing Flynn's distress, Chuck gently patted his friend on the back. "Okay, Denny, I'll let my men in and give them the word, and then let's go have a look. Did you touch anything?"

"Jesus! Chuck you know me better than that! I opened the bedroom window, looked in the kitchen drawers, and I put my ass in a chair in the dining room. That's all. No!– Wait! I lost my lunch in the toilet. Flushed it too. Sorry!"

"Yeah, well– you know, sometimes in the heat of the moment, and all that– " Holland let his men in and turned to the only civilian tech on his squad, Bryan Lynch. "Bryan, have the men get pictures of everything from every angle. You handle the video camera. Start right here at the door, and cover everything. When you get through with this room, have the others get their stills, and then, I want the place dusted. Okay Denny, where are the bodies?"

"Down the hall on your left there," Flynn mumbled moodily.

Lieutenant Holland picked up his forensic kit, pulled a pair of latex gloves from his lab coat, put them on, and then, followed Flynn down the hall. He tiptoed around the blood stains in the hall, paused to stick his head into the bath for a quick look, and continued following Flynn into the bedroom.

As they began work, Herb Nichols, the county coroner, a bundle of barely suppressed energy, entered the room. Women considered him a handsome man at fifty-two years of age, and he looked very much like the gracefully aging, college football player he was, having played for Indiana University while an undergraduate.

"Doc, how'd you hear about this? Who let you in on this one?" Flynn asked.

"The address, Denny, my boy. The address. When your man Gaffney called, I took the call. Thought it might be somebody I know." Doc Nichols's eyes remained fixed on the girl the whole time he spoke. "Any idea who she was?" he asked as he put a wooden match to his ever present cigar. Smoking cigars was a perk his position as coroner gave him. Although he didn't smoke in homes and public meeting rooms, nobody had the balls to remind the man it was government policy that smoking in government office buildings was forbidden. Nichols was about as politically incorrect as one could be. In truth, everybody secretly loved him for it. Soon, Nichols's head was all but lost in a cloud of cigar smoke.

"At this point, I don't have the faintest idea who she was," Flynn answered. "Does she look familiar to you?"

Doc Nichols silently shook his head. "No, but whoever did this deserves to die in the slowest, most painful way man can devise. I think I could come up with a suggestion or two along those lines if anybody is interested. Where's the other body? I heard you had two." Flynn pointed to the man's corpse at the far side of the room. Nichols went over to have a look.

"Who's the long haired hippie out there with the digital video?" he asked.

"That's Bryan Lynch, civilian tech."

"Well, why don't you tell the kid to get a hair cut?"

"Listen, he may look about eighteen to you but he's twenty-five, and that young man has one of the best minds I have ever encountered. He picks up on things nobody else sees. He can put two and two together more quickly and more accurately than anybody else on my team. He can grow that hair all the way down to his ass for all I care. Besides, it's only down to the middle of his back. Give the kid a break!"

"He would never have made our IU football program—looking like that!"

"Look at him! He must weigh all of a hundred-thirty pounds! I doubt he would have ever allowed himself the thought of playing college football."

When the pictures were complete and the entire room dusted for fingerprints, Doc Nichols pulled on a pair of latex gloves, and selecting a scalpel from his oversize, doctor's bag. He very carefully cut the duct tape away from the girl's head, taking care he didn't destroy any prints which might remain on the tape itself.

"Can you give me an idea of the time of death?" Flynn asked.

"Give me a minute here, and I'll give you a first guess," Nichols said.

He cut away the tape around the girl's wrists and ankles and flexed the finger joints, wrists, and ankles. "I'd say rigor set in and relaxed. Considering the fact the heat has been on, the dried blood, and subject to the autopsy, I'll guess her death occurred about eighteen to twenty-four hours ago. Can't say anything about the guy until we get to him"

The coroner's men carefully put the girl in a black body bag, placed her on a gurney, and expedited its leave-taking in secrecy.

Nichols turned his attention to the man's body. He cut the tape which had bound the dead man's wrist to the bed and asked Flynn and Holland to help him move the bed away from the body. "Again, subject to the autopsy, I'd say they died within minutes or an hour of each other. Couldn't tell you who went first though," he said. Still on his knees, he lifted and turned the man's head. "Oh, God Almighty! Do you see who this is?" Nichols asked. Both Flynn and Holland leaned in to have a closer look. "This," said Nichols, "is Deputy Mayor Jack Blakemore, one of the mayor's young movers and shakers!"

A sharp pain hit Flynn in the stomach. A deputy mayor! "You certain?" Flynn asked. The man was unfamiliar to him.

"I had a few drinks with him just last week. It's him all right. Fellas, get me a bucket of warm water. We're going to have to soak Jack here loose from the carpet before I can tell you any more."

"Is this his place?"

"Don't think so. You'll have to check the confidential files for his address. You know the drill." Nichols affected a feminine nasal voice, "*Ever since The Towers, we don't give out that information.* Kinda put the skids to everything, didn't it?"

It took several minutes for the warm water to liquefy the dried blood enough to turn the body over. When, at last, they had the dead man on his back, the cause of death was completely obvious. Jack Blakemore's genitals had been completely cut out of his body! Aside from the missing genitals, there wasn't another mark on the man. The three men stood in silence, looking down at the mutilated body, each dealing with his own private reaction. Flynn broke the silence. "Well, along with being a real sadist, this sure as hell looks like our guy is some kind of a sex nut."

Lieutenant Holland broke the strained silence. "Any chance the girl was his wife?" he asked, finally tearing his eyes away from the horrific scene.

Doc Nichols spoke from around his cigar, "Wasn't married. Had a rep as a real cocks man."

"Girlfriend then? Maybe a hooker?" offered Holland. "One thing, old friend, I don't envy you this one at all. No, sir, not a'tall," Holland said as he patted Flynn on the shoulder. "If I know the chief, he's going to let you carry the bad news to the mayor and then, build a fire about three feet high under your ass to get this one cleared 'cause the mayor is going to have a four foot fire under the chief's ass!"

Flynn turned to the coroner, "Doc, what did this guy do in the mayor's office?"

"He was in charge of getting new businesses to move to our fair city. The dog and pony show man."

"Doc, I'd sure like to have about twenty-four to thirty-six hours of lead time before the media gets a whiff of this. I'd sure appreciate it if you might sorta' hide this for a while. For the time being—at least until I have some idea of just what and who it is we're up against." Flynn turned to Lieutenant Holland, "Chuck, please get those prints on the girl over to the Ident. See if they can come up with a quick computer match. For all we know, she might be a local hooker. If we're lucky, she's been busted and printed before. If we don't have her, and as much as I hate to, we'll go with the NCIC and the Feds—and we all know how great they are at keeping a secret! The word will be on the street in a matter of hours. We've got to know who she was. When you go, disable the lock, and put one of your new high-tech seals on the doors."

It was almost 9:30 p.m. when Flynn pulled his unmarked, metallic-blue, Ford sedan into Chief O'Halleran's driveway.

Eileen, Mike O'Halleran's wife, answered the door, wiping her hands on a flower print apron. "Well, well! Dennis Flynn! What, pray tell ,brings you out at this time of night?"

"Evening, Eileen. What else! I'm sorry to come by so late. Is Mike in? It's rather important."

"Certainly! Come right in. He's in the family room watchin' the Colts game." Eileen ushered him into the family room. O'Halleran was comfortably cradled in his favorite leather club chair, feet up on a matching ottoman, pipe clenched in his teeth, and two fingers, neat, Tullamore Dew Irish at his elbow. Denny cleared his throat. O'Halleran looked up. "Evenin', Denny. Take a chair. How about a shot of Irish?" Without waiting for an answer, O'Halleran pushed his beefy, five-foot-eleven frame out of the chair, went to the sideboard to get a glass, and pour his friend a drink. Flynn silently admired his old friend, recalling their days as rookies at the IPD Academy nearly twenty years ago. Flynn and Mary had married shortly after he'd graduated from Cathedral High School. A year later they had a girl, Monica. Flynn had worked a series of jobs until at age twenty-one he'd passed the police entrance exam, the academy, and had entered his probationary year as a member of the police force. There was now the security of a city paycheck every two weeks. Mike remained a bachelor until he'd made sergeant. He'd gone off on his annual vacation to visit relatives in Ireland and returned thirty days later with Eileen on his arm.

They sipped the fiery liquid. O'Halleran waited with patience borne of experience with his friend.

"Jesus, Mike. Where do I begin? I guess the only way is to come right out with it. We're gonna have hell to pay." Flynn took a deep breath and went on, "Deputy Mayor Jack Blakemore was brutally murdered sometime over the weekend–I won't know for sure exactly just when, until the coroner's report is in." O'Halleran put his pipe aside, took a healthy gulp of his Tullamore Dew, and turned in his chair to face his old friend squarely.

It took Flynn twenty minutes to complete his report and to answer, as best he could, all of the chief's questions. O'Halleran contemplated the options, his face a mask of concern.

"All right. I figure I can keep a lid on this for two working days. But longer than that–no. I just can't risk it. The lid is gonna blow on this like a cheap pressure-cooker! Two days, Denny. Can't do better than that."

Flynn arrived at his office a full half-hour earlier than usual the following morning. The day shift started at eight, and he wanted to set up his office for the meeting of his people. He put his top coat on the hall tree he'd installed in the corner opposite his door. He pulled the smallish, metal, government issue, conference table, ordinarily along the back wall, to the front of his desk forming a "T" with his desk as the crosspiece.

He pulled the government issue chairs away from the walls and placed them at the conference table. Satisfied things were ready, he poured himself a cup of coffee and took his chair at his desk. He propped his feet on the corner of the metal desk and placed a fresh legal pad in his lap.

He took a kind of comfort from the room. He knew its dimensions. With the exception of the chief's office and those of his deputy chiefs, his office, at fifteen by twenty-five feet, was large by the standards of most other offices on the second floor. From the baked-on, beige paint on the moveable, metal walls to the gray, vinyl floor tiles, everything was in need of a good cleaning, waxing, and buffing. Flynn shrugged. It was a working office. The hell with it! He lowered his head and began to make notes.

They all gathered promptly at eight in Flynn's office: Lieutenant Holland and Bryan Lynch from Forensics, Sergeant Gaffney and Detective Sam Elberger of Homicide and Robbery. "Okay, Chuck," Flynn began, "any luck on the identity of the girl?"

Holland allowed himself a smile. "Well, we lucked out there," he began. "Turns out your hunch about her being a hooker was a good one. The computer got a quick match on her prints. She was Jennifer Wick, age twenty, no family. Vice busted her last year in one of those sweeps up on the Meridian Street strip. We have an address. Don't know if it is any good yet. Beyond that, we don't know anything more about her. And the guy was just who Doc said he was, Deputy Mayor Jack Blakemore."

Flynn allowed himself a moment of relief, realizing he'd not have to break the news of their daughter's death to the girl's parents. He turned to Sergeant Gaffney. "Mike, when we're done here, get down to Vice, and see if they have anything on our Miss Wick. If they have a file on her, copy it. Find out if she used a pimp. If she did, follow up on it. I want to know who arranged her last 'appointment' and who it was to be with. See if any of the Vice boys knows anything about her. Let's find out where she lived. That reminds me. We'll need a search warrant." He made himself a note on the rapidly filling note pad. "Get one for her apartment or where ever. See if she kept an appointment book while you're down in Vice, and be very discreet about this".

Lieutenant Holland consulted his own steno style notebook. "One very strange thing. Bryan here picked up on it. Did any of you notice there were no clothes in the place? I mean nothing that belonged to either of the victims. No dress, no suit, no underwear, no bra, no shoes, no socks. Nothing! Unless they came into the building stark naked, our killer took everything with him! I've never seen that done before. Another thing– that apartment is more like a fancy hotel suite. Nothing there but bed sheets, linen, bath towels, skillets, pots and pans, a few canned goods. Nothing of a personal nature. Nobody actually lives there."

Lynch spoke up. "Well, if it was used like a hotel suite by different executives from this West Coast outfit, I can see why there wouldn't be any clothes. But, now–let me really blow your mind. I took a good look at that big marble tub, and all those bloody towels. Everything was watered down. We all thought he just dumped them in there after he wiped up the blood. I think he took a shower to get rid of the blood on his own body. I say that because the drain had the residue of Drano in it–found the same thing in the kitchen sink. Smart! Cooks away all the DNA markers. This guy is nobody's fool. Moving on–I tested all the knives in the kitchen. Checked them with Luminol and even checked them again when we got back to the lab. No blood. At least no *human* blood. So I think this nut case brought his own knives, washed them clean, and dumped more Drano in the kitchen drain. Now, this leads me to another guess. I think he was stripped down to his skivvies or maybe even nude when he killed those two."

Everybody was stunned by the thought.

Flynn took up the point. "Okay. That puts another light on it. Bryan, would you also be led to thinking this guy–we *are* agreed this is a man?" Flynn's question was answered with visible shrugs. Who knew? "Okay, then are we agreed this is a professional killer? I mean who gets naked to kill unless he *or* she has thought this through? Nobody I can think of. I mean most murders are spur of the moment. No thought about getting blood on yourself."

"My point exactly!" Bryan said. "I want to go back today and see what I can find in the tub drain. Who knows, with luck I might find *some* body hair. DNA. I'm guessing we have a pro here. I'd like to check the NCIC for similar *MO*'s."

Flynn resumed, thoughtfully. "Do it. Thanks, Bryan. That's damn good technical detective work!" He turned his attention to Detective Sam Elberger who had been put in charge of the physical search. "Okay, Sam, what can you tell me?"

Detective Elberger rolled his blue eyes toward the ceiling. "Well, Captain, the door-to-door came up empty. About half the people were out of the building– weekend you know, and according to the building manager about half of the retired residents also have condos in Florida. This time of year they're long gone. The manager says the apartment across the hall is leased to a Chicago company, and there was nobody in that apartment over the weekend. The search of the building's trash cans and dumpsters came up zip too. Several uniforms are still out making a sweep of the dumpsters and trash cans in the neighborhood."

Flynn sighed and shrugged his shoulders. "Well, in view of what Bryan has come up with, let's call off the search at the end of this shift. The knife and clothing are probably miles away from the scene by now anyway. Mike, what did you get from the building manager?"

Gaffney opened his notebook and began to read, "The apartment is leased by The Andrews Development Group, L.P. That's a limited partnership of some sort. Anyway, they're out of Los Angeles. Some kind of big real estate investment outfit. The lease is signed by a Ms. Nancy Whittacker, who signed herself as the corporate secretary of the group. All this was done by mail. A cashier's check for a full two-year lease was returned along with the signed lease papers almost a year ago. The lease has another year to go.

"According to the manager, a couple of truck loads of furniture and other things showed up shortly after the lease was signed and paid. Somebody was there from the corporation to oversee everything, and more than that, he can't recall. The manager doesn't really know who uses the place.

"According to him, they have a dozen leases like this in the building. Out-of-town corporations using the apartments like luxury, hotel suites. They have caterers in and out of the building almost every weekend. So, several people come and go during the year. Who is a stranger and who isn't? Who knows? This particular lease includes two reserved parking spaces in the basement. I want to put in a call to this Andrews Development Group this afternoon and ask who was using the apartment over the weekend." Mike consulted his notes again. "The maid service is twice weekly. The same maid has worked that floor of the building for the past three years. I've got her name and address here. I figured you'd want to have a talk with her."

"What about the security?" Flynn asked.

"Security? Well, it's borderline at best. The front lobby has a set of double vestibule doors with a closed circuit TV camera. You need a key card to get through the second set or use the house phone to call whoever you're visiting, and they can check who you are by switching on the TV picture at a security console, which has a remote door release button they push to let their visitors in. You remember the manager had to come let us in. The garage is fairly secure. You need the same key card to get in. There is a visitors' parking area separate from the secure area. Leaving the garage, a pneumatic hose trips the door opener, and an electric eye closes it. That's about it."

Flynn turned to Lieutenant Holland, "Chuck, did anyone think to check the lock on the apartment door before your boys disabled it?"

"We checked the lock and the strike plate. No evidence of forced entry, but, as you know, there's really no way to tell if the lock itself was electronically picked. I'd bet it wasn't. My guess is our killer simply knocked on the door and moved too quickly for Blakemore to do anything. Took him by surprise."

"Okay, let's get to the heart of the thing. What about prints?" Flynn asked.

"Well, we found several belonging to the girl and Blakemore, and several we can't identify yet. The duct tape was clean; so were the faucets in the bath. Ditto the door knobs. Tells me the killer either wiped everything he touched clean, which is pretty iffy, or he wore some damn good gloves–probably surgical. Since I think we're dealing with a professional hit-man here, my money is on surgical gloves. I'm also betting all the unidentified prints belong to people from the development company. Either way, we're screwed."

Flynn leaned forward over his desk and sighed. "Well, that leaves us with a big, fat zero," he said. He sat back to gather his thoughts before he spoke again. "There are just three ways to start this." He began to tick them off on the fingers of his right hand. "One, we need to start investigating the lives of the two victims. Two, I'd say the maid probably knows some of the people who use that apartment, so we'd better get on to her. And, three?– I don't know because I don't have Doc Nichols's autopsy reports yet. Well, fellas, I can only hope something turns up quick, because as of now, we've got nothing! Chuck, thanks for all your help. Mike, you and Sam had better get started." He consulted his watch. "I'm due in the chief's office in five minutes. If anybody turns up anything, let me know immediately."

Flynn walked down the hall leading to the chief's office, passing a row of formal portrait photos of the chief's predecessors and the office of the chief's secretaries. The door to the chief's office was open, so Flynn walked in without knocking. O'Halleran was on the phone, and as he saw Flynn enter he motioned toward a chair immediately in front of the desk. "We have an appointment with the mayor in about fifteen minutes," he said as he hung up the phone.

Flynn rubbed his chin as he began to speak, "I wish I could give you some hope we're getting anywhere on this thing. So far, all we have are two bodies. Both viciously murdered. We know who they both were. The girl was a sometime hooker. No real leads, and we think we're up against a professional killer."

O'Halleran leaned back in his chair and rubbed his eyes. For the next few minutes Flynn brought his boss up to speed on the case.

O'Halleran glanced at this watch. "We'd better get going. If we don't get there on time, we won't get in." Following a quick ride in one of the building's center tower elevators, they were ushered to the mayor's "working office" at the northwest corner of the suite. It offered a magnificent view of Monument Circle and a city reborn. Mayor Robert L. Kirkland was in his shirt sleeves. Mountains of paperwork overflowed his desk onto adjacent chairs and entirely covered a table immediately behind his desk. Kirkland rose to greet his visitors, his impressive six-foot-five frame dwarfing the two policemen. "Morning, Chief. Dennis. I must admit my curiosity is killing me after your call last night, Chief." The mayor indicated the two chairs before his desk.

O'Halleran turned to Flynn as they all took their seats. "Denny, I'll leave the details to you."

Flynn positioned himself in the chair, cleared his throat, and decided to give it to the man straight out. "Mayor, sometime this past weekend, probably Friday or Saturday, your Deputy Mayor, John Blakemore, and a young girl he was with were murdered." He paused to watch the reaction from the mayor. He saw a flexing of the man's jaw muscles and a widening of the eyes. The mayor sat forward, placing his elbows on the desk.

"Oh, God!" he said.

"Well, sir, turns out the girl with him was a local hooker. We only discovered the murders late yesterday afternoon."

The mayor sat back in his chair, absently tapping his desk top with a pencil. "That explains why he didn't show up for work this morning. How did it happen? Why hasn't the media gotten the story?"

O'Halleran spoke up. "Well, sir, they were both knifed to death. It was pretty bloody," he said, hoping the mayor wouldn't press for more details. "We wanted to speak with you about it first, and to be as honest with you as I possibly can, I– we need the time to get out in front of the situation. I mean once the media does learn about this, they're going to be madder than hell we kept it quiet for a few days, and that's just for openers! We're going to be covered up with reporters, insisting we answer their questions. He was one of your appointees. When the news about this does break, we'll have nut cases confessing. It'll take time away from the investigation. Any way you cut it, we're all screwed!

"Now, about the case. The murders took place in the Windom Towers, in an apartment leased to a real estate investment outfit from L. A. We don't know why Blakemore was there. Or for that matter, *how* he got in the place. Some pretty high-powered people live in that building. The pressure to solve this will be considerable! I expect we won't be able to control the thing beyond tomorrow at best. Somebody will talk. They always do."

"Mayor, what exactly did Blakemore do for you?" Flynn wanted to know.

The mayor appeared lost in thought for a moment. Heaving a sigh he answered, "He specialized in attracting business and industry to the city."

"I take it he traveled a lot then?" Flynn asked.

"Yes. Yes, I'd say about forty to fifty percent of the time he was out of town."

"Are there records of his trips?"

"Certainly. He had to fill out vouchers for everything. I'm sure his secretary has copies of all his records and travel itineraries. Do you need all that?" The mayor hesitated for several seconds. "Jack had a reputation as quite the ladies' man," he said.

"We're aware of that. We'll take it into account. The circumstances of the murders would seem to rule out any kind of lover's revenge." Flynn pulled his reporter's notebook from his inside coat pocket and consulted his notes, ticking off the items he'd written there. "If you don't mind, we will also need copies of credit card charges and his personnel file too. I'll need his current residential address, and if you did a background investigation on him before you hired him, I'll need that too."

"I'll have my secretary get them for you right away." The mayor turned, picked up his phone, buzzed for his secretary, and asked that the requested files be brought to his office immediately. That accomplished, he turned to the chief. "Do you have a feeling for this?" he asked. "What are the chances it will get messy? The man was a high-profile part of my administration. Can you keep the blood from splashing on me and my administration?"

"Nobody could promise you that," Flynn told him.

O'Halleran nodded agreement. "He was found murdered in the company of a local hooker—and that's bound to come out."

The killer was savoring a late breakfast at the Airport Holiday Inn. Early that morning, he'd turned in the first rental car and would take the airport bus back into town before renting another car from a different agency. At the moment, he was going back through the home edition of *The Indianapolis Star* searching for any indication the bodies had been discovered. In a way, he was disappointed the deaths had not yet made it into the paper. He always thoroughly enjoyed reading about his work. Yet he knew this lack of discovery would give him time to solve his witness problem.

He sipped his third cup of coffee, mentally totaling up his track record. Thirty-four hits, counting these two, in the ten years since the Army dumped him— all without a problem. He considered himself a perfectionist. Never left clues. Always tied up any loose ends. At a hundred thousand and up a hit, he was a wealthy man!

The fact a girl just might be able to identify him was a bothersome loose end, one that must be taken care of quickly. The hotel P.A. system announced the arrival of the airport bus. The killer collected his bag and rain coat, left a generous tip, and went out onto the drive, joining the queue for the bus. He looked like any other reasonably well-dressed, traveling businessman.

Sergeant Gaffney sat at the conference table in Flynn's office–which now served as headquarters and nerve center for the investigation–poring over the file on Jennifer Wick he'd copied from Vice. Her criminal history, the famous "yellow sheet," showed only three arrests, all for prostitution with the earliest at age eighteen. The full face front and profile photos showed a pretty girl, bewildered and frightened by the processing. According to the record, she had no family. She had come to Indianapolis three years earlier from Cleveland, following the death of her parents in an automobile accident. No other relatives were shown on the record. There was no notation of the girl's having worked for any of the known local pimps. The apartment address listed for the girl was a year old but might still be good. Mike decided a visit to the girl's apartment would be in order. As he was making himself notes, Flynn came bursting into the office, a load of files under one arm.

"Mike! I'm glad you're still here." He dumped the files on the table. "These are all the mayor's office files on Blakemore–his life, working for the mayor." Flynn began separating the files into distinct piles. Pointing to the first pile, he said, "This is the background investigation on him before he was hired, and these two are his travel itineraries, credit card receipts, and personal office files since he started work."

"Okay, which pile do you want?" Mike asked.

"I'm going to start with his application and the background investigation. I want you to start with that pile of itineraries and credit card receipts, and start compiling a list of places he traveled to frequently–concentrate on this past year for now."

Mike pulled the piles Flynn had indicated toward him. "You know this is going to take some time? Do you want to give me some idea just what it is we're looking for? A place to start?"

"Mike, I wish I knew. Considering what happened, it would be fair to say Blakemore had a real enemy–or two out there."

"I've got the Wick girl's file from Vice," Gaffney said pointing to the file laying to one side of the table.

"Anything useful in it?"

"Aside from a possibly current address, nothing."

"Well, we'll get into that when I get back. If Sam shows up have him help you on the Blakemore list." Flynn grabbed his top coat and left for the one block walk to the coroner's office.

The killer got off the bus at the Westin Hotel in the heart of the city. Using one of his stolen credit cards, he checked in under a false name and arranged for a rental car before going up to his room. Today, he would trace the license plate on the red Mustang and make a surveillance of the address listed for the owner. The hunt was on! His spirits were high as he rode the elevator to his floor.

Flynn sat in one of the two chairs facing the coroner's desk, waiting for details. Nichols sat back in his chair, ran his right hand over his thick hair, and then rubbed the dark stubble on his chin.

"Denny, your murderer is off his fuckin' nut!"

"You sure as hell won't get an argument from me. Has anybody from your office notified Blakemore's family?" Flynn asked.

"I got a call from the mayor about fifteen minutes ago. Told me he'd called Jack's parents. He says they're flying in from New York tomorrow morning to make the ID, claim the body, and make the arrangements."

"You going to tell them how their son was murdered?"

"The details? No–I don't think so. Not unless they press me."

"How can you hide a thing like that?"

"Most people don't really want to look at the nude body of a murdered loved one, especially after a full autopsy. Thanks to TV, I think everybody knows it's pretty gruesome. They usually don't ask. We're sewing his genitals back in place anyway. I'll cross that bridge if and when we get to it. But back to the nitty-gritty. To be honest with you, this one stands a good chance of screwing up your clearance rate."

Flynn was quite proud that the IPD Homicide's 93% clearance rate was the best in the nation among big cities and was something Flynn felt was a real accomplishment. "But that isn't the problem just now. Doc, can't you give me anything at all?"

Doc Nichols put on his reading glasses and consulting both files, began to turn pages as he spoke. "I'd say you're looking for more than one knife. The cuts on the girl were all made with something *very* sharp. I'm putting my money on surgical knives. Under the microscope, the wound edges show very little roughness, jaggedness, or tearing. Incidentally, we counted twenty-three separate cuts on her body. The cuts made in her vaginal area were made with a much larger and more interesting blade. I'd say it's about four to six inches in length. Quite sharp. Might be one of those used to cut through a lot of skin and body fat. Used it on both victims. I say this because it took some effort to cut this guy's dick and balls out of his lower body cavity. That's not an easily accomplished task."

"What about stomach content? What did our condemned couple have to eat?"

"Might have something here. Both stomachs showed a partially digested oriental type meal. I'd say the murder took place within a half-an-hour to an hour of the meal, give or take fifteen minutes or so. We also checked both victims for any signs of having been beaten. Nothing there. The only marks on the girl were from the tape the killer used on the wrists and ankles. Tests on the blood show no indications of any diseases, no HIV, and no drugs. She was a fine, healthy, young girl right up to the time she bled to death."

Flynn sat in thoughtful silence for several moments. "That's it? That's everything?."

"Essentially. They differ little. Blakemore bled to death from the excision of his genitalia. His blood test showed some alcohol but not enough to impair." Doc Nichols looked up and fixed Flynn with a fierce look. "Thought you'd heard it all? No way! Here's the *sickest* part of it. We found Blakemore's genitals stuffed up into what was left of the girl's vagina! You've got one *very sick* bastard here!" Nichols closed the files, leaned back in his chair, and picked up the cigar. His face a mask of anger.

Flynn sat in stunned silence.

The killer shifted the phone to his left hand so he could make notes on the hotel note pad. His voice was oily, confiding. "As I was telling the other lady, my car was hit in the parking lot at breakfast this morning, and all I have is a description of the car and a license number. I need to find out who it was–for the insurance."

"Sir, we aren't allowed to give out that information over the phone," said the voice at the Bureau of Motor Vehicles. "But if you can come over to the State Office Building, fill out the forms, and pay the four-dollar fee, I can give you the information."

"I understand, but you see, it's a rental car, and this is going to cost me plenty if I can't give them the information. I was going to fly home today–in two hours– but now–"

"Oh, you're a visitor?"

"Yes, from New York."

"Where are you staying?"

"The Westin."

"Well, you're just across the street from our offices. Shouldn't take more than a few minutes to get the information."

"Are you certain I can get this quickly?"

"Yes. No problem at all. All we need is a license number and if you have it, the make of the car."

"I have that."

"Good. Just come to Room W-160 in the South Building. Like I said, that's just across the street from your hotel."

"Thank you very much for your help. You people certainly know how to treat a visitor. Maybe I can catch that plane for home today after all."

Sergeant Gaffney was in his chair at the conference table. Sam reported the car found in one of the apartment's two reserved spaces was Blakemore's. Mike ordered the car towed to Police Impound for examination. The Blakemore files were piled to one side, and a large street map of Indianapolis lay spread out, covering much of the table. Flynn's return from the coroner's office had prompted this line of investigation. Find out where they had eaten. Had they been seen together? So, Mike had drawn a circle on the map with the center located at the apartment building. The circle represented his best guess at a thirty minute driving time from the outer limits to the apartment building. The circle extended into the bedroom towns of Fishers on the north and Avon on the west side.

"Now," Flynn began, "Doc said the food was Chinese, oriental anyway. So, let's assume the fastest way to do this will be to locate all the places inside the circle that specialize in oriental food."

"That's a lot of territory, Denny. Is there anyway we can narrow it down a bit?"

"Well, if I was with a hooker, I don't think I'd go where someone I know might see me."

"So, we can eliminate the higher class places?"

"It's a fifty-fifty chance as I see it. But since time is so damned important, let's concentrate on the less high profile places for starters."

Mike went to one of the bookshelves lining the walls in Flynn's office and pulled out a business directory. It took the two of them a good hour to list all the high class and low profile restaurants. This afternoon and tonight, armed with photographs of the victims, the eighteen men and women on the middle shift assigned to Homicide and Robbery would wear out shoe leather and put hundreds of miles on the branch's cars visiting each of the low profile restaurants, showing the photos, and trying to learn just where the two had been just before they were murdered. According to the coroner, the best guess would be from noon Friday through Saturday night.

Flynn checked his watch. "I'd better have Sergeant Crooks get ahold of the PIO and get a news conference setup for three-thirty in the chief's conference room. The word has come down from twenty-five; orders are not to keep the murders quiet any longer. The coroner has to release Blakemore's body to his family tomorrow, and we'll have to make some temporary arrangements about the Wick girl's body until we can locate some relatives. The mayor wants it done today. So, guess what? *We*, not the chief, get to face the lions. I'm sorry all this is making things hard for my daughter and my favorite, future son-in-law."

"I think I'll ask Monica to go along with me tonight on the grand tour of oriental restaurants," Mike said. "We might even find one we'd like to have dinner in."

"That's a great idea! Just don't give her all the grizzly details."

"Don't worry. I never do that. She thinks Homicide and Robbery is one of the safest jobs in the department. After all, her daddy is looking out for me." Mike smiled and patted Flynn on the shoulder as he spoke.

Carefully following the street map and street guide he'd purchased at the hotel news and sundries shop, the killer headed his rented Honda east on Kessler Boulevard and slowed the car as he approached the address the Bureau of Motor Vehicles listed for the red Mustang. There was the house, a two-story with a carport at the side but no car. Carefully, he scanned the street for any sign of the flashy car. Eventually, he noticed parking was prohibited on both sides of the street. Just to be certain, he made a circuit of the block. Deciding the girl was most probably at work, he determined to return late that night when the likelihood was better she would be home.

He parked the car around the corner from the girl's address and walked back to have a closer look at the house and surroundings. His pace was leisurely but steady to avoid attracting attention. He slowed just a bit as he walked the ninety yards or so approaching and passing the house. He paid careful attention to the short drive leading off the street, ending in the open carport halfway down the side of the two story house. He noticed there were no first floor windows near the carport, only a solid door from the carport into the house. He continued on past the house and turned the next corner. Halfway up the block, an alley ran behind the row of houses, splitting the block in half. He entered the alley and walked to the rear of the house. A solid, board fence about eight feet high separated the back yard from the alley. There was a door, but he found it bolted from the inside. Thinking over his options, the killer decided the car itself would be the best way to eliminate the witness. He'd return that night and install a time delayed bomb—one of his favorite killing devices. Having reached the solution, he felt an invisible weight lift from his shoulders as he walked back to his car.

Immediately after the press conference concluded, Flynn returned to his office, seated himself behind his desk, and braced for the onslaught. The phone would start ringing any minute now. He had counted on the announcement of a press conference so late in the day producing few reporters. The tactic had worked. Only three radio station men were there, and one reporter covering the cop shop for *The Indianapolis Star*—a blessing for Flynn since *The Star* couldn't get ink on the street until midnight.

A young intern reporter from WTHR, the local NBC TV affiliate, was the kid who caught the conference. Aside from her, the TV people were all busy assembling their early evening shows. Flynn knew it would take a few minutes for the reporters to phone their respective assignment editors and then, a few minutes more before the assignment editors went to their news editors or in the case of the morning paper, the city desk. Indianapolis wasn't New York and this was real news! Then the phone would start. At this point, he wasn't about to make things worse by playing favorites, although he knew favoritism was the least of his worries. He was packing his pipe when the first call came through. It was the city desk editor at *The Star*.

"Dennis, this is Ben Nelson at *The Star*."

"Congratulations, you beat everybody else."

"Well, it's nice to know we didn't waste all that money on speed dialers for nothing. Dennis, I have questions—I need information. A hell of a lot more than you gave our beat writer! Now, what about this girl? Who was she? What was Blakemore doing with her in someone else's apartment?"

"Ben, we're still running an investigation on the girl. We're running print checks on her now. For now, she's officially a Jane Doe. I say that because we do know who she was but we haven't located any next of kin yet. You know the policy: until we notify them we don't publish victims' names. I can't tell you any more than I told your young man at the press conference. I don't know what they were doing in that apartment, but we're busting our asses to find out."

"Word here has it that old Jack was quite a ladies' man. Any truth in that?"

"I really couldn't say."

"You mean you won't. My kid says the cause of death for both of them was knife wounds. How many and what kind of cuts? And where on the bodies?"

"The girl received several wounds, and Blakemore had only one. Their bodies are still over at the morgue. I understand Blakemore's parents are flying in from New York to make arrangements for their son."

"What kind of a knife was used?"

"The coroner thinks it was a fairly large one."

"Kitchen knife? Switch blade? What?"

"I'm sorry, we haven't gotten that far with the coroner yet. He'll be getting the paperwork to me just as soon as he has it all neatly tied up from his end," Flynn lied. He desperately wanted to keep the fine details out of the media.

"Any witnesses?"

"As of now– None."

"Did you find any drugs–Coke? Crack? Heroin?"

"No. No drugs of any kind. Why did you ask that? Do you have information he was a drug user?"

"Take it easy. No, I don't have any information about Blakemore and drugs. Was it a robbery?"

"Well, it sure looked like it. Both victims' money was missing. We think robbery is a distinct possibility," Flynn lied again. All his instincts told him otherwise.

"Okay, one last question. If this happened over the weekend, how is it we didn't find out about it until late today?"

This was the question Flynn had been dreading. "Ben, it was my decision to keep a lid on it until now."

"Why? Because it was the mayor's man?"

"Well, partially. How many years have we known each other? I remember you when you were just a fresh kid out of Ball State all excited about being the police beat reporter for

The Star. You know how my side of the street works. The truth is I didn't need all your reporters and everybody else's underfoot until we got our act together. And there's certain information I don't want on the street."

"Dennis, you just admitted there's a lot more to this than you're letting on. After all these years, you know how my side of the street works too. My job is to dig out the facts and print them. If I were you, I'd tell me now, before I start my people digging. You might not like the way it comes off in print."

"Can't do it, Ben. Just remember this. There's a killer out there somewhere. It's my job to catch him."

"And it's my job to pound you until you tell us what you know. Don't forget the old man still buys ink by the fifty-five gallon drum and paper by the ton."

Arriving home, Flynn carefully hung his top coat in the front hall closet–as Mary had always insisted he do. He pulled the gun and holster from his waist and placed it on top of the television set. He noticed Monica left a note taped on the picture tube.

> Daddy,
> Mike and I are going out for dinner. Yours is
> in the oven. You may have to turn the heat up for
> a few minutes to get it hot. Sorry about missing
> you today. –Love, Monica.

Flynn went into the kitchen, checked the contents of the oven, turned the heat on, set the timer for ten minutes, put the kettle on for tea, and went back into the living room. He took off his suit coat and tie and settled into his favorite chair. Flynn hoped the telephone wouldn't intrude too much. It looked as though he would have an evening to himself for a change. For a few moments he allowed the loneliness to creep into his soul. God how he missed Mary! Her smell and that mischievous smile, which greeted him at the door every night. Realizing he was about to depress himself again, he picked up *The Indianapolis Star* did a quick scan of the front section before turning to his favorite column by the local TV critic, Steve Hall. The man truly had a way with words–particularly when he employed them to burst pompous balloons. Flynn admitted he agreed with the man's reviews of shows more often than not. Since Mary's death, he'd found himself allowing television to occupy more and more of those lonely evening and late night hours. Checking the TV listings for the evening, he noted with pleasure that a new episode of N.Y.P.D. Blue would be on at ten. Last week's installment had ended with a cliff-hanger: Detective Sipowitz had apparently been blown away right at the close of the show. Flynn ardently hoped the feisty detective hadn't been done in. While he waited for the food to warm, he turned his attention to the column.

Wednesday, 1:45 a.m.

The killer turned off the headlights and pulled the Honda into the dark alley. The car's black paint work blended perfectly into the darkness of the night. He stopped the car next to a telephone pole just outside the tall fence at the rear of the girl's house, turned off the engine, and carefully exited the car, taking care to close the car door as quietly as possible. He had made several purchases at a Wal-Mart on the east side of town earlier that afternoon; a ten-foot length of half-inch nylon line into which he'd tied knots about every eight inches or so, and the things that he was now wearing, a navy blue warm-up suit and nondescript high top, basketball shoes in black. In his hand was another purchase, a small, canvas duffel bag.

He silently climbed to the roof of the Honda and looked over the fence, examining the rear of the house. All the rear windows were dark. He listened for sounds coming from the house, heard nothing, and decided it was safe to proceed. Taking the knotted nylon line from the duffel bag, he tied one end around the telephone pole, dropping the remainder of the line inside the fence. Carefully, he climbed over the fence and silently lowered himself to the ground. He dropped to a crouch and moved quickly to the side of the house. Pressing his ear to the clapboards, he listened for signs of life – movement or talk. Hearing nothing, he quietly moved to the carport. The red, Mustang convertible was there. He scanned the street for any signs of life. Satisfied there were none, he lowered himself to the ground and slid under the car. Opening the duffel bag, he withdrew a small rectangular package from which two wires protruded. At their ends, he'd affixed large alligator clips.

Taking a penlight from his pocket, he located the terminals on the back side of the starter motor. Dipping back into his bag, he withdrew two, long, heavy-duty, nylon zip ties, and using these, he fixed the package to the frame next to the starter. He completed the installation by clamping the alligator clips to the starter's electrical terminals. Imbedded in the package was a battery-operated, digital timer, which would begin its preset countdown when the starter was engaged. He'd set it for twenty minutes, allowing for a ten minute warm-up in the freezing, November morning. Quickly, he replaced the pen light, took the duffel bag, and slid from beneath the car. He stood quietly for several seconds, listening. At last, satisfied his activity had gone unnoticed, he returned to the back yard, climbed the rope, retrieved it from the telephone pole, silently entered the Honda, started the engine, and drove quietly out of the alley.

Wednesday, 6:45 a.m

Flynn was seated at his breakfast table with the front page of *The Star* laid out before him. The headline, "DEPUTY MAYOR IN LOVE NEST MURDER", spread across the full six columns. A professional business portrait of Blakemore filled three columns beneath the headline. Flynn noted there was no byline. The subhead read **"Police Stonewall"**. Flynn sipped his second cup of coffee as he read the story.

After most of a column had been given over to a summary of the murders, this:

> Sources close to the investigation told *The Star* the murders took place over the weekend with the best estimate placing the time of death at sometime this past Friday. Police could not offer a reason why Deputy Mayor Blakemore and Miss Wick were together in the apartment as neither had been seen there before according to building residents. No one was able to offer any connection between Blakemore, Miss Wick, and the

development company. Phone calls placed by *The Star* to the Los Angeles investment company have not been returned.

Mayor Kirkland's office issued a brief statement expressing the Mayor's deep shock and sorrow over the death of Mr. Blakemore, "We have complete confidence the police department is doing everything necessary to solve this shocking and brutal murder."

Under the bold face subhead, "POLICE STONEWALL", Flynn read three paragraphs excoriating him by name for not cooperating with the newspaper.

Flynn sat back and lit-up his first bowl of tobacco for the day. Well, he'd been warned. As promised, the powers that be at *The Star* had unleashed the dogs on him for certain! He silently thanked the chief and the mayor for their understanding and cooperation. But he also knew unless he was able to get a good lead, and quickly, the media would shortly put the mayor's feet to the fire in which case his job was on the line.

Monica, dressed in her housecoat, walked into the kitchen, placed her arm around her father's shoulder, bent, and kissed him on the top of the head. "Morning, Dad."

Flynn looked up at his daughter, her hair a tumble of golden brown curls. Her deep violet-blue eyes were still puffy from sleep. She reminded him so much of Mary. Especially, in the way she would toss her head in anger. Now he thought of her safety, the vision of the murdered girl still fresh in his mind. "Morning, honey. How was your evening with Mike?"

"I've never in my life been dragged through so many restaurants in one evening!" she sighed.

"Did he, at least, treat you to a decent meal?"

"After all those oriental places, I had him take me to St. Elmo's downtown. Good old American steak and baked potatoes!" Taking notice of the newspaper, she said, "You know, I was in that apartment building last Friday–it gives me a really weird feeling, knowing I was so close to the murders."

Startled, Flynn sat forward. "What were you doing there?"

"I took a revised will to one of our clients."

"What time were you there?"

"Pop, I swear you're as bad as Mike. When I told him I'd been there Friday, I thought he was going to come over the table at me. Anyway, like I told Mike, I'd say I left there about four-thirty or so–give or take a few minutes."

"Monica, this is important. Did you see anybody?"

"You and Mike really are alike. Yes, I did see a man. He was on the elevator when I got on to leave. Mike made me describe him."

"Well, what did the man look like? Describe him for me."

"He was about five-eleven, maybe six feet, hazel eyes, long light brown hair. He was wearing a three-piece, business suit, pinstripe, dark-blue or black. Had a black, cashmere, top coat over his arm and had one of those fold-over carry-on, airline bags next to him on the floor."

"Did you speak?"

"No."

"Monica, what floor were you on?"

"The thirty-first."

"And this man was already on the elevator when you got on?"

"Yes."

"I know your car is in the shop, so, how did you get there?"

"I borrowed Norma's."

"Where did you park? Was the car in the basement?"

"Yes. In the visitors' parking area."

"I thought you needed one of those special cards to open the garage door."

"Yes, you do. The client sent his to the office so I could get in. I returned it when I got there."

"Did this fellow go all the way to the basement with you?"

"Yes."

"Did you see him leave?"

"No—I don't remember. I wasn't really paying attention. I was in a hurry to get Norma's car back to her before the office closed."

"This may not amount to anything, but are you going to be in your office today? I might want to have one of our artists visit you and make a sketch of this man."

"Dad—do you actually think this man might be the killer?"

"Honey, it's a very long shot, but you know me. I'll turn over every stone until I find the right worm. How are you getting to work by the way?"

"Norma is coming by to get me around eight-thirty."

Flynn got up from the table, grabbed his suit coat, kissed Monica, and headed for his car. For the first time since it all started, he felt a glimmer of hope. A coincidence? Perhaps something was working in his favor at last. He didn't believe in coincidences. Amateurs see coincidences. Detectives see links. And if Monica did see the killer, the killer saw Monica!

Wednesday, 7:30 a.m.

The men and women of Homicide and Robbery were already gathered in Flynn's office when he arrived. The morning edition of *The Star* had been reduced to clippings with some lines highlighted in bright yellow. Flynn poured himself a cup of coffee, took his seat at the head of the conference table, and opened the meeting. Pointing toward the newspaper clippings, he said, "Pass the word–I will have the balls of whoever it was talked to the paper! Now–has anybody got anything good to tell me?"

Detective Harriet Anderson spoke up. "I got a possible ID on our victims at the Ginza, a Japanese joint out on West 38th Street. One of the waiters thinks he's pretty sure they were there. He couldn't say what the time was, but he thinks it was during the lunch hours on Friday."

"Did he know who Blakemore was?" Flynn asked.

"No, but according to the waiter, he ate there frequently, sometimes alone, sometimes with other men, and occasionally, with women."

"Did he identify this girl?"

"I'd say he's sure."

"Had she been there with Blakemore before?" Flynn asked.

"I didn't ask. Sorry. I was so excited–finding where they'd been– I'm sorry."

"That's okay. We can ask about that later. Did you ask if there was anybody with them?"

"According to the waiter, they were alone. Just the two of them."

"How'd he pay for the meal? Use a credit card?"

"Sorry, Boss. Waiter says the man paid cash and left a pretty fair tip. That's how he claims to remember."

"How about somebody who might have gotten up and followed them out of the restaurant?"

"I did think to ask that one. He says he didn't notice anybody. Boss, that's a very busy place, especially around the lunch hours."

Flynn sat back in his chair. "Anything more?"

Mike opened his Blakemore file. "So far, we have four trips to the Detroit area, five to the West Coast, and ten to Miami. His reports on the meetings he held in those places list a lot of names. I've asked his secretary to give me a thumbnail sketch on each of the people he met with. That's as far as I've gotten on the business trips. I did get search warrants for his house and the girl's apartment from Judge Jones early this morning. I thought, maybe, you'd like to come along."

"Wouldn't miss it for the world," Flynn said. "Where'd he live anyway?"

"He bought one of those new town houses on North Alabama Street across from Riley Towers."

Flynn nodded and turned his attention to Detective Elberger. "Sam, what did you turn up on Blakemore's car?"

Elberger waved his right hand through the air. "It's over at the impound lot right now. I asked Lieutenant Holland to go through it personally. He'll look for any unusual modifications in the body work, traces of chemicals."

"Anybody got anything else?" Flynn asked.

Mike selected a computer-generated Detectives' Report from the pile on the table. "Only this. Some old guy took a header off the garage at the Embassy Suites Hotel sometime late last night. I don't think it's connected. Looks to me like a homeless guy decided to go home. I've got Jim Becker following up on it."

"Okay. Now, Harriet, I'd like you and Sam to go check out the girl's place. Mike's got the warrant. If there's nothing more," Flynn said. "You all know what we need. Mike, let's you and I go take a good look at Blakemore's house."

8:10 a.m.

Morning rush hour traffic was still at its peak as Norma Tilson, paralegal at the legal firm of Daniels, Springer, Holds & Steel, backed the red Mustang out of her drive and headed west on Kessler toward Meridian Street. Three minutes later, she turned south on Meridian and found herself joining the double lane of traffic rushing madly from traffic light to traffic light. She switched on the radio. Bob and Tom, the top-rated, local, radio personalities and purveyors of high school boys' bathroom humor, were in good form, and Norma found herself, as usual, laughing aloud as she drove. She was stopped, second car back from the light, at the traffic signal at 38th and Meridian when the explosion ended her life.

On the short drive to Blakemore's house, Flynn and Mike discussed the fact that Monica had seen a man in the apartment building elevator and had mutually decided it would probably be a good idea to have the police artist do a sketch–just in case. Now, they were standing in the middle of the dead man's living room. The room was what modern real estate types liked to call a great room, with a high, vaulted ceiling complete with fake beams. The room itself was expensively furnished and very masculine. Together, the two men walked from room to room. The house was quite, clean, neat–with nothing out of place; four bedrooms housed within two-stories and attached two-car garage. It was a very large house for a bachelor. "If you ask me," Flynn said, "this place was an investment. The kind of an asset a man could sell when he moved on to the next political job."

"Well, I wish I could afford something like this for Monica and me," Mike said somewhat wistfully.

"Her mother and I started out in an efficiency apartment. All-purpose living room with a couch that made into a bed at night, a kitchen, and a small bathroom. I think you two will do a lot better than that when you start out."

"I guess maybe so. Well, where do we want to begin with this place?" Mike asked.

"Let's go back to the den and start there."

Blakemore's den was furnished with a large, modern desk, two leather, club chairs, a large-screen, RCA, digital, projection television with a combination DVD-VCR, and a separate Sony stereo system. Two walls were lined from ceiling to floor with book shelves, holding a collection of business-oriented books, a few novels, and a large collection of prerecorded video tapes, most of them Hollywood movies, but there was a goodly number of X-rated tapes as well. Flynn walked behind the desk and carefully took visual inventory of everything on it. "I'll start here on the right side drawers. You take the ones on the left side," he said to Mike.

Working together, they opened each drawer and began a careful examination of the contents. The drawers contained the usual paraphernalia desks do. But when Flynn opened the bottom drawer, he found an expensive looking, Ampex, reel to reel, tape recorder and six boxes of five inch reels of tape. The reels had been labeled with what appeared to be Blakemore's own code and dated. The Ampex had been wired directly into the phone on the desk and into an FM receiver for a wireless microphone.

"Mike," Flynn said, "we'd better get this stuff boxed up so we can take it back to the office. Would you mind getting the boxes out of my car?"

"Why don't I pull the car into the garage? That way, we won't have to carry all this stuff quite so far—besides, it will keep snoopy neighbors from dropping by to see what's going on."

"Now, why didn't I think of that? Good idea! While you're doing that, I'm going to take a quick look through the bedroom."

Mike was pulling the Ford into the garage when a call came through on his portable, two-way radio. Headquarters wanted Captain Flynn to call in by land line immediately. He was to contact the chief's office. Mike acknowledged the call and went into the house to find Flynn.

He found him in Blakemore's bedroom, which was a shambles. Flynn was searching the pockets of a sport coat as

Mike entered. "Chief wants you on the land line ASAP. I just took the call on my radio. "

Flynn reached for the bedside phone and punched in the chief's private number. O'Halleran answered on the first ring.

"Chief, it's Denny. What's up?"

"Denny, isn't Norma Tilson one of Monica's best friends?"

"Yeah, they went all the way through school together, even work for the same law firm. Why?"

"I hate to be the one to tell you this, but it looks like she was killed in an explosion this morning on her way to work." Flynn felt his stomach go cold. Monica was supposed to ride to work with Norma that morning. Flynn dropped to the bed. "Was there anybody with her in the car?"

"Denny, her car and several others are just so much melted metal according to the report I got from the fire chief. I couldn't tell you right now if Norma was alone or not. I just thought you might want to break the news to Monica before we release the names to the news media."

"Monica was supposed to be with Norma this morning. Where did this happen?"

"38th and Meridian."

"I'm on my way now!" Flynn broke the connection and immediately dialed Monica's office, where he learned she hadn't arrived yet. Mike was looking at him intently, waiting for some word. Flynn dialed his office and told Julie to have two detectives report to him at Blakemore's house immediately. Without saying a word, Flynn got up from the bed and went into the kitchen, where he began going through the cabinets. He found a bottle of Wild Turkey Bourbon, got down two glasses, got some ice from the refrigerator, and poured two fingers of straight whiskey into each glass. Flynn sat at the kitchen table and motioned for Mike to take the other chair, sliding the second glass across the table. Flynn took a healthy pull on his own glass and proceeded to tell Mike about the call. By the time he'd finished, the two men from Homicide and Robbery were at the door. Flynn gave them instructions to box up the contents of Blakemore's den, desk, the Ampex recorder, and the FM wireless receiver–everything! They were to get it all to the Homicide Office. That done, he took Mike by the elbow and steered the shaken man out to the car. Flynn drove.

Arriving at the blast scene, they clipped their department ID's to the lapels of their top coats and worked their way through the crowd. Fire apparatus and other emergency vehicles mixed with radio and television news vehicles. Ambulances totally blocked the huge intersection. Television crews were everywhere with their ubiquitous mini-cams. Reporters, standing at the edges of the horrific scene doing live remotes, worked to keep the background of disaster just over their shoulders. The scene looked like a bomb crater. What had once been cars were now twisted, burned, and melted lumps. The asphalt street surface under the cars had melted down several inches to the original paving brick. Several bodies, covered with fire department blankets, were lying in the street. Windows in the Summit House, a high-rise, apartment building on the east side of the street, had been blown out. Across the street, a church lawn was seriously scorched. Flynn went looking for the deputy fire chief who he knew would be directing operations. He found the man conferring with men from the fire department's Arson Squad and IPD's Bomb Squad and Anti-Terrorist Units. He waited to ask about the car while the deputy chief completed making notes and giving instructions. Flynn introduced himself. Flashing his gold shield, he asked about the red Mustang belonging to Norma Tilson.

The deputy chief pointed to the wreckage centered in the middle of the disaster scene. "That's it—or what's left of it, right there."

Flynn was astonished. "How many people in the car?"

"Just one."

"Do you have a positive ID?"

"No. At the moment, we're going by registrations on most of these. The driver of that car was literally blown to pieces and burned beyond recognition."

"And you're absolutely certain there was nobody else in the car?" Flynn asked.

"Certain as we can be at this point."

Flynn's heart lifted with relief. "So—what the hell happened here?"

"Probably a few pounds of C-4. The detonation was right under the Mustang, probably fixed to the frame."

"C-4? I thought that was impossible to get outside the military," Flynn said.

"Time was it was. But today? Well, if you got the money, it isn't any harder to get than an illegal gun."

"Any idea how it was set off?"

"You name it. Remote radio signal, timer, fuse. It could have been any number of ways. It'll be days before we know for sure.

I'll have to call in the FBI and ATF. Bombs are Federal territory now."

Flynn slowly scanned the disaster scene. His heart was beating like a bass drum! "Look, I know this is out of my jurisdiction, but may I see the list of the ID's you have so far?" The deputy chief handed Flynn his clipboard. "Help yourself. We've got most of them. Looking for anybody in particular?"

"My daughter."

Flynn checked the list. The only name he recognized was Norma's. Flynn handed the clipboard back to the deputy chief and went looking for Mike. He found him lifting blankets and checking bodies. "Mike, I think we're in luck. Looks like Monica wasn't in the car. Get on your cell phone and call her office. Maybe she's there by now." Mike dialed the law firm, Monica's extension number and handed the small phone to Flynn. Monica answered on the second ring.

"Monica, it's your dad." He gave Mike a thumbs up to indicate everything was okay. "Wasn't Norma supposed to pick you up this morning?" Relief released his body. His shoulders lost their tension, and his heart began to slow.

"Yes, she was. I waited for her until almost eight-forty-five, and finally called a cab. She still hasn't showed up at the office."

"Listen, honey, do you think your boss could spare you for a couple of hours today?"

"Well, I don't know—I'll have to ask. Why? What do you want?"

"I'd like you to come down to my office and help us create a picture of the man you saw in the elevator." While this was true, he really wanted to break the news of her best friend's death in person and as gently as he could.

"Oh, sure. I'll be glad to help. I'll have to ask my boss for the time off."

"Why don't you let me do that? Can you put him on the line?"

"Hang on. I'll transfer the call."

Flynn waited impatiently for Monica's boss to pick up the phone.

"Captain Flynn!" said a hearty voice. "This is Luke Daniels. Monica tells me you want me to give her some time off today."

"Yes, that's so."

"Well, we're pretty snowed under at the moment—is it important?"

Flynn's personal stress made his patience disappear. "Mr. Daniels, believe me, it's very   important. Official, police business. If I have to, I'll come down there and physically remove her myself."

Daniels paused before he answered. "Captain, I want to cooperate, believe me. You don't need to get belligerent. I'll tell Monica she can go at any time. But please, don't keep her any longer than necessary. Monica has one of the sharpest minds of all our paralegals, and well, to tell you the truth, I really depend on her."

Denny realized the adrenaline was still effecting his actions and thoughts. He felt ashamed of himself. "Mr. Daniels, I apologize for my bad manners. I'm under a lot of stress at the moment. I promise I'll have her back to you as quickly as possible. Now, if you would just put her back on the line?" In seconds, Monica was back. "Mr. Daniels was kind enough to let me borrow you for a short time. Can you meet me in my office, say, in a half hour?"

"Sure, Daddy."

"Okay, honey, I'll see you there."

Flynn felt helpless as he sat behind his desk watching Mike console his daughter. She'd taken the news about her best friend's death very hard. The two had been bosom girlfriends since parochial school. It shook Denny to the core that his daughter's first reaction was to turn to Mike for consolation and not her father, and he could not rid himself of the ever growing belief the bomb had really been meant for his daughter.

"Monica, think you can talk?" Flynn asked.

"Yes. Yes, I think so."

"Remember describing the man on the elevator to me this morning?"

"Yes."

"Do you think you can describe him to one of our artists?"

"Well, I'm pretty sure I could."

"I'm just working on a hunch. I'd like to have a picture of that man to show around the apartment building. It might help us on the murders."

"You think he's the murderer, don't you?"

"I think there's a damn good chance."

"Did he kill Norma?"

"Well, yes, I think so. I can't afford not to at the moment. Mike, would you take Monica up to Ident and stay with her while she works with one of the artists? Ask the lieutenant if they can let Kurt work with her. Better yet, I'll phone Lieutenant Koslowski, tell him you're on your way, and ask him myself."

The killer was watching the local television, live coverage of his handiwork from the comfort of his hotel room. A self-satisfied smile played at the corners of his mouth. He truly enjoyed watching the confusion and havoc. To him, this was much more fun than an NFL football game. He wished he had a VCR so he could record the whole thing. Considering the devastation his bomb had caused, he had no doubt the girl was dead, but it would be best to know for certain. He flipped channels back and forth between the four network affiliates, listening for confirmation of Norma Tilson's death. He was supremely confident she had been killed by the explosion— nobody could have survived the two and a half pounds of C-4 explosive he'd strapped to the frame of that car. As soon as he was certain of his success, he'd continue looking for the place Blakemore actually called home. He'd go through it with a fine toothed comb, get what that goddamned lawyer wanted, and then, he'd reconfirm his flight to L.A. and get out of town. Another perfect hit with no loose ends.

"The shape of his face is just a little more square and not quite as gaunt. The lips a bit more full," Monica was saying to Sergeant Kurt Youngblood. Sergeant Youngblood made a few adjustments with the computer's mouse. The face on the computer screen "morphed" into a bit fuller look. "Yes. Yes, that's more like it." Warming to the task, Monica said, "Now, the eyes are just a bit larger, and the lids droop a bit. The eyes need to be more grayish too." Monica found herself fascinated by what this Apple G-4 computer and the morphing program could do. "Now, the hair is a lighter brown, and it's longer. Over the ears and down the back of the neck more." Youngblood worked his magic. "There! You've got him!" Monica said.

"Monica, take a real good look at him," Mike said. "Is there anything missing from the picture?"

Monica frowned and stared at the picture for several seconds. "I'm pretty sure there's a small freckle or mole just to the left side of his nose." She pointed to the left side of the man's nose, right in the crease at the edge of his nose. "What color?" Youngblood asked. "Dark brown? Light brown? Tan?"

Monica thought for a few seconds, rolling her lower lip between thumb and forefinger as she thought. "I'd say it was a medium brown. Not as dark as a mole. More like a freckle." Youngblood placed the cross hairs of the cursor beside the nose and gave the mouse a tap. A small circular mark appeared in the place Monica had indicated. "Yes. That's definitely him. Mind if I ask you something?"

"Shoot."

"Well, please don't think I'm prying, but I was wondering about you–your long, black hair, dark eyes, name, and all–I was just wondering–are you of Native American ancestry?"

Youngblood smiled, revealing perfect, white teeth. He was all too aware his ancestry showed and was proud of it. "UGH! Paleface squaw! Me, Potawatomi. Born and raised right here in Indiana." He let out a great booming laugh, "Why do you ask? Isn't it obvious?"

Monica blushed, her face turning a beet red. "Well, Mister Youngblood, you are a strikingly handsome man! I just thought if you were of Indian ancestry, it was unusual to find one right here in the police department."

"Name's Kurt," Youngblood said. "I come with the U.S. Marine Corps behind me and a full scholarship from the Herron School of Art. Of course that came after five years as a street cop."

"Well, it was a real pleasure to meet you," Monica said.

Mike was suddenly jealous of this admittedly very handsome man. He decided to rescue his lady from further possible enticements. "Okay, Sergeant," he said, "can you print me out a couple of those to take with me? And then get color reproductions made up. Tell the photo lab we need a thousand copies, and get them down to me yesterday!"

"Sure. No problem." Youngblood moved the mouse. He placed the arrow on the small icon picture of a printer and tapped the mouse's button. Quickly, a dialog box appeared. He instructed the computer to print out two copies. To Monica's surprise, never having seen this sort of technology before, within two minutes, two perfectly natural-looking, color pictures of the man in the elevator had rolled out of the nearby printer.

The killer was enjoying a room service lunch in his room. All the local midday news programming was still occupied with live remote coverage of the car bombing and aftermath. Identification of the victims had been made, relatives notified, and names and photographs were now being released. He put down his fork, picked up the TV remote control, increased the volume, and sat back to watch. A local anchorwoman, superimposed over "file footage" of the scene recorded earlier that morning, was delivering the latest summary of known details. The killer waited for the name and photo of Norma Tilson. When it came he was thunderstruck. The girl identified as Norma Tilson was auburn-haired, green-eyed, freckle-faced, and definitely not the girl who'd seen him in the apartment building elevator! The identification was the same on the other local channels.

Angrily, he turned the TV off and began pacing the room. The damnable loose end was still there, only now his mistake had made it potentially much more dangerous, especially if the girl made the connection. He went to the window and stared at the view ten floors below. He had to assess the situation. The bomb blast was all over television. The talking heads were speculating about it being yet another act of terrorists. Even the local Muslim Clerics were being interviewed. That was to his benefit. But there was that damn girl. A small voice told him he should just get on the plane and go. But pride in an unblemished career and the knowledge that there was an excellent possibility there could soon be a representation of his face together with a physical description circulating to all police departments in the country prevented that simple, prudent move. Like any true professional, he'd taken the time to study high profile crimes and examine why people got caught after committing murder. The bottom line still held that without a living eye-witness to identify him, they had no case. No, the problem wasn't whether or not to leave. The problem was how to find the girl. No girl—no identification in court. If he were going to stay ahead of the situation, he knew it was time for some fast moves! He crossed the room and called the front desk, asking that his room bill be made ready.

Flynn and Mike sat across from each other at the conference table in Flynn's office. Mike had just returned from taking Monica back to her office. More than anything, he'd returned for a private meeting with his boss, friend, and future father-in-law. "How is Monica taking all this?" Flynn asked.

"She agrees with us. The bomb was intended for her. Right now, she's mad as hell her best friend is dead."

"What are the chances he's still in town? I mean, what's your guess?" Flynn asked.

Mike thought for a moment before answering. "I'd bet the farm on it. That bomb didn't attach itself to the girl's car at random. He stayed around to eliminate a witness. He'd stick around to be certain."

"So you agree—he knew Monica saw him in the elevator. He just chased the plate thinking he'd get the girl?"

"Yes. There's no other explanation."

"He'd have to go over to the BMV and get somebody to give him the registration on that plate. I think we'd better send somebody over there and see who asked for the information."

"If it's okay with you, I'll ask Marge to go. She's a whiz with bureaucrats. That gal can charm the skin off a snake!"

"Do it. Now, we have to believe it won't be long before this scum bag finds out he got the wrong girl—if he hasn't already. I want to put Monica under some sort of protection. Out of town, maybe? You agree?" He scrutinized Mike's eyes as he spoke.

"She's the only one who can put this guy at the scene–at least in the apartment building. So I was going to insist on it if you didn't bring it up."

"I'd like to get her out of town and protected if she'll agree to it. I'll have to give this some thought this afternoon. Maybe I can come up with a plan by the time she gets off work tonight. In the meantime, I want this guy's picture distributed to every uniform in Operations, Traffic, Vice, and Narcotics. When will copies be ready?"

"I've ordered up a thousand copies. The photo section promised to have them before the shift change."

"Good. I think I'd better explain things to O'Halleran and ask him to call in the shift commanders and have them get the word straight from the chief. That ought to light a fire under everybody. In the meantime, I don't want anybody– and I mean anybody– to know about Monica. For now just you and me." Flynn thought for a moment. "Maybe a call to Kurt Youngblood is in order. I think I'll strongly suggest he keep mum about what he knows."

Mike let out a sigh of relief. "If it's okay with you, I'd like to go over to her office, stay with her after work, and keep her with me."

"I think that's a great idea. Think I'll go see if the chief will let me bend a few more rules."

The killer was shopping at Castleton Shopping Mall on the far Northside of town, surrounded by several thousand fellow shoppers. Surreptitiously, he checked each passing uniformed security officer, avoiding eye contact but watching for any signs of recognition. Earlier at a corner CVS drug store, he'd purchased some hair lightener and was now in the process of looking for a hair styling salon. The time had come to change his appearance. A shorter hair cut, a different style, and a change of wardrobe would do the trick. That night in his new motel room, he'd apply the lightener. Tomorrow, he'd start penetrating police security.

He'd done it before in many other cities. Police departments are, and always have been, the world's biggest rumor mills–and uniformly leak information like a sieve. A reasonably good con artist can learn just about anything. All he has to do is ask the right people. Cops are always ready to brag about what they know–or think they know. Before long, he would know the true identity of the girl he'd seen on the elevator–of that, he was confident.

The stack of tape reels taken from Blakemore's house was only slightly diminished. Flynn was frankly surprised the man had recorded so many phone calls and private conversations. He reached over, turned the Ampex machine off, and took off his set of earphones. Detective Elberger removed his earphones as well. "How many names have we got so far?" Flynn asked. Elberger began counting down the list he'd made on his yellow, legal pad.

"Twenty-eight so far."

"Well, let's knock off for tonight–go home to your wife and kids." Flynn checked his watch. "I've kept you an hour past quitting time. Be back here first thing in the morning." Flynn picked up the phone and dialed Monica's law firm. Within a few moments, he had Mike on the phone. "Mike, do me a favor," he began without preamble, "Take Monica home, and wait for me there. I've been working on a plan, and I want to talk it over with both of you. Okay?" Mike readily agreed and ended the call.

Anxious to move quickly, Flynn punched in a new line on the phone. He desperately hoped John Green was home. Twenty minutes later, he was knocking on retired Lieutenant Green's front door. A dog, large by the sound, barked in answer to Flynn's knock. Seconds later, the door was opened by a giant of a black man, his broad smile flashing perfect, white teeth. "Get on in here, white man! Don't you know you stand out like a prostitute in church out there?" Flynn stepped through the door and found himself crushed in the big man's welcoming bear hug. He stayed for thirty minutes before going home.

Monica cleared away the dinner dishes and poured a round of coffee for each of them. Flynn lit up his pipe and blew a plume of aromatic, blue smoke toward the kitchen ceiling. "Oh, Daddy, get on with it!" Monica exploded. "Tell us what the plan is. I can't stand it any longer!"

"Sorry. I didn't realize–" Flynn began. "This afternoon, I visited with Johnny Green."

"Big John?" Monica asked.

"The same." Flynn allowed himself a brief mental reading once again of John Green's pedigree. Former navy seal, outstanding cop. Before retiring from the department, Green had spent his final five years working out of the Prosecutor's office. He was not only a damn good detective but he never lost a witness–never even had one threatened.

"So, where does he fit in?" Mike asked, breaking into Flynn's thoughts.

"Well, I have a lot of respect for that man. He's one of the most honest men I've ever met in my life and a deep thinker. He was usually a step ahead of his prey. Green was the first black lieutenant on the force. Did you know that?" Flynn went on without pause. "I've told him everything, and he agrees it would be better if we hid you for a while. Just to be safe."

Monica exploded, "I can't do that. I've got a job. I can't just drop out of sight!"

Mike reached across the table and gently took her hand. "Please, honey, listen to your dad."

"Monica, now you just listen to me," Flynn began, his voice starting to rise in fatherly anger. "How do you think Norma came to be blown all over 38th and Meridian? I'll tell you how. The killer saw you drive Norma's car out of the apartment garage. He gave the license number to those fools over at the BMV. From that, he got an address. He found the car. He put a bomb on it–and he thought he blew his witness away!

"Monica, down deep, you know it's true. You just have to face it. This scum bag is a professional. Now, I think–and Mike agrees–the chances are damn good that by now, he knows he blew up the wrong girl. Most importantly, he knows what you look like. He's got to figure you've given us a description of him. As a pro, he knows we've got, or soon will have, a description of what he looks like, a physical description, and maybe even a reproduction of his face. He knows that by now, it's been disseminated to every law enforcement agency in the country. The Feds will see to that. Now, as I see it, he has two choices. One, he takes his chances and just gets the hell out of town. Or two, he can stick around to eliminate the witness. Because without the witness to testify she saw him in the building, we have no case. If he gets you, he's long gone and Scott free!"

"Maybe he's already gone," Monica offered in a small voice.

"I don't think so. And even if I did, I won't take the chance. The guy's a pro. The safe bet is he's going to come looking for you."

"So," Mike asked, "what is Johnny Green going to do?"

"He's agreed, as a favor to me, to personally take over Monica's security. He's going to locate a safe house, a place where you'll be out of the way, totally unconnected with me, this house, Mike, anything. Then, he's going to ask one of his friends, probably another retired officer, to help out."

"So, I'm to be a prisoner," Monica said, her angry eyes flashing. "For how long?"

"There's just no way of knowing," Flynn answered quietly.

"How about my job? Can you do anything about that?"

"I'll do my best. Do you have Mr. Daniels's home phone number?"

"Yes."

"Good. I'll call him now. I'll have to lie to him. Can't tell him the truth." Flynn pulled on his pipe for a few seconds before going on. "I think we just got the news of a death in the family. Someone far away and you're going to assist and comfort an aunt–something like that."

77

Sergeant Gaffney was already hard at work listening to the tapes from Blakemore's condo when Flynn got to the office. Mike frantically gestured for him to pick up the other set of earphones. Flynn dropped his coat over a chair, picked up the earphones, and put them on as he sat down across the conference table from Mike.

The amplified voice Flynn heard was deep with a strong note of menace behind it. *"Now, if you can't deliver, as you originally promised, several very influential people will be quite angry. I think you understand."* Mike stopped the tape. "The next voice is Blakemore's," he said as he turned the machine back on.

"Something this big takes time to put together. I'm not backing out. It's just that finding the right people will take time."

"The shipment will be ready in ten days. My investors will insist on knowing how much more time you want."

"A few weeks. I can't go flying off to Miami without a damn good reason. If I make the Miami trip too often, somebody here is going to ask questions."

"Do it on a weekend. Nobody would care about that would they?"

"Well, no, I suppose not."

"It's the right time of year anyway. Nobody will blame you for a weekend in the sun at the start of winter."

"I guess I could do it at that."

"Fine. Call me no later than Thursday and give me your plans. I'll have one of my people pick you up at the airport and put you up at the house. Okay?"

"Yes. Yes, that sounds good."

"Excellent. I'll expect to hear from you on Thursday."

The call ended, and Mike stopped the machine. He took off his earphones, and Flynn followed suit. "Denny," Mike began, excitement filling his voice, "this is the second conversation Blakemore has had with this guy. It's the only thing out of all of these I've listened to so far that even remotely resembles something suspicious."

"What was the first conversation about?" Flynn asked.

"Very close and guarded like this one. Some big money deal Blakemore was involved in."

"Any idea who this guy at the other end is, or where the call came from?"

"No, both of these were incoming to Blakemore. Blakemore never called the guy by name, and with direct dial, there's no way to tell where the call came from. Wish to hell there was a way to read a caller ID on this damn tape!"

"Sound like city business?"

"If it was, it sure sounded crooked. Just like this one."

"What other kind of people were calling Blakemore?" he asked.

"Lawyers wanting to remind him of favors owed. Builders and architects wanting a crack at this or that project. Some people asking for tax deals to move to town. Women. Lots of women."

"Anything besides these two conversations that struck you as out of the ordinary?"

"Aside from those people offering bribes or asking for tax breaks? No, none so far."

"What kind of a recording system is this anyway?"

"Our technical people say this particular secret, government issue, Ampex system is designed to automatically turn on when the receiver is picked up and turns off when it is replaced. The phone instrument actually broadcasts both sides of the conversation through a wireless, FM bug to a receiver on the recorder. Unless you took the phone apart, you'd never know there was a tap on the phone. Seems only certain government agencies can get spy equipment like this."

"Is there any way to trace this unit back to a buyer?" "I've asked our tekies to see what they can find out."

"So, nobody but Blakemore knew the conversations were being recorded. Mike, you've listened to Blakemore's voice on that thing through several conversations. Do you think his voice showed any stress when he was talking to this mystery caller?"

Mike thought for a moment. "Yes, I'd say there are definite signs of stress even though he tried to sound in control. My take on old Jack is—he saw himself as a man with power. In all his other conversations, he was very much on top. He lost that projection of power with this guy."

Flynn nodded his understanding. "Have you found the call he was supposed to make by Thursday?"

"Not yet. You got here while I was listening to that second call."

"Well, we'd better find that other call. What's the date on that tape reel anyway?"

"Last month, October. No finish date. It was the one on his machine when we picked it up. Put the label on it myself."

"You go ahead. See if you can locate that Thursday call. I want to make a visit to the Crime Lab," Flynn said as he got up from the table. "I just had an idea, and I want to follow it up."

Monica peered through the peep sight in the door. John Green's smiling face was in her direct view. Laughing at the big man's antics, she opened the door. John stepped into the small vestibule, tossed his hat onto a small side table, and swept Monica into his arms.

"Lordy!" he said, "Your daddy didn't exaggerate one bit. No, sir, not one bit!"

"Lieutenant Green, put me down," Monica laughed. Green stepped back, holding Monica's wrists. He looked her over like a proud relative. "Monica, you've grown into a beautiful, young woman. Look a lot like your mother too," he said.

Monica felt her face flush. "Daddy always said you were the first true black, Irishman he'd ever met. He claimed you had as much blarney as the best of them."

Green laughed his huge, melodious laugh. "Monica, I'd be pleased if you'd just call me Johnny. I'm retired now, and the lieutenant's rank is long gone–so let's just keep it Johnny. Okay?"

"Sure–Johnny. So, what do we do first?"

"Well," he said, taking her by the elbow and walking toward the kitchen, "let's go into the kitchen, make some fresh coffee, and catch up on the last few years. I want to hear all about it."

Monica filled the Mr. Coffee machine and got out two fresh cups and saucers. She raided the pastry box and set out some fresh donuts. John Green took off his suit coat, draping it very carefully over one of the kitchen chairs. Monica watched the huge, black man with great fondness and awe. Strapped beneath his left arm was the once standard, street-issue, stainless steel, Smith & Wesson, .357 Magnum revolver and a holster polished to a bright burgundy sheen by years of use. She could see the years hadn't yet diminished the man's size or considerable strength. He *did* make her feel safe. John smiled and broke the silence.

"Your daddy still use that back-yard charcoal broiler?"

"Oh, every once in a while." Monica smiled at the memory of the back yard filled with policeman and their families. Johnny Green was always there with his wife and twin boys.

"So, tell me all about this young man of yours," Green said.

"Mike? Well, he's just about the most handsome man in town. He's six-two, light brown hair, blue-green eyes, a very gentle man– has a great body! And–I love him. We're getting married this coming June. He just made the lieutenant promotion list."

"And how does Denny feel about all this?"

"My getting married or this mysterious killer we're hiding from?"

"How does he feel about losing his daughter?"

Monica laughed, "He doesn't feel he's losing anything! He loves Mike–in his own way–as much as I do. Personally, I think he's gaining the son he always wanted. Except this one is fully grown and on his own. Tell me–what have you got planned for me?"

"Well," he began, "I've got G.W. out scouting for a good safe place to take you for a few days."

"G.W.?"

"You remember George Washington Butler, don't you?"

"Oh, Sergeant Butler!"

"Yeah. Only we call him G.W. He's retired now too. Needed something to do. So, I pressed him into service. Personally, I think he was glad to get out of the house and away from his wife. She can be pretty demanding. Anyway, soon as he finds a good place, he's going to call me here, and then, we'll go meet him."

"And until then?"

"Well, we just sit tight. Your daddy wants me to answer the phone if it rings. If anybody wants you, you're out of town at an uncle's funeral."

"So, what'll we do while we wait for G.W.'s call?"

"Well, you any good at gin rummy?"

"Beat the socks off Daddy all the time."

"Well, what are you waiting for girl? Break out the cards!"

The killer examined himself in the large bathroom mirror. The shortened, lighter hair and eyebrows radically changed his looks. Referring to his reflection in the mirror, he carefully applied the new, high-strength, theatrical spirit gum to his upper lip. When the glue was sufficiently tacky, he applied a full-sized, sun-streaked, brown mustache he'd purchased along with the spirit gum at the costume shop on the city's near Southside miles away from his motel. He was a totally different man.

He took the new clothing out of the shopping bags, cut the price tags off, and began to dress to suit his new identity. A blue, flannel work shirt went on first. Then pre-washed jeans with a wide, leather belt, and finally high-top, work boots. He made a mental note to find a suitable dirty place to rub some dirt into the jeans and the pale yellow boots–had to give them some age and the look of use. He opened his soft-side, carry-on bag and removed a twenty-two automatic, which had been fitted with a short silencer of his own making. He ejected the custom-made clip and examined the hollow-point, magnum-load, long rifle shells. The clip was full, thirteen rounds in all. He slipped the automatic into a custom-made shoulder holster and slid the sling over his left shoulder. His final piece of apparel was a down-filled vest. Checking his new disguise in the mirror, he was pleased with the result. He looked ten years younger, nothing like the man the police were undoubtedly looking for. One last item remained to complete the deception. For that, he'd get a cab to take him to the center of town to the Hertz Truck Rental Agency where he'd reserved a Ford pickup. The Honda Civic would remain here at the motel as backup.

"Okay," Flynn said, "back it up, and let's go through it again." Mike reversed the tape for the third time. Again, the sounds of the electronic, touch tone dialing started the segment.

Eleven tones followed by four rings and the connection was made.

"*Hello,*" the now familiar voice answered.

"*I'm set for Miami this weekend. Can you get things arranged?*"

"*That shouldn't pose any problem. I take it you're in the final stages of preparation?*"

"*Yes. This meeting ought to firm everything up.*"

"*What flight will you be on?*"

"*Delta 412.*"

"*That's on Friday?*"

"*Yes.*"

"*Excellent! Jack, I needn't remind you of the consequences should this fail to materialize. On the other hand, I should think the rewards would be enough to motivate any man.*"

"*You needn't worry about my motivation.*"

"*Probably not. But I find everyone needs to be reminded from time-to-time.*"

"*Look, you've got me by the short hairs! So, just get off my case. Okay?*" Blakemore was getting more than a bit testy.

"*Just so we understand each other. See you Friday.*" The conversation ended.

The two detectives pulled the earphones from their very tired ears. Flynn rubbed his face with both hands and got up from his chair, stretching. "Anything strike you about the other guy's voice?" he asked Mike.

Mike rose from his chair and began to pace the floor on the other side of the table. "The only thing I noticed was he had a kind of an educated way of talking. Sort of like some of the lawyers around here."

"That's what I thought too!" Flynn exclaimed.

"Christ! Now we've got a crooked lawyer somewhere in the world to check out."

"No, I think we can nail him pretty fast. Or, at least, find out where Blakemore called."

"How are we going to do that?"

"That's why I went up to the Crime Lab. They've got a computer program up there that can recognize the telephone tones on that tape and tell us what number Blakemore called."

"Then, we just pick up our end of the string and follow it to the other end," Mike offered.

"It would be nice if it were that simple. We still need to know why Blakemore went to Miami, who he met with there, and what happened. My gut tells me whatever deal old Jack made in Miami went sour, and he paid the price."

"How the hell are we going to accomplish all that?"

"Well, first of all, I'm going to pay the chief another visit. He's vice president of IACP this year, and he ought to be able to get us some cooperation out of Miami PD or Dade County, or whoever the hell is in charge down there. And while I'm doing that, why don't you take that tape up to the lab and see what they can come up with for a phone number?"

The killer parked the rented Ford pickup in an angled space near the corner of Washington and Alabama Streets. From his driver's seat, he angled the rear view mirror so he could observe the main entrance to the Police Department on

Alabama Street. The department appeared to have an entire wing in the City-County Building to itself. He counted five stories—he couldn't be certain owing to the facade of the building. He took note that just to the south of the main entrance was a large, two-lane entrance to an underground garage. As he watched, marked and unmarked cars, motorcycles, and "paddy wagons" arrived and departed through the basement entrance. The arrival and departure of paddy wagons meant there was a security system for receiving prisoners, so the entrance would be off limits to the public. As the killer smoked and watched, he began to formulate plans, conjuring up ideas for penetration, considering, and discarding them as he observed the activity. One primary goal obsessed his mind. Somehow, he had to learn the name of at least one detective assigned to the Blakemore murder or the car bomb case. From there, it should be simple to obtain the information he needed.

Flynn returned from the chief's office, smiling at the promise of top level cooperation his chief had received from the chief of the Miami Police Department. Mike had not yet returned from the Crime Lab, but Detective Sam Elberger was back at his desk.

"Sam, I want you to make a run out to the airport," Flynn began, "Get with John Gormley. He's the chief of the Airport Police out there, and ask him to accompany you to the Delta manager's office."

"Okay, Denny. What are we looking for?" Elberger asked as he pulled his reporter's note pad from his hip pocket and prepared to write.

"Well, it seems Blakemore took a Friday flight on Delta to Miami. That's flight number 412. We need to know just what Friday it was– the date. Probably within the last two or three weeks–maybe six weeks. Work through Gormley, and ask the Delta manager to check his manifest records for a John or Jack Blakemore. Also find out about a return flight he made probably for the Sunday following the Friday. Okay?"

"And if the manager doesn't want to give me this information?"

"Call me. I'll have a search warrant out to you in forty-five minutes."

Mike almost knocked Elberger down as he ran into the office. "Denny, we've got the number! I checked it through the phone company. Now get this! The guy Blakemore called is an attorney, and the number isn't in Miami– It's for this guy's house somewhere in the valley outside L.A.!"

"Okay! Sam, on your way. Phone me with the information when you get it," Flynn said. "Now, Mike, settle down. Got a name for me?"

"M. Santini."

"What's the 'M' for?"

"Beats me!"

"God! This is getting too stretched out. Come with me. We're going to ask the chief to run up a debt to another fellow chief of police."

It was a pretty, three-bedroom ranch located on the south side of the city very near the bedroom town, Southport, which had long ago been surrounded by the rapidly growing city. Monica was unpacking her suitcase in one of the bedrooms, Johnny was carrying bags of groceries into the large kitchen, and G.W. was unpacking dishes and cooking utensils. John's car, a big, midnight-blue, Chevrolet Suburban was parked in the garage; the overhead door was closed. G.W. was still ribbing Johnny about the big, truck-like station wagon. "A big, blue SUV! Well, I mean it surely doesn't fit a black man's image," G.W. said.

"I tell you those Suburbans are the greatest idea GM ever had!" John Green shot back–somewhat heatedly.

"But man, you need a Cadillac or at least a big Lincoln Town Car."

"Image ain't everything. When Ella talked me into getting our first one of these in '78, I didn't believe it either. Besides, I ain't outta style! Just check out the parking lot at any country club. You'll find Suburbans cheek-by-jowl with Mercedes, Cadillacs, Jaguars, and all the rest. Anyway, it beats hell out of that little shoe box you drive! Tells you something when the waiting time on one of these babies is a good eight to ten weeks." Monica had entered the kitchen and was enjoying the good natured banter between the two old friends. They were a Mutt and Jeff combination if there ever was one. Green towered over G.W. by a good seven or eight inches. But, as Monica had discovered on the ride to the house, G.W. gave up nothing when it came to intelligence.

"G.W.," she asked, "how did you find this house?"

"One of my friends is in the real estate business. He was supposed to rent this place out. The owners are away in Europe for a year."

"Are we renting it?"

"Well, that's gonna depend on how long we're gonna be here."

"So, how long are we going to be here?" she asked.

"Monica, there's just no way to tell about these things," John Green said.

"Am I going to be allowed to go out– or have any friends come to see me?"

"It would be better if you didn't have anybody come see you, and if you go out, G.W. or I will go with you."

"Can Mike come here?" Monica asked her voice trembling.

Green thought for a moment. "Okay, Mike and only Mike," he said.

"One last question."

"Okay. Shoot."

"Now don't take this wrong–but won't the three of us stick out like a sore thumb in this neighborhood?"

G.W. flashed his smile. "Nah. This just happens to be a racially mixed neighborhood. Just another drop or two of chocolate in the white milk."

Flynn sat across from the chief, waiting for him to finish his call to Miami. He was worried because he hadn't yet heard from John Green. He kept glancing at his watch as the minutes ticked away. At last, Chief O'Halleran finished his call.

"Well, Denny, the man has promised full cooperation and will extend every courtesy to whoever I send down. Got anybody in mind?"

"To tell you the truth, this has been moving so fast that I haven't really given it all that much thought. Probably Mike. He's the best I've got—and I think he can get the strings pulled together."

"Why don't you go yourself?"

"I can't! Somebody has to stay behind here and keep everything coordinated. Besides, I've sent Monica off into hiding with John Green, and I still haven't heard from them. I don't know where they are."

"You're still convinced the car bomb was meant for Monica?"

"More than ever. She's my only child, and I just won't take the chance."

"Okay. I understand. What about this L.A. lead; this mysterious M. Santini? How are you going to handle that end of it?"

"I was hoping you might ask LAPD to provide us with as much as they know about Santini without anybody having to go to L.A. and without Santini being any the wiser."

"Well, Chief Hughes and I are good friends. I suppose I could ask him to have his people do a quick work-up on Santini. If they have a Special Investigations unit like ours, shouldn't be any problem."

"Good. Tell him that speed is very important. See if he'll fax the information to us."

"Just so I won't look too foolish, fill me in on what we know about Santini and what connections we want to make."

"Well, so far, we've got zip. This guy is an attorney–and I know that complicates things. All we *do* know is that he called Blakemore, probably several times. I'm pretty sure it's his voice we've got on tape in several conversations with Blakemore. I know this is a hell of a stretch, but I think he had old Jack's dick in a vise forcing him to do something he didn't really want to do. If I'm right, they had a meeting at a house in or maybe near Miami. You might see if LAPD can locate any record of property or businesses this Santini owns in Florida."

At that moment, the intercom buzzed. The chief's secretary informed Flynn that Mr. and Mrs. Blakemore were waiting for him in his office. Flynn hurried back to find a distinguished looking, elderly couple seated in the small waiting room. The man was gently stroking the woman's hand. Flynn offered a pleasant smile as he introduced himself. Quickly, he escorted the grieving couple to his private office.

Mike excused himself and went next door to start the recorder. Flynn frequently conducted interrogations in his office. A hidden, sensitive recording system had been installed for that purpose.

Flynn offered to provide coffee. Both accepted. Flynn always dreaded this part of his job; talking with the parents of a victim. It was never easy to both console and obtain needed information. Blakemore's father took the initiative. "Captain Flynn, forgive me, but I want to know about the murder of our son."

"Mr. Blakemore, I'm afraid there's not much we can tell you at this point."

"Why is that?"

"The unvarnished truth is this. We're really in the initial stages of the investigation. We're following up on some leads, which appear, for the moment, to be promising. We just don't have anything positive yet. In a lot of murders, the people involved know each other well. That isn't the case here."

"What was my son doing with that prostitute?" Blanche Blakemore asked through her tears.

"Mrs. Blakemore, I really don't have an answer to that question– beyond the obvious one." Her husband resumed his own questions.

"Can you tell me why they were in somebody else's apartment?"

"I'm afraid we don't know that yet either. Mr. Blakemore, do you think you could answer some questions for us? It might help," Flynn asked.

"I'll certainly try. And please, call me Harry."

"All right, Harry. Call me Dennis. Now, I want to know your son a bit better. Where did he go to college?"

"Princeton."

"Major?"

"Business Administration and Political Science."

"Was he good at it? School, I mean."

"Graduated top of his class. Never married."

"Was he all work? You know–a workaholic?"

"No, not at all. But he wanted to build a sizable nest egg before he settled down."

"What did your son do for fun?"

"What kind of fun?"

"Well, did he ski, race cars, boats, gamble– what?"

"Well, he liked to drive his BMW faster than he should have–got a lot of speeding tickets–but I wouldn't say it was recreation for him. No, I guess for these past few years, Florida was his pleasure. And as for gambling, I'm sure he didn't."

Flynn's ears picked up on Florida. "Florida?"

"For the past two years, he's been going to Miami."

"Was there somebody or something special in Miami?"

"Not that we knew of."

"Well, was there someplace special he always stayed?" Flynn asked.

"I couldn't say. You see, when he got down there, he would call us to say he made it, and he would give us a phone number to call in case of an emergency."

"Harry, this just might be very important. Can you remember if these numbers were always the same each time he was down there?"

"No, I'm afraid I can't."

At that point, his wife spoke up. "I always kept them in a notebook in the night table by my bed," she said.

"Mrs. Blakemore, can you remember if the number was different each time?"

"No, I can't. But I do still have the notebook. Is it important to know about these numbers?"

"It just might be a very big help to us. I don't suppose you have the notebook with you by any chance?"

"It's home in the night table," she said.

"Would it be asking too much if I were to ask you to send it to me when you get home?"

"If it will help you catch Jack's killer, you can have it. The minute we get home, I'll arrange to send it to you overnight!" Harry Blakemore said.

"Thank you, Harry. May I ask what you do for a living?" Flynn asked.

"I'm in the investment banking business."

"And was Jack going to join you in the business someday?"

"Regrettably, no. I had hoped he would join me, but Jack had other worlds to conquer as he put it."

"I only have a few more things I'd like to know. Where's home?" Flynn asked.

"We have an apartment in the city and a home out on the North Shore."

"Excuse me?"

"We have an apartment in Manhattan and a home out on Long Island– near Stony Brook."

"And that's where Jack grew up?"

"Mostly at our home on Long Island. You see, he was away at boarding school for high school and then, off to Princeton for college. Since he was about sixteen, he was really only home for the holidays and summer vacations."

Flynn felt a thread forming in his mind and began to follow it. "Is Stony Brook on the water?"

"Oh, yes. It's right on the Sound."

"And do you have a boat?"

"Yes."

"And was Jack a good sailor?"

"As a matter of fact, he spent most of his time on the water when he was home. He was a good sailor and an excellent navigator," Harry answered, a puzzled expression increasing with each question.

"Did Jack or any of his friends do drugs?"

Harry Blakemore looked uncertain. "I was never sure. There were times when he was in college–"

"You suspected he might be using drugs?"

"Yes. As I said–while he was in Princeton, but ever since he got into politics, he seemed to straighten out."

"Now, what about Jack's finances?"

"From time to time, he would send me funds to be invested. He's, or he was, quite well-fixed for a young man. Why do you ask?"

"Well, you see, we really don't know all that much about your son. He didn't grow up here, so we're hampered in building any kind of a background on his life. We need to know these things to help us find a motive for his murder. I hope you understand?"

"Well, I guess that makes sense."

"Good. Now, did he send you unusually large sums for investment?"

"Well, that rather depends on what you mean by unusually large."

"Well, we know Jack was paid forty-two thousand a year by the City. Now, knowing that–how much he made, would you, as an investment banker, think his deposits could be considered unusual–for a man making forty-two thousand a year?"

"Only the last one. Let's see, about two months ago, I believe he sent fifty thousand."

"How did he send the money? Check or what?"

"They were always bank drafts on an account in one of the Bahamian Banks."

"Isn't that illegal?"

"Oh, no. We do business with offshore banks all the time."

"Harry, didn't it ever occur to you that your son was making an awful lot of money for a man his age?"

"You mean, didn't I suspect anything? No, I didn't. Jack always had a very good head for investments and business. I did ask him about it a few years ago, and he told me he was doing very well in the market–the stock market. He also bought and sold real estate properties. Jack often bragged he had access to a lot of inside information. So, I just accepted his explanations. Are you saying it's possible my son may have been mixed up in something illegal, and that got him murdered? I can hardly face that, but I guess I'll have to."

"It's possible. But it's also possible he had outside income we didn't know about here. Right now, the important thing is to find and convict your son's killer. Tracing the money just might help me do that. I hope you'll cooperate and give me all the information you can."

"It's too late for any of this to hurt Jack anymore, even if it turns out he was mixed up in something illegal. We want our son's killer caught and punished! You have my word as soon as I get back to the office, I'll copy my son's investment file and FedEx it to you," Harry said.

After a few more minutes of attempting to answer their questions, Flynn thanked the Blakemores for their help and offered to assist in any way he could while they were in town. He ushered them out of the Homicide office at 3:30 p.m.

When he returned, the news was both good and bad. John Green called to report they were now set up in the Southport safe house, and the bad, Monica was already exhibiting signs of cabin fever. Flynn told John that he and Mike would be by for dinner that evening.

Friday, 8:30 a.m.

The investigative team was assembled in Flynn's office when the fax from LAPD came in. Chief O'Halleran had his secretary deliver it to Flynn personally. Flynn was in the process of reading it aloud to his team.

"Mario Santini moved to the Los Angeles area from New York City in 1975. He set up a law practice after passing the California Bar in 1976. He's a very high powered, high-profile, criminal trial lawyer. His clientele, initially, was made up of minor thugs for the crime families operating on the West Coast. Since 1980, he has moved almost exclusively into working in behalf of big time drug dealers.

"He now owns several acres of prime development land and a good deal of real estate in the Malibu area. Who said crime doesn't pay?" Flynn asked rhetorically. He resumed his reading– "Let's see, according to the LAPD Special Investigations people, Santini makes frequent trips to New York, Florida, Brazil, Mexico, and Columbia. He claims he's serving a long list of legit clients. However, LAPD and the DEA both believe Santini is up to his ears in the drug business but so far, haven't been able to positively connect him with any dealing. He is occasionally under surveillance, but that too has proven unproductive. All his meetings are held out of town, in open, public places like restaurants and never twice in the same place.

"He reports a taxable income of slightly in excess of three million each of the past three years, and he pays taxes on it. He owns no aircraft but does maintain a seventy-five-foot yacht in L.A. Photographs and further information are being sent via Federal Express." Finishing the fax, Flynn observed, "That's quite a busy lawyer if you ask me."

"If they've been keeping tabs on him, what do you think the chances are they can put him on a plane to Florida on any of the dates Blakemore went down there?" Mike asked.

"Who knows? But it sure as hell can't hurt to ask," Flynn told him.

"Captain, you know this guy is bent," Sam Elberger said.

"No. I don't know that, but yes– it seems very probable. *But* don't forget, if LAPD and the DEA haven't been able to catch him dirty, we're sure not going to. Besides, right now, I think we're looking for some connection between Blakemore and Santini. To do that, we need to put the two of them together in Florida, and we need to know what the meeting was about. We can't lose sight of the fact we're looking for a motive that will stand up in court, and I tell you now it will have to be right by the book."

"Even if we put the two of them together in Florida, that's a hell of a long way off, and Blakemore was murdered here, not in Florida," Elberger put in.

"You're right! Why here? Ask yourselves, why our fair city? Could the deal have involved an unusually large drug delivery? If so, were any of the local dealers in on it?" Flynn paced the floor as he spoke.

Detective Elberger offered, "The only thing I can think of would be a big event like the 500 or maybe the Formula One race. Lot of got bucks people in town for that. Some event like that where you could move a lot of drugs quick."

Flynn paused in his pacing. "That's a possibility. But May is seven months away. Has to be something sooner. Right now, it goes on the back burner. Just the same, we'd best give Captain Webber in Narcotics a visit. See if he has any advance intelligence on any unusually big drug shipments headed this way. Sam, handle that for me, will you?" Detective Elberger nodded in agreement. "Now," Flynn went on, "back to *our* problem. If Santini had Blakemore killed, I think we're all agreed he used a pro, and that means no trail back to Santini. I think the man who murdered Blakemore is probably still here in town." For the next several minutes, Flynn took the rest of his team into his confidence. He told them of the connection he believed existed between the car bombing and the killer and that there was a witness. He did not tell them who the witness was. That would remain between him and Mike. Someone would have to go to Miami and attempt to put the two men together, find a connection and a reason for murder.

"So, that's it," O'Halleran said. "You'll have to go. There's just no one else with the brains to put this puzzle together." They were meeting in the chief's office, he and Flynn. It was the end of a long, busy day for the chief, who had asked yet more favors of his fellow chiefs of police in Miami and Los Angeles.

O'Halleran went on, "The mayor tells me the media is starting to ask some very pointed questions about Blakemore and our investigation. Still think withholding information from the media is a good idea?"

"Chief, I'm convinced our killer is still in town. The attempt to get my daughter proves it! I'd advise sitting on what we have for a few more days."

"Where is Monica now?"

"John Green is watching over her in a safe place here in town."

"Good move. Now, how long will it take you to get on a plane to Miami?"

"I'll ask Julie to get me a seat on something going out tomorrow. Since it looks like I'm elected, there's a lot I want to go over with Mike before I go."

"Good. Drop by before you go. I'll have a letter of introduction for you to hand carry to my old friend the chief in Miami. He's quite a fan of the 500 so, I think I'll just dangle the carrot he won't be able to resist."

The killer was at that moment seated on a bar stool in the Press Room Tavern about a block away from *The Indianapolis Star* building. Past experience in other cities taught him this would be the best place to catch the local gossip. Reporters were extremely loose talkers and braggarts when well lubricated. The bar was now beginning to fill with reporters and employees finished for the day. Nobody took notice of the man dressed in common laborer's clothes seated at the bar. Before too long, his patience was rewarded when he overheard two young, raucous reporters arguing about the known facts of the story. He listened as the younger of the two damned his insensitive boss for not understanding that the "boys in Homicide weren't talking to anybody." The older of the two was offering advice, "Why don't you give the tried and true method a try?" The killer watched the two in the reflection of the bar mirror.

"And just what the hell is that?" the younger man asked as he reached through beside the killer and placed his bottle of beer on the bar.

"Ask around. Somebody over there is bound to have a hard-on for Flynn. Find out who that is, and then go to work on him. He'll open up, and Flynn will have to affirm or deny."

The killer decided it was time to learn more. Affecting a pseudo Southern accent, he swiveled in his seat and addressed the two men. " 'Scuse me," he began, "I couldn't help overhearin'. What's all the excitement about this Blakemore fella anyway?"

"And who might you be?" the older man asked, his eyes narrowing.

"Me? I'm a steel worker up from Dallas, workin' over there on the skyscraper. We have murders in Dallas all the time. Nobody seems to get all that excited."

"Well, Blakemore was a deputy mayor, and that makes it a special murder," the young reporter said.

"Well, who is this Flynn fella you been talkin' about?"

The older man answered, "Captain Dennis Flynn. He's head of the Homicide and Robbery Branch over in the cop shop."

"And he won't talk to reporters? That don't seem so strange to me."

"Well, he put the word out to all his people not to talk to any reporters about the deputy mayor's murder," said the younger man.

"Well, I guess you got yourselves quite a stone wall then. Nobody else to ask? You know, to go around this Flynn fella." His question was met with stony stares.

"Have you worked on Sergeant Gaffney?" the older man asked the younger.

"Hell, you can't get anything out of Mike even on a good day. Besides, he's going to make lieutenant in a few days. No way he's going to talk to anybody about anything until they pin that gold bar on his shoulder."

"Sergeant Gaffney?" the killer asked.

The older reporter called the bartender for another round of Miller Lites. "Number two man in the Homicide and Robbery Branch. Works for Captain Flynn," he said.

"Well, it sounds like you fellas got quite a job ahead of you. So do I. Time for me to be getting back to the job. Nice talkin' to you both." The killer put two dollars on the bar for his beer and excused himself. He had gotten what he came for: two names within the investigation. One of them would lead him to the witness.

7:30 p.m., the Safe House

They were finished with dinner. Flynn packed his pipe for an after-dinner smoke while Mike helped Monica load the dishwasher. John Green lit one of his three-a-day cigars, G.W. Butler tilted his kitchen chair back, thumbs hooked through his trouser belt loops.

"You sure have improved as a cook, John," Flynn said.

John Green smiled in slight embarrassment. "Well, to be honest, Monica did most of it. When you called to say the two of you would be here for dinner, she perked up like a puppy."

"I guess it has been hard on her, stuck out here like this."

"And this is only day one. She hasn't complained too much. But she's been like a caged animal walking from room to room looking out the windows. I think I'm going to have to take her out for some air and civilization soon."

"Monica tells me she helped Ident do a computer picture of a suspect. May I see what this man looks like?" Green asked.

"Oh, sure! I'm sorry. I wasn't holding back. I just forgot to give you and G.W. your own copies of the sketch." Flynn got up and went into the living room where he retrieved the five by seven inch photo copies of the computer generated picture from his coat pocket and returned to the kitchen. Resuming his place at the table, he gave each man a copy. "I think this is our man," he said.

G.W. turned the photo over to read the description printed on the reverse side. "According to this, we're looking for mister average."

"G.W. we're not looking *for* anybody. We're looking *out* for this man just in case he gets a line on Monica," said Big John.

"He's right," Flynn cut in, "I want you two to watch over Monica like she was the President of the United States! Every uniform on the street has this picture. Every detective and undercover cop on the force has it. Let them look for him."

"Denny, I didn't mean Big John and I were goin' looking. I only meant this man is a real average-lookin' man. Going to be hard to spot."

"He's got this freckle beside his nose," John observed.

"Yes. Yes, he does. But you'd have to be staring right in the man's face to see it," G.W. said.

"Well, anyway, I want you two to keep your eyes peeled. I seem to recall when the two of you worked for the prosecutor you didn't lose a single witness or even have one threatened. And *this* witness is *special* to me!"

Monica turned from her task at the dishwasher. "Oh, Daddy, with all this protection, I feel very safe. Please don't worry. I'll be fine."

Flynn reluctantly announced, "Now, I'm going off to Miami tomorrow to get a line on Blakemore's comings and goings down there and a lawyer I think may have a hell of a lot to do with this. A guy by the name of Santini. Mike will be in charge of the office while I'm gone. So, if any of you have any problems, get ahold of him while I'm away."

"Any idea how long you'll be down there?" G.W. asked.

"No, but I'm hoping it won't take more than a day or two at most. All the action is back here, and I hate to be away from it.

O'Halleran greased the skids for me, so I think the cooperation from Miami PD will be pretty good."

"What time does your plane leave?" John asked.

"One-thirty in the afternoon."

"Beware of Florida," G.W. said. "The weather changes very fast from sun to rain at this time of year."

"I hadn't thought of that. Thanks. I'll pack accordingly. And speaking of that, it's time I went home to do just that. Mike, are you coming, or are you staying?"

"I thought I'd stay a while, if it's all right with Monica."

Monica hooked her arm through Mike's. "I'll break his arm if he doesn't stay," she said.

"In that case, I'll see you at the office in the morning, Mike. I have a few things I want you to follow up on for me while I'm gone."

Good-byes were exchanged all around. Flynn kissed Monica, gave her a hug, and departed for home.

9:30 p.m.

The killer parked the rental pickup across the street and one house away from the address on Washington Boulevard listed in the telephone book as the residence of Dennis P. Flynn. Since there were only two Flynns with an initial "D" listed in the book, he knew his chances were fifty-fifty this would be the one he was looking for. The turn-of-the-century style street lights pooled their light in small circles, leaving the truck in darkness. The house he watched was dark and had been so for the past hour-and-a-half. He was about to light another cigarette when in the side mirror, he saw headlights approaching from the south. Quickly, he closed the lighter and watched as the car came ever closer. It slowed and turned off the street into the short drive leading to the two car garage at the rear of the house. As the car turned, he saw it was a dark metallic-blue, Ford sedan, with blackwall tires and cheap hub caps. Typical "unmarked" police car by the look of it. A brief flash of red tail lights reflected down the drive, and the headlights were turned off. A car door slammed. Lights began to go on in the house. The killer's heart felt a lightness born of success. He'd located his man. He'd have to be certain. He decided to wait until the house was dark again, and then, he would check out the car.

Shortly after midnight, the last light on the second floor went out— the house was dark and quiet. The killer gave himself another twenty minutes before he quietly slipped out of the truck and keeping to the shadows, crossed the street to the foot of the drive. Exercising extreme care, he approached the Ford.

He stood next to the driver's door, and shielding a penlight with his hand to eliminate reflections, he examined the interior of the car. Spartan cloth and vinyl upholstery, typical police car; however, there was no sign of a radio mounted under the dash. This didn't mean much. He knew modern, big city police departments had changed to individual multi-channel, hand-held units issued to each man. Raising the pool of light, he examined the visors and found clipped to the driver's visor a plastic card resembling a credit card. There was no visible printing, just an embossed series of numbers and letters. He switched to the windshield and searched the floor area with his light. There! Just barely showing beneath the driver's seat was a split lens red/blue portable police light. He'd found his man! As he was leaving, he memorized the license number and wrote it down in a notebook when he got to the truck. Tomorrow morning, he would return early and begin following the police captain.

Saturday, 7:00 a.m.

He watched as the dark metallic-blue, Ford sedan backed out of the drive. Through binoculars, he saw the driver appeared to be a medium-sized man with dark brown hair, dressed in a turtleneck sweater and leather jacket. The killer tossed the binoculars on the seat and started up the Honda Civic. As the Ford turned south on the street, the killer pulled his car out of the alley and started to follow at a distance of about ten car lengths.

The Ford turned south on Pennsylvania Street and picked up speed, the driver doing well over forty in the thirty-mile-per-hour zone. The killer slowed to thirty-five. Keeping the Ford in view on the almost deserted street was quite easy. Within a few blocks, they were on Alabama Street. The killer was now certain they were headed to police headquarters. The Ford dropped out of sight into the underground police garage. The killer pulled into a parking space across Washington Street opposite the City-County Building. From this position he could watch the comings and goings of police through his rear-view and side mirrors. As he watched the entrance to the police garage, he let his mind wander over the problem of finding Blakemore's house or apartment. A solution would come. He was sure of it.

The pot of coffee was about half gone, and the pile of files had diminished to a small stack as Flynn and Sergeant Gaffney separated the unimportant from the important, or as Flynn was fond of calling it: "Separating the fly shit from the pepper". Julie entered Flynn's office with two FedEx, overnight packages. The larger of the two was from LAPD; the other from Blakemore's father in New York. Flynn slit open the package from Blakemore. He reached inside and pulled out a file folder and a small spiral notebook. Clipped to the file was a handwritten letter from Blakemore's father. Mike got up from his chair and stood behind Flynn's so he could read over his shoulder. Together they read the letter. Blakemore wrote:

> Dear Captain Flynn:
>
> I must admit, upon reviewing my son's financial activity, he was amassing a very large fortune for so young a man. I fear a father's pride in a son doing well in his profession clouded my eyes to the truth.
>
> I now believe it is quite possible my son was making his fortune through illegal means. Were he alive, I would be both ashamed and humiliated. All that remains now is for his killer to be brought to justice. Enclosed are my son's financial records and my wife's bedside notebook with the telephone numbers. They come with a mother and father's prayers that

they will prove helpful in finding and prosecuting our son's killer.

Blanche and I want to thank you and your staff, the mayor and his people, for your kindness and understanding.

God speed you!

Sincerely,

Harry Blakemore

"An honest man," Flynn observed. "Mike, will you take this notebook and start comparing phone numbers with those we got off the tapes? I'll start on this financial portfolio."

"What about the LAPD file on Santini?"

"We'll start with that as soon as we've gotten everything we can from this one first. If I need to, I'll take the Santini file with me on the plane."

After two solid hours of work, they had sifted through everything and had compiled quite a lot of useful information. Mike had found seven instances of the same phone number in Miami, four instances of the same number for a different area code in Florida, and two for a California number. He had twelve other Florida numbers and five different numbers in the Bahamas. Blakemore's deposits with his father's investment firm began shortly after he graduated from Princeton with an initial deposit of five thousand dollars. Within six months, there was a second deposit of ten thousand dollars. They grew in size and frequency from there; fifteen thousand, twenty-five thousand, thirty-five thousand, and the last several were all for fifty thousand. In the past five years, Jack Blakemore had deposited almost a million dollars with his father! All transactions were made via wire transfers from two different offshore banks in the Bahamas. Flynn knew this sort of thing was well beyond his level of knowledge. He'd need expert help. He called Sergeant Crooks and asked her to locate Bob Silverman who headed the Indianapolis office of the Secret Service. If anybody could tell him the intricacies of money laundering, it would be Bob.

Mike was busy working the telephone; getting cooperation from the phone company operators as he put cities, towns, and addresses with the phone numbers in Florida. While Flynn waited for Julie to track down the Secret Service Agent, he opened the file on Santini, furnished by LAPD. There were several eight-by-ten, glossy photographs of the man taken outside a building as he addressed an assemblage of news people. In each photograph, the person standing at the lawyer's side had been circled in red marker. Flynn examined the back of the photographs. Taped to each was an LAPD Narcotics Division memo. Each held a lengthy paragraph or two explaining who the circled individual was and his or her litany of crimes. Flynn noted that all were accused drug dealers.

He concentrated on Santini in the photos. The man appeared to be tall when compared to the defendants at his elbow. He had a well-groomed crop of wavy, black hair, sported a full but well-trimmed mustache. His suits ranged from banker's pinstripe in dark blues to gray. In one photo, Santini was gesturing so that his right hand was visible above the assembled news people. Flynn noted the hand was large and strong. In keeping with an image of class, the man wore no jewelry on the fingers or wrist. Santini's very clear eyes had small crows feet at the sides, a feature that stood out on his well tanned face. The man bore a strong resemblance to a young Caesar Romero, the movie actor. Flynn was about to begin reading the file itself when Julie announced she had Bob Silverman on the line. "Hello Bob. I have a question for you about laundering a lot of money. Let's say I'm a big drug dealer and I'm raking in millions of dollars every year. Now, I know the banks have to report any transaction over ten thousand dollars, so how do I get my money into a bank?"

"Well, some use couriers to take money out of the country to foreign banks and then send wire deposits back to accounts in the States. But we're getting pretty good at catching the couriers, so that's been cut back in favor of a new method. If I were going to move money today, I'd do it through currency exchange operations."

"I don't follow. Can you explain?"

"Well, take the Tijuana, Mexico, to San Diego, California, area, for example. There's literally hundreds of currency exchanges operating along that corridor. The dealers call it Wall Street West. Now, since these businesses are licensed by the cities they operate in, they don't fall under any federal banking rules or any real regulation. They're private businesses. They're there to exchange pesos for dollars and dollars for pesos. Cash paychecks. Loan out money until payday at unconscionable rates. That sort of thing. These places can make perfectly legitimate wire transfers out of their legal, American bank accounts to offshore banks. They make deposits in American banks, banks in the Bahamas, Switzerland, France, and Japan.

Then the drug dealer can have a transfer made back here to his account from one of those foreign banks. It's beautiful. We can't prove where any of it came from. The real money doesn't exist. It's all on computers."

"So, who owns all these currency exchanges?"

"We figure organized crime–probably."

"Anybody looking into Miami money laundering?"

"How the hell would I know? You on to something we ought to know about?"

"I'm in the middle of a murder investigation. You know, the Jack Blakemore thing. Looks like there might be a Miami connection. My victim made several trips down there over the years. And he has a sizable investment portfolio, more than he ought to from his regular income. I just thought it might be a thing I should check into."

"You going down there?"

Flynn consulted his watch. "Yep. My plane leaves in about two hours as a matter of fact. Any chance you could give me an introduction to your man in Miami?"

"Where will you be staying? I'll have him come by and fill you in."

"I don't know where I'll be staying. I'm to be a guest of the Miami PD."

"In that case, when you get settled in, call the Office down there and ask for John Heller. He'll be expecting your call."

Flynn made a written note of the man's name, thanked his friend for his help, and rang off.

"How much time left before you have to go?" Mike asked.

Flynn looked at his watch,"About ten minutes. Gotta be at the airport at least an hour-and-a-half before flight time. All the new anti-terrorist rules—remember? Looks like I'll have to take the file on Santini with me."

"Is there enough time for me to run some copies so I can go through it while you're gone?"

"Sure there is. Why didn't *I* think of that?"

As Flynn's dark blue Ford pulled out of the underground garage and turned right on the one-way street, the killer started the Civic and backed out of the parking space on Washington Street. He watched as Flynn's car stopped for the light on the next corner, the car's turn signal light indicating a right turn. The ease with which he had spotted the police car and driver filled him with excitement. He took it as a good omen.

The trip west through town and then south to the airport expressway went quickly. The Ford entered airport property. The killer watched the police car pull into the long-term parking lot. The killer pulled his Civic to the side of the road and turned in his seat to watch for Captain Flynn. Moments later, he saw the man, carrying a small suitcase and a briefcase, walk from the parking lot to a shuttle bus stop. Within minutes, the shuttle bus arrived, picked up the policeman and three others, and sped off toward the terminal building amid diesel clatter and a cloud of smoke. The killer cursed his luck, slamming his fist repeatedly against the steering wheel. He realized with Flynn out of town he was left with the only other name he'd gotten; Sergeant Mike Gaffney. The killer pulled the Civic back onto the main access road and headed back into the city.

5:18 p.m., Miami International Airport.

Flynn immediately felt the heat and humidity as he stepped from the forward door of the Delta 727 into the jet way. A tall, distinguished looking man with a distinct Hispanic look approached. "Captain Dennis Flynn?" he asked.

"Yes."

"Deputy Chief Jose Alvero, Miami PD," he said offering his hand.

Flynn put his suitcase down to shake the man's offered hand. "My boss, Chief Burke, asked that I personally meet you and see to your every need while you're in town. Chief Burke has arranged for you to stay at The Atlantic Hotel. It's a very nice place with the added advantage that it's owned by his brother-in-law. So, you'll be getting a special rate well below normal for this time of year."

"I don't know what to say."

"Just thank the chief when you see him Monday morning. Now, if you're ready, let's go get you settled in and have some dinner."

Flynn picked up his suitcase and followed the deputy chief out of the terminal into the warm, humid, salt-scented air.

7:30 p.m., the Safe House

Mike and Monica were seated on the living room sofa, her head resting on his shoulder. The television volume was turned down; the lights in the room low. John Green and G.W. had retired to the kitchen table where they were engaged in a spirited game of Gin Rummy. Monica reached over and took Mike's hand, gently rubbing it with the tips of her fingers.

"Mike, how long do murder investigations usually take?" she asked.

Mike considered his answer for a moment before he answered. "Well, except for drug dealers knocking each other off, they usually last a week or sometimes a few weeks. Some are easy to clear. Most murders are committed by people who know each other; relatives, lovers, that sort of thing."

"How about murders like this?" She looked him directly in the eyes.

"Contract murders are a different can of worms. This is the first one like this I've ever been even close to. Here we have two people without any apparent connection, murdered together in an apartment that doesn't belong to either of them. We have no motive, and aside from your description of the man on the elevator, not much else to go on. Murders like these can take years to clear–if ever."

"So, why did Daddy go off to Miami?" she demanded.

"He's chasing down some leads. Old Jack may have been into moving drugs or money laundering or both. He made several trips to Miami. We've got some phone numbers down there your Dad wants to check out."

"I hope all this is all over by next Friday."

"Why next Friday?"

"Have you forgotten? Your promotion takes effect next Friday. I was planning on being there when the chief pins your lieutenant's bars on your uniform and you get your lieutenant's gold shield."

"By all that's holy, you're right. In all this excitement it slipped my mind!"

"Mike, what are the chances I can talk you into staying the night?"

Mike thought it over carefully. "Well, that all depends—"

"Depends on what?"

"Well, do you mean staying here for the night on the couch, or did you have something more personal and intimate in mind?"

"I had something *very* personal and *very* intimate in mind."

"Well, I'll have to clear this with Big John—"

"Let me handle Big John. He and I understand each other." Monica got up from the couch and went into the kitchen. Mike saw G. W. go out the back door, and then, he could hear only whispers from the kitchen. Soon Monica returned, a triumphant smile on her pretty lips—lighting her face. Mike didn't need to ask. Monica held out her hand. Mike took it and let her lead him into the center bedroom. Monica crossed to the bed and turned on the small bedside lamp. Mike silently closed the door. Monica came into his arms and began a long, hungry kiss, which ended in a very passionate French kiss. Their breathing became shaky as their passions rose. Finally, Monica backed away and began to unbutton Mike's shirt. "I've wanted to do this ever since I met you," she said. "I've been undressing you with my eyes for months. Now, at last, I have the real thing, right here!"

"I hope I won't be a disappointment," Mike said as he kicked off his shoes.

Monica gently slid his shirt off his shoulders. "I don't think so," she said as she ran her fingers over his bare shoulders and then, through the light brown hair covering his well-muscled chest. Mike reached for her, and she laughingly backed away. "No! This is *my* fantasy. I get to undress you first. Then, you can undress me," she said, reaching for his belt and unbuckling it. She unzipped the fly and let the trousers drop to the floor. Mike stood before her, tall, trim, and very well-muscled. Monica admired her lover's body, gently touching and stroking. "I'm glad you wear bikini briefs. I think they're sexy! I hate to see men in those boxer things and the old fashioned jockey shorts," she said as she hooked her thumbs through the tiny waistband of his briefs and pushed them to the floor. Mike stepped out of the pile of trousers and briefs, his passion already causing his manhood to lengthen and stiffen. Monica stepped forward and pressed her body against his as he reached for the zipper of her dress.

They made gentle, yet demanding love several times before at last falling into a deep sleep, cradled in each others' arms.

Sunday, 9:30 a.m.

The killer was in his motel room going through the Indianapolis phone directory. He'd found ten "Gaffneys" listed, and three of them had listed the initial "M" for the first name. It was a place to start. He wrote down the telephone numbers and the addresses for each. For a minute, he considered calling each to learn if there was a Mike there and if he was a policeman. No. That would raise suspicions. There had to be a better way, one that would not let the man know he was being singled out. He got up from the small desk and began to pace the room, pondering the problem. His eyes fell on the Sunday edition of *The Star* when an idea came to him. Since it was Sunday, the chances were good the police department had only a small skeleton crew on duty at headquarters. Perhaps, he could phone in asking for this detective–make up some sort of story. Quickly, his devious mind formulated a plausible story. He paused a moment to gather his thoughts again and then dialed the homicide office number. The phone rang only twice before a woman answered.

"Hello? Listen," he began, "I feel foolish. I was supposed to meet a detective last evening, and I missed the appointment. Let's see– it was a fellow by the name of Gagney or Cagney or something like that."

"You must mean Sergeant Gaffney."

"Yes! That was it. By any chance, is he there now?"

"No, sir, he won't be on duty until Monday morning."

"What time will he be in?"

"He usually gets here about seven-thirty every morning."

" Could you describe him for me–so I'll know if it's the right guy?"

"Well, he's a little over six feet tall, has light brown hair, and well built. Not skinny if you know what I mean?"

He did know what she meant and what it meant to him. Now, the problem was to observe Gaffney without getting nailed.

Sunday, 2:30 p.m., Miami

Flynn and John Heller, the officer-in-charge of the Miami Secret Service office, were meeting in Flynn's hotel room. A large pitcher of fresh orange juice, delivered from room service, had been half emptied as they talked. Early on in the meeting, Flynn had decided he would open up to Heller. They were discussing the possible role Santini played in the murder.

"You understand I'm not at all trained in murder investigations," Heller admitted.

"I understand all that. I'm not knowledgeable about this money laundering thing. I need help putting this all together. Now, here's what I think may have happened. I think Blakemore was dealing drugs. Picking them up down here, or perhaps arranging for shipments to other places. I'm starting to believe Santini was probably the banker or the broker for the deals, furnishing his own house as a headquarters for a meeting. If Santini is the banker, he might be doing business through a money exchange. Paying Blakemore and God knows how many others through money transfers to offshore banks. Can you help me find out if Santini owns any of these money exchanges? If he does, is there a way to backtrack deposits to local banks made by these exchanges? And transfers to offshore banks?"

"Well, there are ways to learn these things. But I can't do anything that isn't an officially sanctioned investigation."

"What would it take to get such an official investigation going?"

"It's the same for us as it is for you. We need evidence or probable cause that a crime has been committed—or is about to be. A federal banking law broken. Or that there's an ongoing criminal enterprise."

"And there's nothing illegal about these off shore bank deals?"

"No. The crime would have to start at the other end when the money gets put through a currency exchange."

"And I don't know who is doing it. Damn! That leaves me at square one again."

"Look, you give me a good lead on anything you uncover down here, and I'll get the wheels moving on my end. I promise you I will."

"Okay. Now, I'd like to ask one more favor. Can you put me next to anybody down here in the DEA? Somebody you'd trust with your wife's life and honor? I want to find out how this drug business really operates at this end–here in Miami."

"Well, Vincent Daly is the head man down here. Vinnie's a good man–honest and usually very cooperative. But why don't you ask Miami PD to make the introductions?"

"I'm not certain I want Miami PD involved beyond some basic gumshoe work just yet. I may be a dumb, Hoosier hick, but I do know a criminal enterprise like this can't exist unless somebody is getting his palms crossed with a hell of a lot of money– maybe a top cop or several mid-level cops. I'm an outsider. You've been around– you know the score. A cop from out of town, snooping around, is about as welcome as a naked whore in church! And anyway, all police agencies are paranoid about an outsider asking official type questions–tends to upset the local balance of power arrangements. That sort of thing."

"So, the bottom line for you is you're not sure you can trust anybody in the Miami PD just yet. Is that it?"

"You got it! Hell, appearances aside, they won't trust me either!"

"All right. I'll personally set up a meeting between you and Daly. Any special time?"

"If he's agreeable, ask him to come to my hotel room tomorrow night. If you will give me your number, I'll call you sometime tomorrow afternoon to find out what he had to say."

"I'll wait for your call then. Jesus! I hope you're not overreacting. You're starting to make me nervous."

Monday, 7:15 a.m., Indianapolis

From a gas station pay phone, the killer called the homicide office, claiming information about the murder of the deputy mayor.

"May I have your name, please?" Sergeant Julie Crooks asked.

"I'd rather not say just yet."

"Well, Sergeant Gaffney is in charge, and he isn't in the office yet. Can anyone else help you?"

"No. I don't trust this to anybody else. Look, just ask the sergeant to meet me at the California Cafe Bar and Grill up in the Circle Centre Mall. I'll be there for lunch around noon. I'll wait for him there."

"But I'm not sure he'll come."

"Tell him if he doesn't come, I'll give what I have to the newspapers. I don't think he'd want me to do that."

"I'll tell him. How will he know you?"

The killer conjured up a mental picture. "I'm dressed in a gray, pinstripe suit, I have a red, silk handkerchief in my handkerchief pocket. I can only wait until about one. So tell him to come on time." With that, the killer broke the connection. He checked his watch. Less than a minute had elapsed since he began the conversation; not enough time for a trace. He would dress in his workman's disguise and be on the third level of the mall—a very busy food court, well ahead of Gaffney. In his short time in town, he'd learned how extremely crowded and popular the Circle Centre Mall was. There would be the added cover of several thousand conventioneers just a city block away at the convention center. They'd be swarming the mall. His pulse picked up a beat or two as the thrill of the hunt was on him again. It was almost like being back in the service. The Army showed him his true life's calling. He discovered he enjoyed hunting down and killing the most intelligent animal on earth, and he was good at it! It was a rush higher and stronger than coke!

Monday, 8:30 a.m., Miami

Dressed in his only lightweight suit, Flynn sat, cooling his heels in the chief of police's reception room. When he'd started to pack his pipe, the receptionist had haughtily pointed to the *Thank You For Not Smoking* sign on her desk. It only served to increase Flynn's frustration. He'd been kept waiting since 8:00 a.m. Not a very auspicious start to the day. As he was sipping his second cup of coffee, icily provided by the same prim receptionist, the intercom buzzed at her elbow. There were a few softly mumbled words in the phone, and Flynn was informed the chief "would see him now". Flynn followed the woman down a hallway paneled in dark woods. At the end of the hall were two large, walnut doors. Flynn thought it resembled the entrance to a Fortune 500 Board Room. Polished brass lettering on the right hand door proclaimed this to be the office of E. W. Burke, Chief of Police. The woman knocked softly at one of the double doors, opened it, and motioned Flynn to enter.

Burke's office was a very large, high-ceilinged room, paneled in softly shining walnut, and carpeted in expensive, wine-red carpet. The walls were festooned with plaques, framed, autographed photos of the chief with sports celebrities, politicians, numerous certificates–and prominently displayed on the wall behind the chief's desk, a large, three dimensional rendering of the FBI Academy seal.

Burke, like most big city chiefs of police, had attended the FBI's special school for chiefs of police and other high ranking folks in law enforcement whom the Bureau wanted to both flatter and influence. Admittance to the school is by invitation only and considered an anointment to be among the chosen few.

Chief Burke rose from his high backed, judge-style, leather chair and extended his hand. Flynn observed the man was about his own size with carefully trimmed gray hair. The suit, an expensive looking, tropical weight, blue pinstripe. Flynn introduced himself and handed over the sealed personal letter from his own chief of police. Burke accepted the letter and asked Flynn to have a chair. Flynn waited in silence while the man read the several page letter. The chief smiled as he finished the last page.

"Well, Captain Flynn, it seems you've got quite a murder case on your hands." He went on to express his friendship with O'Halleran and promised full cooperation. "I'll put you with Deputy Chief Alvero and have him make all the necessary arrangements with our people," pressing a button on his phone as he spoke.

"Jose," he said to the man who had slipped unnoticed into the room, "take Captain Flynn under your personal care. I want him given every cooperation and courtesy this department has at its command. I think it would be a good idea to break Detective Madigan in Special Investigations loose to work with Captain Flynn while he's our guest. If Captain Flynn asks for anything too far out, call me for a decision. I'll call Chief Anderson in Administration and have a car made available."

After a few closing amenities, Alvero took Flynn by the elbow and steered him toward the door at the back of the room through which he'd entered. "I think it would be a good idea if we went to my office, and I got acquainted with your case. I want to hear your story for myself," he said as he opened the door.

Monday, 11:05 a.m., Indianapolis

Mike threaded his way through the hundreds of people filling the third floor of Circle Centre Mall. He headed straight for the restaurant, conveniently just a few steps away from the elevator. From his vantage point across from the ornate railing outside the cafe, the killer, dressed in his workman's clothes, watched the tall, young man as he stepped off the elevator and quickly strode toward the entrance to the cafe. Gaffney's description was very close to the one he'd gotten over the phone. He watched as the man paused at the cafe entrance and slowly looked over the patrons. It was obvious he was looking for someone in particular. The killer's pulse quickened as he watched the man enter the cafe and begin to walk through the tables. No doubt, this was Sergeant Gaffney–the look of authority, and the straightforward approach marked the young man as a cop. Perhaps five minutes passed before he saw the detective come back out to the entrance of the restaurant. Gaffney headed for the waiter doing maitre d' duty. The young detective spoke very earnestly with the young man. Turning away, Gaffney pulled a cell phone from his inside coat pocket and began tapping out numbers. Gaffney turned and began walking toward the down escalator. Cautiously, the killer got to his feet and began to follow.

The detective took the escalator to the street level, talking on his cell phone the entire time. Gaffney walked to the street entrance, passed through the glass doors, and headed toward a sedan parked at the curb. The killer paused inside the door, watching as the policeman opened the driver's door on a lime-green, Ford sedan, got in, and drove off. The killer smiled as he considered the ease with which he'd pulled off the first part of the hunt. It had been easy to trick the detective, and now this ridiculously ugly, lime-green, Ford sedan only improved the odds in his favor. The car would stand out beautifully. Tonight as the day shift at the police department finished their day, he would watch for the lime-green Ford and begin his surveillance, confident that sooner or later the policeman would lead him to the witness.

3:15 p.m., Miami

Flynn was laboriously poring through property tax records in the Dade County Court House. At his elbow was Detective Sergeant Megan Madigan of the Miami's PD Special Investigations Unit, assigned to him by Chief Alvero. Together, they were checking property ownership against the addresses listed for the phone numbers Mike had gotten from Blakemore's mother's notebook. They were searching for property, which might be listed as owned by Santini. They'd worked their way through seven of the twelve addresses with no luck. As they worked, Flynn became increasingly aware he was becoming terribly distracted by Megan Madigan. She was a strikingly beautiful woman. From that first meeting in Alvero's office when she flashed him a smile that could stop a man in his tracks, he was hooked. Now, working side by side with her, he found himself sneaking sidelong glances at her.

He took in her beautiful, long, brown, almost black hair, her flashing green eyes, and a figure he fantasized seeing in a bikini–or less. Her very subtle perfume served to constantly remind him of her nearness. They'd been together for most of the day and had soon become friendly enough to operate on a first-name basis. Flynn learned Megan was a seven-year veteran, just thirty-two, and according to Deputy Chief Alvero, one of the very best detectives to be had in any division of the Miami Police Department. He was about to refocus his attention when Megan snapped her fingers in front of his nose.

"Hey! Wake up. I can't do this all by myself."

"I'm sorry, Megan. I guess I let my mind wander," he said attempting to cover his real thoughts. "This all seems so futile. I mean, here we are going through these property tax books and can't come up with so much as a smell of Santini. Maybe I'm all wrong about the man."

"Denny, let me level with you. Okay? I realize you're an outsider down here and all that, but you don't have to be so guarded about what you know. Don't you think I know you don't trust anybody down here? Me included. Maybe we do have some cops on the take–dirty as hell even. But I'm not one of them! Open up. Let me really help you."

Flynn nodded slowly making up his mind. He fixed his eyes on hers and found no falseness. "Okay, what do you want to know?"

"Start by telling me about this Santini character we're busy chasing down."

Flynn looked around to see if anybody else in the room was paying the two of them any attention. He lowered his voice and began. It took several minutes to tell the whole story to date.

"Thanks. I assume you've got more?"

"I've got a whole file–about a inch thick– back in my hotel room."

"In that case, let's finish up on these property owners and adjourn the meeting to your hotel room. I'd really like to see that file."

Flynn remembered he had to phone John Heller at the Secret Service office to see if Vincent Daly of the DEA was agreeable to meeting that night. "Let me make a quick phone call first, and then, I'll know more. Okay?"

"Great! You go make your call, and I'll finish up on these property owners."

Flynn left to make the call and was back within five minutes. "We're in luck. I was supposed to have a meeting with someone else tonight, but he can't make it until tomorrow afternoon. We have the afternoon and evening to ourselves if you don't have any other plans."

"Buy me dinner tonight, and my time is yours."

Flynn's heart filled with unexpected happiness. He admitted to himself he could really get interested in this lady with the flashing green eyes.

4:50 p.m., Indianapolis

From his vantage point on Washington Street, he watched the comings and goings of police vehicles as they used the ramp to the underground parking area. The killer patiently awaited the appearance of the lime-green, Ford sedan. He'd been there since 3:30 p.m. As the time drew nearer to 5:00 p.m., traffic on Alabama Street became increasingly heavy as the street filled with hundreds of civil servants and ordinary office workers all headed for home. He lit yet another cigarette as he watched the garage.

A sharp rapping on the passenger window startled him. He turned to see a uniformed patrolman, night stick in hand, standing at the door; peering at him through the window. Flustered, the killer reached over and cranked the window down. Regaining his composure, he addressed the situation.

129

"Yes?"

"I've been watchin' you for some time now. Seems to me you've been keeping a close watch on the building. Care to tell me why?"

"Just waiting for the wife to get back. She gives me hell if I'm not right there when she's ready to be picked up." Out of the corner of his eye, the killer saw the lime-green Ford come to the top of the garage ramp and turn right onto Alabama. He almost panicked as he waited for the patrolman to make the next move. "As a matter of fact, I see her coming out now."

"Just checking. Ever since those rag heads took out the WTC in New York, well–you know?"

"Yes. Yes, that's all right. I understand. But I'd better get moving."

The patrolman touched the bill of his hat and walked off resuming his foot patrol around the City-County Building perimeter. The killer turned his attention back to the street. His luck held! The lime-green Ford had been held up at the traffic signal. As quickly as he could, the killer backed the pickup out of the angled parking space and began to bully his way into the one-way, heavy traffic. He could still barely see the Ford headed west. At the first opening, he stomped hard on the accelerator, and the truck shot forward, cutting off two cars. He flung the truck around the corner and began to weave in and out of traffic as he sought to get nearer the Ford. The height of the truck allowed him to see over much of the automobile traffic ahead, letting him catch occasional glimpses of the lime-green roof ahead.

He redoubled his efforts to get closer. The Ford made a left turn on Pennsylvania Street with the killer four cars behind. They proceeded south beneath a railroad underpass, the speed picking up with every passing block. The Ford stayed in the center of the three lanes of southbound traffic. The killer followed suit. Soon, they were speeding along Madison Avenue, down to two lanes of traffic on the wide boulevard. After twenty minutes the Ford pulled to the right lane, and the killer followed. At Southport Road, the Ford turned right with the killer one car length behind. Within a quarter mile, the Ford turned left into a large complex of apartments and town houses, Wyandotte Apartments. The killer slowed as he followed the Ford almost to the south end of the large complex. The Ford turned left into a parking area and parked as the killer slowed to watch. The detective got out of the car and walked straight to a ground floor, two-story apartment that faced the parking area. The killer pulled the truck into the same parking area and slowly drove toward the far end. He watched the detective use a key to enter the apartment. The man had not noticed the truck. The killer took note of the address on the apartment door and slowly exited the parking area. Tomorrow, he would return to check out the apartment. If the girl were there, he'd kill her, find Blakemore's place, search it, and be on his way. Right now, Blakemore was the least of his problems.

Flynn unlocked the door to his hotel suite and stepped back to allow Megan to enter ahead of him. A small sitting room, a tiny kitchen, a fair-sized bedroom, and a well-equipped bath constituted the suite. Megan made a quick inspection tour and then, observed that the Indianapolis Police Department did pretty well by its traveling officers.

"Actually, I'm told the hotel belongs to your chief's brother-in-law. He's giving me an excellent rate. I can't complain at all," Flynn said as he tossed his suit coat over the nearest chair, and Megan set down her handbag.

Flynn went into the bedroom closet where he got his suitcase, unlocked it, and retrieved the file. When he returned to the sitting room, Megan was on the phone. "You're sure you'll be all right by yourself?– No. Just working late– I'll get something to eat before I get home–Okay, you take care now, see you later, honey."

"Everything okay?" Flynn asked.

"I just wanted to let Neil know I'd be late tonight."

His heart sank. Flynn tossed the file on the coffee table and sat down on the couch. "Your husband?" Flynn asked.

Megan joined him on the couch. "My twelve-year-old son. Classic latchkey kid. He's a good boy. I always check in if I'm going to be late. He takes pretty good care of himself."

"And Mr. Madigan?" Flynn was very conscious of the delicate scent of her perfume and the heat of her body.

"Neil's father deserted me the day I told him I was pregnant. Haven't heard from the bastard since."

"I'm sorry," Flynn managed to say.

"Don't be. I'm better off without the son-of-a-bitch. So is Neil. What about you Flynn? You married?"

"I was. My wife died almost eleven years ago. I have a twenty-one-year-old daughter, Monica, who is about to marry my best detective. No animals–pets. Pretty much a staid, old police detective."

"You don't seem all that old to me."

"I'll be forty-two my next birthday. I'm only six months away from putting in my papers. That is if I decide to retire."

"Like I said, you're not all that old. Retiring kinda young, aren't you? By any chance, does that kitchen have anything to drink hiding in it anywhere?"

"Well, there's a gallon of orange juice in the refrigerator, and I've got a bottle of Irish– Tullamore Dew– but no mixers."

"A little Irish on the rocks would be nice if you'll join me."

"It would be my pleasure," Flynn said as he got up to fix the drinks.

When he returned to the sitting room, Megan had her shoes off and her legs propped up on the coffee table. He almost stumbled as he leaned over the table to hand her the drink.

"Make yourself comfortable–you can see I have," she said as she accepted the drink. Flynn sat next to her on the couch and kicked off his own shoes. "Why are you retiring at such a young age?"

"I've given the last twenty years to the Department. I've seen what happens to guys who hang on and on. Police work is their entire life. I want something better for the second half of my life. The pension will be decent, and I've made some good investments over the years. That's something Mary got us started on– so I'm actually looking forward to a whole new life."

Megan listened and watched as Flynn told of his desire to start anew. There was more to this man than the average cop. She found herself admiring the man as he spoke. Time to change the subject! "Now, please tell me everything about this murder case–from the beginning," she said.

"It's a long story and getting longer every day."

"Dennis, do they have good room service in this hotel? I'm hungry!"

"I really don't know. I haven't used it yet."

"Well, let's find out together."

He found the room service menu and handed it to Megan. "You pick." As Megan read off what she thought would be a good dinner for two, Flynn went to the phone, ordered dinner, and then placed a second call to Mike Gaffney. The conversation lasted several minutes. Flynn gave Mike his number at the hotel and promised he'd call Monica later that night.

While they waited, Flynn retrieved his pipe and tobacco. After determining that Megan didn't object to his smoking, he began to pace the room as he packed the pipe, lit it, and amid great plumes of aromatic smoke, began his narrative. By the time he'd finished, darkness had settled over Florida in the twenty minutes his narrative consumed along with two pipefuls of tobacco. Megan had interrupted only a few times to ask very perceptive questions, which further impressed Flynn. The Santini file remained unopened on the coffee table.

"I'm sorry Monica is in such danger. I can understand why you are so secretive about all this. I can't say I blame you," she said.

Flynn ran his fingers through his hair and continued his pacing. "I'm really up against it. I have to find the connection between Santini and Blakemore because I don't think I'm ever going to catch the actual killer. Did your boss tell you how long he'd spare you to give me a hand?"

"No, not exactly. Look, I don't know how it is back in your shop, but in mine, women are still pretty seriously discriminated against. We're unwanted, second-class citizens. I'm on Alvero's shit list anyway. I'd bet that's the main reason you got me."

"On the contrary! Chief Burke told Alvero to assign you to assist me."

"The chief?!"

"I was sitting right there in his office when he said it."

"Well, I'll be damned!"

"Oh, I very much doubt that."

"Well that explains why my captain told me I was off the clock for this assignment. TAD as my dad would say. Tell you a secret. Maybe you lucked out. I have this terrific memory. Nearly photographic. I can't go into all the details, but I recalled some paperwork on a highly placed citizen at a bad time for the citizen. My boss thought he'd managed to make everything disappear–until I spilled the beans. Been on his shit list ever since."

"Why keep your photographic memory a secret?"

"Denny, it's my edge. My ticket to get ahead in the department." Before more could be discussed there was a discrete knock at the room door. The dinner had finally arrived.

Over the meal, Flynn told Megan of his phone conversation with Mike back in Indianapolis. Mike had responded to a tipster, who claimed he would meet with Mike at a restaurant at Circle Centre Mall, but the tipster failed to appear. And tonight's local, television news broadcasts had run the police computer rendering of the man they were looking for. Much of the story was given over to the fact that the police had a "mystery" witness. All of which troubled Flynn. It meant someone inside the department had talked to a reporter. Monica might now be in increased danger. He confided all this to Megan.

"Is Mike up to handling this alone?" she asked.

"So long as he doesn't let his love for her get in the way of good police work, yes."

"Okay then, if you're satisfied Mike has what it takes, let it drop. Don't worry about it any more. You're a good twelve hundred miles away. Couldn't do anything about it anyway."

"I guess you're right. I'd like to ask you a question or two. Okay?"

"Shoot!"

Flynn knew this one was a possible quagmire. "Well, have you been ordered by your deputy chief to report my activities or what we find to him?"

"Alvero? He didn't *order* me. He did rather pointedly tell me to keep him apprised of any developments. Why?"

"Trust, Megan, trust. Who do I trust? Can I—*we* trust the man?"

"Like I said earlier, I'm sure we've got guys on the pad for drug dealers. I don't think Alvero is one of them. If he's susceptible, I'd think it would be in the political area. He's got his nose up the mayor's ass! Are you asking me not to tell him anything?"

"Let's think about that for a while. We don't have any developments yet anyway. Next question. Since we are pretty much joined at the hip in this, I need to know if I can count on your help for any length of time. So, I really would like to know how long will you be available to assist?"

"Like I said, I've been detached from special investigations for as long as you're in town. TAD. That's navy speak for temporarily assigned duty. And don't forget, I'm on Alvero's shit list. He'd be happy if I dropped off the face of the earth. Now, if that's everything, are we ready to tackle that Santini file? If so, let me call Neil. I need to tell him I'll be home later than I told him before. I don't want to worry him, and then, we'll get right to it."

"By all means. Are you sure he'll be all right–by himself like this?"

"Neil has been taking care of himself since he was about ten and is very mature and responsible for his age."

Flynn was suddenly conscious of her nearness on the sofa. He could feel the heat from her body. "Frankly, I can't imagine how you've stayed single all this time. Surely, there must have been a lot of guys who wanted you," Flynn said surprising himself with his boldness.

Her response was flat and deliberate. "That's just it–they wanted *me*, not a woman with a young boy."

Flynn felt ashamed of himself for intruding into her private life. "I see. I'm sorry–go ahead. Make your call."

While Megan was calling her son, Flynn took the carafe of hot coffee off the table along with the sterno stove and the coffee cups, carried them into the kitchenette, and then, pushed the room service cart out into the hallway. He resumed his place on the sofa to wait while Megan finished her call.

She was smiling when she turned to face him. "Neil is just fine. Says he'd like to meet you before you go home."

"Well, I'm flattered. Perhaps, I'll do that before I leave. Now, are we ready for work at long last?"

"Let's see what you've got." She moved closer on the sofa. Their hips and legs touched. Flynn's heart rate increased.

He opened the file and began to sort the paperwork into categories. Suddenly, Megan reached in, grabbing the thin stack of photographs. A frown creased her pretty forehead. Quickly, she shuffled through the pictures and examined the LAPD memos taped to the back of each.

"Dennis, is this your man, Santini?" she asked with some urgency in her voice.

Flynn was alerted by her reaction to the photos. "That's what it says. Why?"

"I've seen this man right here in Miami, and he doesn't use that name here."

"Are you certain?" Flynn was astonished.

"Positive!"

"But how? I mean, why are you so sure?"

"My photographic memory—remember? Never forget a picture or a page."

Flynn was stunned. "Well—I'll be damned! I'd forgotten."

"Let me think now." She looked intently at the photo in her hand as her mind raced through associations. After some tense moments on Flynn's part, she resumed, "He goes by the name Dominic Mazzicone down here. Wait a minute!" Megan jumped up and grabbed her handbag. Quickly, she tore through its contents until she came up with her notes from the day-long, property-records search. "Yes! Here it is! I knew I'd seen it–Dominic Mazzicone has property in South Miami. Off the Coral Gables Waterway. See, here it is! Riviera Street."

Flynn was thunderstruck. Not only was she beautiful but smart as Hell. "Let's check the address against these telephone numbers. See if we have a match," he said, excitement growing within his chest. Seconds later, Megan had cross-referenced one of Flynn's Miami telephone numbers with the house on Riviera Street.

"So, Detective Madigan, how do you recommend we proceed?" Flynn asked.

"Well, I suggest we take a little trip out there tomorrow and look the place over. Ask the neighbors a few questions. You know, old-fashioned police work."

"I agree. When do you want to start?"

"I'll come by in the morning and pick you up. Any chance you'll be available for breakfast?"

"Sure. Got someplace special in mind?"

"I know a simply smashing place. Great food–and it's on the way," Megan said as she slipped on her shoes and grabbed her purse. "Be ready about eight."

"I will. Are you leaving?" Her sudden departure took Flynn by surprise.

"Yes. We've done all we can here tonight. Time to get home to Neil."

"Well, let me walk you to your car."

"Thank you. I'd appreciate that."

Flynn slipped his naked body between the cool sheets. As he lay waiting for sleep to overtake his tired body, his thoughts turned to the extraordinary woman with whom he'd spent a most rewarding day. God! She was beautiful, smart, and to Flynn very appealing. He could call to mind the scent of her subtle yet somehow compelling perfume. As his mind fantasized, he became aware he was having an erection. Laying in bed and fantasizing about a real woman hadn't happened for many months. Immediately, a feeling of guilt passed through his heart. Guilt that he had abandoned his long gone Mary for this beautiful woman in his thoughts. When at last sleep came, he dreamed of Megan Madigan. The dreams were joyous and extremely erotic. Flynn's subconscious ran riot with his day long, suppressed desires.

The killer parked the Civic to the north of Detective Gaffney's apartment. From there, hidden by the morning darkness, he could watch as the lime-green Ford passed without being seen himself. All around him residents of the Wyandotte Apartment complex were leaving for work. Kids were queued–up waiting for school busses. At 7:15, he saw the Ford pass his location. He waited for another fifteen minutes. He then backed his car out and drove on down to the parking area in front of the detective's apartment. He waited until all the activity about him had died down and then, approached the apartment door. Dressed in a business suit and carrying a small, cheap brief case for cover, he knocked on the door. He waited and knocked again. No response. He examined the door. There was no dead bolt, only a cheap lock. He reached into his inside coat pocket and withdrew a set of lock–picks. In less than twenty seconds, he'd defeated the cheap lock.

The apartment was small, arranged in a "shotgun" fashion with a living room in front, dining room and kitchen in that order toward the back, and bedrooms on the second floor. The living room offered no clues, so the killer turned his attention down the hall. He climbed the stair to the second floor. He entered the front bedroom and quickly scanned the room. His attention was arrested by a large color photograph atop the chest of drawers. He crossed the room and examined the picture. It was the girl. Pictured with her was the detective.

Triumph snapped in his eyes. *So*–the two were lovers. That should make his task all the easier. Sooner or later, Detective Gaffney would lead him to the girl. As the comfortable and familiar feeling of the hunt came back over him, he started a thorough search of the remaining rooms for any clue, which might reveal the girl's name or residence. With the exception of several packets of Target Store processed photographs, showing the two in various locales and states of dress–none of which gave a clue to a location or a name, he found nothing of significance. He determined to spend the rest of the day in attempting to locate Blakemore's house or apartment. He knew political figures often kept their addresses and phone numbers as confidential information. In a way, he looked on the hunt as yet another challenge to his superior abilities.

8:00 a.m., Miami

Flynn was standing at the main entrance to the hotel when Megan pulled a jet black, Mazda, RX–7, turbo coupe into the circular drive. Like so many of the cars in Florida, the car's side and rear windows were tinted a deep, almost black, dark gray. The sunroof was open. He could see her sparkling dark hair. She took off her sunglasses and smiled a welcome to him as he approached the car. She had dressed in a pale blue, lightweight suit with a cream blouse. Her hair was caught in a light-blue band. Flynn's heart skipped a beat as it struck him again how astonishingly attractive she was. He opened the passenger door and got in. The soft bucket seat cradled his body.

"Good morning, Denny," she said with a smile accompanying the greeting.

"Good morning, Megan." He felt himself smiling like a love-sick high-school boy. "I must say you Miami cops are certainly pampered–racy sports cars and all."

"This isn't department issue. This is all mine."

"Then you are well-paid, indeed!"

"Not nearly enough. Well, are you ready for breakfast?"

"Starved. Simply starved."

"Then, we're off!" And they were. The Mazda shot out of the drive amid a screech of tires and the throaty roar of the turboed rotary engine. She handled the car expertly. Within minutes, they were speeding along a wide freeway headed southeast. The scent of sea air growing stronger by the minute. As she drove, she played tour guide, pointing out buildings and places of interest. Flynn was content to enjoy the ride and let himself be caressed by her voice. They'd been driving for about fifteen minutes when she suddenly pulled off the freeway, made a few quick turns, and slid the car into a parking space at the rear of a large restaurant. "We're here," she said, getting out of the car. Flynn quickly got out of the car and followed as she led the way toward a rear door. Bringing up the rear, he watched her hips gently swaying as the beautiful, shapely legs carried her to the door. Without hesitation, she opened the back door. They made their way through the kitchen toward the front. Employees called out welcomes and hellos to Megan, who returned them by name. Megan led the way into the main dining room and to one of the small alcove banquettes, sheltered from view by hanging fish nets. Moments later, a pretty, young girl brought glasses of ice water and handed each a richly done menu.

"Dennis, would you mind if I ordered for both of us?" Megan asked. "They have one of the greatest breakfasts in the world here."

"No. By all means, please do. Mind if I ask you a question?"

"No. Go right ahead."

"Well, how come you can just walk right in the back door? And why does everybody know you?"

"Simple. I worked my way through school here."

Flynn was about to observe that more than a few years had passed since she was in school when a smartly dressed, older woman approached the table. Megan got to her feet to greet the lady. Flynn fumbled himself to his own feet as the two women embraced. Megan turned toward Flynn and stunned him by saying, "Mother, I'd like you to meet Captain Dennis Flynn.

He's down here from Indianapolis on a murder case, and I've been assigned to assist him."

"How do you do, Captain Flynn?" she said extending her hand.

"Mrs. Madigan," Flynn said as he took her hand.

"Please, please. Sit down both of you. It's been quite a while since Megan has been to see us."

"Well, you know how busy I am, Mom. I just don't get the time. We're only here now because it's on the way to our first stop this morning," Megan said.

"In that case, I should thank Captain Flynn."

"Oh, Mom, will you stop. Most of this is just paperwork. No danger."

"Megan, since you are here now, I need to know– will you be having a party for Neil on his birthday this year?"

"We haven't talked about it yet. His birthday isn't for another three weeks. But don't worry, if we do, you'll be invited no matter what."

"Good. I'll drop by tomorrow night, I promised Neil I'd take him to a movie he wants to see. It was nice meeting you, Mr. Flynn. Now, you two enjoy your breakfast." With that, Megan's mother gave her daughter a kiss on the cheek and left the two alone.

"Quite a striking woman, your mother. How is it we ran into her here?" Flynn asked.

"Yes, she is. But she still isn't too keen about my independent life or my choice of profession. She still thinks police work is no place for a woman."

"And your father, what does he think?" Flynn asked.

"Well, if Pop were still alive, I think he'd approve. He was a pretty independent man himself."

"I'm sorry. I didn't realize–" Flynn trailed off in embarrassment.

"Oh, that's all right. I didn't tell you. Pop died shortly after I got pregnant. He was a great guy, my Dad, and I think about him often. As for Mom, to answer your question, the reason we saw her here is because she owns the place." She was about to say more when the waitress returned to take their order.

Later, as the car turned off the blazing white freeway, Flynn began to take notice of the surroundings. There was a profusion of large, old, palm trees, large, cactus-like plants, flowering shrubbery, lush lawns, and neatly trimmed hedges, shielding large homes from prying eyes. Megan slowed the car to a sedate twenty-miles-an-hour and began concentrating on street addresses. At a four-way stop, she turned the car south toward the waters of the Coral Gables Waterway. Flynn was struck by the quiet beauty of the area. At the next corner, Megan turned right on Riviera and slowed the car. These houses were situated on even more land, many of them separated from their neighbors by high brick or painted concrete block walls. Fancy crushed shell or paved brick drives wound their way toward the houses. The street fairly screamed of money, lots of it! Flynn was impressed.

Megan nudged Flynn's shoulder and pointed toward the house on their left just coming into view. "That's it," she said, slowing the Mazda to a walking pace. Flynn fixed his eyes on the house. It was a large, two-story brick, done in Spanish style, red tile roof, ubiquitous in Miami, with wrought iron work grills at the windows, along an ornate second floor balcony, which appeared to run around all four walls of the house. More cast-iron work covered five sweeping brick archways which supported the balcony. The property was separated from its neighbors by thick, tall, brick walls, which Flynn estimated were at least ten feet high. The drive was paved in brick and ran to a circular entry way before large double doors, which appeared to be quite substantial. Megan picked up speed as they passed the next house.

"Any plans?" she asked.

"Anyway we can see the place from the back?"

"That's the waterway out there behind the house."

"So, how do we get there? Rent a boat?"

"Or we could use mine."

"Megan, you never cease to amaze me!"

"Good. I like to keep people guessing. We can't do it now, though. My boat is quite a few miles from here, and we're definitely not dressed for it. So, what say we do it tomorrow, and for now, let's ask the neighbors a few questions."

"Sounds good to me."

Pulling the car to the curb, Megan faced Flynn. "Let's start right here. Please, let me do most of the talking. I'll introduce you as Captain Flynn, but I won't say from where. I'll buzz 'em with my badge and ID."

"It's your territory. I'll follow your lead."

They got out of the car and walked back to the house immediately to the south of the one owned by Mazzicone. The late morning sun was hot on Flynn's shoulders and face. He felt perspiration start on his upper lip. They walked up a dazzling white drive of crushed sea shells to the cover of a large entry way at the front door. Megan pressed the door bell. Flynn could faintly hear the sound of chimes ringing somewhere deep inside the house, and at length, the door was opened by a large, black woman dressed in a maid's uniform. Megan reached into her large purse and extracted her ID case, opening it for the maid to see.

"Good morning. I'm Detective Madigan, Miami P.D., and this is Captain Flynn. Are Mr. or Mrs. Anderson home?"

"No, Ma'am, they both over in England."

"Oh, I see. Perhaps you can help us. Do you live in or come to work days?" Megan asked.

"I live in. Can you tell me what this is about? The Andersons wouldn't want me talkin' 'bout none of their business."

"Oh, I'm sorry. This isn't about the Andersons. It's about the people next door. Mr. Dominic Mazzicone."

"Don't know nothin' about the folks next door," she was definite.

"Haven't you seen the owner?"

"Couldn't say. What with that big brick wall and all. There's so many folks comin' and goin' over there at all hours. Besides, they ain't sociable anyway."

"Oh? Why do you say that?"

"Well, Mr. Anderson, he went over there shortly after the place was bought, you know, to be neighborly, an' he come back madder than I ever seen him. Said they practically threw him right out!"

"You say there's people coming and going at all hours. Could you explain that in more detail?" Flynn asked.

"Strange cars come here all the time, and then, they take that high-powered boat out late at night and come back just afore sunup."

"I'm sorry, I didn't ask your name." Megan said.

"Sarah Jenkins."

"Well, Sarah, it's pretty warm out here, and I have a lot of questions. Do you think it would be all right if we came inside?"

The maid thought it over for a few seconds and then, stepped back from the door. "I reckon the Andersons wouldn't mind. I'm workin' back in the kitchen. Can we talk back there while I work?"

The kitchen overlooked the waterway, and from his position at the kitchen table, Flynn could see the brick wall of the adjoining property.

"How long have you been with the Andersons, Sarah?" Flynn asked, sipping the fresh lemonade Sarah had served.

"Goin' on thirteen years now," she answered with pride.

"Was that brick wall always there?" Flynn asked pointing out the window.

"No, sir. That wall went up right soon after the new owner took over."

"How long ago was that?" Megan asked.

"'Bout six or seven years ago. Made Mr. Anderson all upset. He even talked 'bout takin' them folks to court."

"But he never did?" Megan asked.

"Well he talked to his lawyer 'bout it, an' he said there wasn't no law agin' buildin' a wall on your own property. So, Mr. Jack, I mean Mr. Anderson, he just forgot the whole thing."

"Do you ever see any of these people who come and go next door?" Flynn asked.

"Sometimes I can see 'em when they way out on the roof of the boathouse."

"But I can't see any boathouse from here," Flynn said.

"I kin see 'em from my room upstairs."

Flynn chanced it. He took a photograph of Blakemore out of his suit coat pocket and held it out for Sarah to see. "Have you ever seen this man visiting next door?"

Sarah wiped her hands on her apron, pulled some glasses from her blouse pocket, put them on, and examined the photograph.

"I seen him here plenty of times. Matter of fact, he drives that big boat. Seen him do it lots of times." She smiled as she handed the photo back.

Flynn gave Megan a triumphant look. His pulse quickened. Now, all they had to do was put the two men together in the same place at the same time.

"Sarah, what does this big boat look like?" Megan asked.

Sarah described an offshore racing boat. Megan quickly understood the significance. "Do they have more than one boat?" she asked.

"Them folks got three or four boats! Must be rich as Midas!"

"Sarah, can you keep a secret?" Megan asked.

"Like to think I can."

"Well, we think these folks next door might be dangerous men. It would be best if you didn't tell anybody that Captain Flynn and I have been here."

Sarah gave them both a hard, fierce look. "I ain't afraid. But I'll do what you say. Can I tell Mr. Jack you were here?"

"What does Mr. Anderson do for a living?" Flynn asked.

"He owns the Jaguar dealership downtown." Sarah pronounced it "Jaggeer", and Flynn had to perform some mental gymnastics to translate.

"Well, for now, I don't think it would be a good idea. If we catch these men, we'll tell you all about it, and then, you can tell the Andersons. Deal?" Megan said.

Sarah smiled with pride. "You got a deal! Don't fret none. I can keep my mouth shut. I learned to do that when I was a little girl back in Loosianna."

As they walked back to the car, Flynn told Megan he was nervous about meddling in what could turn out to be the world of narcotics. It was almost a foreign language to him. He told her of his proposed meeting with Vincent Daly of the DEA Miami office.

"Do you work closely with the Feds up in Indianapolis?" she asked as she pulled the car away from the curb.

"Not in my line of work. Ordinary murder isn't a federal crime– yet."

"How do your IPD Narc officers feel about the DEA, in Indianapolis?"

"To tell you the truth, they don't have much use for them. Even though we're supposed to be having all this lovey-dovey inter-agency cooperation now, what with the war on terrorism and all, not much has really changed. The Narc guys in my department claim the DEA and the FBI still are looking out for their own number one. Always making headlines, for themselves at the expense of the guys in the department."

"It's the same down here, only much worse."

"How so?"

"This is where most of the Colombian shit comes into the country. Container ships, drops at sea. The law enforcement infighting is something else. The DEA, the Coast Guard, the Customs people; everybody's out to make headlines that get the attention of the budget people in Washington."

"I take it you're not in favor of my meeting with this man?"

"Look, Denny, I can't tell you what to do, but if I were in your shoes, I'd pump him for the information you need and guard my own information like Fort Knox. If you don't, he'll move in on you and blow away any chance you have of clearing your murder case. I mean, what the hell does he care about a two-bit murder way up in Indianapolis?"

Flynn was lost in deep thought all the way back to the hotel. It was shortly past one o'clock when Megan pulled the sleek Mazda into the hotel drive. Megan asked him to join her for dinner that evening. They agreed, and Megan told him to dress very informally. "Tee shirt, shorts, and sandals if you've got 'em. Be ready at six."

"I'll be waiting for you right here at six."

Flynn watched her drive away until the car was lost to sight. Returning to his room, he called Mike.

"Mike, how's it going at your end?"

"Not too good. *The Star* blew the whole thing out of the water this morning. Our suspect's picture is three columns of the front page. They've turned up the fire on the murders. The chief is so mad he could chew nails. The mayor had him on the carpet for about an hour this morning. If the chief ever finds the guy who talked and gave *The Star* the picture, he'll be walking a beat in East Overshoe, New Jersey in the dead of winter with no coat. Or better yet, Bumfuck, Egypt, in the heat of their summer! Monica's climbing the walls. She's got a real bad case of cabin fever. Her boss called, wondering when he can expect her back. In short, nothing's going very well. The only thing we've turned up since you left was the hooker's car. It was parked in the lot behind that Japanese joint. So, I think she met Blakemore at the restaurant. I've had the car pulled in. Chuck went over it and wasn't able to find anything useful."

"Well, I've had a bit more luck at this end. We've located the house. Santini apparently owns property down here under the name Dominic Mazzicone. I interviewed a neighbor who definitely put Blakemore at the house several times over the past few years. So far, I haven't checked into the money laundering angle, but I will if I can. I'm working with Detective Megan Madigan out of special investigations. She's one smart lady! Wish we had her back in Indy."

"Is she good looking?"

"To be perfectly honest—she's fantastic! But not to worry, she's too old for you. Besides, what would Monica say?"

"I wasn't asking for myself, Denny. I was thinking of you and all the years you've been without someone to love you." Mike was serious.

Flynn was both surprised and deeply touched. His throat choked a bit as he answered, "Thanks, Mike. What a nice thing to say. I admit I'm very attracted to her. Can you imagine that!

Me, at my age and after all these years? But enough of that, at my age not much chance it could go anywhere. Any chance you can take Monica out for a change of scenery?"

"I'll be going over there for dinner tonight. I'll see if John will let me take her out for a few hours to a movie or do anything she wants to do," Mike said.

"Good. Well, if anything new comes up, call me. You have the number here?"

"Don't worry. You're still in charge even if you are almost, what? Thirteen hundred miles away. Will you call Monica tonight?"

Flynn promised to call. He checked his watch as he hung-up the phone; three hours until he was due to meet with Vincent Daly. He decided to do something he hadn't done in several years—treat himself to clothing suitable for tonight's "tee shirt, shorts, and sandal" dinner. He smiled to himself as he got a mental picture of the billing clerk at American Express. He hadn't used the card for so long they'd probably check the files to be sure he was still alive.

It was exactly 4 p.m. when he returned to the hotel, a large shopping bag in hand. The combination of the shopping and the anticipation of an evening with Megan had him in high spirits. He had just stowed the shopping bag in the bedroom closet when there was a knock at his door. "Damn! The man is punctual if nothing else," Flynn muttered as he opened the door.

Vincent Daly was at least six-five with a florid, beefy-looking face, salt and pepper crew cut, and a handshake like a vise. Flynn was immediately reminded of a Marine drill instructor gone to seed. Daly's voice had all the intonations and accents of a man born in Brooklyn, New York.

Daly seated himself on the couch and came right to the point. "Flynn, I got a few questions for you before I answer yours. Okay?"

"Well, it's your territory. I guess we'll play by your rules," Flynn answered as he chose one of the arm chairs for himself. He took an instant dislike to this walking ego.

"Good. Now, I want to know why a homicide cop from Indianapolis, for God's sake, Indiana, is nosing around down here, asking about drugs."

Flynn, irked by the man's overbearing, superior attitude, answered with some sarcasm. "The answer to your question is I came here to learn how drugs get into the country, how money changes hands, and to trace a suspect in a murder investigation. I believe, it is very possible that drugs and the murder are linked. Is that good enough for you?"

"Who's your suspect?"

"I can't tell you that."

"Look, you cooperate with me, and I'll cooperate with you. Now, who is your suspect?"

"Sorry."

"Is this suspect involved with the drug business?"

"I'm beginning to think it's a distinct possibility."

"And you're not going to tell me who it is?"

"Nope."

"Mind telling me why?"

"Vinny, may I call you, Vinny? Every kid I grew up with named Vincent liked to be called 'Vinny'. I never reveal too much to anybody until I have my case lined up–the T's crossed and the I's dotted, the legal paperwork complete, and the suspect in custody. Once that's done, my suspect is all yours if my chief agrees. Deal?"

"You realize I can have you bounced out of town?"

"I don't see how. I wasn't aware the Feds had taken over Miami."

"I can make life miserable for you down here."

"I've no doubt. Look, everybody told me you were an okay guy, a straight shooter. You and I aren't enemies. You really don't need to come on like Patton. Now, why can't you just tell me what I want to know without all this bullying?"

Daly relented a bit. "Okay, but if you turn a dealer, I want him. Will you promise me that?"

"Like I said, if my boss agrees. Remember murder takes precedence over drug dealing."

"All right, what do you want to know?"

"Well, to start with, how do they get the stuff into the country?"

"The currently popular method is secreting the shit in shipping containers that come in here by the thousands every day of the week. Smaller operators use an air or ship drop at sea out in international waters. The stuff is picked up by fast cigarette boats and then, smuggled ashore. But for the greatest part, it hits our shores in those goddamn containers off loaded from container ships. From there most goes north right up I-95 in motor homes, campers, and in trunks of cars. A variation on this is the use of an air strip on one of the British Bahamian Islands and then, to the boats."

"What's a cigarette boat?" Flynn asked, embarrassed he had no clue.

"Basically, it's a ocean-racing vessel with either a twin hull or a single deep V, multiple engines–either inboard or outboard. They're about thirty to forty feet in length, and in a favorable sea, they can do a hundred miles an hour– or better."

"Where do they bring it to shore?"

"Are you kidding? Florida has thousands and thousands of miles of coastline all told. The shit comes in everywhere! It's like water running through a sieve."

"Do you have a list of known dealers or importers?"

"Between us and the other police agencies in this state, we've got a book of names as thick as the Manhattan phone directory. But these guys are all small-time lieutenants. They make the list when they get arrested. We don't have a long list of the kingpins; the money men behind everything–they're well hidden. So, unless your suspect has been arrested, he won't be on anybody's list. Now, level with me. Have you got someone specific in mind?"

"Yes, I do. But my murder case comes first. The murder took place in my jurisdiction. This possible drug business is only important to provide a motive and a link between my victim and the man or men who had him killed. And to tell you the truth, I don't have any hard evidence that drugs are involved– yet. It's just a cop's gut feeling."

Daly was silent for several moments before he asked his key question. "Okay, I'll do what I can to help you, but I want your promise if your suspect is involved in any drug importing–and I mean everything from grass to coke you will give him to me after you've made your case."

Flynn thought it over before answering. "I think I can safely promise my chief and the prosecutor back home will agree."

"Okay, I'll accept that. Now, exactly what is it you want from me?"

"Right now, just your promise of cooperation. Is there a way I can get to you without going through your subordinates?"

"The best I can do along that line is to give you my personal pager number and the unlisted number for our communications center." Having said it, he pulled a pocket notebook from his coat, wrote the numbers, tore out the page, and handed it to Flynn.

"Thanks. I promise to use this only if it is really necessary. I apologize for my attitude. It's just that I want to keep control of my investigation and my suspect."

"I guess I did come on a little strong. I apologize," Daly said as he stood to shake Flynn's hand. "I have to get going, or I'll miss my next meeting."

Flynn thanked him again for the promise of help as he let the man out.

5:15 p.m., Indianapolis

From his vantage point in the apartment complex parking lot, the killer watched the lime-green Ford return at the end of the work day. Gaffney, dressed in a brown suit and topcoat, got out of the car and immediately entered his apartment. Within thirty minutes, he reappeared in more casual attire, jeans, turtleneck sweater, and leather jacket. He quickly reentered the car and drove out of the complex. The killer waited a few seconds, started the pickup, and began to follow.

Several minutes later, he watched as the Ford pulled into the drive of a large, ranch-style house. The killer pulled his pickup to the curb several houses away to watch as the detective walked to the front door, knocked, and let himself in. A satisfied smile insinuated itself onto the killer's face as he considered the possibility of success. Unless he was badly mistaken, he'd now been led to the girl's home or hiding place. He began formulating a plan of attack. He carefully examined the neighborhood. Well-established trees and lawns, curving streets, and fenced-in back yards told him it was a subdivision of some age, perhaps into its second or third generation of owners. On his way in, he'd passed several Neighborhood Crime Watch signs. It wouldn't do to remain parked too long where he was. At length, he hit on a scheme that would allow him to verify the situation. He remembered passing a small strip shopping mall as he followed the detective to the present location. If the policeman returned to his apartment via the same route, he would pass that mall. A pickup parked on the strip wouldn't attract any attention, and he would be able to observe the policeman from a safe distance. He started the truck and made a tour of the subdivision. Several of the streets ended in cul-de-sacs, but the two main streets paralleled each other in a large "C" with both ends exiting onto Madison Avenue, a four-lane, main city thoroughfare. The killer backtracked and drove the quarter mile to the small strip mall. As he entered the parking lot, he examined the shops. There was a CVS Pharmacy, advertising a twenty-four-hour day, a Big John's Pizza shop, a closed supermarket, and a bank branch. Toward the end of the strip, he spotted a tavern with a large, front window facing Madison Avenue. His luck was holding. If he could find a table with a view out that window, his problem would be solved.

6:00 p.m., Miami

The sleek black Mazda followed a meandering street beside yet another waterway. Towering high rises and sprawling estates lined the street. Flynn was astonished to see so many huge cruisers capable of ocean navigation lining the waterway. Megan drove with casual ease. She was dressed in runner's shorts and shoes and a tank top, which flattered her trim figure. Flynn had worn his new purchases: string tied athletic shorts, a dark blue Polo shirt, and some amazingly comfortable Asolo sandals. In all, not only was Flynn quite comfortable but also he felt more like he "belonged" and less like a tourist, his untanned, white skin notwithstanding. All efforts to get Megan to tell him where they were headed had been met with smiling evasions. From the length of time they'd been driving, Flynn estimated they were a good twenty-five miles from his hotel. The scenery became more sparse, the high rises were gone, and the houses had become smaller and were closer together. Sand and wild-looking plants fought for control over the side of the narrow road they now traveled. Suddenly, the Mazda slowed and turned left onto a short drive of crushed shells. In the evening light, he could see a small, white house of two stories. A wall, perhaps six feet high, ran the length of the back side of the property. Megan slid the Mazda into the attached garage.

She got out of the car. "In answer to all your questions, welcome to my home."

He could hear the sound of pounding surf beyond. The smell of the sea was strong on the air. Megan's eyes sparkled. "I haven't cooked for an honest-to-god man in a long, long time. I hope I haven't forgotten how." They entered a sun room, which faced the ocean. Jalousie windows ran the length of the room and from floor to ceiling. The inviting room was furnished with wrought iron patio furniture. Two walls were paneled in unfinished pecky cypress, which gave off a delightful aroma. Megan led the way into the kitchen where she directed Flynn to a bar stool seat at the center cooking island. Extracting a wine bottle and chilled glasses from a large commercial sized refrigerator, she placed them on the counter and handed Flynn a levered cork screw.

"So, how is it you have this fabulous place?" he asked as he got the bottle open.

"Pop bought this place years and years ago after the war before all the development spread this far south. He left it to me in his will. I spent my years as a little girl here until the restaurant got so famous, and Mom pushed Pop into buying a condo closer in."

"He must have loved it. Hanging on to it even though he had the condo."

"This was one of two of his favorite places in all the world. The other is a cabin down in the Keys. He'd spend hours here out on that beach or out on his boat," she said with a far away look in her eyes.

"I think you loved your dad very much." He poured the wine.

"Yes, I did. He never once condemned me or said 'I told you so'. I wish he'd lived long enough to see his grandson. He would have been so proud of him. And Neil would have been wild about him!"

"Speaking of Neil, is he going to be here tonight? Isn't he scheduled to go to a movie with your mother?"

"When I told him you were going to be here tonight, he canceled the movie. Really wants to meet you." Megan glanced at her watch. "I expect he'll show any minute now. If I know him, he's out along the beach somewhere."

"I'm looking forward to meeting him too. Now, if it isn't being a bad guest, I'm starving. May I inquire about the bill of fare for tonight?"

"You may indeed. We'll start with tossed salad and then, move straight to the main entrée: broiled shrimp and broiled stuffed lobster. Dessert will be Key lime pie. How does that sound?"

"That sounds like at least one hundred and ten dollars per person back where I come from!"

"Surprise, it's not that much cheaper down here! It helps to be in the restaurant business though."

"You mean your mother–?"

"No. Pop left me half of the restaurant too."

"I meant, did your mom provide the shrimp and lobster?"

"In a way. I purchased the shrimp and lobster from the same outfit we use to supply the restaurant at wholesale prices of course."

"So, your mother might know we're having dinner at your house tonight?"

"No. I most always get my seafood from the same seafood supplier." She looked at him a bit quizzically, "Would it bother you if she knew?"

"No, I suppose not. At my age, it just seems weird worrying about what a girl's mother might think all over again."

Megan looked him straight in the eyes and said very matter-of-factly, "Mom would be worrying that you might be after my money."

"Oh, are you independently wealthy?" Flynn was stunned. The thought hadn't occurred!

"You could say that. I get half the restaurant profits on a quarterly basis, my paycheck from the city, and the interest on a trust Dad setup for me and Neil. Speaking of that little dickens, I think I hear him coming now."

Flynn heard the sun porch door open and close with a slam, followed by the sound of something being tossed into a chair. "Neil," Megan called out, "we're in the kitchen." Flynn turned on his stool as he heard the sound of bare feet on the polished wood floor. A well-tanned, strikingly handsome boy in the spurt of preteen years appeared at the door. Like his mother, Neil had shoulder-length, windblown, sun streaked, dark brown, curly hair. Startlingly deep blue eyes, topped by full, dark eyebrows assessed Flynn. At twelve about to be thirteen, the boy had the beginnings of a fine athletic build. Flynn estimated the boy's height at about five-seven or eight. Tall for a young kid. He was dressed only in bikini swim trunks. Flynn saw a look of apprehension cross the boy's face as he anticipated the inevitable awkwardness of introductions. Wanting to spare the boy embarrassment, Flynn took the initiative.

"How do you do?" Flynn said, extending his right hand.

The boy crossed the kitchen, stood before Flynn, and took the offered hand of friendship, saying, "Pleased to meet you, sir." Flynn gave the boy's hand a firm but gentle shake.

"No, the pleasure is all mine. Your mom has been telling me so much about you. I've really been looking forward to meeting you."

The boy shot a quick look at his mother, "Well, she's been talking about you for two straight days now, Captain Flynn," the boy said, clearly enjoying a "gotcha" on his mother.

Megan broke in. "Enough fellows! Neil, you have time for a shower before dinner. So, off with you, and don't dawdle!"

Neil flashed a bright smile to them both and went bounding upstairs into another part of the house. Soon, Flynn heard the sound of a shower running.

"That's a beautiful boy you have there. I can see why you're so proud of him," Flynn said.

"Never had a son, did you?" she asked.

"No. After we had Monica, we tried and tried, but after two miscarriages in quick succession, Mary said God was trying to tell us something, so we just gave up. Used to talk about adopting, but after a while—"

Megan was busy preparing a cracker crumb stuffing for the lobsters as they talked. "I have a feeling you wanted a son pretty badly," she observed.

"Yes. Yes, I did. What man doesn't?" Megan observed a dreamy look pass over Flynn's face as he spoke.

She was chopping celery for the stuffing and stopped for a moment to appraise Flynn. He didn't see her frank look of appraisal, being far away in his dreams and remembrances.

"Denny, have you ever fixed stuffed lobster before?" she asked.

Flynn tore himself out of his memories, "No, I never have."

"Well then, you are about to get your first lesson," she said as she opened a large, metal box. Three large, live lobsters in a bed of wet seaweed cringed in the sudden light. Megan quickly grabbed one of the lobsters behind the claws and lifted it onto the counter top. Deftly turning the creature on its back, she took up a large, chef's knife and neatly sliced the lobster open from head to tail through the underside. She was in the process of cracking it open to accept the stuffing when Neil bounded into the kitchen.

"Oh, Baaad! We haven't had lobster in weeks and weeks!" he said, as he grabbed up a stalk of celery, seated himself on the stool next to Flynn, and began to chomp away. Flynn turned to look at the boy. Neil had dressed only in brief running shorts. His hair was still wet from the shower, and here and there, beads of water still clung to his body where he'd missed with the towel. He'd obviously been in a great hurry to get to the table.

"Welcome, Neil. Your arrival has saved me from a terrible fate," Flynn said.

"Oh, what's that?" Neil asked.

"Well, your mom was about to teach me the fine art of killing and stuffing a lobster."

"You're kidding? Anybody can do that!"

"Well, I never have and I don't think I want to—right now."

"Okay. Can I ask you a question?" The boy's eyes shone with anticipation, life, and joy. It pained Flynn's heart to realize what he'd missed by not having a son.

"Shoot."

"Well—have you been to the 500?"

"Oh, sure. I go almost every year."

"Are there really a million people there just for that one day?"

"Well, its really closer to a half million. Maybe a bit more."

"Can you get right up next to the race cars and the drivers?"

"I usually get a pit pass. That lets you go almost anywhere."

"Do you know any of the race drivers?" The boy's enthusiasm was growing.

"Well, let me think a minute. Let's see—I've met Johnny Rutherford, A.J. Foyt, Mario Andretti, both of the Unsers, and a few others."

"Oh, wow! Did you get their autographs?"

"You know I never thought about it. So, I'm afraid I didn't."

Neil was really warming to his quest. "How did you meet them?" he asked.

"Well, each year the night before the 500 Festival Parade, the mayor has this big party for the drivers and the car owners and a lot of other bigwigs. I usually get invited, so I go. To tell you the truth, I've only met them. I don't really know them, and I'm sure they wouldn't remember me. I'm just another person at the party."

The boy's face betrayed his disappointment. "I watch the race every year," he stated.

"You do?"

"Oh, sure."

"Neil, I'm sure Denny would rather talk about other things. Don't monopolize the conversation," Megan said, placing the lobsters and shrimp in the broiler. Checking her watch, she said, "Fifteen minutes and we eat."

11:30 p.m., Indianapolis

From his seat at the tavern window, the killer saw the lime-green Ford pass as it drove through the pool of light cast by the bright, overhead lights of Madison Avenue. He finished his beer, left a decent tip, and went out to his pickup. Within five minutes, he was back in the subdivision. As he approached the house, he was pleased to see the developer had not spent much on street lighting. With lights only at the corners, most of the street was in velvety darkness. He cut the lights and coasted to the curb three houses away from his objective. He turned off the ignition, rolled down his window a bit, and sat in silence for several minutes, listening. Several of the houses still showed lights, but no one was visible on the sidewalks on either side of the street. Many of the short drives were filled with boats, trailers, motor homes, and motorcycles. They would provide excellent cover if needed. The lights were still on in the house, which was his objective. Feeling secure, he started the engine for warmth and waited for the neighborhood to retire.

By 12:30 a.m., all the houses were finally in darkness. The lights in the girl's house had gone out at 11:45. Deciding it was safe, the killer left the truck to make his way to the house. Within minutes, he was in the side yard, silently making his way to a window looking into the garage. Placing the lens of his mini, Mag-Lite flashlight against the window pane, he switched it on and examined the garage contents. A Chevrolet Suburban literally filled the far side of the two car garage. Turning off the flashlight, he crept toward the back side of the house. Carefully, he pressed himself against the wall beneath a window. After a moment, he lifted himself on tiptoes to look into the room. A window shade was pulled to within two inches or so of the window sill, restricting his view. The room was in complete darkness. He pressed the flashlight to the window pane and clicked it on. Instantly, a dog barked, a very large dog by the deep bark. The killer was momentarily paralyzed by the sudden and unexpected barking. Recovering, he jerked the flashlight from the window, turned it off, and was dropping to his knees beneath the window when he heard the dog at the window above his head. The barking grew in intensity and in rapidity.

Running in a low crouch, the killer ran across the neighboring back yard, passed between two houses, and made it back to the truck. Lights had gone on in the house. A huge, black man, dressed in pajamas and a bath robe, came out the front door. In his hand, the killer could see a large, police-type flashlight and the glint off the finish of a very large, stainless-steel revolver. The big man's breath hung frostily on the night air. The big man turned and said something toward the open door. A second, smaller, black man appeared at the door with a large, black Labrador straining at a leash. He turned the leash over to the bigger man. There was no leaving now. He'd have to wait the man out. He watched as the big man, Labrador pulling and straining at his leash, made his way around the side of the house. An eternity seemed to pass while he waited for them to reappear. Would the damn dog track him through the neighboring yard and straight to the truck? He held his breath and slid down on the seat so that only his eyes and top of his head were visible as he watched between the houses. One hand was on the ignition switch. He decided if they came through between the houses he'd start the engine and get the hell out! After an eternity of scarcely breathing, he saw both men and the dog return to the front of the house. The larger man swung the powerful flashlight toward the street. The killer dropped beneath the window. Several times, he could see the light illuminate the cab above the dashboard. The man was checking everything on the street. After several minutes, the light was extinguished, and the killer heard the house door close. Carefully, he inched his way up to look over the dashboard. Good, no one in sight. He started breathing again. Thirty minutes after the lights had gone out in the house, the killer started the truck and quietly drove off.

Wednesday, 1:30 a.m., Miami

At the hotel's main entrance portico, Flynn said good night to Megan and Neil, thanked them for a wonderful evening, and filled with an excellent meal and the joy of this new relationship, made his way to his room. The red message light on the telephone winked in the darkness as he unlocked his door. Suddenly, all the good feelings vanished. Life and its woes had returned. He turned on the room lights and hit the phone's zero button. There was a voice mail message from John Green. Please call immediately. Green left the Indianapolis phone number. Minutes later, he was talking with Green.

"We had a little excitement tonight. Thought I'd better tell you," John said.

"Is everything okay?"

"At the moment, yes. Everything and everybody is fine. A little after midnight, I'm pretty certain we had a visitor. Old Sam scared him off."

"Prowler? Or do you think it might be our killer?"

"I can't say. I went outside and checked. There are some very good footprints right under Monica's bedroom window. If you want, I'll have Mike see about making casts."

"Wasn't your dog able to track the prints?"

"Nah. Ole Sam is a retriever. Good watch dog and great friend but no bloodhound. Sam was the one who heard the noise at the back bedroom window."

"We'll have to alert Mike and have him ask Chuck Holland to come by at first light and make those castings. Anything else you can tell me?"

"Well, like I said, I checked around outside. I didn't see anybody, so I went back inside, turned out the lights, and waited. There was a dark-colored, Ford pickup parked down the street a house or two away. About thirty minutes after I came back in, the truck drove off. My gut feeling is this was the prowler."

"Get a plate?"

"I may be retired, but I haven't forgotten good police work. I'll give the number to Mike in the morning. I was just wondering if you thought we ought to move to some other location just to be safe?"

Flynn considered the suggestion for several moments. "Let me ask you, do you think the driver of this pickup knows you made the number?"

"I'd bet the farm he thinks he got away clean."

"Then we have an advantage—we know where he will come looking, and we have an idea of how he'll come. I just can't imagine how he located you. Any ideas?"

"I've been asking myself that one ever since he showed up. I'm damned if I know."

"Well, here's what I think you'd better do. Tell Mike to ask Chuck to come in an unmarked unit so the neighbors don't suspect anything. When he shows up, ask him to make as little fuss as possible. Don't draw any attention to yourselves. I think we might be in a position to set a trap. Do you think we can put some men in the neighborhood under cover in such a way that they can watch the house and the street?"

"Well, it will take a little time to set up, but sure, it can be done."

"Tell Mike to work it out. Now, I do think we ought to get Monica out of there? The question is where to?"

"I'll put G. W. on it first thing."

"Tell Mike to run that plate, and then have him talk to the chief about putting out a 'observe and report' message at all roll calls. Anybody makes that truck, I want them to watch it and report where it goes. Don't have any hot dog try to stop it. You know we really don't have a thing we could make an arrest for at this point? Really, all we've got is a suspected prowler. Five will get you ten the damn truck comes up stolen anyway."

"I realize we may be getting alarmed over nothing at all, but I wanted to play it safe. I'm just keeping you in the loop—as they like to say these days—just in case."

"John, I picked you for this job because you're the best. Just keep on doing your thing. I'll be out for most of the morning tomorrow, so if you need me, contact me through Detective Megan Madigan at Miami PD. Is Monica awake? I'd like to talk with her if she is."

"No, she finally got back to sleep about twenty minutes ago. I'll go wake her."

"No. Don't do that. Just tell her I called and what we talked about. Tell her I love her, and I'll call again tomorrow night."

They said their good–byes. Flynn undressed and got into bed. For several minutes, he lay wide awake thinking about the implications of the prowler. In spite of the danger to his daughter, he hoped the prowler *was* the elusive killer. At least now, they had a slim lead.

Toward morning, Flynn enjoyed a highly pleasurable, erotic dream about Megan.

Thursday, 8:00 a.m.

Dressed in a fresh tee shirt, shorts, and the comfortable Asolo sandals, Flynn stood in the shade of the hotel portico while he waited for Megan to arrive. The day was already hot and bright with a few wispy clouds in the sky. His mind bounced between the happenings at home and the anticipation of the day to be spent with Megan. He felt like a teenager madly in love with a gorgeous girl. For the past two days, Flynn had felt far younger and more alive than he had in many years, and it wasn't the excitement of the hunt. Flynn knew he had fallen in love, but like a fearful teenager, he was scared to show his love for fear of rejection. While he waited, he took his pipe and tobacco pouch from the shorts pockets and packed the pipe as he recalled the highly erotic dream of the night before. He'd been waiting for about ten minutes when the sleek, black Mazda roared into the drive.

Megan was dressed in a bright-blue tee shirt, dark-blue shorts, and white, canvas deck shoes. Neil was dressed in shorts, a wild, Nine Inch Nails tee shirt, and sandals. Flynn saw a large wicker hamper in the back of the car. He emptied his pipe, stuffed it back in his pocket, and got into the car.

"You look very pretty this morning, Megan. Neil, shouldn't you be in school today?"

"I'm giving him a day off," Megan said. "What's new back home?"

For the next several minutes, Flynn briefed her on the latest. As he finished, they arrived at a large marina. Megan parked the car at the head of a group of long piers. She opened the rear hatch, and together they lifted the large basket out of the car, carried it between them as they passed the guard house at the head of the piers, and made their way out on the sun-bleached wood of the pier. Neil raced ahead. Flynn was amazed at the huge collection of boats of every size and description, bobbing gently in the small waves. All about them, there was activity as owners and hired hands cleaned, polished, and visited back and forth. Bronzed bodies and sun-bleached hair was in evidence everywhere. Flynn realized his white skin must stand out, marking him for the snowbird he was.

"Which one of these boats is yours?"

"We're almost there. It's that one just up ahead and on the right." She pointed with her free hand.

There it was. A dazzlingly white hull topped by varnished, dark woods and blue topped cabins. It had been backed into the slip and lay gently bobbing in the dark oil and gas stained water. The entire back part of the boat was covered by a tight-fitting, white canvas. As they placed the hamper on the pier, Flynn looked at the name proudly affixed in brass letters on the wide mahogany transom; *The Lady Grace* and in smaller, painted letters beneath, *Port of Miami*.

"Your dad named it after who?" he asked.

"After mom. Everybody calls her Gracie."

"Pardon my ignorance, but what kind is it, and how *big* is it?"

Megan's voice assumed the tone and delivery of a bored tour guide. "This is a forty-eight foot Chris-Craft Catalina double cabin cruiser with a flying bridge. She has twin Cummins diesels and a one inch thick, double-planked, oak bottom. She has a twelve-foot-six beam and just covered in beautiful

Philippine Mahogany, tough as iron, teak decks, and sleeps ten. Below deck, she has a stateroom forward and one aft with a large combination galley, dining room, and living salon in between. I'll give you the ship's tour just as soon as we get squared away. We have several minutes of preparation to get through before we can go. So, we'd better get to it."

It did take quite some time to unsnap, fold, and stow the huge, three-section, canvas cover. Unaccustomed to the humid heat of south Florida, Flynn was soaking wet with sweat when they'd finished. Megan led him down to the master's stateroom at the back of the boat, where she pointed to a built-in chest of drawers. "I'm pretty sure there's some swim trunks in there that will fit you. You'll find several different sizes of deck shoes over there in the closet." She pointed behind Flynn. "Those Vibram soled Asolos are nice but no good on a slippery deck. I'll wait for you up on deck." She gave him a playful pat on the rear and was gone, closing the door behind her.

Megan and Neil were busy stowing the contents of the wicker hamper in the galley when Flynn, wearing the swim suit and deck shoes, entered the salon area. Megan stopped to watch as he entered the salon. Flynn felt her eyes appraising him as he approached.

"You've got good legs."

"Well, thanks, I guess. Nobody has ever said that to me before."

"Oh, you'd be surprised how many of us women check out a man's legs and buns. I just hate to see a good manly torso supported by bird legs. But, as you observed earlier, you've got no tan at all. Here's some sun screen lotion. Get plenty on. I have a feeling you're going to need it today." She tossed him the bottle of lotion. While Flynn covered himself with the lotion, Megan and Neil finished the unpacking.

"So, how long will it take us to get down there and check this place out?" he asked.

"About an hour or two if the water traffic doesn't get too heavy," Megan checked her watch. "I'd say we'll be there by eleven or so."

"How far away are we?"

"About twenty nautical miles."

"I have another confession to make. I've never been out on the ocean before. Hell, I've never been on a boat this big before. The biggest thing I've been on was a fishing boat on a big reservoir back home."

"You'll be fine. We won't be out on the ocean today, just the waterway. Well, we're ready. Go forward, and cast off the line."

"What?" he asked.

"Neil, take Denny and show him, would you?"

Feeling very foolish, Flynn followed the boy out on the deck and using the hand holds, made his way past the main salon to the forward deck. There Neil pointed out a rope wound in a figure eight around a wing shaped device bolted to the deck. The boy carefully explained how to untie and cast off the line. The diesel engines came to life. Flynn looked up to see Megan take her place up on the flying bridge as Neil called it. Together the two made their way to the rear of the big cruiser. Flynn climbed the ladder to join Megan. A wide, curving dashboard filled with instruments and levers completed the control station. Megan was scanning the engine instruments. Flynn chose a seat to her left side. She reached forward and pressed a button on the dash. From high above his head, Flynn was startled by the sound of an extremely loud air horn. The blast lasted for several seconds. Releasing the button, she gently eased two levers forward, and the big boat began to move.

9:00 a.m., Indianapolis

"So, have you two come up with any ideas yet?" Lieutenant Chuck Holland asked as he poured himself a cup of coffee and took a seat across from Gaffney at the safe house kitchen table.

"G. W. thinks he can have another place lined up by this afternoon," John answered.

"I'm looking on the far west side," G.W. said.

"How's Monica taking all this?" Mike asked.

"She's got her Irish up. Belligerent as hell all morning," John answered.

"So, what are your immediate plans?" Mike asked.

"Well, I want to get her away from here as soon as possible. If Monica will do it, I think it would be a good idea to take her out while G.W. does his thing. Maybe I'll take her to the Greenwood Mall; let her spend a few hours shopping. Women seem to like that. I think she'll jump at the chance to get out of here for a few hours."

"I think that's a great idea. Take the two-way, and whatever you do, carry it with you at all times. The undercover team is on tac three. Sergeant Harry Grant is in charge. If anybody sees that truck or, for that matter, anything suspicious, they'll warn you on the radio." Mike checked his watch. "I wonder what's keeping that woman?"

"Go easy. She had a rough night. She ought to be out of the shower any minute now." The telephone rang. John sprang to his feet and answered before the second ring. The call was for Sergeant Gaffney.

Mike took the phone, listened for a few seconds, and reported he was on his way! Abruptly, he hung up the phone and turned to both men, his voice filled with excitement. "They've located the truck!" he said.

"Where?" John asked.

"It's in the parking lot at the Holiday Inn up at 465 and Michigan Road. I'm on my way up there now. Tell Monica I'm sorry I missed her." Reaching in his pocket, Mike withdrew his wallet and counted out fifty dollars. "Give her this for the shopping trip, and tell her not to worry—tell her what happened. I'll check in with you when I know more." Without waiting for an answer, Mike raced out of the house.

The killer was taking no chances. The scare of the night before had shaken his confidence badly. Early in the morning, he checked out of the Holiday Inn, leaving the truck behind. He'd spent about forty minutes very carefully wiping down the interior to remove or destroy any fingerprints. He dumped the ash tray and then left the truck, doors locked, on the far back side of the parking lot. With his baggage stowed in the trunk of the Civic, he was headed south back to the house where he was now sure the witness lived. He'd planned a pass or two through the neighborhood to be sure the area was safe and then make a direct approach to the house. He was dressed in his dark business suit, the silenced twenty-two automatic snug against his ribs in its holster. If everything went well, he'd finish off the girl and any cops guarding her and be on his way to the airport before noon. After spending two days trying to find Blakemore's home address, he'd learned that the WTC attack had resulted in making the residential addresses and telephone numbers of elected and high-placed public officials closely held confidential information. So, locating Blakemore's home was a problem he decided he could do without—too risky. Let Santini pay somebody else. He decided he'd gladly forgo the balance of his fee just to get the hell out of town.

Shortly after turning off Madison Avenue and into the subdivision, the killer was startled to see the lime-green Ford, a flashing red and blue light affixed to the roof, siren at full whoop, come hurtling toward him. The car blew by at high speed in the opposite direction. The killer's instincts for survival sharpened. Others might be watching. He turned into the subdivision and at a steady, sedate pace, began a circuit of the neighborhood. Within a block of the house, he spotted a work crew from one of the utilities with their blue truck and red cones taking up half the street. Two men in work clothes and hard hats were standing near an open man hole. He cruised on by and continued his circuit of the block. As he approached the house behind his target, he observed an IPL truck belonging to the local power and light company. The truck was equipped with a cherry picker lift. A lone man was high over the street above a combination power and telephone line. He seemed to be alone. The killer's instincts screamed loudly in his mind's ear. Setup! The house was being watched! Get out now! It took great self control not to smash his foot on the accelerator and speed away. Regaining his composure, he completed his journey to the subdivision exit.

The police radio in the kitchen had dutifully reported the license number on the small, black, Civic coupe, and its progress through the neighborhood. Big John listened patiently, while he waited for Monica to finish her breakfast. In another few minutes, they'd leave the house for the mall and safety.

The killer stopped on Madison Avenue at a Wendy's to have some coffee and reconsider. Stay and kill or run for it. He'd already spent much more time than he'd planned for, too much time. He worried about the description and picture he'd seen of himself in the newspapers. The airport cops would have it as well. His gut told him he should just cut his losses and get on a plane for L.A. With luck, Santini would understand. He involuntarily shuddered as he thought of Santini. The lawyer was the only man on earth he really feared. Santini paid extremely well and protected his people, but if you crossed the man or failed an assignment, it was all over. He had the money and people to find you anywhere in the world. His fear was legitimate. He'd been dispatched by Santini over the past several years to several foreign countries himself to settle scores and silence people forever.

Considering what to do next, he was gazing absentmindedly out the big windows of the fast-food restaurant when he saw a bright red and white Chevrolet Suburban roll to a stop at the corner traffic signal. Although the big car's windows had been darkened, he could make out the shadows of two people in the front seat. He was sure it was the same Suburban he'd seen in the garage back at the house. Quickly, he grabbed his coffee and headed for the exit. The Suburban continued down the street as he got into his car. Moving as quickly as he could, he pulled his car out of the parking lot and began to follow the distinctive Suburban. Within a short block, the Suburban turned right and drove into the parking lot of a very large shopping mall. The killer followed at a safe distance.

Hundreds of cars were already parked in the huge lot with more streaming in. The access lanes wound snakelike through the lot and confused the killer as he attempted to keep the Suburban in sight. At length, it came to rest in a space far from one of the mall entrances. The killer quickly parked in a nearby, empty space and watched as the two people got out of the car. A huge, black man, the same one he'd seen in pajamas the night before, got from behind the wheel. As he closed his door, a honey-blonde haired, white girl came from the other side into the killer's view. It was the girl in the elevator! He killed the engine, grabbed his topcoat off the seat, and got out of the car. The two were about fifty yards ahead of him as he followed them into the mall.

Mike spotted the uniform car as he pulled into the Holiday Inn's parking lot. The black, Ford pickup had been backed into a space at the back of the lot. It was now blocked by the uniform car. He pulled his car to a stop and getting out, introduced himself to the patrolman.

"You're the man who spotted the pickup?"

"Yes, sir."

"Have you run the plate yet?"

"Yes, sir. I did that first thing. It's a Hertz rental."

"Haven't touched it, have you?"

"No, sir. I know better than that."

Mike put in a radio call for Sergeant Hawks who, in his off-duty hours, ran the security operation for the motel. Hawks was to report to him at the motel as quickly as possible.

Lieutenant Holland pulled his car into the lot. "I came myself when I heard it was you who asked for an Ident unit."

"Thanks. I appreciate it."

"Is it locked?"

"Door locks are down on both doors," said the alert patrolman.

Holland took a Slim Jim from his case of tools and inserted it between the window and the door skin. Within seconds, he'd defeated the lock on the driver's side. Holland went to work. Thirty minutes later, he was finished. The dusting was negative. "Well, if you ask me, this removes any doubt for me," Mike said. "I think he's still in town."

"I wouldn't put that in the bank just yet. You realize this could have been dumped here. I mean it's a toss–up whether the guy is staying here."

"I realize that only too well. But I can't afford not to follow up on every lead we get. It seems to me that to be safe, I have to act as though he was still hanging around to finish the job. When Sergeant Hawks gets here, we'll start through the registration cards, the credit card slips, everything. By the way, anything turn up on those plaster casts?"

"The guy wears a size eleven shoe and from the depth of the impressions, probably weighs in at about a hundred and seventy or so. I can't tell you much more than that. The soles are from a cheap work boot; the kind they sell by the thousands in discount stores. K-Mart, Wal-Mart, Pay-Less–you name it"

"In short–nothing!" Mike said.

"Not exactly, if we catch him and if he's still got the boots, I can build a circumstantial case for him being at the house." Sergeant Hawks arrived in a department uniform car as the two were talking. Quickly, Mike explained what they needed and took Hawks to the motel office as Lieutenant Holland left to return to headquarters. Hawks immediately called a meeting of his on-duty security men, all retired policemen. Within ten minutes, they were all meeting in the motel manager's office. Mike explained they needed to put the Ford pickup with someone registered at the motel if possible. At that point, one of the men interrupted, "A Ford pickup, you say?"

"Yes. Do you know it?" Mike answered.

"Well, we've had one here for about three days that don't belong with anybody registered here." Giving the manager a look, he went on, "We don't talk about it, but we've got a big theft problem here. So, we double-check the make and license numbers on the guests' cars. I walk the lot checking plates on the midnight to six shift when I have that shift, and I check the plates against the registration forms. If it's a black, Ford pickup, then it doesn't belong here. At least, I haven't seen a registration card that listed it."

"It's a Hertz rental, and that's all we have. Where was it usually parked?" Mike asked.

"Over on the east side by the 300 units. But sometime after midnight, I saw it parked way out on the north side of the lot, backed in by the fence."

Mike sat thinking for a few moments. Turning to the manager, he asked, "May I use your phone?"

"Certainly."

Mike picked up the manager's telephone and called his office at police headquarters. Getting Sam Elberger on the line, he ordered a police wrecker be dispatched to take the Ford pickup away to the impound lot, and then, reading the VIN number on the truck to Elberger, he ordered the detective to personally get over to the Hertz, truck-rental office and pick up the rental contract. He told Sam to call him the minute he had a name to go with the truck. Maybe, just maybe, the guy rented the truck under a name they could find in the motel registrations. To the team on site, he instructed that they go through the registrations for those rooms in the 300's to see if there was a match. At last, he felt they were closing in.

The big, black man and the girl were easy to follow, because the big man stood out a full head above most of the crowd. Staying back a safe distance, the killer paced himself, waiting for the right moment. A silenced twenty-two fired in the noise made by the hundreds of milling people would very likely go completely unnoticed. They'd been wandering aimlessly through the mall with no particular destination evident. Side trips were made off the main mall into department stores and shops. The killer had no option but to follow at a safe distance. After an hour of aimless shopping, they rounded a corner at a large food court, filled with sidewalk type shops. Tables and chairs were set out on two levels filling most of that section of the mall. Live trees reached for a high ceiling, festooned with multicolored banners and flags. The noise level rose considerably as hundreds of shoppers, many with small children, enjoyed the festive area. The killer watched as his prey stood in the center of the court and selected a shop. After some discussion, they settled on a Chinese egg roll shop and walked over to place their order.

The killer stepped to the McDonalds counter and ordered a medium-size, black coffee, which he then carried to a table at a corner of the area. He examined his position. Immediately behind where he was sitting and to his left, was a main mall entrance. An unnoticed exit from the mall would be easy. As he began to think through his escape, he suddenly realized finding the Civic would be a problem. What was the shape of this mall? Was it an elaborate "X" or a crooked "E" shape? With all the random shopping, covering virtually what seemed to be miles of street-sized, shopping aisles lined with shop after shop, he was hopelessly disoriented. A quick getaway was now problematic. He moved to a table nearer the exit—estimating it to be about fifteen yards away, which allowed him to watch the girl and her protector with ease. He slipped the automatic from its holster, folded his top coat around it, and placed it on the table in front of him. He sipped the coffee while he waited for his target to be served and a table selected.

Minutes later, the two selected a table about ten yards away and took their seats. The girl selected a seat facing the killer, the big, black man sat opposite with his back toward him. The man was so large that the slightest movement on his part frequently blocked a clear shot at his intended victim. At times, there was just enough side angle to allow for a clean shot at the girl. He considered his order of execution. Owing to the conditions, this would be a true challenge. First, he had to eliminate the girl, then the big body guard. Slowly, he placed his hand inside the bundled topcoat. The familiar rush, better than any drug high, began to fill his entire being as his fingers closed around the familiar butt of the twenty-two auto. There was no way he could lift the gun from the coat and take aim, so this would require pure instinct aiming, which he had learned so well in the army.

Carefully, he shifted the gun inside the coat until he was certain that he was centered on the girl's chest. He took a deep breath, held it for a second, and slowly began to let it out while the meaty portion of his index finger gently tightened on the trigger. The body guard moved, lifting his left arm in a sweeping gesture just as the first silenced bullet left the muzzle of the silencer—the shot a mere muffled coughing noise. The bullet hit the big man in the upper arm, flinging it and the man forward toward the girl. A look of amazement crossed the girl's face as she instinctively leaned forward to help. At that moment, the killer fired again. Monica felt a breeze pass her ear, and the tempered window surrounding a video arcade behind her shattered. John Green threw the table aside with his good arm and grabbed Monica, shielding her with his body. Frantically, he searched for the source of the shots while he struggled to extract his gun from beneath his left arm. Few bystanders realized anything was amiss in the noise that the crowd was making. When John finally managed to get his .357

out of its holster, a woman with two small children at a nearby table saw the gun and screamed. All hell broke lose as other people took notice of the big, black man, bloodied and brandishing a gun. More screams from the women, men began yelling and shouting wild orders. Tables and chairs were overturned and thrown aside as panicked humans fled the area. The killer got to his feet, dropped the topcoat, and took aim.

John Green saw a man at a table a few yards away stand, drop a topcoat, and lift a gun. He lifted his own weapon to fire. The killer snapped off two quick shots, both of which hit John, one in the left thigh and the other in the lower right side. The impact threw him back, and he knocked Monica to the floor. Their feet and legs tangled as John fell on top of her. Frantically, he lifted his head in the direction of the killer; the man was gone. Green rolled off Monica and struggled to a sitting position. He put his gun on his lap and pulled the portable police radio from his belt.

He keyed the transmit button. "Code One. Code One. Officer down, Greenwood Park Shopping Mall. Ambulance needed. Officer shot. Suspect is white male Caucasian, five-ten to five-eleven, blonde hair, mustache. Blue business suit," John said as weakness and sudden nausea overcame him. The radio slipped from his fingers and fell to his lap.

"Officer calling Code One, give your ten-twenty," a female voice responded from the tiny speaker. Monica was badly shaken; tears flowed freely down her face. With trembling fingers, she reached for the radio covered in John Green's blood. Forcing herself to calm down and control her voice, she keyed the transmit button. "Communications, this is Monica

Flynn, Captain Flynn's daughter. I'm with retired Lieutenant John Green. He's been shot. We need an ambulance–fast! We're inside the Greenwood Park Mall in front of the video game arcade–the food court area. Hurry!" She released the transmit button.

"An ambulance is in route. Greenwood PD has been notified. Did you say the injured officer is Lieutenant Green?" asked the dispatcher.

"Yes. Please hurry. He's bleeding badly. He's passed out,"

"Are you all right?" she was asked.

"Yes. I'm not hit. Please notify Sergeant Mike Gaffney in Homicide. Tell him I'm staying with Lieutenant Green." Monica placed the radio on the floor and cradled John Green's head in her lap. When she looked up, three police officers, weapons drawn, were converging on them.

Nothing galvanizes a police force into action like a "Code One" call. A brother officer is in need of immediate assistance. A generations-old code of conduct requires immediate and unreserved response. The loss of policemen and firemen at the World Trade Center the year before had only heightened the wariness of the men and women of the thin blue line. Most were itching for a taste of revenge. The problem in modern times has become how to maintain control in such situations. Chief O'Halleran published revisions to the Departmental Rules and Regulations with such situations in mind. Only those officers in the immediate area were to respond. All others were to remain in their sectors and to maintain their patrols.

Unfortunately, this was observed only on paper. As soon as he was notified, which was within minutes of the "Code One" message being received in communications, the chief took control. With Flynn in Miami and Gaffney out at the Holiday Inn, the capture of the suspect was of paramount importance. Armed with the knowledge and believing the killer was a contract man from out of town, the chief ordered a road block at the entrance to the airport and sent a detail to the bus and Amtrak stations. Green's description of his assailant was circulated to all on-duty members of the Department, the Marion County Sheriff's Department, and the State Police. O'Halleran assigned two uniforms to guard both Monica and Green, who had been taken to the Community Hospital emergency room only a half mile from the shopping mall. Satisfied the Department had been deployed as best he could arrange it, he put in a call for Flynn at the Miami PD.

Suppressing an almost overwhelming urge to speed, the killer headed for the airport. Locating the Honda Civic in the huge mall parking lot had cost him a precious fifteen minutes. He knew every one under the sun would be looking for a man answering his description. This time the cost was too high. The hell with Santini! The hell with Indianapolis. He was getting out. He'd cut his losses and hope for the best. If he were quick enough, he just might be able to clear out his bank accounts and safety deposit boxes and get the hell out of the country long before Santini learned about the screw-up. He knew the Far East and he knew the languages. Santini would play hell finding him there.

He turned the Civic off the Interstate and began the cloverleaf turn onto the airport entrance. As his car topped the Interstate overpass, he saw the main entrance road was blocked by several police cars, their rooftop lights flashing. He brought the car to a stop in the long line of cars waiting to gain entrance. Each car was being stopped, the occupants questioned, and the cars searched. Panic seized him for a moment. There was nothing to do but to get out of there. Cars blocked his way to the rear. He concentrated on the roadway ahead. Just before the multi-lane road bottlenecked down to the main entrance street, a turn off toward the north was open. He saw it was a main street bordering the airport property. As his car inched forward, he elected to take it as his escape route. Five minutes later, he was headed away from the airport.

11:10 a.m., Miami

Flynn and the boy were seated in a forward jump seat in the bow of the big cruiser. Neil had asked his new friend to come forward to sit with him. Flynn found it was rather like the old rumble seats of the 1930s cars. Neil had very carefully explained the exact position of the seat with all the correct terminology–above the chain locker and ahead of the forward stateroom. Carefully, Neil showed Flynn how to operate the manual mechanism which opened the seat or closed it against heavy weather and rough seas. Flynn learned the seat could be entered from the deck or from below by way of a door in the foot well. Far behind and above the two, Megan was piloting the big cruiser at a steady pace. Neil wanted to talk. He began with startling directness. His face an unreadable mask.

"Can I ask you something?" the boy began.

"Sure."

Neil asked without preamble, "How old are you?"

"I'll be forty-two come my next birthday in September. And since you asked, I'll lay down a ground rule. I get to ask one for each one you ask. Agreed?"

It was Neil's turn to be surprised. After some thought he said, "Okay–I guess."

"Good. Then, it's my turn. How old are you?" Flynn asked, already knowing the answer.

"I'll be thirteen in two weeks. Now, my turn. Do you have any kids?"

"I have a daughter named Monica. She's twenty-one and is going to be married next summer."

"Mom says your wife died."

"Yes, she died of cancer several years ago."

"I'm sorry," the boy said.

"That's nice of you. But no need to be sorry. Mary had a particularly bad kind of cancer and in the end, when we knew there would be no cure, I was very grateful that God took her quickly so she wouldn't suffer."

"You like my mom?" He watched Flynn carefully.

Flynn was not altogether prepared for this question even though he'd anticipated it. "To be absolutely honest with you, I really like your mom a lot. I'm very attracted to her."

"You two done it yet?" He looked Flynn in the eyes waiting for an answer–watching for honesty.

Flynn was really not prepared for this one! He decided the boy deserved truth. "You know, just for future reference, that isn't the sort of question a gentleman *ever* answers. But I believe that at this moment, right here and now, allows an exception to the rule. The answer is, no. No, we haven't. That is if you are asking whether or not we've made love–gone to bed with each other. Is that what you're asking?"

"Yes." Neil's eyes looked deeply into his own.

Dennis thought carefully before he spoke. "As I said, we haven't. But, I want to ask you a question. Are you against it? Your mom and me 'doin' it' as you said?"

"It's really not up to me. It's between the two of you. I just don't want to see my mom get hurt again." Neil's face was grim.

"Have men hurt your mom?"

"What do *you* think? Mom is pretty and she's dated a few guys since my father hit the road. Some of them hurt her pretty bad. You might think I'm just a kid–but I know what's going on. I've heard my mom crying in the night. Tell you what I think. I think they wanted *her* but not *me*. She's lonely, and I don't want to see my mom hurt anymore."

Flynn knew he held the boy's emotions in his hands–he was on eggshells. This next question would have to be carefully asked. Risking his own feelings he asked, "Neil, what does your gut tell you about me?"

Neil considered his answer for several moments before he spoke. "Well, I don't know you very well. Mom says you're a good man. She says we ought to take today to get to know each other better–you and me. You're the first man my mom has ever done this sort of thing with–I mean setting things up so I would have some private time with someone she's dating."

"Think you mom wants your opinion of me?"

"She's gonna ask what we talked about and what I thought of you."

"That's fair. But I want to answer your question about whether I love her. Listen very carefully. Okay?"

"I will."

"I am *very* attracted to your mom. I agree with you. I think she's a very pretty woman and quite a wonderful woman. But, you see, I don't know if she's interested in me. After all, we've only known each other for only two days now. So, I think it's a little too soon to be thinking about getting serious. Even if we decided to get serious, there are so many things we'd both have to take care of before we could get married. Was that what you wanted to know?"

"Some of it," the boy answered.

"What's the rest of it?" Flynn asked.

"Well–" the boy's voice faltered.

"How do I feel about you? That what you want to know?" Flynn asked, taking the initiative.

Neil turned doubtful blue eyes toward Flynn. "Yes," he said in a quiet voice.

Flynn knew Neil had risked his own emotions. Dangerous ground for the boy. What he said next could ruin everything. "Let me think about that for a minute before I answer. This is *very* important–to us both. How do I feel about you?" Flynn paused to consider his answer. "Hummm–Well, truthfully, like you said, we don't really know each other all that well, do we?"

"No." The boy's voice trembled a bit.

"Neil, all of my adult life, I've had this personal rule. It goes like this: I won't judge a person until I get to know him or her.

Now, I'd say you and I have a lot to discover about each other before we can make a judgment about how well we like each other. I'll tell you something. I always wanted to have a son. I think the answer to your question is– I like you a lot. I can't truthfully say I love you yet. I mean after all we don't really know each other, not really. So let me strike this deal with you. If it begins to look like your mom and I are getting serious about each other, I will make the time to be sure you and I talk about anything at all that you want to know. I want to get to know you as much as you want to know all about me. Deal?"

Neil thought about the offer for several seconds before he answered. The silence was so lengthy that Flynn feared he'd said the wrong things. Finally, Neil spoke, "Okay that seems to make a lot of sense."

Flynn spoke quickly, "And if your mom and I do get married, you'd be my son–the one I never had."

"And you could be the dad I never had!" Neil said with hope in his voice.

"Be a good deal for the both of us, wouldn't it? Anyway, before we get too far along here, like I said, I think you and I ought to do some serious talking–man-to-man. I also think you need to know I wouldn't dream of hurting your mom for the world–or you either. Now, if you don't mind, I'd like to spend some time with your mom."

"You gonna tell her what we talked about?"

"Well, that brings me to a new rule I just this minute decided I'd follow. The new rule is I won't reveal anything you tell me in confidence–ever. Not unless you've done something criminal. So, the answer to your question is I'm not telling. I think that's your job. Don't you?"

"I'll tell her when we talk more."

Flynn made his way to what he now knew to call the "flying bridge".

Flynn was enthralled by the scenery he beheld as Megan piloted the big cruiser down the waterway. The width appeared to be about fifty to sixty feet in places, a bit less in others. On both sides, he saw absolutely beautiful homes, many with large boats moored at private piers. After about an hour or so, Megan told Flynn they'd just about arrived behind Mazzicone's property. She slowed the big cruiser to about five knots, as they passed the rear of the property. She explained to Dennis that traffic on the waterway moved slowly by law, so one more cabin cruiser moving slowly shouldn't attract any special attention.

"Sit over here on my right so you're looking toward me as we pass. That way you can take a good look without anybody noticing," she said to Flynn.

Denny shifted to the right hand side of the seat and concentrated on the property as they passed. The entire width of the property along the waterway was defined by a higher than normal concrete sea wall, which Flynn estimated was about fifteen feet in height from waterline to the top. A large, flat-roofed boathouse, which looked to Dennis to be larger than a two car garage, was roughly centered in the wall and flush with it. A windowless overhead door extended to within inches of the water. As only the door face of the boat house could be seen, Flynn figured the space for it had been excavated out of the earth behind the sea wall. From the water, the flat expanse of the wall prevented passers-by from seeing more than the edge of the roof. Flynn estimated the flying bridge on which they sat was probably twelve to fourteen feet above the water. Looking back toward the boat house, he could see a large umbrella in the collapsed position and several metal chairs. He assumed the flat roof provided a sun deck at the edge of the water. Something was missing. He couldn't quite put his finger on it. They were now too far beyond the property for him to see any more detail.

"Can we turn around and make another pass?" he asked Megan.

"Why? Did you see something?"

"Something I didn't see."

"Well, if we turn around right now, someone might see us—take notice. There's a small inlet up ahead about two miles. It's a small yacht basin. I'll turn around there and come back."

Megan piloted the cruiser to the inlet and executed a flawless turn around. On the way back, they hatched the plan to anchor at the west side of the waterway just beyond the boathouse door. It was lunch time, and a stop for lunch would provide decent cover for their task.

They set up a table and chairs on the large fantail deck, rigged the big awning to provide shade from the noonday sun, and broke out the lunch. From the galley refrigerator, Megan served the contents of the large hamper: turkey, lettuce, and tomato sandwiches, a relish tray of carrots, celery, and a variety of olives. A chilled bottle of white wine completed the luncheon.

Flynn suspected the food had been prepared at the family restaurant but dared not ask. Megan excused herself for a minute, instructing Flynn to go ahead and begin. She returned wearing a flower print bikini, which took Flynn's breath away.

Noting his stare, she said, "Time to get back to business. Remember? What's missing?"

"Well–I haven't put my finger on it yet. May I call on that secret weapon of yours for a minute?"

"No problem. Ask away."

"Well, think back over what you saw as we passed his place. What do you remember seeing?"

Without looking at the property, she described it in detail.

"Now, keep all that in your mind, and ask yourself what's missing," Flynn said.

Megan thought for a minute before answering. "Well, the Mazzicone place is the only one with a high sea wall like this, but I don't suppose that's what you're after." She thought some more. "Well, the backyard didn't have any trees that I could see. Both the neighbors' places did."

Flynn slapped his forehead with the heel of his hand. "That's it! No trees!" He sat pondering this for a few moments. "I wonder if it means anything?"

"Without asking, I can't think of any way to find out if it does or not."

"How long would it take to get to a phone from here?" he asked.

"Oh, about twenty seconds. Why?"

"I'd like to talk with that maid at the neighbor's house next door."

"May I finish my lunch first?" Megan asked.

Flynn cleared away the dishes, helped put the leftovers back in the refrigerator, and took a seat next to Megan in the galley to listen as she spoke with the maid at the neighboring house, Sarah Jenkins. Quickly, Megan had established the Andersons were still away in England and just as quickly renewed her rapport with Sarah. It was as though the women were sharing a wicked secret.

"Sarah, there are a few more questions we'd like to ask. Are you up to it?....Good. Now, was that sea wall behind the Mazzicone place there when Mazzicone took over, or did he have it built?–I see. Can you remember when that was?–Right after the wall? The boat house too?–All at the same time?" Several more exchanges took place before Megan was satisfied. She replaced the phone in her bag and turned to Flynn. "Here's the dope. The new owner built the sea wall and boathouse after he built the walls around the house. Most of the comings and goings take place on Tuesdays and Thursdays. She says about once a month a helicopter lands on top of the boathouse–it remains there overnight and leaves the next day. I think that explains why there are no trees. They use the same car, a gray Lincoln Town Car with blacked-out windows."

Flynn considered the information before responding. "Did she say whether or not it was the same helicopter all the time?"

"Yes. It's the same one. From the description she gave, it's most likely a Bell Jet Ranger."

"Back in Indiana, things like boats and airplanes are considered personal property, so they're taxed. That means records. Does Florida do the same?"

"Yes. Oh, I see. You want to check the records for the helicopter."

"The car too, if we can."

"You think Santini or Mazzicone, or whoever the hell he is, owns them?"

"I think it's worth checking out. Presumably, these are a matter of public record?"

"Let me put in a call to the office. Henry's there. He can get the ball rolling on boat, car, and airplane registrations while we check out the plans," Megan said, reaching in her purse for her phone. Flynn waited as she placed the call.

When she'd completed her conversation with Sergeant Hightower, she said, "There's an emergency message for you. You're to call your chief."

He took the phone and dialed the chief's private number. The phone rang five times–

"O'Halleran." Came the brusque answer.

"Chief, it's me, Denny. I just got your message."

"Thank God! Well, first off, Monica is fine, so don't worry. An attempt was made on her life late this morning. She and John Green were out at the Greenwood Mall. The shooter hit John three times with twenty-two hollow points. He's out of surgery down at Community South, and they say his condition is good. Monica is at the hospital and refuses to leave until she's sure John will be okay. I've got uniforms guarding her and John down there now. The shooter got away in the confusion.

I've got roadblocks at the airport and the bus and railroad stations. That's about the story for the moment."

Flynn felt a tremendous relief. "Did Monica see who the shooter was?'

"No. She says the whole thing took her completely by surprise. She was too busy reaching to grab John before he fell."

"Where's Mike in all this?"

"He's following up on two very good leads. John reported a late-night visitor at the safe house in the early morning hours. Early this morning, we located the pickup John remembers seeing parked on the street at the time. Mike is following up on that. We may have found where the guy was staying. We know he used a different car to get to the mall. According to the tapes in Communications, the stakeout at the safe house this morning indicates a black, two-door Civic made a pass around the house this morning. We have the license number, and we're running a check on the plate now."

Flynn was torn between the urge to get home to Monica and a strong desire to pursue this to the source of the murder. "Chief, are you certain you don't need me back there? I mean I can drop everything and get back on the next plane."

"Denny, everything is under control. No need to quit what you're doing."

"Is the Department gonna look after John?"

"Yes. So don't concern yourself. The word is nothing vital was hit. He'll pull through okay. Mike makes lieutenant on Friday. I'll continue to keep him in charge at Homicide and Robbery. If he has any problems, I'll be right here to give advice. So, please, get on with your investigation down there, and don't worry about this end. We'll manage to muddle through until you get back. And, like I said, as for John, we're looking after him. He's one of our own!"

With conflicted emotions, Flynn agreed to stay and said his good-byes. Megan listened compassionately as Flynn recounted the morning's events so far away. She put her arm around his shoulders as he agonized. When he'd finished, she asked, "What do you want to do right now?"

Anger flashed in his eyes as he answered, "Right now, I want to hang the bastard by his balls! Right now, I want to put my hands around the shooter's throat and crush it for what he did to my daughter!" He slammed his fist into his knee in frustration. "And I can't do either!"

"Denny, do you think it would have happened any differently if you *had* been there?"

He thought about it. "No, I guess not."

"Then, let's let them do their job, and let's you and I get on with ours."

Flynn stood and extended his hand. "You're right. What next?"

"Let's get back into town and start checking those building permits and architects plans for starters."

Flynn went forward to bring in the anchor under Neil's instruction while Megan got the boat underway and headed back to her marina near Miami.

1:10 p.m., Indianapolis

Using the manager's pass key, Mike unlocked the door to room 345 and entered the vacated room. The bed hadn't been made, and there were the usual signs of occupancy: wet towels and other discarded items. Quickly, he took his cell phone from his coat pocket and called Lieutenant Holland to ask that he send his very best print men and forensics team on the double. He stationed Sergeant Hawks outside the door to prevent any unauthorized entry and went back to the lobby to question the desk clerk and cashier.

The clerk remembered the man well. "He was very impatient with me because I couldn't get his final bill prepared fast enough to suit him," she said.

"Please, can you describe him for me?" Mike asked.

"Well, he was a little shorter than you, but not by much. He has medium-blonde hair, kind of gray-green eyes, and he can be very nasty."

"What do you mean, 'nasty'?"

"Well, he frightened me. He didn't raise his voice or anything; he just leaned across the counter and talked to me in this low, threatening voice."

"How old would you say he was?"

She thought about it for a minute. "Well, I'd say he was in his late thirties."

"Can you remember anything else about him?"

She thought some more. "Well, there was this mole next to his nose. I remember looking at it when he was leaning across the counter right in my face."

Mike's heart leapt in his chest when she mentioned the mole. "Is that your copy of the guy's bill there on the desk?"

"Yes."

"May I see it, please?"

Mike scanned the bill. There were three charges to room service, five local call charges, and the basic room charge. "Have you verified the credit card?" he asked.

"Oh, yes. We do that right away. We run it through the card reader before we imprint it for the customer's bill. It's a good card."

Mike examined the charge card imprint. "Does this name D.L. Stanton check as correct?"

"I wouldn't know about that. The reader only checks the magnetic number on the strip on the back of the card. If it's okay, we get an authorization number from the issuer. We assume the name on the front of the card is good."

He pondered the situation for a few moments. "Miss, can you get in contact with the credit card company and check this card for me?"

"Sure, no problem. It will probably take a while, though."

"How long?"

"Well, on a *good* day, it takes about thirty minutes. Are you familiar with voice mail hell and dial around the phone menu?"

"Can't you reach a human being?'

"Like I said, on a *good* day, it takes about thirty minutes."

"Please, see if you can get them to hurry it up for us, will you? Tell them it's a police matter. In the meantime, I'm going back to the room. Call me there when you get anything, and thanks for your help. You've been just great."

Sergeant Hawks was still standing guard at the door when Mike got back. The men from Ident hadn't shown yet. Several possible actions raced through his mind. Pulling his two-way from his belt, he called Communications and ordered a broadcast on the Civic and its license number be put out on all channels. He instructed a "locate and report only restriction" be broadcast as a part of the bulletin. The Ident mini-van pulled up as he was finishing his radio call. Bryan Lynch was at the wheel with Lieutenant Holland riding shotgun. Two other techs got out as the van rolled to a stop. Within minutes, they'd begun their work. The room was, it seemed, bereft of fingerprints. Everything had been wiped clean. Lieutenant Holland smiled in satisfaction as the portion of the phone under the receiver cradle, a drinking glass, and the bathroom mirror yielded some beautiful prints.

"It's a lead pipe cinch this guy won't be in our files," Holland said as he transferred the prints to evidence cards.

Mike returned to the lobby to check with the clerk. She had a handwritten note waiting when he returned. According to the credit card company, the card was issued to a division of General Motors in Detroit.

"Is this all they could tell you?" he asked, puzzled by the fact that the card belonged to GM.

"That's all they said they were allowed to tell me. I wrote the name and the phone number of the person they said you'd have to contact if you wanted to know more. It's there on the bottom of the note."

Mike thanked the girl, stuffed the note in his shirt pocket, and returned to police headquarters. All over the city, every uniform car, traffic solo cycle, mounted horse patrolman, and foot patrolman was keeping an eye out for a black, two-door Civic with the right license number. Nearly all the men knew John Green personally.

3:30 p.m., Miami

The ceiling fans wafted cool, dry air over their heads as they looked over volumes of building permits and architectural drawings and blueprints. After about an hour of searching, Megan located the building permits and blueprints for the house on the waterway. The property owner was listed as Dominic Mazzicone. The blueprints revealed extensive new construction had taken place behind those tall, poured concrete walls. Most of the rear of the property had been excavated to a depth of five feet below mean sea level behind the sea wall. A large underground room of seventy by fifty feet extended from the sea wall, ending at a short tunnel, which led into a basement of the mansion. Centered in the boat house room was a rectangular pier about four feet wide; a continuous concrete pier platform formed the perimeter of the remaining three sides of the room. According to the plans, the room was covered by four feet of earth.

"How many boats could that thing hold?" Flynn asked.

Megan examined the dimensions of the three pier areas for a moment. "Well, this center area here," she said, pointing to the water between the piers, the docking area, "could hold two of those cigarette boats or several smaller boats. The door opening isn't high enough to admit a cruiser."

"Does the paperwork list a reason why the owner wanted to build this?" Flynn asked.

"Denny, down here, if you've got the money, nobody ever asks why. So long as you meet the covenants of the neighborhood and aren't threatening some environmentalist's idea of land or animal rights, nobody complains."

"Well, just look at this! That room takes up almost half the width of the property and goes almost all the way to the back of the house. Why would anybody want such a big room buried under ground?"

"Denny, you're looking at a built-in boathouse. A damn big one, I'll admit, but a boathouse nonetheless. Not all that unusual down here. If anybody asks, that's all it is."

"Could Santini build anything he wanted in there–I mean without a permit?"

"Sure. Do you have something in mind?"

"No. But I'd love to see what he keeps in there."

"Have you seen enough?" Megan asked.

"I guess so. Let's go see what your Sergeant Hightower has found for us."

4:30 p.m., Indianapolis

Frustration and tension ran high in the office. Mike was pacing Flynn's office, his hands thrust in his hip pockets. Time dragged by as they waited for something to happen–something; anything. The communications monitors were turned up so everyone in the room could listen. If anybody on the street sighted the car, they'd know about it immediately. Lieutenant Holland had sent an electronic transmission of the suspect's prints to the Bureau in Washington. Chief O'Halleran made a personal phone call to an FBI deputy director he knew personally, asking that they give the prints a priority. He was told there was little hope of any results before sometime tomorrow. Mike walked back to Flynn's desk and for the hundredth time reexamined the rental agreements they'd obtained from Hertz and Avis. Two completely different credit cards and names had been used, but, according to the handwriting experts, the signatures on both were written by the same hand as was the registration card and credit card slip from the Holiday Inn.

Mike looked up from the papers. "Who's the best man we've got in the department on credit cards?" he asked of everybody assembled in the room.

Sam Elberger shifted in his chair. "I'd say Captain Hebert in Special Investigations knows more about credit card fraud than anybody." Around the room heads nodded in assent. Mike picked up the phone and dialed Captain Hebert's number, praying the man hadn't yet gone home for the day. Luckily, he caught him on his way out. In response to Mike's impassioned request, he stopped by the Homicide office.

Once the man was comfortably seated at Flynn's conference table, Mike explained the situation and began asking his questions.

"Captain, if you used credit cards like this guy does, how would you go about it?"

"Well, if it was me, the first thing I'd do is find a good connection within the credit card company, somebody who needs cash. I say this because everything you've shown me indicates this fellow has an accomplice inside the business. Anyway, then I'd buy some account numbers from this person. I'd buy card blanks, a strip reader/recorder, and an embossing machine, and I'd be in business."

"Where would you get all this?"

"Oh, it's not too hard to find somebody inside a credit card company willing to sell account numbers and blanks. The account numbers are the easy thing; the blanks are a little harder. They generally keep track of those pretty well. But it is relatively easy. The strip reader/recorder you can get in any Radio Shack for about fifty bucks, and you can pick up used embossing machines at most used business equipment stores."

Mike considered the answer for several seconds before he asked his next question. "I've got three different account numbers. The one from the motel shows as a GM corporate card. Should we run a check on these other two? How do we find out who these other two account numbers really belong to?"

"What is it you're after here?"

"Well, I see the numbers on these two rental contracts are different. One is a Visa, and the other is an American Express. I was thinking that perhaps all these accounts are being charged to this GM corporate office in Detroit."

"Fat chance. I'll lay you even money the other two are charged off to similar safe accounts in some other huge corporation. Or even the federal government!"

"What do you mean by a safe account?"

"To me, a safe account is one used by a very big company—like GM. A big outfit like GM or the government has thousands of employees using perfectly legit credit cards owned by the corporation. Trouble is the corporation has so many outlying offices, all with people using this plastic. The problem of keeping track of each and every individual account number is almost overwhelming.

"They don't keep track of these in their computers?" Mike asked.

"They're just now getting around to it. Up till a few years ago, they were more concerned with getting their manufacturing and sales on the computers."

Sam Elberger asked, "So, you think the chances are pretty slim we'll get anywhere chasing these particular credit cards?"

Captain Herbert leaned forward to rest his forearms on the conference table. "Well, yes and no. It depends on how smart the guy using the cards is."

"Captain, this is all a bit over our heads in here. Would it be asking too much for your people to do it?"

"Well, things are a little slow in my office right now. I think Veronica might enjoy doing this. Give me the paperwork, and I'll drop it off on my way out."

"Ask her to call me the minute she gets anything," Mike pleaded.

Captain Hebert scooped the paperwork off the desk and said good night as he left the office.

Mike looked over the assembled police officers. "Well, there's nothing more to be done here tonight. I suggest we return to our normal shift routine. I want a watch maintained on the radio traffic. If and when the car is sighted, I want to be notified no matter what time it is. I'll be spending the night at Captain Flynn's house, so you can reach me there. Now, if they spot the car, be sure nobody moves on it until the chief and I have been notified. I guess that's everything. Who has the duty?"

Julie Kincaid and Sam Elberger raised their hands. Mike nodded his approval. "I want one of you two here at all times. I'll leave it up to you guys how you work it out. Okay? The rest of you go home and get some sleep."

Mike waited as they filed out of the office. When they'd gone, he phoned Monica, who was now back at her own home. With any luck, he'd be with her in just a few minutes.

5:30 p.m., Miami

Carefully following the map she'd drawn for him before they parted company at the Hall of Records, Flynn was headed for Megan's house, driving a Pontiac Bonneville sedan, arranged for by Megan's boss, Deputy Chief Alvero. Dennis was enjoying the last rays of a red and gold sunset off to his right and the softness of the early evening. He was dressed in the casual attire he'd found so comfortable. As he drove, he anticipated the evening he was to spend with Megan. The traffic was relatively light, so he was able to maintain a steady pace along the freeway. He'd spent the late afternoon in three different bookstores until he'd found the one gift he had in mind as a surprise for Neil, a large, coffee-table-sized, hard-cover edition of *The History of the Indianapolis 500*. The slick book was filled with photographs of winners, their race cars, an excellent history of the track, and some shots inside the museum located in the track infield. For Megan, he'd found a wood carving of an old sea captain with a sensual twinkle in his eye and a most suggestive smile. The minute he saw it he knew it was perfect! The two gift wrapped packages were in a large shopping bag with cord handles, safe on the floor on the passenger side of the front seat.

In the distance, he thought he could just make out the exit sign she'd indicated on the map. He turned his head and lowered his eyes to check the hand-drawn map next to him on the front seat. At that moment, the car suddenly filled with shattered glass as the rear window was blown into the car. The shock and surprise caused him to jerk the wheel to the right. The car lurched toward the railing. With his heart pounding, he fought for control. The car fishtailed wildly. As he was regaining his composure, two spider webs appeared in the windshield. Somebody was shooting at his car! With his heart in his throat, he mashed down on the accelerator; the big, police-package V–6 growled to life, and the sedan shot forward. Flynn thanked God he'd been issued a car with the complete police package–hot engine and strong suspension system, suited for high-speed work. Flynn began dodging the slower traffic, as he raced down the freeway, picking up speed by the second. He divided his attention between the road ahead and the rear view mirror as he sought a glimpse of a pursuing vehicle.

Far back, weaving in and out of traffic, he saw a car of some sort coming on fast. He mentally cursed himself for not keeping current on automobiles. Not too many years back, he could have identified just about anything Detroit made–not so today. The speedometer was passing 90 miles-per-hour and heading for more as he pushed the car as hard as he could. Still, the chasing car seemed to be closing the gap. Why? kept pressing his mind. Why would anybody want to kill me? The question rang in his mind as he hurtled down the expressway. Suddenly, he realized he was a sitting duck unless he got off this limited access highway. He had to get off this highway as soon as he could and lose himself on side streets.

Up ahead, perhaps a quarter of a mile away, he saw an exit. He dodged a slower moving car like it was standing still and swung into the center of the three lanes. He both heard and felt the car take two bullet hits in the trunk as he set up for a last second swerve to the right. With luck, he'd be on the exit ramp before the following car could react and follow. He gripped the wheel with both hands and swung it violently to the right. The big Pontiac heeled over on its left side, the tires screaming as the car began to slide. Flynn jerked the wheel back to the left, the direction of the slide.

The car righted itself and shot forward almost at right angles to the exit ramp. He threw the car into a second slide, this time to the right. The car heeled over again and was now aimed straight down the exit ramp. Behind him, he was conscious of cars making panic stops, and he could hear the beginnings of a major multi-vehicle pileup. Good! That's going to make it impossible for the other car to get off the ramp behind him. The thought of safety passed through his mind at high speed as he began frantically pumping the brakes to slow the car as it hurtled down the curving ramp. The Pontiac hit the bottom of the ramp and shot across an intersection. Flynn mashed down on the accelerator again. Parked cars and astonished pedestrians flashed by as the car picked up speed again. He checked the rear view mirror for a car speeding to follow and was relieved not to see it there. He slowed the car and took the first left turn.

Now, the problem was to find a phone. Not for the first time since he left home did he realize the value of that damn cell phone–where was it now that he needed it? In the damn charger on his dresser back in Indianapolis! Damn–damn! For the next several blocks, he searched, checking every intersection and side street for signs of a chase car. After several turns, he was satisfied he'd made a clean getaway. He turned in at the first supermarket he came to and parked the car deep in the lot. Grabbing his package and the map, he walked to the supermarket and through the automatic doors. He found a bank of pay phones at the rear of the store and dialed Megan's number. The phone rang several times. Flynn felt panic grip his chest. Just as he was about to give up, the phone was answered by a breathless Neil.

"Neil, it's me, Denny Flynn. Is everything okay? Is your mom there?"

"Oh, Hi, Mr. Flynn. Yeah, we're both here. You want to talk to Mom?"

"I sure do. Would you put her on?" Seconds later, Megan was on the phone.

"Megan, would you do me a big favor?" Flynn began.

"What is it? You're not going to miss our dinner tonight are you?"

"No. We'll have dinner. But first, would you have a look around outside? See if there are any strange cars near your house. See if anybody is watching your place."

"Yes. Hold on. I'll be right back."

While he waited, Flynn checked the store aisles and the shoppers for anybody who appeared to be interested in him. After what seemed an eternity to Flynn, she came back to the phone. "Everything seems normal," she reported.

"Well, I'm not sure they're going to remain that way. Can you get yourselves in the car and meet me somewhere?"

"No problem. Where are you?"

"I'm in a supermarket someplace in South Florida. I'm lost."

"Tell you what. Grab a cab, and meet us at the boat. Do you remember the name of the marina?"

"Yes, I do. That sounds like a good idea. Megan, would you happen to have an extra gun? I'm feeling rather naked at the moment."

"Believe me, guns are no problem. Just get yourself into a cab as fast as you can. We'll meet you at the boat in about forty-five minutes."

Flynn dropped the receiver back on its hook and walked to the front of the store. Once out on the sidewalk, it took him ten minutes to flag down a passing cab.

It was a full hour later when Flynn stepped out of the cab at the marina parking lot. As the cabby drove off, Flynn stood looking for any sign he'd been followed. Nothing. He breathed a sigh of relief. Megan's car was nowhere in sight. Carrying his gift package, Flynn walked to the guard shack at the gate to the piers. An elderly gentleman had him sign a visitors' register and passed him on through. As he walked the length of the pier, he felt the tension fall away like a raincoat falling off his shoulders. Soon, he saw her boat bobbing silently in the gentle waves of the marina, abandoned. He was about to return to the guard shack to ask if Megan and her son had checked in when the zipper at the rear of the boat cover opened. Megan stuck her head through the opening and beckoned Flynn inside.

The moment Flynn's feet were firmly planted on the deck, he found himself locked in an embrace as Megan threw her arms around his shoulders and hugged tightly.

"Thank God, you're all right!" she said, her face buried in his chest.

"Oh, I'm fine. Just scared, that's all. I can't say as much for your department's car though."

Megan stepped back to look in his face. "Well, it's time we got the hell out of here. We've got a lot of thinking to do and plans to make."

Within minutes, the twin Cummins diesels were thrumming away, and they were underway. Flynn climbed the ladder to the flying bridge and joined Megan as they departed the harbor. The late evening sun painted ships, shore, and distant houses a brilliant red gold. The air was soft and warm on his face as Flynn contemplated the paradox he was living. Here he was with one of the most beautiful and exciting women of his life in years, and death was lurking nearby. Megan broke into his thoughts.

"We're going to pull in at the next marina and top off the fuel and fresh water tanks. Frank Harrison from the restaurant is going to meet us there with enough provisions for several days. We can live aboard for as long as we need to. How does that sound to you?"

"Fine. I'm completely in your hands."

"Go below, and get into some of Pop's old duds, while I get us to the next marina." Flynn departed to do as he was instructed.

Within minutes, she had deftly put the big cruiser alongside a refueling station. Soon, a young attendant hooked up the fuel and water lines. Moments later, a white van pulled onto the pier and drove to the side of the boat. A gray-haired man dressed in restaurant whites slid the side door open and stepped onto the pier. Megan turned, looked up to Flynn, and without saying anything, motioned him to join her on the pier. By the time he'd gotten to the pier, a sizable stack of fresh and frozen food had been unloaded from the truck. Flynn unsnapped the well deck cover and began carrying the boxes aboard. Megan gave the old man a hug and pressed some money into his reluctant palm. "Now, remember, Mr. Harrison, not a word to anybody. Especially, my mother!" She escorted the elderly gentleman to the van's driver's door.

Flynn began carrying the provisions down to the main salon while he waited for Megan to complete her business on the pier and to return. The frozen things went into the large, upright freezer at the side of the galley. The milk, butter, eggs, and meats, he stowed in the matching refrigerator. He left several loaves of bread on the galley counter, not knowing where else to put them. He heard the big diesels start as he completed his work. Megan's voice intruded into the salon over an intercom. "Denny, would you go bring Neil up now? I think he fell asleep, or he's listening to that damn walkman again. I can't raise him on the intercom."

Flynn walked over to the intercom and examined the several switches. None were labeled, frustrating his effort to respond. Shrugging his shoulders in defeat, he turned to descend the short stairs to the stateroom at the back of the boat.

Neil was sprawled on the big, double bed, a *Sports Illustrated* hiding his face. Flynn walked over so the boy could see him. The magazine came down, and a set of earphones came off. "Come on, Neil, your mom wants us," Flynn said as he turned to leave the stateroom.

9:00 p.m, Indianapolis.

Back in the Flynn home, Mike and Monica were seated on the living room sofa. Monica stretched out with her head resting in Mike's lap. On the television, an HBO movie was showing, largely ignored. Each was preoccupied with private thoughts and concerns. Suddenly, the phone rang, startling them both. Mike snatched the receiver from the cradle before the second ring.

"Yes," he said, tension filling his voice.

"Mike, it's Sam. We've located the goddamn car!"

"Where?"

"It's parked in the lot at the Travel Time Inn out on the west side."

"Who reported it?"

"One of the uniform cars out on the beat in that sector."

"Where are they now?"

"About a block away. Standing by for instructions."

"Okay. Here's what we'd better do. Have the sector cars cover the block around the motel. I don't want this asshole to see a uniform car or uniforms within a block of that place. Is Sergeant Crooks there with you?"

"Julie's right here."

"Good. See if the two of you can borrow a Vice or a Narc car, something that doesn't look like one of our standard unmarked units. I want the two of you to drive up to that place like married tourists. Have Julie stay in the car. You go inside and check the register for the guy. Find out if he's there. If he is, what room he's in, how long he's been there. All of it. Then, I want the two of you to meet me someplace close by. I don't know that area. Name something I can find easy."

"Well, the Hanger Bar is about two blocks away from there on High School Road."

"I know it. I'll meet you there. If you have any problems getting a car, call the chief. He'll see to it. Jump to it. I'm leaving now."

Mike explained the situation to Monica. He kissed her tenderly and swore he would be careful. He asked her to stay off the phone until he returned. Before leaving, he informed the three uniformed officers standing guard about his planned movements and how he could be reached. Within minutes of the phone call, he was speeding west toward the killer and, he hoped, the end of the long nightmare.

Mike pulled into the parking lot at the Hanger Bar thirty-five minutes later. Ten minutes later, Sam Elberger and Julie Crooks rolled up in a flashy Lincoln Town Car within minutes. Mike got out of his car and joined them in theirs, climbing into the back seat. Excitement loaded his voice. "Okay, tell me everything!"

Sam Elberger turned in his position in the driver's seat to look at Mike as he reported. "He checked in about an hour ago under the name Jeffrey L. Warren. He put down an American Express card for that name. It checked good according to the desk clerk. He asked for and got a room on the second-story corner facing the main entrance. I glanced at it as I left the office; corner room, floor to ceiling windows, looking east and south. The east window overlooks the drive at the front door. He can see anybody coming into the place. The room is dark, but the drapes are open about a foot or so at both windows. So, he's probably sitting there in the dark, watching."

"Has the place got a restaurant?"

"Yes."

"Has this Warren made any phone calls?"

"No."

"Did he match the description we got from the desk clerk over at the Holiday Inn?"

"It's a match except for the mustache. He's not using it anymore. The freckle beside the nose is there."

"Where's the back way in?"

"The supply doors for the restaurant are on the back side of the building."

Mike sat back to think. Several minutes went by before he spoke again. "Thinking this over, I'm convinced the asshole made me somehow–I don't have a clue how, but I know it in my gut. Once he made me, I think he followed me to the safe house. Hell, he probably even knows where I live! I don't dare show my face around that motel. But we need people on the inside. Sam, do you think the manager will cooperate with us?"

"He seemed very helpful before. Told the desk clerk to cooperate with me when I went in to ask my questions. I think he'll go along with us."

"What did you tell him?"

"I told him we had reason to believe a dangerous man, a fugitive, was in his motel. He immediately asked what we wanted him to do."

"In that case, let's get back there. We're going to need to get people into the place without being seen by this Warren—or whoever the hell he really is."

Elberger drove back to the motel's rear entrance. The back lot was a mixture of dumpsters, employee vehicles, and a few scattered shrubs. Sam parked on the street along side a length of evergreen shrubbery. While Mike and Julie waited in the car, Elberger went to look for the service entrance. Mike contacted headquarters using his two-way radio. A total of eight sector cars were in position, out of sight, surrounding the motel. He instructed them to maintain their positions until further notice. They were instructed not to obstruct any traffic. Minutes later, Elberger returned, motioning them to get out of the car. The manager was waiting for them at the entrance. "Sergeant Gaffney, I'm Herbert Walker, the hotel manager. How can I help?" he said introducing himself and leading the way to his office. Mike held his tongue until they had entered the office. Sam closed the office door.

"Mr. Walker, the truth is things are a little more serious than Sergeant Elbeger told you. We're pretty sure you've got a vicious killer staying up there in that corner room. The man the newspaper and the TV people have been going on about. We need to take him as quickly, quietly, and as safely as we can with no harm to any of your guests."

"I see–," he hesitated. "Does this mean we're to be surrounded by a SWAT unit and all that?"

"No. I have no plans to do that at all–well, not unless everything else fails. I'm hoping to take him with no muss nor fuss. Now, we need to know a few things. Has this Warren made any phone calls since Detective Elberger was in earlier?" Mike said.

"Well, he's placed an order with room service."

"Ah! That's great! We need to get a look at the man and the inside of the room if we can. I don't think any of your people ought to be going up there anyway, do you? Knowing what you do now."

"No. No, I guess not."

"Good. How much time have we got?"

The manager phoned the kitchen and checked. "About ten minutes according to the cook," he said.

"Good. Can you see to getting Elberger here into a waiter's jacket and brief him on how to be a room service waiter?"

"I guess so. Will there be anything else?"

"Are the rooms on each side of Warren's occupied?"

"Yes."

"Then, if you don't mind, I think we'd better come up with a way to get those people off that floor without raising an alarm."

Quickly, a plan was devised. The clerk was to phone the guests all around the room occupied by the target, telling each guest that they had "won" a free dinner with drinks in the motel's dining room. That to 'collect' they must present themselves at the dining room within the next twenty minutes. For those who had already had dinner, they were to be told that they would be able to trade the free dinner for ten dollars worth of drinks in the motel bar. Mike decided that once everybody had been accounted for, he would gather them together and explain there was a very dangerous fugitive up on he second floor and just as soon as the police had him under control the guests would be allowed back to their rooms. Mike also promised the manager he would see to it that the Department picked up the tab for the motel's out-of-pocket expenses. Ten minutes later, Sam Elberger and the manager were back. Sam was dressed in a white shirt, black-bow-tie, and a waiter's red jacket with name tag and was carrying a covered service tray. Seconds later, he was gone.

Ten minutes later, Elberger was back. Mike questioned him as he changed back into his own clothing and reclaimed his badge and gun.

"Now that you've had a good look at him, give me a description," Mike began.

"He's a good five-eleven, short, light-brown, almost bleached hair–I think he's bleached it–he has blue-gray eyes, and he's definitely nervous. In my opinion, he matches the computer drawing except for the hair. The freckle beside the nose is right where it needs to be. He's our guy."

"Okay, how about the room?"

"He turned the lights on when I knocked on the door. The room is pretty much unused. Standard two double bed arrangement. Beds are against the north wall. He's got a suitcase on the bed nearest the door. It was unzipped, but he had it closed when I entered the room. He seemed to be in a big hurry to sign the check and get me the hell out of the room."

"Give you a tip?"

"Nah. He just signed the tab and charged everything to the room."

"Did you see any weapons?"

"No."

"Anything else?"

"I waited in the hall after I left, and I saw the lights go out. I swear he's sitting up there in the dark, eating his shrimp and fries, and watching everything outside the building."

"How was he dressed?"

"Light blue shirt, no tie, street shoes. His suit coat was laid out on the bed."

"I want to take this man alive. We have to find out who paid him to kill Blakemore and why. Any ideas?"

"I could go back to get the dishes and tray back. We could rush him then. Before he could react."

Mike thought this over for a few minutes. "No, that's too risky. He's probably just waiting for something like that to happen." Mike was about to offer another idea when the telephone operator stuck her head in the office and announced that the man was using the phone. Mike and Sam quickly followed her back to her small cubicle.

"Can you tell whether that's a local or a long distance call?" Mike asked.

"Oh sure, each phone has a meter on it. See, that's a long distance call he's on," she said, pointing to the meter on a large board.

"Can we find out what number he called?" Mike asked.

"Not until he's off the phone and the computer records the call."

"Where's the computer?"

"In the room just behind us."

"Let's go!"

Once they were inside the computer room, Mike asked for the list of calls, especially the just completed one. The girl stepped to a keyboard and rapidly tapped out a command. A small printer to the side of the room came to life and quickly printed off a single sheet of information. The girl tore the paper from the printer and handed it to Mike. The room number appeared at the left, followed by 24-hour military time, the area code, phone number, and the call duration in minutes and seconds and, to the far right, the hotel's charge for the call. Mike recognized the 213 area code as the area code for Los Angeles. The call had lasted for just over four minutes. He handed the printer paper to Julie and asked her to get on to the phone company and find out to whom the number belonged. As she took the paper from Mike, Julie flippantly observed, "They ought to just gas the bastard and get it over with."

Something like lights flashed in Mike's mind! Gas! Why not? Quickly, he grabbed the computer room phone and dialed the chief's home phone number. Within minutes, he'd brought the chief up to date on the situation and made his highly unusual request. The chief promised to get back to him as quickly as possible. Mike had asked for a colorless, odorless gas of a non-flammable nature, which could put an unsuspecting person to sleep long enough to be taken into custody. Mike asked the manager if there were blueprints for the building. Receiving an affirmative answer, they all waited while the man went to another location to retrieve the requested paperwork. While they waited, they busied themselves by checking on the status of the "free dinner" winners in the dining room. Mike wanted them off the second floor for as long as possible. When the manager returned, he unrolled the blueprints on his desk and began explaining the layout of that particular room. Sam was looking intently at the plans and stabbed his finger at the walls separating the killer's room from the one next door. "Is this the water wall?"

The manager looked where Sam's finger was resting. "Yes."

"Looks to me like these two baths share a common vent."

"Yes, they do. The steam and other vapors are vented into this area and expelled out a roof vent."

"How much room between the walls?"

"Oh, it's a good foot."

Sam looked triumphant. "You get the gas, and we've got a way to do the job!" he said to Mike.

Five minutes after his call to the chief, the coroner himself was on the phone. He asked several questions about the size of the suspect, his weight, and the volume of the room he was in. The coroner advised it might take about an hour or more before he could be at the motel with something that would do the job.

9:00 p.m., Miami

The Lady Grace rode at anchor in a small inlet miles away from the marina. Megan was clearing away the dinner dishes while Flynn finished his coffee. Neil had gone to the forward part of the main salon to watch television. Except for the distant muffled sound of the generator and the noise of the TV, it was reasonably quiet aboard the boat. Flynn sat thinking over and reviewing his movements and actions since coming to Miami. Objectively, he could think of no reason, nothing he had done, which would have drawn attention to his investigations. He was left with an informant within the Miami PD, and he was reluctant to bring it up with Megan. His solitary silence was broken as Megan sat across from him at the table. She brought two cold bottles of Michelob with her. She eyed him quite frankly as she spoke. "Denny, you and I both know we're in deep shit! And we both know somebody in my department put the finger on us!"

"That's the conclusion I came to, but I was trying to find a way to say it that wouldn't—oh, I don't know—"

"Piss me off? Hey, I'm a big girl now. I can put two and two together with the best of 'em. Somebody, either in my office or at the hall of records, tipped somebody off. The question is, who's the traitor, and who got the tip?"

"Megan, how safe do you think we are on this boat?"

"This is the best hiding place in the world. We've got fuel, water, and provisions good for a week at least. Longer if we have to stretch it. Believe me, it's harder than hell to find a boat, even one this size, if the skipper doesn't want to be found."

"What about protection? I don't know about you, but I don't have my service revolver with me, and I'm starting to feel more than a little insecure without it."

Megan took a quick pull on her beer and held up her index finger. "I think I have just the thing to solve that. I'll be right back." She got up from the table and went down the stairs to the main stateroom at the rear of the cruiser. A minute later, she was back with a large mahogany case about the size of a large silverware box under her arm. Resuming her seat at the table, she placed the box in the middle of the table in front of Flynn. "I think this is just what the doctor ordered," she said as she thumbed the combination lock and opened the catch. She turned the case toward Flynn. "Go ahead. Open it," she said.

Flynn lifted the hinged lid. There, nestled in a foam lining, was a SIG–Sauer, 9 millimeter semiautomatic. Two loaded clips were nestled in their own slots to the side of the hand gun.

"Do you know the gun?" Megan asked.

"Well, I've heard of it. Several guys on the Department think it's the best hand gun made to date."

"This is the model P226. It holds a fifteen round clip of nine millimeter, parabellum cartridges. I've got about a dozen boxes of ammunition for that weapon on board. Take it—it's yours. My gift to you."

Flynn was speechless for a moment. He wasn't sure, but he was fairly certain the gun was worth several hundred dollars. "I couldn't take this. I mean I shouldn't have the only weapon."

"Oh, don't worry. I have a pretty good armory aboard. Like to see?"

"Yes, I would."

Megan took him by the hand and led him down to the master stateroom. She opened one of the two closets which flanked a large, built-in dresser. A second door inside the closet was unlocked with a key she took from a jewelry box on the dresser. Flynn was surprised by the contents. He could see a lever-action, thirty aught six rifle, two shotguns both pump action, one with a short barrel, a Smith & Wesson .357 revolver in stainless steel, and three more wooden cases like the one she had just presented him. Megan opened one of the two large drawers beneath the display. It was filled with plastic wrapped boxes of ammunition. There was double aught buck for the shotguns together with ammunition for the thirty aught six and all the handguns. "I think you could stand off a small army with all this!" he said.

Megan smiled her approval at his surprise. "Well, when the drug business started getting real serious, I decided to be prepared. You can't be too careful out here. Boats get stolen or hijacked, their owners killed and dumped over the side fairly often down here."

"Are you proficient with all this hardware?" Flynn asked, still amazed by the display.

"I'm confident I can handle any of it as well as any man."

"Does Neil know about this?"

"Not only does he know about it but he's familiar with how each weapon is used, just in case. We've practiced what to do several times in case somebody tries to board us against our will. Actually, he's a pretty good shot." Megan stooped and opened the second drawer. She pulled out two shoulder holsters and handed one to Flynn. "This is custom-made for the SIG-Sauer. It has two clip holders sewed into the strap. Do me a favor and load up the sawed-off Remington while I load up a SIG for myself."

Flynn did as she asked and watched while she selected one of the automatics for herself and loaded two extra clips. She loaded a clip into the hand grip, chambered a round, and set the gun on safety. She slipped the gun into the other holster and deftly slipped into the shoulder rig. The gun nestled snugly under her left arm, butt forward. "Now," she said as she closed and locked the armory door, "let's go back up to the salon and make some plans."

They were seated at the galley dining table, their beers almost finished. Flynn loaded his weapon and slipped it into the custom-made shoulder holster. He felt far less vulnerable.

"Since we're going to make this boat our operational headquarters, I'd best give you a crash course in terminology and everything else. I can't afford to stop and explain everything in landlubber English if things heat up," Megan said.

"Okay, Captain. Go to it." Flynn said, smiling as he said it.

"To start with, everything is done in terms of ship's head or the bow. That's the front of the boat. Now, the left side is called port, and the right side is called starboard. The back of the boat is called the stern. Ceilings are called overheads. Stairs are called ladders, and the ropes are called lines. Oh, wait a minute! I've got the perfect book for you to read." She was out of her seat and down the ladder to the stateroom in a flash. Moments later, she returned with a fair-sized book in her hand. "Here. Spend some time with this. It's the absolute bible," she said as she handed him the book. It was *The Blue Jackets' Manual* published by the United States Naval Institute at Annapolis, Maryland. "Now, we'll need to set up watches between ourselves for the rest of the night," she went on. "What are you, a day person or a night person?"

"I guess I'm pretty much a day person."

"Good. Then, you'll take the first watch. Now, tell me what you think has happened here."

Flynn thought for a few moments before he answered, "Well, I agree with you. Somebody tipped someone off about our snooping. The only thing that makes sense is this Mazzicone connection."

"So, what do you think happened?" she asked.

"Well, think about it. Somebody tipped them about the checking we're doing. Lawyers, especially those in the trial end of the business, pay cops for tidbits of information all the time. Maybe Santini or Mazzicone has a standing offer. You know? If anybody comes snooping about me, let me know about it, and I'll make it worth your while."

"So, that makes it somebody who waited on us at the hall of records, or God forbid, Henry back in my office."

"Fraid so—or it could go even higher."

"Oh, my God! I hadn't even considered that."

"This is going to take some deep thinking. Maybe by morning, I'll have something to toss around," Flynn said.

"Well, I'll give it more thought myself."

Flynn remembered the gifts. They lay where he'd dropped them on one of the two sofas in the salon. Excusing himself, he retrieved them and asked Neil to join him and Megan at the table. With a small speech about how happy he was to have made new friends, he presented the gifts. Neil ripped his open and was very excited by the find. To Flynn's great surprise, the boy gave Flynn a very strong hug and thanked him profusely. Neil's unexpected reaction took Flynn by surprise, and he was as surprised by his own emotional reaction to the boy. Megan was examining the old sailor with great amusement in her expressive eyes. "I suppose you know every tourist to Florida collects one of these. But I must say this one has a wonderful twinkle in his eyes," she said.

"That was why I chose that particular one over all the rest. And check out that devilish smile. He looks like he's just made love."

"I like the thought. I'll give this old sea dog a favored position on the mantle back home. Thank you very much— perfect for the occasion." She dropped the levity and got serious. "Now, it's getting late, and we'd better get the routine started. Since you have the first watch, we'd better get to it. Go on up to the flying bridge, and make yourself comfortable, but keep a lookout for anybody trying to get too close to the boat. If that happens, sound the horn. The large, red, mushroom-shaped button on the dash to the left of the wheel. Just push on it for a good long time. I'll be up to relieve you about three a.m. No lights, or you'll destroy your night vision. We'll make more complete plans tomorrow."

"What are you and Neil going to do?"

"We're going to bed. Now, off with you, and don't worry too much. I think we'll be okay for tonight. I just don't want to take any chances."

Flynn stood and gazed into her eyes. At last, he gave into his desire, took her in his arms, and kissed her. She responded willingly and gave him a tender hug. At length, Flynn took his leave and climbed the ladder to the flying bridge. He situated himself on the large pilot's seat. After a time, the boat's generator went silent, and all the lights except the anchor lights went out. As he gazed into the darkness, punctuated here and there by lights from houses and street lamps in the distance, he packed his pipe and lit up. The sounds of water gently slapping the sides of the boat and noises of unfamiliar insects were his company as he watched and thought about their predicament.

10:15 p.m., Indianapolis

Doc Nichols and an assistant arrived at the motel, driving the coroner's, body-pickup station wagon. They unloaded a collapsible gurney, piled three large tanks of nitrous-oxide gas aboard the gurney, covered everything with a dark-green, army blanket, cinched it all to the stretcher with body straps, and entered the motel through the rear door. They'd brought with them several feet of clear, plastic tubing on a roll. Several minutes of discussion followed about using the guest room adjoining the killer's. The manager led the way to the service elevator, and the band of men made their way to the second floor and to the room next to the killer's.

Sam Elberger lifted the glass shower doors from their tracks on the tub and set them aside. Using a phillips screwdriver provided by the manager, he quietly removed the four screws from the vent grill located high on the shower enclosure wall. All three men were in stocking feet to prevent noise, and they spoke in low whispers. Doc Nichols set up the three tanks just outside the shower and attached the plastic tubing to the first tank's release valve. Mike, being the tallest, straddled the tub with his feet on opposite sides of the tub and began to snake the tubing through the wall and into the grillwork vent in the bath of the adjoining room. He was careful to let only a scant fraction of an inch of the tube protrude thorough the grill.

When he was satisfied with the placement, he taped the tube in place with the duct tape Doc Nichols had brought along and then, carefully covered the grillwork with more duct tape that would seal the gas in the adjoining room. When he was satisfied a casual inspection from the killer's room would not show anything amiss, he gave Doc Nichols a nod of his head. Nichols cracked the valve on the tank until a barely audible hiss could be heard. Doc checked his watch and motioned the two policemen to follow him into the bedroom. He closed the door to the bath and took a seat on one of the beds. "At this rate, it will take about forty-five minutes for that first tank to run empty. We have one more possible leak we need to plug, the crack under the room door. Somebody is going to have to stuff a towel or something under that door."

Mike immediately volunteered. Taking a large bath towel from the neat stack on the adjoining vanity and sink, he silently opened the door and slipped into the hall. Getting to his knees, he carefully rolled the towel into a tube shape and silently placed it against the crack at the bottom of the killer's room door. Just as quietly, he returned to the adjoining room, closing the door without so much as an audible click.

Doc Nichols checked his watch. "We've got lots of time so, you might as well make yourselves comfortable," he whispered.

Mike sat on the bed opposite. "How long do you think this will take?" he asked.

Doc Nichols shrugged his shoulders. "Let's give it a couple of hours."

"Will he be really knocked out?"

"With luck, yes. If not, he'll be very groggy and not really able to think or move quickly."

"Any chance he'll smell the gas?"

"There's always a chance, but in this case, I think not. Nitrous oxide is pretty much odorless, maybe slightly sweet-smelling by itself, but when it's mixed with all the ambient air in that room, I doubt he'll detect it. He'll just feel more and more sleepy and fall asleep."

"Well, if it is going to take that long, I'm going to go down to the office and make some phone calls back to the Department. Joe, you stay here with the Doc. If anything happens, call me at the manager's office."

Mike was seated at the manager's desk. He'd just dialed the chief's home number and was waiting for the phone to be answered. After several rings, the chief answered. "Chief, we're all set up here at the motel. Doc Nichols has the gas feeding into the room now. He figures we're probably a couple of hours away from taking him."

"How do you plan to do it?" the chief asked.

"We're going to use a pass key and simply go in and cuff him while he's asleep. It ought to be a piece of cake if everything works out."

"I just got a call from the Ident office. The Bureau finally came through with an ID to go with the prints. According to the telex, our killer is one Albert Thomas Cutshaw. Now get this—Cutshaw was a Green Beret, trained in covert behind-the-lines assassinations. He was proficient with several different weapons, explosives, and killing methods. The Army discharged him—seems he was getting out of hand and refused psychiatric help. It seems their shrinks didn't believe Cutshaw would really be a threat to society. *Can you imagine that!* Anyway, the Bureau has no other record of any kind on the man. Last known address is in Los Angeles. The guy has no record at all, not even so much as a parking ticket. Mike, if this guy is as bad as the Army says he is, and I think he is, you'd better wait the full two hours before you go into that room."

"Don't worry. I know this bastard is one dangerous son-of-a-bitch! We'll give it the full two hours. Since we have the time, would you send someone up here with some leg irons? I think we'd better go the whole route with him."

"No problem. Where do you want them delivered?"

"Have them ask for me at the front desk. I'll be in the manager's office. Just make sure they come in by way of the back door."

"They're on their way."

Julie entered the manager's office from the computer room, a puzzled expression on her face. Mike saw the look and asked, "What's the matter?"

"It's this number in Los Angeles—the one our man called a while ago."

"What about it?"

"Well, the phone company gave me the official listing. It's a private residence listed for an A. T. Cutshaw. I called the number and got voice mail."

"He called his own phone! I just spoke with the chief, and according to the feebees, the man upstairs is Albert Thomas Cutshaw. If he spoke for four minutes like this printout says, he's left instructions for someone. I'd sure as hell like to know what he had to say and who he said it to!"

Twenty minutes later, the leg irons were delivered to the motel. Mike took them up to the room. Doc Nichols and Detective Elberger were passing the time playing Gin Rummy at the round table near the window. Mike tossed the leg irons on the bed and sat down on it. "How much longer before we change tanks?" he asked.

"About fifteen minutes," Doc answered.

"Any noises from next door?"

"Nope. All's quiet," Elberger answered.

Doc inclined his head toward the leg irons. "Not taking any chances, I see."

"No chances at all." Mike told them what he'd learned from the FBI report to the chief. Detective Elberger asked about the possibility that the door chain was in place. They couldn't afford to wake the man by forcing the door. A trip was made to the hotel maintenance room for a set of bolt cutters to be used if the chain were in place.

By 1:15 a.m. the motel was quiet and dark. Doc Nichols pulled the gurney out into the hallway while Mike and Sam, in their stocking feet, approached the killer's door. Mike pressed his ear to the door and heard nothing. He slipped his service Glock from its holster. Elberger already had his in hand. As silently as he could, Mike inserted the pass key into the lock and turned it. Slowly, the door opened. By the light from the hall lights, Mike could see the door chain was in place. He motioned Elberger forward with the cutters. Sam slipped the cutters over the chain and slowly squeezed until the chain fell in two pieces with a small rattling noise.

Both men held their breath, listening. From the room came the sounds of light snoring. Elberger put the cutters aside on the hall floor and with a nod of his head, indicated he was ready to follow Mike into the room. Silently, both men advanced into the room their weapons pointed at the figure on the bed.

The killer lay sprawled on the far bed, still dressed in his street clothing. He lay on his side with one arm under his head. Mike holstered his Glock and pulled his handcuffs from his belt. Elberger advanced to hold his gun inches from the killer's head as Mike snicked the cuffs over the free wrist. Now came a moment of danger, lifting the man to cuff the second wrist. Mike gently rolled the man face down on the bed and pulled the arms together behind his back, quickly locking the cuff over the second wrist. The man didn't give any indication he would wake. Mike swung the man's legs up on the bed and quickly snapped on the leg irons, which were in reality extra large hand cuffs made to accommodate the larger bones of the lower leg. The manacles had an eighteen-inch, hardened chain linking them together. Elberger retrieved the gurney from the hall and was followed into the room by Doc Nichols. Together they lifted the still sleeping man onto the gurney, covered him with the army blanket, and using the leather straps affixed to the gurney's side rails, strapped the still sleeping man down. Doc Nichols urged everybody out into the hallway and out of the gas filled room. Doc returned to open some windows. Once everybody had assembled in the hall, Mike radioed his "raiding party", filled them in, and ordered the Civic impounded.

"He'll come around quickly now that he's out in the air," Doc Nichols said.

"We'd better search him before we take him down to your wagon, then," Mike said. A quick body search was made, with only car keys, pocket change, and a wallet produced. Mike went back into the room and checked all the dresser drawers, wastebaskets, and closet before closing up the two-suiter and bringing it and the loose clothing into the hall. Within fifteen minutes, the room had been sealed, and the prisoner was on his way downtown in the back of the coroner's station wagon. Mike was anxious to call Flynn in Miami and to let him know they'd captured their killer. In the Vice car on the way back to pick up Mike's car, Sam Elberger checked his watch. "Well, I guess I get to be the first to congratulate you."

"No, we all did it together—it was a definite team effort," Mike said.

"Oh, I agree! We *all* deserve credit and *a lot* of it! I wasn't thinking of the capture. I want to be the first to congratulate you on making lieutenant. According to my watch, you've been a lieutenant for almost three hours." Mike was astonished. He'd completely forgotten about this major event in his life.

Friday, 4:00 a.m., Miami

Flynn heard Megan climbing the ladder to the flying bridge. In the light of a half moon, he could see she was dressed in jeans and a light jacket. Her hair had been pulled back in a ponytail. Even in the near dark, she looked wonderful.

"Since I didn't hear any signal, I assume we're all still safe?" she asked as she sat next to him.

"Nothing but these damn mosquitoes have come near us."

She produced a thermos. "I made some fresh coffee. Care for a cup?"

"Thanks, but I think I need some sleep more than coffee." He watched as she poured for herself, the aroma filling the air.

"So, have you reached any conclusions yet about who's after our asses?" she asked.

"It's the same as it was when you turned in. Someone at the hall of records or someone within your department. I've decided we're on the right track though. The more I think about this, the more convinced I am we're up against a major drug operator. The question now is how do we prove it, and how do I link him to Blakemore's murder?"

"Can we go to the DEA?"

"We could, but I'd lose him for the murder case. Besides, we can't prove anything about the drug business yet. All we've got is a lot of pretty wild speculation. No proof."

"So, we're back to square one. Back to investigating Mazzicone."

"Megan, is there anyone in your Department you'd bet your life on? Someone who'd help you from the inside without anybody else knowing?"

Megan considered the question before she answered. "I can't really say. I've never been in a position quite like this before."

"Well if you think of someone, he or she has to be small potatoes. The higher the rank, the more attention is drawn to a request for information. We need somebody who can freely look at files, make phone calls, check records, and things like that without anybody being any the wiser."

"Speaking of small potatoes, Cindy Small just might fit the description. I'm not joking. That's her name."

"Why Cindy?"

"Cindy *works* in Personnel and Records. She's a sergeant. We were in the academy together. She's very efficient and a great organizer—that's why they made her number two in the branch. She's a buzz saw when it comes to everything being complete and in place. Nobody, but nobody will buck her. I don't think anybody would be suspicious if she checked a file."

"Is she independent, or does she brown-nose? Does she have a political protector, you know, a rabbi? Are the two of you good friends—the kind you could ask this sort of favor, and if she refuses, would she blow the whistle on you?"

"I don't know. Let me think this over on my watch. Maybe I can have some answers for you in the morning."

"Sounds like a plan. Megan, can we talk?"

"That sounds ominous. Sure, shoot."

"Tell me about your dad."

Megan thought for a few seconds before answering, "What do you want to know?'

"What kind of a man was he? Where'd he come from? For that matter, where'd all your money come from?"

"Well, my Pop was the greatest man who ever walked the earth! Originally, he came from a well-to-do manufacturing family in Chicago. Graduated Northwestern University. During the War—that's the Second World War—he served in the navy. He rose to be a full commander as the war ended. He skippered a destroyer in the Pacific. He fought his ship alongside Halsey and Spruance for most of the war. Thought Spruance was the smartest fellow he'd ever come across. When *The Indianapolis* went down at the end of the war–she was Spruance's flagship– well, the heart just kinda went out of Dad's zeal."

"Oh? How come?"

"What the navy did to the skipper of *The Indianapolis* soured him on the navy and when his points had accumulated, he just packed his sea bag and, as he put it, 'Went over the side' and out of the navy."

"Did you know we have a national memorial to *The Indianapolis* back home?"

"No–! Pop would have loved that."

"You're not old enough to know all this history."

"Dad thought it was his duty to pass along his history to me–his only child. Anyway, getting back to Pop, when the war ended, he went back home to Chicago and into the family business. But a year or so after he got back, his father passed away. Pop hated the manufacturing business, so he sold the business for a huge chunk of cash and stock to a big New York outfit. He moved down here to Florida, met my mother, got married–and here I am!"

"That explains a lot. Tell me about the restaurant and this magnificent boat."

"Well, Pop bought the restaurant for Mom and me. I was sort of an afterthought, a real surprise, to hear Mom tell it. Anyway, Mom always wanted to be in the restaurant business. Dad wasn't really interested. He missed the sea. Anyway, the day after Mom told him she was pregnant, he drove himself over to Sarasota, sat down with the bigwigs at Chris-Craft over there, and ordered *The Lady Grace*. Claimed he paid cash on the spot. This boat is almost two years younger than I am!"

"Thanks. You didn't have to tell me all this. I appreciate it." "I know. But I'd like to know why all of a sudden you felt you needed to know all about me and my family."

"Well, it got kinda serious between Neil and me today. He's a good, straight-to-the-point kind of kid. While I was sitting up here tonight, I had time to do a lot of real soul searching and thinking. He gave me a lot to think about."

"Care to share with me?" she asked.

"Well, much as I'm tempted–I rather got the impression he wanted the conversation to be just between him and me–for now anyway."

"And you'll let me know what's to come from all this?"

"Oh, sure! Okay. Now, where do I sleep?"

"I'd appreciate it if you'd take my place in the main stateroom aft with Neil. If something should happen, I'd like you to be there with him. Would you mind?"

"Not at all. Is it proper for the captain to give her first mate a good night kiss?"

"I don't know how proper it is, but this captain will do so with great pleasure." They embraced and joined in a lingering, passionate kiss.

As they stood apart, Flynn touched her cheek with his finger tips. "Proper or not, I'm in love with this captain," he said as he stroked her cheek.

Megan smiled her answer. "I think you'd better get below."

Flynn entered the dark stateroom. Faint moonlight filtered through the large, oblong, port holes, enough that he could make out Neil's sleeping form on the large, king-sized bed. Flynn slipped off his deck shoes and sat carefully on the edge of the bed. No point in getting undressed, he thought to himself as he carefully stretched out next to Neil. Silence filled the stateroom as he prepared to let go of the thoughts, which had been tormenting him for the past several hours. Neil's voice startled him by its unexpected presence.

"Mr. Flynn, are we in trouble?" he asked in a stage whisper.

Flynn thought about his answer. He lowered his voice to a whisper. "We could be. What did your mother tell you?"

"Oh, Mom always treats me like a kid. She says everything is fine and all that. But I'm not dumb. I know we're out here because something bad has happened."

"Neil, I'll level with you—but this has to remain between the two of us. Agreed?"

"As far as I can tell, you've kept your promise to keep our last talk private, so I'll do the same," Neil promised.

"Some *very* bad, *very* dangerous men are after me, and because of me and what I came down here to investigate, they might be after your mom too. We're out here on the boat because your mom thinks this is the safest place to be for now."

"After you called tonight, mom really came unglued. Can't you tell me what happened tonight?"

Flynn sat up in the bed and pulled his knees toward his chest, wrapping his arms around his legs. Continuing in his best stage whisper, "Okay, I'll tell you." He told the boy the entire story from Blakemore's death to the attack on him in the car. He didn't name Santini or Mazzicone.

Neil sat up too, mimicking Flynn's own posture. He turned to look Flynn squarely in the face as he asked what was now his burning question, "If you marry my mom, will you take me to the 500?"

The sudden non sequitur threw Flynn for a loop. "Well, I don't see why not. I have a request for you."

"Sure. What is it?"

"Well, if I marry your mom, and I'm not saying I will– we haven't talked about it–nothing is definite yet. Will you teach me all about the ocean and fishing and boats?"

"Oh, I'd like to do that. Will you stay here after you catch these men?"

"I can't. I have to go back home. There's a killer up in Indianapolis, who's a part of what I'm down here for. If we catch him, I'll have to be there for that case. Then there's my daughter, Monica. She's getting married in June. There's a lot of things I'd have to do before I could come back ."

"Mr. Flynn, are you scared?"

"Yes, a little, and please, call me Denny."

Neil moved closer. Flynn saw a tear stained cheek glisten in the moonlight. "Neil, why have you been crying?" he asked in a gentle voice.

" 'Cause I'm scared, and 'cause I don't want you to go away. I know I shouldn't cry, but I can't help it. My buddies all say men don't cry."

"Neil, your buddies are dead wrong. Men, *real* men, do cry because they know who they are. Why, I've seen great big policemen cry like babies!"

"Gee–you have! Really?" Neil's voice was filled with awe but tinged with some suspicion.

"Oh, sure. We've got this motorcycle drill team back home. They're all men from the traffic division–have you watched our 500 parade on television?"

"Oh, sure, we watch it every year."

"Well,you know those policemen on motorcycles that lead off the parade? The ones that spell out Indianapolis?"

"Yeah."

"Those guys are some of the toughest men on the whole police department. Well, every year, they throw a party out at Riley Children's Hospital for all the kids there. They bring presents, and then, they put on a show, a demonstration with their motorcycles–just for those crippled kids. Some kids are too sick to get out of bed, so they go see them right at their beds. Some of those poor kids are so beautiful, and so sick, that it makes those policemen cry. And you know what?"

"What?"

"They're not at all ashamed of it! So don't you ever let anybody tell you men don't cry. Now, we'd better get some sleep or we won't be any use to your mom in the morning."

Friday, 8:00 a.m., Indianapolis

The promotion ceremony had been brief and to the point. With Monica looking proudly on, Mike was officially promoted to lieutenant along with four other men. The chief

244

congratulated each man and his family on this major career achievement and then, steered them into his conference room for coffee and rolls. Amid the hub-hub of excited voices and congratulations, Mike took Monica aside and handed her the letter written by O'Halleran and addressed to the head of her law firm.

"The chief hopes this will square things with your boss–keep you out of trouble. Now, there's one last thing I need for you to do if you're up to it?"

"Just ask."

"Will you come up to the interrogation rooms and see if you can identify this guy?"

"Let's go!"

Moments later, they were in the hallway outside the interrogation rooms. Mike stopped outside the door to the observation room next to the room in which the suspect sat, shackled to the table. "There's a one-way mirror so you can see him, but he can't see you. Sam is in there with him now."

Mike opened the door and ushered Monica into a small, semi-dark, room. A large tape recorder, its reels turning very slowly, and mounted on a tripod, a digital television camera, with its red light recording indicator burned steadily indicating it was recording. The camera was aimed through the one-way window. Monica immediately grasped the fact that every sight and sound in that interrogation room was being duly recorded. Mike steered her to the window. Speaking just above a whisper, he said, "Now, take a good look. Tell me, is that the same man you saw on the elevator and later at the mall? Don't worry, like I said, he can't see or hear you."

Monica approached the window. Facing the prisoner, Sam Elberger sat his back to the one-way window. A gray metal table of about four by three feet separated the two men. Cutshaw sat facing the window. Cutshaw's body language clearly showing a defiant attitude. He sat with his back pressed firmly against the chair and his arms folded across his chest. Monica was startled when he shifted his eyes from the detective to the window. It was as though he could see her standing there. Monica shuddered involuntarily.

"That's the man! Except for the shorter and lighter hair, it's him. See—he even has that thing at the side of his nose."

"Is this the same man who shot John Green?" Mike asked.

"I'm pretty certain, I only got a glimpse of him when he stood up to take another shot." She studied the man intently for several seconds. "Yes. I'm sure it is."

"I need you to dictate a statement to Julie. She'll lead you through the technicalities. Then, you can get back to your job. I hope you don't mind, but I have to stay here and keep on top of the situation. I'd like us to have dinner tonight if I can get away."

Monica allowed herself to smile. "I'll call you from work before I leave. We'll have dinner at my house. Something special to celebrate your promotion," she said.

"It's a date! Now, let me get you back down the hall to Julie."

Everything in the Civic and from the motel room had been brought to the Ident Office. Lieutenant Holland and Bryan Lynch were still examining and cataloging each item. Holland looked up from his work as Mike entered the room.

"Mike, congratulations on the promotion–and on this scum bag's capture." He shook Mike's hand. "That idea to gas the bastard was inspired!"

"Julie gets the credit. It was her idea. Doc Nichols gets the credit for pulling it off. Couldn't have done it without his help! So, tell me, what have we got so far?"

Chuck picked up a large, clear, plastic evidence bag. It resembled a rather hefty, commercial freezer bag. Written in black marker on the surface of the bag was a series of letters and numbers. These were an all-important link in the chain of custody. Sealed inside the bag was a fair-sized, folded, survival knife. Chuck began to describe the knife. "Here, we have a five-inch, Kershaw Blackhawk, model 1060, folding, buck-type knife. That means it locks in the open position until you press this release lever. Stainless steel. Made in Japan. Notice the rubber handle with the finger grips. This affords the user a lot of control and leverage. I think we can safely say this was at least used on both victims. The blade has been honed to an extremely fine edge!" He picked up a second similarly marked plastic bag. "Now *this*, this is the *piece de resistance!* Inside this rolled-up, velvet bag is a set of surgical knife handles with blades and spare blades of various sizes and uses. This is what did the work."

"Have you run tests on any of this yet?" Mike asked.

"No, we're still cataloging. But I have several other items, which ought to interest you." He selected another plastic bag. "Here, we have eight credit cards. All made out in different names." He tossed the bag back onto the table and selected another. "Here are no less than six operators' licenses. All made out to the names on the credit cards." He tossed the plastic bag back onto the pile. With a flourish, he ceremoniously selected another from the pile. "Now here, we have a possible gold mine. This is a telephone and address book with something like a diary or a journal. Every entry is in some kind of code. The only thing I can make out are the familiar seven digits for phone numbers and the dates he's written in that part. I'm guessing it's a personal diary."

Mike was smiling in spite of himself. The potential for making the case stick just kept elevating. "This is all great stuff! Is it too much to hope there's more?" he asked.

"Just this!" Chuck tossed a covering aside to reveal his icing on the cake. "A twenty-two automatic complete with a homemade silencer, about a pound and a half of plastic explosive, and this very interesting object," he said as he sorted through the plastic evidence bags until he found the one he was looking for. He held it up for Mike's view. "This rather interesting theatrical mustache!" Chuck's grin was a delight to see.

"God! I can't believe the luck! Do you realize with all this, we've got him for Blakemore and the girl, the car bombing, and the attempt on John Green's life?" Mike was overjoyed.

Bryan Lynch joined the conversation. "The prosecutor is gonna wet his pants over this one. You hand him all this, he'll see high political office in his future! I mean, just imagine the publicity!" Lynch said. His views on the smarmy, pompous prosecutor were well known—and in truth, held by most of the department's detectives.

"Well, let him have it. I'm not running for anything. May I have the address book? I think we need to get started on that code," Mike said.

"No, I can't give you the book. However, I will have a Xerox copy on your desk before quitting time. Chain of custody, you know? "

Mike thanked Chuck and Bryan for their excellent work and returned to the interrogation room. He unlocked the door, stuck his head in the room, and asked Sam Elberger to join him in the hall. Together, they went into the adjoining observation room. The prisoner sat calmly awaiting developments. "So, what have you gotten out of him?" Mike asked.

"Absolutely nothing! The man hasn't opened his mouth since we went in there an hour ago."

"He hasn't even asked for a lawyer?"

"Hasn't made a goddamn sound since I woke him up to read him his rights."

"Has he reacted to his real name?" Mike asked.

"I thought I caught a reaction in the eyes when I used it, but I'll have to review the videotape to be sure."

"Let's get a couple of mugs of hot coffee and get back in there. I wanna play a head game with him; just follow my lead." Mike led the way to the coffee pot. Minutes later, they were back in the room with the suspect, two steaming mugs of coffee at their elbows on the table. Mike noticed the man let his eyes wander toward the coffee, but he quickly regained control and looked away, his face a stone mask. For several moments, Mike stared into the man's eyes. Cutshaw didn't look away.

At length Mike spoke, "Well, well, well. Albert Thomas Cutshaw of Los Angeles, welcome to Indianapolis! You know why you're here, of course? How did we capture you? Well, for now, I'm going to keep that a secret, but I thought you'd like to know we've got the knives you used to murder Blakemore and that beautiful, young girl. You know," Mike lied, "our crime lab has this new high-tech device they tell me can detect blood molecules imbedded in metal. I figure, with any luck at all, they'll find enough for good DNA evidence. No question–the knives are yours. Can't fight that one, can you? I'll bet we'll prove those were the very same knives you used to murder those two," Mike said, watching for any reaction from the man. He saw none. "And we've recovered about a pound or so of plastic explosive, which it turns out was also in your possession. I am quite sure we can chemically prove it was the same explosive used to blow up a red, Mustang convertible driven by a perfectly innocent girl–and kill four other innocent people in the process. And we have your twenty-two automatic with your prints all over it. I'm certain we can prove it was used to shoot John Green. Bet you didn't know that big, black man was a retired police lieutenant, did you?"

The killer sat in stony silence. Mike took a sip of his coffee and leaned across the table, looking the killer directly in the eyes. His voice was low and carried in it a deadly menace when he spoke. "We've got you by the balls! You're not in here to make a confession. Hell, we don't need one! Because we have an eye witness who puts you at the apartment building at the time of the murders. I've got you dead bang on those. Indiana is one of those 'backward states' that still executes folks in the electric chair. Did you know that? Of course, you can opt for the shot in the arm if you want." The prisoner squirmed for the first time but maintained his silence.

Mike leaned back in his chair. This time when he spoke, his voice was in a normal, conversational tone. "No, you're history– what is it the kids say today? Toast? That's it. You're toast! All I want to know now is who paid you to come here all the way from Los Angeles. I'd like to know what Blakemore did to get himself dead like that with his dick and balls cut off. And that poor girl–did you know she was only twenty? What kind of a sicko cuts up a girl like that? You know, the jury will see color enlargements and color video of these two unfortunates. Shouldn't take them any time at all to return a 'guilty' verdict. Nope! This is a slam dunk for the prosecutor. You're gonna fry for sure. But now, if you'd cooperate with me, I think the prosecutor might be persuaded to recommend life instead of the chair or lethal injection. So, the question is–Who hired you?" Cutshaw maintained his silence.

Mike took another sip of his coffee. It was time to play his trump cards and to see what developed. "Cutshaw, does the name Santini, Mario Santini, mean anything to you?" Mike saw Cutshaw's eyes widen slightly and then, recover. Score! Mike played his second card. "What about The Andrews Development Group out of Los Angeles?" Again, the killer's eyes reacted. Time to play the third and final card– the book. "I've got your book. You know–the coded one," Mike said.

Cutshaw's face drained of some of its color, but still, he said nothing. Mike continued, "You know, I'll bet we'll learn a lot from that little book, once we get it decoded. I've got some friends who know all about codes. Some former Green Beret types. I'm betting they can break your code. It's what they do— code breaking." Cutshaw's breath became constricted. He looked as though he might faint. Still his lips remained sealed. Mike decided it was time to let the man's own mind apply the pressure. "Well, I'll be going now. Sam, return him to his cell. Cutshaw, if you decide to cooperate, just let the turnkey know, and I'll come up to see you."

12:45 p.m.

Chief O'Halleran was on the phone to Miami. There was no answer at Flynn's hotel room, and now, he was attempting to reach the chief of police. The chief's secretary told him her boss was out of the office, but Deputy Chief Alvero was in. O'Halleran said he'd speak with Alvero. Moments later, Alvero's smooth voice answered, "Chief O'Halleran, this is Deputy Chief Alvero. What can I do for you?"

"Actually, Chief Alvero, I'm trying to reach my head of Homicide, Captain Dennis Flynn. I have some great news for him. Do you know how I can reach him?"

"No. I haven't seen Captain Flynn for two or three days now. He's working with one of my people, Detective Sergeant Megan Madigan. I can see to it he gets a message."

"Okay. Tell Denny we've caught our killer. Monica is out of danger. The guy is alive and in the lockup right now. The prosecutor will be filing charges later today." Quickly, Alvero wrote the message on a notepad.

"Will Captain Flynn want to know who the suspect is?" Alvero asked.

"I doubt it, but you can tell him the guy's name is Cutshaw, Thomas Albert Cutshaw–from Los Angeles." Alvero carefully wrote the name.

"Chief, I'll certainly see to it Captain Flynn gets this message, and congratulations on the arrest."

Deputy Chief Alvero pulled the message page from his note pad, stuck it in his pocket, and informed his secretary over the intercom he'd be out of the office for a few minutes. Three minutes later, he was in the telephone booth in the corner drug store, waiting for a phone to be answered in Los Angeles.

Saturday, 8:30 a.m., Miami

Flynn awoke with Neil snuggled at his side. Bright sunshine poured through the portholes, and only the gentle snoring of the boy interfered with the sound of gently slapping water on the boat's sides. A few minutes later, following a quick shower and a shave, he went up to the main salon.

Over a hearty breakfast of sausage, eggs, and cottage fries, they got down to business. At Neil's urging, Megan reluctantly admitted the fix they were in and how she and Denny were trying to avoid trouble while they worked to find out all they could about this man called either Santini or Mazzicone. Neil asked to help. It was decided that he could be lookout while the two adults made plans. When breakfast was finished, Neil took his post on the flying bridge while Megan and Denny washed the dishes and made plans.

Flynn wanted to check on Monica and John Green, and he was also well aware he needed to report in with his chief, to let O'Halleran know of the events of last night–the attempt on his life. Megan handed him her cell phone. Flynn waited patiently while the unpublished, private phone rang several times back in Indianapolis. Finally, O'Halleran answered.

"Chief, it's me, Denny."

"Oh, good, you got the message. What do you think of our boy, Mike, now?" the chief asked as his voice filled with satisfaction. Flynn was puzzled.

"I'm sorry—I don't understand. What are you talking about? I didn't get any message."

"Well, I called and spoke with a deputy chief named Alvero about one o'clock yesterday afternoon. Oh, never mind that. We've got Blakemore's killer in our lockup right now!"

Flynn was elated. "Tell me everything!" It took O'Halleran several minutes to tell the complete story. Flynn interrupted several times with questions. He then filled in the chief about his own predicament and his belief that Mazzicone/Santini had not only contracted for Blakemore's murder but was also a big drug importer in Miami. Flynn felt it would be important to complete his investigations and to find the connection between Blakemore and Santini/Mazzicone here in Miami. He ended his conversation by giving the chief the number for Megan's cell phone with the admonition the number and his whereabouts be a very closely held secret.

They sat facing each other across the galley table. Flynn asked the question he'd been considering for several minutes. "Megan, have you come up with an inside contact yet?"

"I still think the safest bet is Cindy Small in Personnel and Records."

"And you believe she can be trusted with our lives because that's what we're talking about here."

Megan thought for a moment. "Yes."

"Okay, how do you plan to make the approach?"

"I think I can just phone her and arrange to meet someplace safe."

"Okay, let's get to it," Flynn said as he passed the cell telephone across the table.

Saturday, 11:30 a.m., Indianapolis

Mike was seated with two U.S. Army Officers in a private room in the former base Officers' Club, now an open to anybody restaurant. With President Clinton's decimation of the U.S. military, Fort Benjamin Harrison, the major U.S. Army finance center and home of the multi-service defense information center, had been put on the market. Now, it was a quasi military-civilian entity. Major Ted Couch and Lieutenant Colonel Robert Heath were examining the Xerox copy of the killer's coded journal.

"This does look very much like one of the codes the special forces first used in Nam. There are some differences here, but I'd bet the old code is the basis," Colonel Heath said to his colleague.

"I agree. There's a good chance it's the same basic code, but it will take some time to run it through a computer to be certain," Major Couch offered.

"Do you have the computers here to do this?" Mike asked.

Colonel Heath laughed. "Even though we look like a jack-leg civilian lash-up, we've still got some of the army's best and most powerful computers right here. I'll have to requisition a program from DOD to make the test and translation."

"Who do we have to see to get that done?" Mike asked.

"You give me something in writing from your chief of police, and I'll make the request myself. If DOD approves, the program can be sent from their computers to our computers in milliseconds."

"Please, will you do it?" Mike pled.

The colonel looked Mike squarely in the eyes. "You say this is critical evidence in a murder case?"

"Several murders actually. And it may involve a very major drug dealer as well."

"Can you leave this with us?" the Major asked.

"It's a Xerox of the original. Keep it."

"Get me that letter!"

"I'll have a uniform car hand deliver it to you inside of an hour!" Mike said as he speed dialed the chief's private number on his cell phone.

Saturday, 12:45 p.m., Miami

Flynn and Neil steadied the small outboard at the stern of the big cruiser as Megan stepped out of the boat and onto the deck of *The Lady Grace.* "Well, don't keep me in suspense," Flynn said as he tied the boat to a stern cleat. "Tell me all about your meeting."

Smiling, Megan said, "Cindy has agreed to help."

"Good. Now, tell me exactly what she agreed to do."

"First of all, she'll do a computer search of Records to see if we have anything on either Santini or Mazzicone. Then, if we do, she will check to see who, if anybody, pulled any record on this guy. She's going to do a similar search of boat, aircraft, and auto registrations for Dade County and cross check them for a Santini/Mazzicone ownership. And she's agreed to be our contact inside the department."

"Did the two of you work out a cover for this little operation?"

"Well, not a cover as such. Don't forget she has daily access to just about any department record. So, she doesn't need a cover. As for communicating with us, I gave her my cell phone number."

"Good, I guess that will work. Now, what about checking into the arrivals at the airport? Did she think there was a way to give us any advance warning if Santini or Mazzicone has booked himself into Miami?"

"That one has her stumped for now. She couldn't think of how to go about it. All that information is in reservations computers the airlines use. She promised to let me know if she thought of a way to access those. She'll be calling me between seven and eight tonight for an update on everything."

"So, we just sit tight until then?" Flynn asked.

"More or less. Let's get the boat back aboard and take another trip up the Waterway. I think we ought to have another look at the Santini/Mazzicone place."

3:30 p.m., Indianapolis

Julie came into Flynn's office with a business card in hand. "Lieutenant, there's a lawyer out here. Says he's been retained to represent Cutshaw. Wants to see his client."

Mike reached out and took the card. J. Robert Richmond, Attorney–at–Law, Las Vegas, Nevada. Mike's eyebrows raised in surprise. "Show the man in, Julie. Give me a few minutes with him before we set things up with Cutshaw." The lawyer extended his hand as he entered the office.

"Captain Flynn?" the lawyer asked.

"No. I'm Lieutenant Gaffney," Mike said, standing to shake the lawyer's hand. "Captain Flynn is out of town at the moment. Please, take a seat." Mike watched the man take the seat nearest the desk. From his demeanor, it was obvious he'd spent a lot of time in police agencies and wasn't in the least uncomfortable. Mike took his seat behind Flynn's desk.

"Lieutenant, I'd like to see my client as soon as possible," the attorney began.

"And that would be?"

"A.T. Cutshaw," the lawyer sighed.

"Oh, yes. You understand he hasn't been arraigned yet?"

"No, I wasn't aware. When will that take place?"

"First thing Monday morning." Mike consulted the man's business card. "Mind if I ask you a question, Mr. Richmond?"

"Surely." The attorney flashed a smile, confidence oozing from every pore.

"Since, to my certain knowledge, Cutshaw hasn't requested the use of a phone and hasn't uttered a sound since we took him into custody, I'd like to know how the hell he managed to retain you to represent him?"

"I'm afraid you'd have to ask my secretary about that. I am only aware my office received a call just a few hours ago–I was in court at the time. Well, the long and the short of it is, I've been retained, and I'm here."

"Airline service between Las Vegas and Indianapolis must be pretty good."

"I flew in on the firm's private jet."

" I see. And, if I may, have you represented Cutshaw before?" Mike asked.

"No—and detective, even if I had, it isn't any of your business. Really, I must insist on seeing my client—now, if you please."

"I'll have him brought down right now," Mike said, reaching for the phone.

"Lieutenant, while you're doing that, may I see the charges you plan to place against my client?"

Mike reached inside a leather document folder, extracted a copy of the formal charges, and handed it across the desk. He watched the lawyer read the stilted legal verbiage as he dialed the intercom number for Sam Elberger. When Sam answered, Mike instructed him to bring Cutshaw down to the lawyers' conference room. Strangely, the lawyer's only reaction had been a pursing of his lips as he read the charge sheet. Mike waited until he'd finished reading before asking his next question. "Why all the way from Las Vegas, Mr. Richmond?" Mike asked.

"I'm a member of the Indiana Bar, Lieutenant. There'll be no problem."

"I wasn't asking about a problem. I want to know why you came all the way from Las Vegas."

"Well, I suppose because that's where my office is, Lieutenant." Richmond stood and retrieved his alligator case. "Now, if you'd be so kind as to take me to my client–"

Mike knew he'd been bested by an experienced fighter. "If you will just follow me, I'll take you to your client," he said as he stood to lead the way.

As they walked toward the conference room, Richmond asked if Indianapolis had a really good hotel. Mike recommended the Canterbury on South Illinois Street, knowing it would make a sizable dent in the lawyer's wallet. The mere thought of it made Mike feel a little better.

They reached the door to the private consultation room. Mike opened the door, which could only be opened from the outside. Cutshaw was already seated at the metal table, his left wrist shackled to the table. He fixed his unblinking eyes on Mike. Richmond leaned forward to look into the room to see his client. Pulling back, he addressed Mike. "I assume we will have complete privacy?" he asked.

"You have my word. The room isn't wired, bugged, or videoed. We may seem like small-time cops to you, Mr. Richmond, but I assure you, we observe all the constitutional rules."

Richmond flashed an ingratiating smile. "Please–no offense intended. Might we have Mr. Cutshaw's shackles removed?"

"No. We won't do that. It's for your safety as well as ours. There's a bell push on the wall next to the door. Just press it when you've finished. There is one last formality. I'll have to check you for any weapons, so if you will just hand me your case first–" The lawyer bristled a bit but handed over the elegant briefcase. Mike zipped it open and observed a mini tape recorder and a legal pad. He zipped the case closed and handed it back. "Now, if you'd just raise your arms," he said.

"Now see here!" Richmond exploded.

"I'm afraid, if you don't let me check, you won't see your client," Mike warned. Richmond's eyes showed anger and defiance, but he submitted, raising his arms. Mike slipped his hands inside the man's coat and checked his rib area, small of the back, and belt line for weapons. He did a quick check of the suit pockets, inside and out, finding a pocket secretary and two gold pens. He noticed the suit bore an English tailor's label–meaning the man came more expensively than he'd previously estimated. He then checked the attorney's legs and ankles. He didn't really expect to find anything but took perverse pleasure in the discomfort he was causing the attorney. "Well, you're clean. Remember now, just push the bell button when you're ready to go. Someone will come let you out." Mike waited in the hall as the lawyer entered the room and pulled the door closed. Mike returned to his office, reminding himself to have somebody run a registration check on a private jet, which had just arrived from Las Vegas. Ownership might provide one more lead to Santini.

5:45 p.m., Miami

The big cruiser was riding at anchor just a little over seventy yards upstream of the walled compound. With the turning tide, the stern swung downstream. For the better part of two hours since anchoring, Flynn, Megan ,and Neil had acted the part of a family, swimming and playing in the late afternoon sun. Throughout the afternoon, Flynn caught himself gazing at Megan. Thoughts of a romantic and yes, even of a sexual nature occupied his mind. He hadn't experienced anything like this in the many years since Mary died! There was a moment when Megan's eyes locked with his, and he knew he'd been found out. Feeling like a foolish school boy, Flynn blushed and averted his gaze. But it *was* like family. And Flynn knew how very much he wanted a family about him again. Like the school boy, he began to fantasize a family built around Megan and Neil. Then the fear struck again. Would they even entertain the thought he could fill the void in their lives as well? He wasn't prepared to pursue the answer—just yet.

Shortly after they dropped anchor that afternoon, Megan noticed two young men stroll out on the boathouse roof overlooking the waterway. The two took seats on the patio chairs, smoked cigarettes, and watched while the "family" swam and played. After about twenty minutes, the men appeared to lose interest and returned to the house. Megan brought out a portable charcoal grill and set it up at the stern rail. Within a half hour, Flynn was tending three thick, New York-strip steaks. The smoke and odor of roasting meat carried toward the walled compound.

Flynn thought it a perfect cover for their little operation. He was happier than he'd been in years. The killer was behind bars, and Monica was now out of danger. Flynn relaxed. He let his thoughts run once more where they would. He allowed himself to make a mental summary of his life and a possible future one. Monica was leaving the nest for her own separate life with Mike in just a matter of months. He'd be all alone in that two story house. The sudden realization of his impending solitary life shocked Flynn.

Thoughts of Megan and her son pushed forward again. Dare he let himself consider proposing marriage to this beautiful woman and adopting Neil? After several moments, he became aware he was staring unconsciously into space. Wrenched himself back to the present, he looked around. Neil was seated as near to Flynn as he could get on the stern cushions, a beach towel draped over his shoulders, reading the gift book Flynn had given him on the Indy 500. Megan was down in the galley preparing the rest of the meal. Flynn's peace was shattered as the cell phone trilled for attention. Megan answered. It was Cindy Small.

"I know I'm calling early, but I have some information that might be important," Cindy began.

"No problem, go right ahead," Megan responded.

"I asked a favor of a friend up in Tallahassee, in the secretary of state's office. That's where the corporations have to list all the owners and officers and file a report each year. She did a computer sort using the names Santini and Mazzicone. Her computer spat out a corporation called the South Florida Currency Exchange, LLC. Mazzicone is listed as the Chairman and C.E.O. I took this corporation and did a computer run looking for any vehicle and aircraft registrations. Matter of fact, I checked for anything the outfit owned. Hit pay dirt! There's a Lear 25 and a Bell Jet Ranger registered to the South Florida Currency Exchange. Both of these aircraft are kept out at Miami International, and they're registered here. I called the Miami Flight Service Center, and they told me the Lear filed a flight plan for Los Angeles and departed at noon today. It's a round trip flight plan. According to the flight plan, the Lear is due back here around eleven tomorrow morning."

"Anything else?"

"Well, just this. Deputy Chief Alvero has been asking around about you and that Captain Flynn from Indianapolis."

"What kind of asking?"

"Where you are, what are you up to, who you've been talking to. Looking for any file notes the two of you might have–"

"He's talked to you?"

"No. He sent one of the civilian secretaries down to pull files. She was complaining about all the extra work he'd given her."

"Cindy, this may seem off the wall, but do you know anybody you can trust to could keep an eye on the Lear when it returns? Tail whoever comes in on it?"

"Well, according to the information I have on the flight plan, it's due back around eleven a.m. tomorrow. I might just take an early lunch break and do it myself. How's that sound?"

"Great! The fewer people who know about this the better."

"No sweat! It'll be nice to get back on the street again. I'll call you, let you know what I found."

Megan called Flynn into the main cabin and briefed him on Cindy's report.

"Could it be our man is coming down here himself?" Flynn wondered.

"Cindy has volunteered to shadow whoever gets off that plane. The bad news is–according to Cindy, Deputy Chief Alvero has been asking questions about us, where we are, who we're talking with, what we're up to—even sent a secretary down to pull case files we might have looked into."

"Is this the sort of thing you would expect Alvero to be doing?"

"It is out of character for him—as far as I know. He's political as far as I can see. I mean, for a man with only ten years on the department, to make deputy chief– was well, nothing short of a miracle. He's connected. I figure if he's asking questions, somebody put him up to it."

"Do you think he's crooked?"

"I really don't know, but it wouldn't surprise me. Up till now, I hadn't given it any thought. You and I both know politics runs the upper levels of any PD. You can bet your ass Alvero's probably answerable to some politician—the guy who got him his job. I don't think it would be smart to attack Alvero head on. He'd win.. Let's concentrate on Santini or Mazzicone—whatever the hell his name is, and if Alvero falls in the net, so much the better. Besides, if Alvero is dirty, he's bound to have any number of people in the department working for him."

"A deputy chief in Santini's pocket! Damn! You realize what that could mean?" Flynn asked.

"It means we can't really trust anybody—maybe not even Cindy."

"She doesn't know where we are, does she?" Flynn asked.

"No. Nobody does. All Cindy has is my cell phone number."

"Well then, there's no point in worrying about that for now. I want to go over this underwater excursion you've got planned for tonight. I'm still not convinced it's smart, or that you'll be safe."

"Denny, we've been over this before– one final time. Since *you* don't know anything about scuba gear, I'm appointing myself the volunteer for this mission. End of discussion. We've got to know what's inside that boathouse. It looks like the only way in is underwater through the opening under the door if there is one. I go. You and Neil stay and keep up the show on the boat. And that, dear Denny, is that! Now, let's eat before those steaks are too cold to enjoy."

6:00 p.m., Indianapolis

Mike and Monica had just finished their special meal, celebrating Mike's promotion. Monica prepared his favorite; Alaskan King Crab legs with baked potatoes and white wine. They were washing the dishes when the telephone rang. Mike decided to pass up taking it on the kitchen phone. He went to the front room and took the call on the phone next to Denny's favorite chair, dropping into the chair as he lifted the receiver. "Hello," he said.

"Is this Sergeant Mike Gaffney?" a heavy male voice asked.

"It used to be. It's Lieutenant Gaffney now. Who am I speaking with?"

"Major Couch out at the Fort. I've got good news for you. We broke the code."

Mike's breath caught in his throat as his hopes leaped. "Thank God! I've been sweating bullets waiting to hear–I know this is a bit out of your experience, but can you give me some idea of what's in it?"

"Mike, if I was a cop, I'd be on my knees in church thanking God for that little book."

"Major, may I come pick up the translation tonight?" Mike asked, excitement building in his chest.

"I'd like to bring it to you. According to the woman who gave me this number, you're not all that far away from the Fort. May I bring it by? It'll save time, and I can explain some things about it."

Mike gave the major the address and directions for a shortcut between Fort Ben and Flynn's home.

"Great! I'll be there in about twenty minutes."

Mike returned to the kitchen and put his arms around Monica's slim waist. He leaned over her shoulder and whispered in her ear. "We're going to have company, so we'll have to put off that special dessert for a little while." Monica dropped her dish brush in the dishwater and spun in his arms. "No! This was to be our night!"

Mike raised his hands in a gesture of supplication, and then slipped then around Monica's waist. "That was Major Couch out at the Fort. They've broken Cutshaw's code! He's going to come by the house and drop off the translation in about twenty minutes. Should be here and gone in minutes. I promise we'll have dessert–just a little later. Okay?"

"Oh, Mike! I'm sorry. I was being selfish. That's wonderful news!"

"So, you won't mind too much if I ask him to have a celebratory drink with us?"

"No. Just as long as he doesn't stay very long."

7:30 p.m., Indianapolis,
The Canterbury Hotel, Suite 1204.

J. Robert Richmond, "J.R." to his many friends, was enjoying a pitcher of very dry martinis in his suite of rooms. He'd removed his tie, suit coat, vest, and shoes. He was seated in a leather recliner, his stocking feet up. The mini recorder lay on the elegant service table at his elbow. Cutshaw's voice, reduced to a tinny mockery of itself, issued from the two inch speaker. "I tell you they've got my insurance book!" Cutshaw said.

Richmond's own voice: "I don't understand–"

"Tell Santini the cops got my code book. It's my record of every hit. Every deal–every drug and laundry operation. Times, places, names, dates–the works. If he doesn't get me out of here, and quick–"

"You mean this book names Mario!?"

"Bet your ass!"

"Albert, that's just dumb! Stupid!"

At that point in the conversation, Cutshaw had pointed his finger in the fat attorney's face. "Don't call me Albert! Nobody calls me Albert. You just tell Santini what's happened. Tell him to get me the fuck out of here if he values his ass!"

"You said this is some sort of a–a journal. A diary written in code?"

"Yeah, my own personal code. It's a version of one the Special Forces used in Nam."

"Why on earth would you keep such a thing?"

"I'm damn good at what I do–probably better than anybody. I keep score. And I figure the book is protection–insurance."

"Insurance against what?"

"Against somebody putting out a contract on me."

Recovering from the shock of the revelation, the attorney tried to get to the problem he'd been sent to solve. "Let's talk about these charges for a minute. According to this, they've charged you for murdering Deputy Mayor Blakemore, a Jennifer Wick, for car bombing one Norma Tilson, a Herbert Jacobson, a Robert Samulson, and a Joseph Laughton. In addition, there's the matter of several forged credit cards, and the icing on the cake–the attempted murder of a retired police officer. Don't plan on walking out of here Monday morning on bail. With the possible exception of the attempt on the retired cop, all of these are premeditated, first degree charges."

"You just remind Santini I have the book, I'm sure he'll–" The phone at Richmond's elbow rang. The attorney switched the recorder off and reached for the phone.

"J.R.?" asked the voice at the other end.

"Yes–?"

"Mario. Fill me in. I take it you've seen and talked with Cutshaw?" Mario Santini's voice dripped quiet venom.

Richmond chose his words very carefully as he spent the next several minutes recounting the arrest and the charges to be placed against Cutshaw at the arraignment come Monday morning. He opined the man's chances for bail were nil. Santini became violently angry when he learned of Cutshaw's so-called insurance book and the fact it was now in the hands of the local police. "Do you think there's any chance you can get your hands on that book?" he asked.

"Forget it. They'll have it locked up with all the other evidence."

"What else do the cops have?"

"What *more* do they need?"

"No. I meant what other physical evidence do they hold. Anything from Blakemore?"

"Just what are we looking for here?'

"Any record of his contacts with me!"

"Well, I haven't had any discovery yet. So I'll not know anything about that until they allow me a list of evidence. You know how it works."

"Do we have any contacts inside the department?"

"I certainly wouldn't know that. Do you have someone in the organization out here I could contact?"

"Yes, I do, but the more I think about it, I don't think I want to get him involved. Cutshaw doesn't know about him. No. I think I want to keep him out of this unless it turns out I really need him to do a favor. Has anybody mentioned my name?"

"Only Cutshaw."

"What time is the arraignment Monday?"

"I'm told it will be first thing Monday morning–any time after ten a.m. I expect to see Cutshaw at least once more before then.

"Excellent! Tell Cutshaw you told me about the code book. Tell him I said I understood and that I will do what I can."

"I don't really think there's much anybody can do for Cutshaw," Richmond said.

"I'm aware of that! I haven't practiced law all these years without learning when a case is hopeless! I just want you to convince Cutshaw that if he keeps his mouth shut, I can get him off–maybe that hope will help him stay silent. Right now I've got another problem. There's a cop from Indianapolis in Miami snooping around. My inside man tells me he's looking into me and my business. He's down there to make a connection between Blakemore, the dead deputy mayor, and me."

"I'm afraid I can't help you there. Your name hasn't been mentioned by anybody here," Richmond told him.

Santini's voice dropped to a menacing whisper. "Look, I'm going to Miami in the morning. There's a big shipment of paste due in. I'll be there until Wednesday or Thursday. I want you to call me at the unlisted Miami number the minute the arraignment is over. In the meantime, go hold Cutshaw's hand and find out where they're going to hold him after the arraignment. I may have to send someone inside to make a hit."

9:30 p.m., Miami

The sun had long since set. The cruiser's auxiliary generator could be heard putting along like a muffled lawn mower. The cabin lights were all on as was the television set; curtains were drawn in all the cabins and the main salon. For somebody watching from the opposite bank from "Santini's place" as Flynn called it, only shadows could be seen as people walked about the salon. Megan, in a black scuba suit, was seated at the port rail, opposite the side of the boat facing the Santini property. She had already strapped on the diving belt, a flash light, and the scuba tank. She wet her face mask and slipped the swimming fins on her feet. Flynn kissed her and whispered an admonition to be careful as he assisted her over the side. Her entry into the water made no sound.

Megan tread water for a moment while she placed the mouthpiece between her teeth and lowered the face mask over her eyes and nose. She gave Flynn a thumbs up signal and quietly disappeared beneath the big cruiser. Flynn slipped back into the main salon and began pacing. He checked his watch for the umpteenth time; Megan would have forty minutes of air–an eternity! He was worried. Was he a coward, letting a woman do a job he knew he ought to be handling himself? Even though he knew absolutely nothing about scuba diving? The undeniable fact he was falling in love with this woman only made matters worse.

Megan held her breath for a good part of the distance to the boathouse wall, hoping to prevent any escaping bubbles from giving her away in the event somebody was watching. The water was dark and murky, making her progress toward the wall difficult. Just when she thought she had badly misjudged the distance, her hand brushed the concrete wall. She felt her way along the wall until she came to the overhead door opening. Then, switching on her flash light, she examined the entrance. From the bottom of the metal door, there was about a four foot space between the bottom of the garage-like door to a heavy mesh fence, which filled the rest of the opening from side to side and to the floor of the door opening.

She knew immediately there might not be enough room for her and the set of air tanks. She took several deep breaths of air, slipped out of the harness, closed the regulator valve, and carefully hooked the tanks on the fence. Taking the flashlight with her, she swam through the narrow space between the door and the fence. Once inside, she soundlessly broke the surface of the water.

The room was in total darkness. She could hear the gentle wash of the water and the echoing sounds of her own breathing bouncing off concrete walls. She raised the flashlight and switched it on. To her left was a cigarette boat, tied to the inside pier. She swam further in. Directly ahead was a steel door set in the far concrete wall, the tunnel entrance to the house. Megan swung the beam of light to the right. The beam of white light revealed a pier area on the opposite side. It was partitioned off by a full length, glass wall. Beyond the wall were large, long tables, several steel drums, and several yellow, plastic drums. She crossed to that side of the underground room to make a careful inspection of the glassed-in room. Climbing out of the water, she aimed the flashlight at the lamps above the table. A bank of what looked like infrared heat lamps were suspended over one end of the table, and along the wall hung several white coats and breathing apparatus masks. She took several minutes to memorize everything, and when she was satisfied she could remember it all, she returned to the entrance, swam outside, retrieved the tanks, and made her way back to the far side of the cruiser.

Flynn felt the boat rock slightly as Megan pulled herself up the portable ladder, which had been placed over the port side. Within seconds, she was in the main salon, stripping off the cumbersome equipment and the glistening wet suit. Flynn wrapped her in a large beach towel, handed her a brandy, and guided her to a seat on the big sofa. His eyes wide with curiosity, he waited while she took a sip of the brandy.

"Well, I think I understand what I saw. The cigarette boat was in there, but the strangest thing was what was on the other side of the boathouse. A glass walled-off work area, a room."

"Could you see into it?"

"Yes. I went over and took a good look. Thick glass from floor to ceiling."

"What was in the room?" Flynn asked.

"Looked like a drug processing plant to me. There were three big, long work-tables, several steel and plastic drums, infrared heat lamps, lab coats, and breathing apparatus like firemen use. Everything you'd need. It is a pretty big operation. That boathouse is a lot bigger than it looks from the outside. Inside, it's a good fifty feet wide and extends a long way underground back toward the house."

Flynn rose from the couch and began pacing, rubbing his chin and the back of his neck as he thought. "Could you sketch it?"

"Just give me a few minutes," Megan said as she moved to the galley table while Flynn scrounged up paper and a pencil. Using a book for a ruler, Megan began to draw what she had seen in the boathouse. Flynn asked questions as she worked. When she had finished, she presented the drawing to Flynn.

Flynn studied the drawing. "I think it's obvious Santini brings his drugs in on that boat and processes whatever it is he's bringing in right there in the boathouse." Flynn's voice began to rise with excitement.

"Where can we go, or who can we talk to and get answers?" Megan asked.

"I'd better call Vincent Daly, the DEA man down here. He's a disagreeable son-of-a-bitch, but I think he's honest. He'd want to take Santini for drugs–I might lose him for the murder case."

"Couldn't we just sort of feel him out before we give up Santini?" Megan asked.

"I met with Daly only once, and I gave him my word I'd turn over any drug dealers if we uncovered any. Isn't there anyone in you entire department we could turn to?"

"Outside of Cindy, I can't think of anyone I would trust– sorry."

"Well then–" Flynn was stopped short by the trilling ring of the cell telephone. Megan moved first and answered. A man's voice asked for Captain Flynn. Megan shrugged and handed the receiver to Flynn.

"Denny! It's me, Mike. Terrific news. You remember the coded notebook I told you about when we grabbed Cutshaw? Well, the guys out at Fort Ben ran the code through their computers for me and gave me a translation."

"That's great! Tell me about it," Flynn said–the problems of the moment forgotten.

"It's a record of every hit! Every trip he took and even what he was paid for each," Mike exclaimed, "and here's the best part. Seems a good part of it was contract work for your guy Santini!"

"Was the Blakemore contract in the book?" Flynn asked

"Yes!"

"Was there a reason listed for the hit?"

"No. Just the contract, when it was made, and for how much."

"So when did he make it?" Flynn asked.

"Contract was placed on Wednesday a week ago. Cutshaw flew into Indianapolis on Thursday and made the hit on Friday afternoon–two days before we found the bodies. It's the last entry in the book. There are some other tidbits of information though. It seems Cutshaw made several mule trips for an outfit called the South Florida Currency Exchange. Trips to Mexico City, the Bahamas, Switzerland, and Berlin. All for Santini."

"And Santini is definitely named in the book?"

"Yes. Several times. Sometimes just initials. There's another name I haven't seen before, a Dominic Mazzicone."

"Mike, Mazzicone and Santini are the same person. Anything more?"

"I haven't really studied the complete decoded book yet, so I don't really know. But one thing has me really puzzled. Cutshaw didn't speak with anyone or use the phone when we brought him in. But not a day went by before some high-priced lawyer from Las Vegas, no less, by the name of J.R. Richmond, shows up, claiming he represents Cutshaw. He says his office got a phone call asking him to take the case."

"Mike, do you remember that phone call you told me Cutshaw made to his own phone in L.A. from the motel where you grabbed him?"

"Yes."

"Probably a prearranged time sequence contact. You know, if you don't hear from me by such-and-such a time, I'll be in trouble. That sort of thing. I wouldn't worry too much about it. Just keep a close eye on that lawyer. When's the arraignment?"

"Ten, Monday, Judge Hollingsworth."

"Does the prosecutor see any problems?"

"Are you kidding? He has visions of running for governor when this is over!"

"What about the mayor? Is he off everybody's back?"

"Yes. The chief tells me the only thing worrying the mayor is the motive behind Blakemore's murder. He's still worried about getting dirt on his skirts."

"I'm afraid it still looks, to me anyway, like old Jack was hip deep in the drug business. We're pretty much on top of that situation at this end, right now. Mike, I need a favor. Would you agree Lieutenant Holland is an expert on the chemistry of the drug business?" Flynn asked.

"Definitely."

"Here's the favor then. Please, call him as soon as we finish this call. Give him this cell phone number, and ask him to call back immediately. Tell him not to give the number to anybody– not anybody. And don't you give it out either. Now, how's Monica?"

The last few minutes of the conversation were given over to family matters. Monica and her father had quite a spirited conversation. Megan could tell from Flynn's animation he was deeply fond of both his daughter and future son-in-law. When they'd finished, Flynn explained to Megan who Lieutenant Holland was and what an excellent forensics expert he was. He was saying good night to Neil when Chuck's return phone call came.

Megan answered the phone and called Dennis, who, upon hearing it was Lieutenant Holland, eagerly took the phone.

"Chuck!" Flynn exclaimed to his old friend, "I need your help on something important. Would you know a drug laboratory if you saw one?"

"Denny, that's a dumb question. What do you want to know anyway?"

"I need to know what a drug laboratory setup would look like. I think we may have uncovered one."

"Well, rather than me telling you what a drug lab looks like, why don't you tell me what you saw?"

"Not me. An officer down here–Detective Megan Madigan, she's the one I'm working with. She saw it. ."

"Is she there now?"

"Yes."

"Put her on." Flynn handed the receiver to Megan.

"This is Megan Madigan," she said.

"How do you do, Megan? I'm Chuck. Please, tell me what you saw, and how you saw it." Megan spent the next several minutes describing in detail the layout of the underground boathouse and answering Lieutenant Holland's probing questions.

"When you were in there, did you smell anything?" Chuck asked.

"Well, mostly the gasoline fumes from the boat. There was something else, only I didn't really pay attention at the time."

"Was it a sweet, sour, stringent, or rotten smell?"

"The gas fumes were pretty strong, but I'd have to say it was an unpleasant smell."

"By any chance, could it have been a little like rotten eggs?"

"Yes. Now that you mention it. It did smell a lot like rotten eggs."

"I think you found a coke operation. They'd need acetone, pool acid, and the heat lamps to convert cocoa leaf paste to pure coke crystals. That could explain the drums. They could contain the acetone. And the lamps are probably heat lamps. They're used to dry the finished powder. The face masks are to filter out the fine crystals of coke. There has to be some sort of ventilator system as well. Did you see anything like that?"

"There may well have been one. I don't remember seeing something like that."

"Okay, Megan, put Denny back on, will you?"

Flynn took the cell phone. "Yes?"

"Denny, now before you go off half-cocked, let me warn you about a couple of things. First off, if that place is a coke lab, it's more dangerous than you can possibly imagine—with all those stored chemicals, especially if they're using ether to speed up the drying, it could go up like a bomb! Secondly, you're way out of your depth, old friend, not to mention your jurisdiction—which in case you've forgotten, ended at the Marion County, Indiana, Line. Want to tell me how this fits in with our case back here?" Flynn told his good friend all he knew.

Chuck urged Flynn to turn the matter over to the DEA and get home—to be satisfied with what he had. Flynn adamantly held out for completing the case from his end.

By eleven-thirty, Flynn was in his lookout post on the flying bridge. The big cruiser lay in darkness except for the anchor lights. Megan had gone to bed, and Flynn sat watching, puffing on his pipe, and thinking of Santini/Mazzicone, wondering whether he'd made the correct decision—to continue looking into Santini.

6:45 a.m., Miami

Megan sat sipping hot, black coffee. To the east, a bright white ball of sun was raising majestically over the stately homes lining the waterway. Seagulls and the ubiquitous pelicans wheeled in the early morning sky, filling the air with their raucous calls and cries. At her elbow, the cell phone suddenly rang for attention. It was Cindy, excitement in her voice. "Listen, the jet just got in a few minutes ago. Now get this! Deputy-fuckin'-Chief Alvero met the plane! He gave the guy who got off a big manila envelope, big enough to hold files. They talked for a few minutes, then the guy from the plane got on a helicopter, and it took off about two minutes ago."

"Any idea who the guy on the plane was?" Megan asked.

"No. But I brought my camera with a Polaroid back and a long telephoto lens. I took about a dozen shots while they talked."

"Are you sure they couldn't see you?"

"I stayed in my car in the parking lot. I'm certain they never even thought to look for somebody watching."

"How soon can you get the pictures to me?" Megan asked.

"Probably have them to you by this evening. Gotta work my shift before I can come."

"Okay. Sounds like a plan. Now, what about the helicopter? Any idea where it's headed?"

"Sorry, I don't have a clue."

"Stay safe, Cindy. Call me if you learn anything, and I'll let you know how to get the pictures to me. I'm on the move. So, I'll call you. And thanks a million for putting your ass on the line for me," Megan said, ending the call.

Megan ran down the ladder to the aft stateroom to wake her two "men". She reached over and gently shook Flynn's bare right shoulder. His eyes snapped open.

Her voice was a hoarse whisper. "Time to get up. The jet came back from L.A. I think we've got trouble–Deputy Chief Alvero met the plane! Whoever he met is now in a helicopter, and I think it's just possible it's our man, Santini–if that's the case, I think that helo is headed here right now!" Megan said.

Flynn gently shook Neil until the boy awoke. "Neil," he said, "Time to get moving. Battle stations for all hands!"

Within minutes, plans had been made and were in effect. Flynn and the boy, dressed in their swim suits, made themselves conspicuous at the stern, setting up a table and deck chairs. Preparations for breakfast, should anybody be curious. Megan had gone to her concealed weapons locker and loaded her motor-driven Nikon with high-resolution color film and selected a 250 mm telephoto zoom lens. Her station was in the main salon, where she could photograph the expected arrival of the helicopter and its passengers through the large salon windows without being seen.

Flynn and the boy set the table in the bright, clear, early morning air. As they were making preparations for breakfast, three young men appeared on the boathouse roof and began to remove the patio furniture, setting it far to the side of the property. Flynn went to the galley and brought out milk and a box of cereal. He asked Neil to prepare bowls for both of them while he retrieved a pot of coffee and a mug for himself. He had just taken his seat at the table when the familiar "whapping" sound of a helicopter's rotary wing joined the noises of the seagulls and pelicans.

"It's okay to look; anybody would," he said to Neil. The Jet Ranger appeared over the trees, coming from the west. It swung out over the Santini property, made a 180 degree turn and began its descent. Just before touching down, the pilot rotated the craft 90 degrees, and within seconds, the Bell Jet Ranger settled on the boathouse roof, a short portion of the tail overhanging the railings and the waterway. The jet engine was switched off, and the rotor blade began to slow. One of the young men ran to the left rear door and opened it. A briefcase was passed out. Flynn watched with intense concentration.

From the main salon, he could hear the motor drive on Megan's Nikon make familiar click–whirring sounds as she took several shots in rapid succession. A man, dressed in a dark suit, stepped from the helicopter. He turned to take the briefcase back from the young man. Flynn instantly recognized the familiar face of Santini/Mazzicone! Santini turned and walked to the boathouse roof railing. He paused to look directly at Flynn and the boy. For a moment, Flynn was paralyzed, filled with panic. Neil saved the moment by raising his arm and giving Santini a big wave. Santini stared back for a moment and then, returned the wave. Saying something to the young man at his elbow, Santini turned and walked out of view toward the house, followed by the pilot and the three muscular, young men. Megan, dressed in a bikini, with coffee mug in hand,

282

strolled casually out to the table. She leaned over Flynn's shoulder and kissed him full on the mouth before taking a seat across the table. "That wasn't entirely for their benefit–it was a nice touch, though, wasn't it?" she said, eyeing Flynn with sparkling eyes.

"Can I expect repeat performances?" Flynn asked. "However, if I live to be a hundred, nothing will ever equal the move Neil made. When Santini was staring at me, I froze! Mr. Cool here," he said pointing to Neil, "gave the man a big wave!" Flynn gave Neil a big smile of thanks. "And yes, for your information, that was Santini himself giving us the once over. I'm pretty sure he told the guy with him to check us out. I would have if I were in his shoes. I'd like to suggest we finish this sumptuous breakfast and get the hell out of here."

Within twenty minutes, they were headed down the waterway and out to sea, Megan at the helm, the twin diesels pushing the big cruiser along at a stately eight knots. Flynn was seated at her side. Neil was down in the main salon watching a movie on the VCR. "My big question is, why is Santini here?" Flynn asked.

"There could be any number of reasons. He might be expecting a drug shipment. He might be following up on us. I say that because Alvero met him at the plane–by the way, Cindy got pictures of that meeting. And it might be all of the above," Megan answered.

"So, we need to think of our next several moves. Suppose he's here for a drug shipment. What do we do about that?" Megan asked.

Flynn thought through the options before he spoke. "Well, I'd say if a drug pickup or some big deal is going to happen, it'll happen soon. According to Vinnie Daly, these things are almost always night operations."

Megan chimed in, "And—if Santini is going to send that cigarette boat out to make a pickup, it will most probably be at night, and the closest exit off this waterway out to the open sea is about a mile further on. I think it's a good bet it will be very soon, maybe even tonight, since Santini himself showed up. I believe we'd be playing it safe if we spent the day cruising out of sight of land and then, anchored for the night just off the waterway entrance. We could watch for the pickup boat to go out," Megan said.

"Let's say he sends it out tonight. What then?"

"Then, Dennis, my love, it's time we talked with your friend Daly at the DEA."

"But I'll lose Santini for the murders!"

"What do you care? You've got your murderer. If the DEA gets Santini dirty, he'll go away for a long, long time. Either way, he loses and you win!"

"Then, maybe, I've only got today to do something about my case—," Flynn began.

"That might be. What have you got in mind?" she asked.

Flynn thought about the problem for several moments before deciding on a course of action. "I think I need to have Mike do a number on Cutshaw. May I use the phone?"

"Be my guest, and good luck with whatever it is you're planning."

Flynn dropped down the ladder to the deck and entered the main salon. Taking a seat at the galley table, he reached for the cell phone, his thoughts still a mass of confusion. Somehow he had to get Cutshaw to verbally implicate Santini in Blakemore's murder and, if possible, provide the motive. Flynn had a fair idea of where he'd find Mike, so he placed the call to his own home in Indianapolis. Mike answered the phone himself and was delighted to find it was Flynn. "Mike, have you studied the complete code book translation, yet?" Flynn asked.

"I finished it about an hour ago."

"What do you think? Is there anything in there we could use to scare Cutshaw into talking?" he asked.

"Denny, Cutshaw makes a clam look like a blabber-mouth! I've never met anybody who can sit, look you right in the eye, listen to everything, and say absolutely nothing. It's like talking to a wall. He hasn't even admitted to his name. So, I wouldn't hope for too much."

"But he did talk to the lawyer?"

"Richmond was in with him for over an hour."

"Well, grab your socks. Santini just showed up down here at the house Blakemore visited. In fact, he owns the place under the name Mazzicone. I don't know why he's here—but I sure as hell want to find out. Has Richmond been back to see his client today?"

"He's scheduled for another visit around two this afternoon."

"Look, I'd like you to get to Cutshaw first. Use what you've learned from his code book. You're good at head games. Run one on him. See if you can't shake him up enough, so he'll relay what you've said to the lawyer. I'm playing a long shot here, but I think the lawyer will get alarmed and contact Santini down here. Maybe we can provoke Santini into doing something foolish. In any event, see what you can do to put the fear of God into Cutshaw. Call me at this number when you get done with Cutshaw."

"Okay, Denny, I'll do my best–no promises. Like I said, the guy is a stone wall. Your ass is hanging out down there, so please, be very, very careful," Mike pleaded.

"I'm still planning to attend your wedding all in one piece. Give my love to Monica–and for Christ's sake, lean on that bastard!" Flynn closed the Motorola flip-phone, set the unit back in the charger, and returned to the flying bridge.

By 10:30 a.m., they were traveling at trolling speed a little more than a half mile off the coast, describing a generally oval track in the gently rolling Atlantic. Deep-sea fishing gear had been broken out, baited with artificial lures, and Flynn and the boy had each taken up positions at the stern, watching the lines. Gulls and pelicans wheeled in the cloud-filled sky above them, occasionally swooping within inches of the surface, their sharp fishers' eyes watching for a chance to steal the catch, or as Neil remarked, any garbage they might toss overboard. Megan, seated in the captain's chair, was now piloting the cruiser from the main station at the starboard side of the entrance to the main salon. All the necessary navigational and engine instruments were duplicated at this helm–including a modern-day flat screen, LCD, radar presentation, GPS, radio gear–ship-to-shore radio. As she piloted the big cruiser, Megan would occasionally raise powerful binoculars to her eyes and scan the waterway exit. The cell phone rang for attention. Quickly, she grabbed the tiny phone. "Hello," she answered.

"Megan, it's me, Cindy. Bad news. Alvero phoned down to my office a few minutes ago and ordered a registration search on a boat. By any chance, is your registration number, FLC 188745A?"

"Yes. But how–?"

"I don't know. Will it be shown in your name?"

"Have you run it yet?"

"No. Not yet."

"Where are you?"

"In the women's rest room on the public pay telephone."

"Cindy, the registration is in the name of my Pop's restaurant, The Moorings."

"So, it's corporate ownership?"

"Yes. But I'm half of the corporation."

"Listen, I think I can stall him on this for an hour or two."

Megan thought furiously. "Great! We gotta believe Alvero is on Santini's payroll, so watch yourself. According to Denny, this guy has had a lot of people killed. Don't take any chances."

"I understand. Call me at home tonight if you can."

Megan thanked her friend for the warning and pressed the "End" button on the phone for a moment. She then speed dialed her mother's private number. Within moments, she had her on the phone. "Mom, sometime today, some policemen are probably going to come by or call you to ask about *The Lady Grace*. Just tell them the restaurant owns it and where it's berthed–nothing else."

"Megan, are you in trouble?" her mother demanded.

"Not yet, but if you say too much, I might be."

"Are you and Neil together on the boat?"

"Yes. Denny Flynn is here too. We're safe for now. Just don't tell the police or anybody where we are. Tell them you don't use the boat."

"Megan, I think I can handle the police. Now, I want to hear from you by tonight. I need to know you're safe–understand?"

"Yes, Mother, I do. I promise I'll call later tonight. And watch yourself. Don't let them make you angry." Megan closed the phone, set it back in the charger, and called Flynn to come join her. She filled him in on the development.

"Well, I guess it was to be expected," Flynn said when she'd completed her report.

"Yes. But they still don't know where we are."

"Santini could send that helicopter out looking for us. He does know what the boat looks like. It was too much to expect he wouldn't check on a boat anchored across from his property. Easy enough to read the name on the back."

"In that case, we need to find a haystack. Look, sunset is a good three or four hours away. If that cigarette boat is going to make a run, it won't be until after dark. I think it's time we pulled into a friendly crowded marina, top off the tanks, get lost among similar boats, and wait until evening before we go out again."

It took just a few minutes to get the fishing gear retrieved and stowed. While Neil and Flynn were doing that, Megan consulted her coastal charts and selected a marina about seven nautical miles further down the coast.

4:40 p.m., Indianapolis

A terribly shaken J.R. Richmond unlocked the door to his suite at the Canterbury and upon entering the room, tossed his alligator brief case on the sofa. The short taxi ride from police headquarters had given him little time to think. The evidence in the hands of the police in the form of Cutshaw's notebook was damning! Richmond stripped off his suit coat, vest, and tie and fell into the leather recliner. He desperately needed a drink. As he reached for the phone to summon the floor butler, his hand was shaking, and a fine cold sweat had broken out on his brow. Santini's anger would be uncontrollable when he got the news. Richmond could see no way out of the dilemma. He knew Santini would order Cutshaw killed–it wouldn't be the first time, either! Perhaps, he'd not stop with Cutshaw. With all information to which he was now privy, perhaps, his own life was in jeopardy.

He dialed the floor butler and ordered a large pitcher of very dry martinis. While he waited, he listened to the recording he'd just made of his session with Cutshaw. Within an hour, he'd reviewed the pertinent parts of the tape several times. Fortified by several dry martinis, he placed the dreaded call to Santini. The phone in Miami was answered by one of the young guards. Richmond struggled to put a face with the voice while he waited for Santini. A few seconds later, Santini was on the phone. J.R. took a deep breath and began. "Mario, the situation is worse than I thought. Cutshaw says this police lieutenant, Gaffney, has managed to decode his notebook. Gaffney met with Cutshaw for over an hour this morning and read off several items out of the notebook. Cutshaw confirmed the man wasn't bluffing. Seems they've got all the mule trips Cutshaw made to deposit money in your foreign accounts, a list of contract killings by name and location along with the amount of each contract, and they've apparently got information on Blakemore."

"What information on Blakemore?" Santini demanded.

"Cutshaw didn't know. This lieutenant dangled bits and pieces of information in front of Cutshaw–enough to scare the hell out of him."

"Am I named in Cutshaw's book?" Santini demanded.

"Yes. Apparently several times."

"That stupid motherfucker! That God-damned, stupid son-of-a-bitch! *He's dead!*" Santini screamed. "Where are they holding him?"

"He's about to be transferred out of the police department lockup to the Marion County Jail." J.R. was sweating profusely now.

"J.R., did you make your usual recording?"

"Yes."

"If you want to live, destroy it. Do it now! Stay in town for the arraignment. Do you think Cutshaw is gonna crack?" Santini was slowly regaining his composure.

"I don't know. He's very agitated. I've never met the man before, so I can't really estimate his breaking point. He's very upset. I think this guy, Gaffney, is getting to him," J.R. speculated.

"What kind of a deal did this Gaffney offer?"

"So far– none. Oh, there was the usual 'do yourself a favor' routine. But so far, nobody has even been to visit him from the prosecutor's office. I think the cops want to work on him over the weekend before they even notify the prosecutor."

"Did he mention whether Gaffney told him anything about the operation here?"

"He said Gaffney told him his boss was in Miami tying up some loose ends on the case."

"Shit! Stay with Cutshaw through the arraignment. I don't care how you do it, but you've got to convince him he's got nothing to worry about. I can't afford to have him talk. Do a good job on this one, J.R.!"

Richmond gently replaced the receiver and poured himself another drink. His hand trembled as he lifted the glass to his lips.

7:15 p.m., Miami,

The Lady Grace was back on station about a mile off the waterway entrance. To the west, the sun was dropping in a brilliant red ball. Megan lit off the radar and was watching for echo returns. From seaward, she could make out the returning fishing fleet, their small, slow-moving blips, tracking in a westerly direction, distinguishing them from all the other faster moving radar targets. The lights were out aboard the big cruiser, even to the running lights—as Megan had pointed out, a serious infraction of the rules, should the Coast Guard catch them. Earlier that afternoon, Flynn had given in to her insistence that should the cigarette boat make an appearance, Flynn would immediately contact Vincent Daly of the DEA and give him everything. Flynn was seated at the stern rail, a pair of night-lensed binoculars slung around his neck. Neil was down in the master stateroom listening to music on his walkman. The idling twin diesels, turning just enough revolutions to maintain steerage way, chortled softly in the evening quiet. As the sun dropped to a small sliver of light behind the far shores, the sea calmed first to gently rolling swells and then, to an almost glassy, smooth surface. Flynn loaded his pipe and began once more to review their moves and options as he puffed. By 8:45 p.m., the sky was inky dark except for a few stars winking through a thin overcast. Megan cut the engines and started the auxiliary electric power generator. Quiet reigned.

Shortly after eight, Megan noted a fast moving target leaving the waterway entrance. She waited for several sweeps of the radar before she was certain. "Denny, here he comes!" she said in an excited whisper. "Time to call Daly!"

"You're certain?" Flynn whispered back.

"He's going like a bat out of hell—yes, I'm sure. Call Daly!"

Flynn opened the cell phone and placed a call to the DEA operations center using the special number Daly had given him. Daly was off-duty according to the man who answered the phone. Flynn identified himself and requested Daly be found and that he call back on an emergency basis. For twenty minutes, they waited for the call. Megan started the cruiser's engines to close the distance on the cigarette boat because her radar was limited in range by the height off the water of her mast mounted radar to an effective range of about ten miles. When Daly finally called back, it took Flynn a good ten minutes to tell his story. Daly was highly skeptical until Flynn put Megan on the phone to tell the man what she had seen in the boathouse. Daly asked them to continue to trail the cigarette boat at a safe distance and to stand by for another call from him. In no event were they to do anything other than keep an eye on the suspect boat.

Ten minutes later, Daly was back in communication. He and Megan conferred for several minutes while she made reference to the coastal charts. When the conversation ended, Megan turned to Flynn. "He wants us to meet him at the Cutler Ridge municipal marina as fast as we can get there."

"What's his plan?"

"He didn't say–he just insisted we get there as fast as we can."

"Where is this marina?" Flynn asked.

"About five miles south of Santini's place along the coast."

"Well, the shit's in the fan. Let's get to it," he said.

Megan turned the cruiser to a northwest heading and pushed the throttle controls to full ahead. As the big cruiser came up on the step, traveling at top speed, she lit all the navigation lights and instructed Flynn to keep a close eye on the radar. Flynn divided his attention between the radar screen and watching Megan at the controls.

Minutes later, Megan pointed out the beacons marking the entrance to the harbor as she throttled back the twin diesels. The trip had taken about forty minutes, but in Flynn's troubled mind, the time had passed much faster. Megan throttled back to about five knots and began searching for the marina service area. At length, she spotted the poorly lit Gulf Oil sign and made for the service pier. The cruiser had barely touched the tire-lined pier when Daly, dressed in black from head to toe, stepped from the shadows and leaped to the main deck. "Wind it up, and let's get the hell out of here!" he commanded without preamble as he scrambled to the ladder and climbed to the flying bridge. Megan backed the cruiser off the pier and turned the cruiser toward the main channel. "Megan, I'm Vincent Daly," he began. "Sorry to ask you to get involved, but I need to talk with you and see about setting up a raid on this laboratory you two seem to have uncovered."

"Where to?" Megan asked.

"For starters, lets get out of this harbor and drop the hook so we can do some serious talking." While Megan piloted the boat out of the harbor, Daly began questioning Flynn. "So, Captain, tell me everything—and I mean everything!" For the next twenty minutes while they traveled to a safe out of the way anchorage, Flynn recounted the story from day one. He left out nothing. By the time the story was completed, they were all seated around the galley dining table, sipping freshly-made, hot coffee.

"So, we've got a big time lawyer, operating under two names, who just may be a major coke distributor and money launderer. And you are convinced you've got the proof he ordered the hit on this politician back in Indianapolis. To top it off, you think he's got a deputy chief of police in his pocket. That about it?" Daly asked.

"That about sums it up," Flynn answered. "If you can find a way, I'd sure like to have Santini stand trial on the murder charges back in Indianapolis. Our suspect, the one we have in custody, has, in writing, named Santini as the individual who ordered the murder of the deputy mayor and an innocent, uninvolved, young woman who had the very bad luck to be with Blakemore when the contract was executed. I want Santini!"

"Believe me, I understand. But, you know the rules. If we get him on the drugs and money laundering, we get him first. If everything works out and you can make a good case against the asshole for murder or conspiracy to murder, I promise I will do everything I can to get my bosses to cooperate with you. That good enough?"

"What choice do I have?" Flynn asked.

"None. Now, let's get on with putting the asshole where he belongs. Megan, are you up to taking this boat back to Santini's place tonight?"

"Yes," Megan answered firmly. "But if you have a plan, would you mind letting us in on it?"

"Not at all. As I see it, the only way to do this safely is to actually catch everybody dirty–in the act of converting the cocoa paste to coke crystals. So, we have to let the pickup boat get back and then, give them time to start the refining process. Our *eye-in-the-sky* is monitoring the pickup boat as we speak. But I need to see this place and plan the raid." Having said that, Daly reached for the Motorola two-way on his belt. He raised the operations center and advised they were proceeding to the suspect's base of operation. He ordered his deputy back at the operations center to get from the federal magistrate a search warrant, based upon the eye witness information as supplied by Detective Megan Madigan of the Miami Police Department, listing the place to be searched as the residence and the boathouse upon the property at the street address for Santini's property, which he obtained from Megan. The warrant was to cover the usual things to be sought in a drug factory raid. He named the federal magistrate he wanted them to use, and next, he ordered the standby assault team assembled and instructed to stand by. Scuba gear would be necessary for half the team. At Flynn's urging, Daly ordered strictest secrecy. No one outside the DEA was to know anything! All contacts with Miami PD and the Dade County Sheriff's office were to be broken until further notice. All communication was to be set up on Tac 9. "What's on Tac nine?" Flynn asked.

"A secure channel not shared with any other agency. When we're on that, nobody outside the DEA can listen in. Satisfied?"

"Okay. So, what's next?" Megan asked.

"First, I want to get a look at this place. Once I've done that, I want to coordinate a dual-pronged raid. One on the house and all the above ground property from the street side, and the other by water, the way you got in. I want to catch this son-of-a-bitch with his pants down, right in the middle of refining the shit."

Forty minutes later, Megan was piloting the boat up the waterway, past Santini's walled compound, the cruiser making a sedate five knots. Daly was in the darkened main salon, looking over Santini's compound from the salon windows. From their position on the waterway, no one could be seen on the roof of the boathouse; however, the water beneath the boathouse door glowed from interior lights. Daly raised the Motorola to his lips. "Operations, where's the pickup boat?" he asked.

Came the radioed reply, "Looks like he's completed the transfer. He's headed back. Estimate him to be six miles off the coast."

"Traveling fast?"

"Very!"

"Okay, notify the Coast Guard to move in on the ship he rendezvoused with. How many men have we got standing by?"

"Fifteen."

"I want them in night battle dress, automatic weapons, and ready to go when I give the word." Daly instructed the strike force to meet him on Riviera Street, three blocks south of the address and to await his radio update. He turned to Megan. "Can you find a place nearby to park this thing for a while?"

"If you plan to meet your men south of Santini's place, we'd better do a one-eighty and find a good spot south of the waterway entrance. We'll be nearer your rendezvous point, and we can watch the cigarette boat return. How does that sound?" Daly nodded his head in agreement.

"Do it," he said.

Twenty minutes later, they were at anchor just outside the waterway about twenty yards off the port side breakwater. The cruiser's lights and engines were off. The three adults were assembled around the galley table. Penlight in hand, Daly was examining Megan's sketch of the boathouse interior. He asked questions about locations and dimensions. He asked for a sketch of the grounds as best they could remember. As they were answering Daly's questions, the sounds of powerful engines came across the night air. Daly switched off the pen light and turned to the salon windows. Suddenly, the engine growl reduced to a deep-throated thrumming as the engines' RPM's were cut back. They watched as the fast boat entered the waterway and made its way north. "Okay!" Daly exploded. "Megan, I've got a lot riding on the say-so of you two. Pray to God this doesn't all go into the shitter! Get me to my rendezvous point, and wait for me, will you?"

Flynn went forward and hauled up the anchor. The diesels thrummed to life, the cruiser backed down to clear the breakwater, and then, turned to follow the smuggler's boat. Just beyond the 42nd street bridge, Megan pulled the cruiser alongside an unoccupied, private pier. Daly asked her to remain at that location while he went to brief his assault team. A half hour later, he returned accompanied by four men dressed in dull black wet suits and laden with scuba gear. Daly wasted no time as he and his men came aboard. His face showed the tension of a man about to go into battle. His voice rasped, "Megan, I'd like you to take us up the waterway very slowly. I need to drop these men about twenty yards from Santini's place. We must be there by nine forty-five—twenty-five minutes from now," he said, consulting his watch. "Can you do it?"

Megan nodded in the affirmative. Flynn untied the cruiser. Again, the twin diesels rumbled to life. As the cruiser pulled away, the agents began to strap on their gear. Everything was flat black: tanks, suits, weight belts, and even the M-16 automatic rifles and extra bandoleers of ammunition each carried. Megan piloted the cruiser to the middle of the waterway channel. She maintained bare steerage way while checking both her location and the time as the boat slowly and almost silently made its way up the waterway. "Tell me when we're about a hundred yards from the objective," Daly said.

"Can you let us in on your plan?" Flynn asked.

"Ten men will take the house and grounds from the land side. These four men," he said, indicating the divers, "will take the boathouse. We figure there has to be some sort of warning system the people in the house can use to warn the people in the boathouse, so we're timing this so the underwater men get inside the boathouse just before the land force takes the house. I hope to take them completely by surprise–that's the plan, anyway." Daly's anxiety made his voice tight.

Tension filled the boat as the men completed their preparations. Only the muffled burble of the nearly idling diesels and the gentle wash of the bow wave broke the silence. Ten minutes later, Megan gave Daly the word–"One hundred yards." Daly lifted the radio to his lips once more. "We're on station. Assault at exactly nine forty-five!"

"Roger!" came the reply from the land side force.

They were approaching the property adjacent to Santini's when one-by-one the men slid silently over the stern. Daly asked Megan to pass Santini's place and to let him off at the yacht basin at the first open pier. She managed to find a vacant spot in about a hundred yards further on. As the cruiser closed on the pier, Daly jumped off the boat onto the pier. "Don't follow me!" he commanded in a loud stage whisper. "Stay here. I'll come back when it's over and fill you in." Daly pulled an automatic from his belt holster, turned on his heel, and was immediately swallowed up in the darkness.

Flynn offered an arm and a word or two of comfort to Neil. Then, Megan said, "Denny, when this is all over tonight, let's get away for a day or two before you go home. It looks to me like Mike and your people have things pretty well in hand in Indianapolis. Who'd fault you for taking a day or two off before you go back?" Megan suggested.

"You know, I'd like to do that–I'd like it very much!" Flynn said.

"There's this little island down in the Keys, Walkers Island. It's really small, just three houses. No electricity, no phones. I mentioned it before–the fishing shack. Another of Dad's dreams. It's mine now. Let's take Neil and get away. Spend time getting to know each other better, and just relax. How does that sound?"

"It sounds terrific!" Flynn said as strong emotions flooded his heart. He would be happy to have this nightmare behind him as well as a chance to find out if there really were a future for him with Megan at his side.

"Great. When we're finished here, I can drop you off about five blocks from your hotel. You go pack your things and check out. Take a cab back to the marina, and meet us there. I'll go home, pack some things for Neil and me. We'll meet you back at the boat."

"Which marina are we talking about?" Flynn asked.

"The home port for this boat–where you met us the first time. My car is still there. Here, I'll write down the name and address for you. Just give it to the cab driver," she said as she wrote the information on a scratch pad.

That decision made, the tension, which had formerly filled the air, dissolved. Smiles replaced frowns. Expectant thoughts of happy togetherness filled each heart around the galley table. The future suddenly looked safe and promising.

Coffee was ready to serve. As they sat sipping, Megan held Flynn enthralled as she further described the delights of the tiny remote island. As they talked, laughed, and planned, the desire to ask this woman to marry him began to take solid form in Flynn's mind and heart.

An hour later, Daly returned to the boat, a huge smile on his usually stern face. Megan offered him a cup of coffee as he took a seat next to Megan at the galley table. "Well, we got them all! We got everything!" Daly began. "I mean we got them with their pants down. We took the house with no trouble at all. The two dummies they left to stand guard were both watching television and drinking beer! By the time I got to the basement and found the tunnel door, my water team had already taken the boathouse. I estimate there was about three hundred pounds of coke paste on that table, and they'd started in on about fifty pounds of it by the time we took the place. The street value of this stuff will go into the range of seventy to one hundred million dollars! This'll be one of the biggest busts I've been a part of down here. Flynn, I owe it all to you and Megan here. So, I promise I'll keep my word on this Santini or Mazzicone—or whatever the hell his real name is. You make an official request through Justice, and I'll back your play to get him sent to Indianapolis to stand trial on your murder case."

Flynn grinned and felt a great weight lift. "Vinny, I thank you from the bottom of my heart. Is there any chance I can see him? Talk to him tonight?"

"Maybe, after we get everybody processed and booked. Right now, we have two paddy wagons full of prisoners—didn't take the time to try to identify everybody yet. We'll sort them out back at the federal lockup." He looked at this watch. "I have to get back to the house. We've got trucks and U.S. Marshals coming to seize everything and haul away the evidence. Probably take all night. Look, give me a call in the morning, and I'll give you a shot at Santini." He put his coffee cup on the galley sink and shook hands with Megan and Flynn. "I cannot thank you two enough. Rest easy—it's all over." He flashed a smile and left as quickly as he'd come.

It was well after midnight when Megan dropped Flynn off at the public pier a few blocks from his hotel. Because his heart was light, his step was light and brisk. Within fifteen minutes, he'd reached the hotel. It took only a few minutes to pack his few belongings. By one in the morning, he was checked out and standing beneath the hotel portico waiting for a taxi. When it arrived, the driver, a recent arrival from Cuba, "had little English". With the aid of a Miami street map the Cuban carried and sign language, Flynn managed to convey the route to his destination. After several bad turns en route, they finally managed to reach the marina. As Flynn paid the meter price, it occurred to him the man had made a pretty good fare off him in spite of, or perhaps, because of the language handicap. That driver would be a wealthy man in short order at this rate. Flynn collected his bag and walked to the guard house at the head of the fenced in piers. Megan's car was nowhere in sight. He hoped she would not be long in returning. He identified himself to the guard and signed in as a guest aboard *The Lady Grace*. Picking up his bag, he made his way down the pier to the boat.

The cruiser was in total darkness when he arrived, but he could see the dock-side facilities, electricity, telephone, and fresh water had been hooked up. He stepped over the starboard railing and made for the salon door. He opened the door and went down the carpeted steps into the main salon. When he got to the middle of the room, he dropped his bag and was about to turn back to the bulkhead to turn on the lights when the lamp at the galley table was switched on. The pool of light spotlighted a stainless .357 magnum clenched in a large, hairy hand. The gun was aimed directly at Flynn's chest and didn't waiver.

Flynn's heartbeat pounded in his ears. A voice addressed him from behind. "Ah, the estimable Captain Flynn." Flynn, paralyzed by fear, could move only his eyeballs. The overhead salon lights came on. With the salon now fully lit, to his right, Flynn could see the hand holding the gun was attached to Deputy Chief Alvero. Footsteps came from behind. Santini appeared. With great dignity, he took a seat on Flynn's left in one of the chairs in the living room grouping. "Please, Captain, take a seat," he said, indicating the club chair across from the one he occupied. Flynn unlocked his knees and did as he was told. Santini was dressed in a summer-weight, dark, pinstripe suit, white shirt with French cuffs, and regimental tie. Black alligator shoes gleamed in the light. Alvero was in full police uniform. Flynn was thunderstruck! He became conscious of that prickly sweat, which breaks out when you're cornered. His arm pits began to let go. He felt the small rivulets of sweat run down his sides.

"And Ms. Madigan? Will she be joining us soon?" Santini asked.

"I honestly don't know," Flynn managed to croak through a dry throat.

"No matter—we'll wait," Santini stated in a grand manner.

"What do you want with us?" Flynn asked.

"Why, I should have thought that was obvious. I cannot have the two of you alive."

Flynn decided to play for time. "What have we done to you?"

Santini's cultured voice took on a hard edge. Speaking through clenched teeth, he asked, "Do you think I'm a fool? Haven't you been watching my house? Haven't you been looking into my affairs?"

"Now, why would I be doing a thing like that?" Flynn asked.

"*Exactly!* That's what troubles me. I hope to learn the answer to all my questions very soon—when Ms. Madigan and her son return."

"You've got Alvero here in your pocket. Looks like he's ready to kill on your command. I'm certain he's filled you in."

"I'm afraid his answers haven't been very satisfying."

Flynn turned to look directly at Alvero as he spoke. "Must not be a very good deputy chief! More than that, he's a traitor to everybody who wears a badge."

"Spare me the sanctimony!" Santini said. "Everybody eventually has a price—even you. Money, life—what do you value most? You name it. Now, back to my question. Why are you nosing around in my business?" Santini asked, ignoring the jab at Alvero.

"Well, when you dispatched a fella named Cutshaw to eliminate a problem–a young fellow named Blakemore, you got my attention–seeing I'm the head of our homicide unit. Blakemore was a deputy mayor. And in case you aren't aware of it, big city mayors don't take kindly to having their deputies bumped off. Things like that tend to put people like me on the spot. Can't have the mayor look like he's got an incompetent police force. Guaranteed to cost elections. They don't like that! Have to prosecute the guilty. Since I know you paid Cutshaw to murder Blakemore–well, why waste my breath? You're a defense attorney–a criminal defense attorney. You know the rest."

"I know all you have is Cutshaw's word and that notebook he kept. Without Cutshaw to testify to the authenticity of the notebook, you'll have no case against me."

"What makes you think he won't testify?"

"Cutshaw will not live to go on trial. As a matter of fact, Cutshaw will not live to see Tuesday." Santini's voice was coldly matter of fact. "He will not testify. Without him–your code book is useless." He flashed a toothy, self-satisfied smile. It was the smile of a shark.

Flynn took a chance, "Oh, then–you obviously don't know what happened tonight?"

Santini lit a small, thin, black cigar and blew a stream of blue smoke toward the ceiling before he answered. Outwardly, he seemed completely unfazed, remaining very much in command of the situation. "I am unaware of anything unusual happening tonight."

"Then, you don't know about your house getting knocked over by the DEA?"

"And just why would they do that?" Santini asked.

"Because they discovered your drug factory. They took it down a couple of hours ago. I understand they seized unprocessed coke. They think the processed street value is close to one hundred million. The last I heard, they were carting off everything that wasn't nailed down." Flynn felt a great satisfaction as he watched the great and powerful attorney's reaction. Santini's face drained of its artificial tan.

Santini looked at Alvero and snapped his fingers. Alvero reached for the boat's land line telephone and without letting the gun waiver, passed the instrument to Santini. Santini rapidly punched in a series of numbers. When the call was answered, Santini spoke without introduction, "Tell me what happened tonight." As the muffled voice at the other end answered the question, Flynn watched Santini's face redden and twist in anger. Without speaking further, Santini placed the receiver back into the cradle and passed the phone back to Alvero. "Call your office. See what they know about the DEA raiding my house." Alvero did as he was told, his gun never wavering. Completing his call, Alvero reported there was no information at headquarters about a raid on the property. Santini appeared to be considering his options. "Mind if I ask a question?" Flynn asked.

"You want to know how Blakemore figures into this, don't you?" Santini stated.

"Yes. And I have been wondering–which is the real name? Santini or Mazzicone?"

"Santini. As for Blakemore–behind my back, he was attempting a direct alliance with some Colombians. Wanted to go into business for himself. I gave Blakemore his start, made him a few million. He got greedy, and he became disloyal. I can't have that. I won't have it!"

"How long did Blakemore work for you?"

"Since his college days. He was an excellent producer too– politically connected in several cities. He'll be difficult to replace."

"You don't seem to understand. After tonight, you're out of business," Flynn said.

"Ah, but *you* don't understand. There's nothing here to connect me with the drug business–nothing at all. Everything here belongs to a legal phantom. Mazzicone doesn't exist except on paper. Once you and the Madigan woman are eliminated, all the loose ends will have been tidied up. Chief Alvero here will see to my interests. I will simply return to California."

"A couple other things–how did you get aboard? How did you find us?" Flynn asked.

Alvero spoke up for the first time since the encounter began. "This uniform gets me anywhere I want to go. You're a cop, you know nothing can stay hidden for long. And as for how we found you, well, it was simply a matter of putting surveillance on this pier and waiting until the boat returned. In sum, a simple stakeout."

"Just how do you plan to get rid of us?"

307

"I think a simple disappearance at sea is best," Santini began. "This boat will be found several miles out to sea—nobody aboard—a frequent happening in recent years, I understand. The police, with Alvero's help, will decide the boat was hijacked, most probably by some desperate drug operators, and the owner killed. Dropped overboard at sea. And now, I'll ask you again—when do you expect the Madigan woman to return?"

Flynn was frantically searching his mind for some kind of an answer when the salon window at his back exploded in a shower of tempered glass. Alvero's head was knocked back, exploding in a mass of blood, bone, and brains. Both Flynn and Santini were frozen by the unexpected gunshot. Flynn recovered first and made a leap for Santini just as the man began to reach inside his coat. Flynn's head impacted Santini's chin and chest, knocking both him and the chair over backwards. The two men sprawled on the floor with Flynn on top. Before he could raise his arm to deliver a punch, Santini had him locked in a powerful bear hug, both of Flynn's arms captured at his sides. Megan's strong voice rang out in the room. "Everybody freeze!—Don't move!"

Flynn turned his head. She was standing about seven feet away from where the two men lay on the floor. Her feet were spread in the classic, combat, shooting stance, the deadly SIG—Sauer held in both hands, leveled unwaveringly, directly at Santini's head. Santini unlocked his arms, allowing Flynn to roll off away from Megan's line of fire. Flynn sprang to his feet and quickly rolled Santini over on his face. He pulled the man's suit coat open and located the gun, a small, snub nosed, .38 airweight, hammerless, Smith & Wesson revolver. "We need something to tie him up with," Flynn said.

"Keep that gun on him while I go to the weapons locker. I've got some cuffs there," Megan said. Flynn placed the barrel of the revolver at the base of Santini's skull. Neither man said anything while they waited for Megan's return. When she returned with the hand cuffs, Flynn secured the lawyer's hands behind his back and rolled him over.

"Megan, since I'm out of my jurisdiction, would you do the honors?"

"You have the right to remain silent," Megan began. Once the formalities had been completed, Megan asked, "How the hell do I explain killing a deputy chief of police–rat fink though he was?"

"I'm sure the investigation will clear you. Where's Neil?"

"Out in the car," Megan said.

"How the hell–? I mean what great luck! Did you suspect something?" Flynn asked.

"I spotted Alvero's unmarked car in the lot when I pulled in. I put two and two together."

"Well, if you don't mind, I think we ought to call Daly at the DEA and have him put Santini under federal arrest. That ought to keep him away from any other local boys on Santini's payroll. That leaves us with the late deputy chief of police. What do you suggest we do? Who do we call about Alvero?"

"I'll call Chief Burke. It's his headache now."

"Speaking of phone calls, I'd better call Mike and let him know Santini has a contract out on Cutshaw." Megan handed over her cell phone.

"Do it!"

The local prosecutor came with a team of his own investigators. Dennis and Megan were seated side by side on the seat cushion at the stern of the boat. Flynn was in the unusual position of having to answer pointed questions posed by the detectives of another police department. He found himself more than a little annoyed. A ruddy faced detective named Duke Mayer, his breath reeking of stale beer, was standing over the two asking leading questions.

"Isn't it just possible Chief Alvero was really arresting Santini? That you just made a horrible mistake?"

"Me?" Flynn asked.

Megan spoke up. "Hey! Duke, I told you– *I* shot Alvero."

"I'll get to you when I'm ready. Until then, shut the fuck up!"

"Do you treat all your fellow officers like this?" Flynn asked.

Mayer bent over so his face and beer sodden breath were right in Flynn's face. "Look, Buddy, I'm Jesus come to judge! When I want your opinion, I'll ask for it. I got news for you. Your hunk of gold tin doesn't carry any weight down here. None! You're playing the big leagues now! You think because you're head of homicide back in podunk Indiana-no-place, you can skate?"

"No."

Mayer withdrew his face, and stood erect with his ball point pen poised over his notebook. "Well then, Chief Alvero is dead, and we're going to make *goddamned certain* it went down like you two claim!"

Megan spoke up. "Like I told you before, I was coming down the pier, and when I got next to the main lounge window, I saw Alvero and Santini. Alvero had his gun on Captain Flynn. I saw him raise it to take aim,and that's when I decided to take him out. He was dirty!" Megan was shaking with anger as she finished.

"Dirty? Jesus! We're talking about a goddamned deputy chief here."

"Look, Duke–it's no secret Alvero was your rabbi. Maybe you'd better start thinking about your own ass!"

Detective Duke Mayer looked as if he were about to take a swing at Megan–woman or not. Flynn rose from his seat and stood directly in front of the outraged detective. He raised his voice and called out for the prosecutor.

A tall, thin, balding man obviously in his middle age, came up the short ladder to the main deck. "Yes?"

"I think this is getting out of hand," Flynn said.

"Oh? How is that?" he rasped.

"Not that it really mattered until now, but you and I have not been introduced. My name is Flynn–Dennis Flynn. I'm a Captain with the Indianapolis Police Department. I'm down here on a murder investigation. If you'll check with Chief Burke, I'm certain he will confirm all this. My point is– if Mayer were any more stupid, he'd have to be watered twice a week! What's your name?"

The man appeared to consider how to answer before he spoke. "I'm Cline. Lawrence Cline. And–?"

"And this is getting completely out of hand. Detective Madigan here tells me it is common knowledge in the department that Deputy Chief Alvero was this man's rabbi–his protector. Now, when we have a situation like that back home, we make certain the investigating officers are not related in *any way* to the victim–that includes rabbis–especially rabbis!"

Cline blinked his sleep-deprived, blood-shot eyes as he thought the matter over and then, pulled a cell phone from his pocket. With the press of a button, a number was auto dialed. When it was answered, Cline launched into an account of the situation. He grunted a few times in response to whoever was at the other end. After a few more such responses, he broke the connection and addressed himself to both Flynn and Megan. "The boss says to let the two of you go. He wants to see both of you in his office in the morning. He turned to Detective Mayer, "Turn in your notes and go home. You're off the case."

Megan reached her hand out to take Flynn's. "Let's get Neil and go home."

Early morning found the three at the breakfast table in Megan's sunshine filled kitchen. The night before, when they arrived at Megan's home and after Neil had gone to his room, Megan asked Flynn to share her bed. Flynn was astonished by his pent up ardor. They made love–several times that night.

The mood about the table was jovial. Megan and Neil began planning the vacation to her father's fishing shack and were well into painting a fantastic picture of life on the tiny island when the phone rang. Megan took the call. She listened intently to the muffled voice at the other end of the call. Flynn watched her facial expressions alter as she listened. When the caller was finished, Megan thoughtfully replaced the receiver on the kitchen, wall-mounted phone and returned to her seat at the table. "Well, I should have expected this."

"What?" Flynn asked.

"That was the DC of Internal Affairs. Seems I'm under investigation, and the prosecutor is going to convene a Grand Jury to examine the Alvero situation. He's calling your chief to make certain you don't leave town till this is all settled."

"If that's the case, my smart play would be to call O'Halleran before the shit hits the fan. Mind if I use your phone?" Megan simply gestured toward the phone. "If you don't mind, I think I'd better do this somewhere private. Is there another phone?"

"Use the one in the living room." Flynn excused himself and headed for the privacy of the living room to make his call. He found the phone next to a comfortable easy chair. Collecting his thoughts, he entered the chief's private number. The answer came on the second ring. With the salutations done, O'Halleran jumped in with both feet. "Jesus, Denny! What the hell are you mixed up in down there? I've got the Dade County Prosecutor all over me, and now, the newsies are calling. Tell me everything, and do it now."

It took Flynn some time to make a complete report and answer the chief's follow up questions.

"So, it looks like you're stuck down there for several more days?"

"Well, it all depends on when he can get a Grand Jury to sit on the case. Now that you've got Cutshaw, and we've got Santini down here, I don't really see anything pressing back home. Why not let me take some of those vacation days I've been accumulating these past many years?"

"Gaffney told me you called late last night with word that Santini had put out a contract on Cutshaw. Do you think he was bluffing or what?"

"Chief, I'd take no chances. Santini didn't strike me as a man who would bluff."

"Cutshaw has a hot shot lawyer here from Vegas. I think I'll send Mike over to pay him a visit at his hotel. Let him know what we know."

"Do it now. I think Santini put all this in motion early yesterday afternoon."

Mike was getting concerned. There was no answer in J.R. Richmond's room. He knew Cutshaw's attorney hadn't left the exclusive hotel. He turned to the desk clerk once more. "Is there any way we can double check on this?"

"Sir, the only information I have is that he ordered a breakfast about ten minutes ago. He might be indisposed."

"Got a pass key?"

"We use key cards."

"I don't care if you use shoe horns! Have you got a way to get into that room?"

"I'll have to get the hotel manager."

"Do it!" Mike fumed as he cooled his heels in the tiny lobby. After a few minutes, an imperious man introduced himself as the hotel manager and asked what the trouble seemed to be. Mike introduced himself, showing his police credentials, "I think we may have a situation involving one of your guests. I need to get into his room, and I need to do it *right now!*"

"And you have the necessary search warrant?"

"I don't need one!"

The manager seemed to consider challenging the statement, but considering the look on Mike's face, decided against it. "Where do we need to go?" he asked. In less than two minutes, Mike was outside Richmond's room, the manager at his side. Mike held his index finger to his lips, indicating to the manager that he should stay silent. He reached for the key card. Still reluctant, the manager handed it over. Silently, Mike slid the card into the reader slot. The tiny, red, indicator light changed from red to green, indicating the electronic lock was now open. Mike reached inside his coat and withdrew his Glock from its shoulder holster. Silently, he pushed down on the door handle and quickly entered the room, his gun leading the way. There, before his eyes, was a man dressed in a red waiter's waistcoat in the act of garroting a nude, wet J.R. Richmond. The man's eyes widened as he caught sight of Mike's weapon. He let go the handles on his wire garrote and lifted his hands in the air.

J.R. Richmond slipped to the floor gagging and gasping for breath. Mike dropped the key card, grabbed the manager by his lapel unceremoniously jerking the man to his side, and snarled, "Get help up here right now! *Go!*" The badly shaken and thoroughly frightened manager fled the room as quickly as his forgotten dignity. Mike kept his weapon squarely aimed at the center of the assassin's chest. "Mr. Richmond, are you okay? Can you speak?" He dared not move his eyes from the suspect's face. Richmond was garbling and gasping incoherently, but he was alive. Mike reached into his side coat pocket and withdrew his cell phone. Thumbing a speed dial digit, he called police dispatch and ordered a uniform car and an ambulance–never taking his eyes from his suspect. With the call completed, he ordered the man to lie face down on the floor, his hands at the back of his neck, fingers laced together– he began the ritual. "You are under arrest for the attempted murder of Mister Richmond here. You have the right to remain silent. You have the right to an attorney...."

In spite of the heat and humidity outside, the hallway outside the Grand Jury room was cool. There was even a breeze as the building's air conditioning system did its job. Mike checked his watch again. Time was dragging by so slowly that he began to doubt his watch. Megan had been in there for nearly an hour. Familiar with how the prosecutors back home conducted a Grand Jury, which was pretty much quick and to the point, Mike was worried. Surely, they couldn't doubt her testimony. Killing Alvero had been the right thing to do; legally and morally. How could they not believe her? For that matter, how would he fare in all this? Try as he might that old saw about a prosecutor being able to indict a ham sandwich with the help of a Grand Jury kept forcing itself to the fore. As he was stewing in his own concerns, the door swung open, and Megan was ushered into the hall. The door closed. Flynn, knowing he was on egg shells, stood and gently took her hand in his. "Well, will the marriage be on the beach or in prison?" he asked. An attempt at levity he instantly regretted. Megan smiled, "Well, it's really different when the target of the inquiry is you."

"Hey! It was the right thing to do. We both know it."

"I just hope those good Floridians in there can see that."

"I think I'm next. Is there someplace we can meet after they get through with me?"

"There's a pretty good, little restaurant across the street on the corner. I'll be over there waiting." Mike was preparing to give her a hug when the door opened. It was his turn.

Mike took his seat in the witness box and surveyed the unfamiliar room. The jury was made up of a typical cross section of the local registered voters as far as Mike could determine. There was the usual mix of blue-haired, old matrons, balding elderly men, and a sprinkling of younger men and women. The younger jurors were there because they could find no way to get out of the obligation. These younger folks were quite often the cause of rushed judgment, so anxious were they to get the hell out of duty and back to their lives. His wandering mind was jerked back to the present when he heard his name. For the first time, he looked at the woman who had called his name.

"Mister Flynn, would you stand and be sworn, please?"

Flynn stood, and when the elderly gentleman came forward bearing the Bible, he placed his left hand on the cover and raised his right to the heavens. The old man spoke, "Do you swear, or affirm, that the testimony you are about to give before this Grand Jury will be the truth, the whole truth, and nothing but the truth, so help you God?"

"I do."

"State your name for the record." The old gentleman returned to his seat at a side table before Flynn could reply. "Dennis Patrick Flynn."

The woman came forward, a closed, legal-sized, manila file folder in her left hand. "Mister Flynn, I'm Sandra Goreman, chief deputy prosecutor." She was dressed in a form-fitting, beige, two-piece, business dress. Not at all bad looking, Flynn thought. She continued on. "What is your occupation?"

"I'm a police officer."

"With what police agency are you connected?"

"The Indianapolis, Indiana, Police Department."

"And what is your position there?"

"I presently head the Homicide and Robbery Branch."

"And your rank?"

"I hold the permanent rank of Captain."

"Are you in Miami in an official capacity?"

"Yes."

"Tell us exactly what that capacity is."

"I was sent here by my department to follow some leads we had developed in a murder case."

"What murder case?"

"Our deputy mayor for economic development."

"Were you acting alone here or with the assistance of the Miami Police Department?"

"I had a letter of introduction from my chief and the full assistance of the Miami Department."

"So, they knew what you were doing here?"

"Those who had a need to know were aware."

"Were you provided with an official liaison or an assistant to be with you from the Miami Department during your investigations?"

"Yes, I was."

"And the name of that person?"

"Detective Sergeant Megan Madigan."

"And did Detective Sergeant Madigan assist you in your investigations?"

"Considerably!"

"Would you please describe for the Jury her contributions to your efforts?"

"Certainly. Sergeant Madigan's knowledge of the way things are done down here, her ability to locate information. I think she's exceptionally bright."

"Would you expand upon that for us?"

"Gladly. You see, when a police officer from an outside jurisdiction comes to a locale such as Miami he, or she, is pretty much at a loss, even though he, or she, is there on legitimate official business. By that I mean every police agency operates differently. Functions are frequently given entirely different nomenclature, which makes access and cooperation without help, an iffy thing. Then there's the matter of turf. By that I mean every police agency is jealous of its jurisdiction. There is a natural suspicion of, and resentment of, an outsider just beneath the surface. Then too, each police agency is more-or-less a creature of the local political party which happens to be in power at the time. For a visiting cop, coming into a strange jurisdiction is a little like navigating in a mine field at night without a flash-light."

"Truly? Is it really that problematic? I've not heard a police officer ever express such an opinion."

Flynn thought about the mine field he had just laid for himself in that Grand Jury room. Well, he was just a few months away from retirement. So, why the hell not go on the record. Just for the refreshment of it? "Speaking in generalizations is always a bad idea. But, I'm going to do it anyway. In general, every police agency has some degree of corruption. Some major, some minor–but corruption all the same." His eyes swept the jurors for their reaction. He saw he had their undivided attention. He saw renewed interest. They were anticipating learning some inside dirt. Heartened by this, he forged on. "Trouble is, everybody inside the agency knows it. It's a little like working for a big corporation in their headquarters. All the mid-level people, secretaries, and assistant managers–they all know who's stealing from the company. Whether it's pencils, ball point pens, or petty cash. They know. It's water-cooler and coffee break gossip. Police agencies are no different. The stakes are higher. Cops *do* get paid to look the other way. Some run parking scams– letting certain well connected folks park in tow-away zones for a fee. Some take money from drug dealers and gamblers to allow them to operate. And sad to say, some even provide these dealers and gamblers protection and information. In short, they sell out. So, when an outside cop shows up on official business, those, who are taking money, get nervous. Even the good cops don't want you to expose the dirt in their agency. That's pretty much what happened here. Detective Madigan helped me through your local mine field and was a major contributor toward uncovering this entire mess." Flynn realized he'd been running off at the mouth. "I'm sorry. I didn't mean to make a speech."

The prosecutor scanned the jury to pick-up on their reaction. She turned back to Flynn. "That's quite all right. Let's continue. In the process of your investigations, did you encounter the name Santini?"

"Yes."

"And Mazzicone?"

"Yes."

"How did you encounter these names?"

"I discovered they are one and the same man. A man using the alias Mazzicone here in Miami."

"And Mazzicone is really who?"

"A California attorney named Mario Santini."

"Is your testimony that they are one and the same man?"

"Yes."

"What led you to this man?"

For the next several minutes, question by question, Flynn laid out his entire case; from the death of the people in Indianapolis through the discovery of the drug processing laboratory hidden behind the walls of the boat house on the Mazzicone property. He told of the raid by the local DEA and of the capture of a killer for hire in the employ of Santini.

The prosecutor stood quietly letting Flynn's testimony capture and hold the jurors' attention. You could hear a pin drop in the room. The prosecutor launched into her final round of questions, "I call your attention to the incident of three nights ago aboard a motor vessel during which a man lost his life." She opened her file folder and briefly consulted the information. "*The Lady Grace* moored in the slip, which had been leased to the corporate owner of the boat. Tell us what transpired that evening–the thirteenth."

"When the DEA raid was finished, Detective Madigan and I decided it was all pretty much all over– except staying around for a few days to assist and testify against Santini for the government's case. We could relax and get on with life. She dropped me a few blocks from my hotel, and I packed a few things for a day or two of vacation. We were to meet at the boat's slip at the marina. From there, we were going to spend a day or two at her father's cabin on an island somewhere in the Keys."

"So, you returned to the boat?"

"Yes. It was late, and Detective Madigan and her son had not yet returned to the boat when I got there. I decided to wait inside–in the salon, I think it's called. Anyway, I went in and was about to turn on the room lights when a small light came on at the galley table. It really surprised me! I whipped around to see who it was. I saw a .357 pointed directly at my chest."

"Were you able to determine who had the gun pointed at you?"

"No. Not then. His face was in the dark."

"What happened next?"

"The rest of the lights in the room came on and I heard another man's voice. Turned out it was Santini. He came up from behind me and sat in one of the chairs on the other side of the salon. I thought he'd been taken in the DEA raid at his place. Then, the lights came on, and I saw it was Deputy Chief Alvero sitting at the galley table with the gun on me."

"Had you ever seen Santini before?"

"I had photographs supplied to my investigation by the Los Angeles PD. I recognized him from the photos."

"And then?"

"And then, Santini ordered me to take a seat in front of where he was sitting. He began to question me about who I was and what I wanted in his business. It was clear he had no idea his place had been knocked over by the DEA. So, I told him the DEA had just raided his place, and it was all over. He told Alvero to call somebody and check on my story."

"Did he?"

"Yes."

"Who did he call?"

"I have no idea. I assume it was somebody back in the Miami PD Headquarters."

"And then?"

"And then, Santini said we were going to wait for Detective Madigan to show up with her son, and there would be a staged hijacking and death at sea for all of us. Said it happens all the time down here. Then, all of a sudden the window behind me shattered, and a bullet smashed Alvero right in the forehead. His brains spattered everywhere! Before Santini could react, I jumped him. Then Detective Madigan came aboard, and we handcuffed Santini. Detective Madigan read him his rights."

"Are you saying Detective Madigan shot the deputy chief of police in order to save your life?"

"Yes. Yes, I am."

"Captain Flynn, in your experience, would you say it would be fair of me to describe Deputy Chief Alvero as a co-conspirator? A paid ally of this Santini?"

"Without a doubt!"

"Would it be fair to say the DEA did not take the Miami Police Department into their confidence with respect to the raid they conducted on Mister Santini's property?"

"Yes. That'd be fair."

"Do you have direct knowledge as to why they didn't share this information?"

"Only what the agent in charge told me."

"And that was–?"

"That, based partly on the information Detective Madigan and I shared with the DEA, they had reason to believe that the integrity of the Miami Police Department had been compromised."

Ms. Goreman turned to face the jury, "Does anybody have any questions of Captain Flynn?" No one indicated any interest in more questions. "You're excused, Captain Flynn."

Mike's quick thinking foiled the attempt on Cutshaw's attorney's life. The hit man was now in custody, and a grateful J.R. Richmond was cooperating for all he was worth! His resolve to tell all was enhanced by the information that Santini was in the hands of the DEA and would also face other state and local charges when the Feds were done with him. In return for entering the federal witness protection program, Richmond agreed to give testimony when called upon and as Cutshaw's attorney, to visit Cutshaw simply to tell the man what had happened and to relay the offer made by the Marion County Prosecutor–instead of the death penalty, life without parole in return for full cooperation. Cutshaw had been singing his head off ever since.

In Florida, the Grand Jury investigation into Alvero's death was complete and the shooting ruled justifiable. The Dade County Prosecutor totally cleared Megan; however, the grand jury investigation uncovered several other police officers on Santini's payroll. At the moment, the prosecutor with Megan's help was backtracking the paper trail on Santini's phantom man, Mazzicone.

Her work accomplished, Megan arranged for a full week's vacation and asked Flynn to do the same. She was determined to spend those days away at her father's famous fishing shack with her son and Flynn. To Flynn's surprise, Chief O'Halleran readily agreed.

The "shack" turned out to be a very sizable beach house built in the shelter of a small cove. They spent the first day stocking the house, cleaning and dusting, and just settling in. Flynn could not recall when he'd been so happy. On the second day, late in the afternoon while he and Neil were out scrounging shells on the beach, Flynn made up his mind to ask Megan to marry him. They'd talked about it or rather, all round it in bed the night before. But now, he felt certain he'd ask her to share his life. However, he knew Neil's desires would be a deciding factor. He knew he would have to win the boy's total acceptance. That was still a question in spite of the closeness he felt for the boy. Flynn stretched out on the warm sand to let his thoughts sort themselves out. He hadn't been there long when he knew the boy was standing over him. He opened his eyes and looked up.

"Something up?" he asked.

"Do you think we could talk?"

"Sure pull up a hunk of sand and sit." Flynn sat up and waited while Neil moved close and sat cross-legged, so that they were facing each other. "What's on your mind?" Flynn asked, deciding that maybe there was no time like the present to take the matter head on.

"You're gonna ask Mom to marry you, aren't you?" the boy began.

Flynn was surprised by the boy's perspicacity and directness. "Well, we talked about it last night. We both want to. But I wouldn't be marrying just your mom. The real question is—how do *you* feel about it?"

"Does it matter what I think?"

"Hell, yes! If I marry your mom, I'd adopt you as part of the deal—if you agree. We'd have to be a real family. It wouldn't work if you and I can't get along—if we can't come to love each other."

Neil didn't answer for some time. Finally, he began to ask his own series of questions, "If you two do get married, would we have to move away?"

"Well, I hadn't thought much about that, just yet. Let's talk about it. I'm eligible to retire from the Department in about six months. Even less if I cash in my vacation time." Flynn thought for a few moments before going on. He hadn't expected this line of questions at all. "I don't think it would be right for me to ask you and your mom to give up your lives here and move to

Indianapolis." He fell silent for a few more minutes thinking a new thought through. "If we get married, I'll–give my house to my daughter, Monica. That is I'll offer it to her and her husband, Mike, when they get married–if they want it. It's all paid for. Might be the best all around." He found he was warming to the idea the more he thought about it. The house would make one hell of a wedding present!

Neil began to draw geometric doodles in the sand as he spoke, "I've always wondered what it would be like to have a dad. All my friends have dads or stepdads. Mostly the stepdads are pretty mean. The stepdads don't really love their sons. I see it when I'm at their houses. The real dads, now that's different. Most of them do things together with their sons. Will you and I do things together?"

"Well, if your mom says 'yes', it means I'll be here with you–full time. I won't have a job–at least, I don't think I will–not for a while anyway–and that would mean you'd have me around full-time. So, I guess I'd be available to spend time with you–probably anytime you wanted. The short answer is yes."

"Well, I think you are a really nice guy. I mean you're sure the best one mom has ever spent time with. Most of her other boyfriends were nice to me just to get to her, and some just didn't want me around," the boy said as he continued to doodle in the white sand.

"Are you really asking what I feel for you?" Flynn asked.

"Well, yes." The voice was small and tentative.

"How do I feel about you?" Flynn looked out on the curling afternoon waves gently lapping on the beach and considered his answer. How *did* he feel about this boy? The years of wanting a son pushed once more into his thoughts and weighed heavily on his heart. When he looked back, Neil's deep blue eyes were looking into his. Flynn knew the boy was looking for honesty. "Well, the truth is I like you a lot. I mean I *do* feel very close to you. It's a kind of love, I guess. I can see the two of us learning to love each other as our lives develop together. We'd have to learn to trust each other. Love and trust are two-way streets. How do you feel about me?" Flynn finished.

Neil's finger drew circles in the sand as he spoke. "I think I like *you* a lot. I mean I sometimes think about us doing stuff together. Kinda like daydreaming about what it might be like. I do feel kinda safe when you're around. You don't treat me like a dumb, little kid. I wouldn't be ashamed to have my friends meet you—show you off as my dad. I don't think you'd go off and leave me—or mom."

"You've been giving this a lot of thought, haven't you?"

"Well, yeah. It's *important* to me." He thought for a minute before continuing, "Will you be honest with me if I have questions? Can I trust you to keep things just between us? You and me—even after you and mom get maried?"

"What kind of questions?" Flynn asked.

The boy's finger dug more deeply in the sand. "Well—I need someone I can talk to about sex and that kinda thing. I can't talk to mom. *Geezz!* It's just too embarrassing! Guys don't ask their moms about sex. For instance, my friends do a lot of bragging. I mean I'm pretty sure they're all blowing smoke—as my mom says."

Flynn wasn't prepared for such sudden frankness. He thought for a few moments before posing his question. Talk about land mines! "Is there something in particular bothering you right now? Something you'd like to get straightened out? Something you want to talk about?"

"No, not right now. I just wanted to know if you'd tell me the truth when I want to know something, no matter how silly it might seem to you." Neil concentrated on his toes as he spoke.

"Yes. I promise to tell you the truth," Flynn said, placing his left hand on his chest and raising his right toward the sky. That made Neil laugh.

"And will you promise to love me too?" the boy asked again looking Flynn directly in his eyes.

"You mean will I love you even if I think you're doing something wrong or stupid?" Flynn asked.

"Well, yes."

"Neil, I promise to love you no matter what! How's that?"

Neil obviously thought he'd made some headway and ventured to speak of one of his major concerns.

"Well, I sleep naked. You won't make me stop, will you?"

Flynn barked out a loud laugh in spite of himself. The boy's admission so surprised him. Then, realizing it was important to the boy, he answered, "I'm sorry. I didn't mean to laugh. Your question just took me by surprise. About sleeping naked–no, I wouldn't make you stop. Not at all. Matter of fact, I sleep naked myself. Can't stand pajamas or wearing anything to bed. I don't see anything wrong with being comfortable in bed. Somebody tell you it was wrong?" he asked.

"Couple of my buddies say it isn't nice," Neil said.

"Nice! What the hell's 'nice' got to do with it?"

"Well, they say it's not right."

"I assume your mother knows you sleep naked?" Flynn asked.

"Yes."

"Well then, what does she say about it?"

"Nothing. I mean she sleeps naked too. Besides, we keep our bedroom doors closed."

"Neil, if it's good enough for your mom and good enough for me, don't you think it is pretty much okay to do?"

"Yes, I do," the boy answered.

Flynn thought it was time to talk about what was about to happen in the boy's life; something that could come between them, the other side of the coin. "Neil, there *is* something, which could screw things up for us–you and me. Maybe we ought to talk about it."

Neil turned to look Flynn in the eyes as he responded, sudden concern showed in his face "Something bad is gonna happen?"

"Oh, no! Actually something perfectly normal and rather wonderful is going to happen to you. You just turned thirteen and are going to start to become a man."

"I know. What's so bad about that? I mean how can it hurt you and me?"

Flynn thought about his response before he spoke. "Well, this business of going through puberty–becoming a man, generally causes some strange things to happen."

"If you mean I get hair everywhere and all that, I already know all about that. And in case you hadn't noticed, it's already started."

"I'm sorry I can't say I *had* noticed. I was thinking more about the way all those hormones that cause the hair and all those other things make you say and do strange things. It's really a chemical reaction. Mostly affects your head. You'll forget things. You'll do weird things. Stuff like that. Anyway, those of us who have already gone through puberty sometimes forget how confusing it all is, and we sometimes get angry when you forget things and all that. Now, you *could* take this for not loving you, but that wouldn't be right. I just wanted you to know that just because your mom or me might forget ourselves and yell at you that it doesn't mean we don't love you. I'd hate to think you and I would stop learning how to love each other just because you're going through puberty."

"And you're sure this is going to happen to me?"

"Yup! We all have to get through it. I thought I ought to bring it up because no matter how much we come to love each other–you and me, when all this crazy chemistry gets ahold of you, how much you love me or your mom just seems to go straight out the window."

"And this is the truth?"

"I swear to God!"

"And you will still love me even when this happens?"

"Yes."

"Is there any way to keep this from happening?"

"Well–short of castration, and maybe it's already too late for that– I don't know of any. Except that it's important we talk. You and me, you and your mom."

"And you and I can still talk about *anything*?"

"Yes. And I do mean *anything*. I promise I will always treat you as though you had a brain in your head, and I will respect your opinions. *But* I may not always agree with them. You have to accept that as part of the bargain too. And, if I ever forget, just remind me about our talk here today. I promise I will never judge you. I'll never ever say 'I told you so'. Now, do you think it would be okay with you for me to ask your mom to marry me?"

The boy raised himself on his knees and gave Flynn a strong hug and a kiss on the cheek. "Yes! I want you for my dad!"

Flynn returned the hug. He finally held the boy at arms length and looked into his eyes as he spoke, "Now, there is something I want from you."

"What?"

"Well, like I said, this matter of love and trust is a two-way street. While I expect you to be and act like a teenager, I want you to give *me* a little space when you don't agree with me. When that happens– and believe me it will– I want us to do what we're doing right now–talk. Man-to-man. About anything. Let me make this point. At your age, you are entering the most wonderful and confusing time of your life."

"And?"

"And– that's a wonderful and troubling time of life."

"Oh, you mean the girls."

"Well, there's way more to it than that. But girls *will* be a very big part of it."

"What else?"

Flynn got to his feet. "Let's walk a little. Okay?" Flynn led the way down the beach. The two walked side by side in silence for some distance before Flynn spoke again, "Well, you need to know as you begin to mature, your body is going to change even more—more than just the hair and all that. Maybe you know all this already, maybe not. But these changes will have a big impact on all of us—if we are family. These changes are caused by hormones starting to do their thing. A side effect for most kids—boys *and* girls— is these huge emotional swings. You are happy as a clam one minute and mad as hell the next, and for the life of you, you can't think why. You will think us older people are full of shit and don't know anything."

"No, I won't!"

"Yes, you will. But when that happens, remember what I said here today. I remember how it was when Monica turned thirteen. She was suddenly so ashamed of me she didn't want to be seen in public with me."

"You're kidding! Why? I wouldn't do that to you."

"You might. Like I said, when you're in your teens, you think your folks are old fashioned and totally out of it. So, don't make any great promises right now. Let life take its course. I take that back. I think there are some promises we can make. Let's make each other a promise right now."

"What's the deal?"

"Let's promise each other we will never ever go to bed angry with each other. Let's promise we will always try to respect each other's opinions about things. Let's promise we will always try to talk things out."

"I think I can live with that."

"Shake on it?" Flynn asked.

They did.

It was shortly after eleven when Neil went off to bed after giving his mom a big kiss and a strong hug for Flynn. It was the end of a wonderful day for Flynn, and he was alone at last with Megan. To further enhance the evening, Flynn built a small fire in the stone fireplace. Still dressed only in the bikini swim suit, which Megan had given him to wear, he felt the need for some warmth. All the lamps in the room had been extinguished, and only the flickering firelight lit the room. When he had the fire just right, Flynn sat in a nearby easy chair and gazed into the dancing flames. Megan entered the room, dressed in a flowing terry cloth robe, a brandy snifter cupped in the palm of each hand. "I thought it would be nice to sit in front of the fire and enjoy a brandy. Nice finish to the day." She handed Flynn a glass and then, sat cross-legged on the floor in front of the fireplace. Flynn slid off the seat cushion to join her. They sat shoulder to shoulder, leaning on each other. Megan broke the silence, "I was watching you two this afternoon. Looked like you were doing some pretty serious talking."

"Yes. We had quite a talk."

"Can you share it with me?"

"Some of it."

"Okay, tell me what you can."

"Well we talked about us—the *three* of us. And quite a bit about him and me."

"Share"

"Okay. I'll tell you what I think he wouldn't mind if you knew. *Some* of it, I've promised to keep just between him and me. Can you accept that?"

"Do I have a choice?"

334

"No. Well, Neil is very unsure of the future, but he very definitely wants us to marry. He's decided I might do right by you. Then, there was the question about would I take the two of you away from here after we got married. And so on. The more I think about that idea the more I think it is best that *I* make the move. I know the key to us being a happy family depends on what you want to do with your career and how Neil and I get along. He's your son. Somehow, he will have to accept me into your life as your husband and his father. Right now, he thinks it will be like falling off a log, but we both know it will not be as easy as he thinks."

For the next few minutes, Flynn talked about the boy's concerns and a few of the other things they had talked about. When he was finished, Megan said, "You know for a man who never had a son you're pretty perceptive."

"I went through it with Monica. I watched my friends with teenage sons go through it. I promised myself if I ever had a son I'd try to treat him with respect and to love him in such a way that he'd never ever wonder if I really loved him. It's a shame he has never had a man in his life. Somebody he could talk these thing over with. You know boys don't want to talk about personal things with their mothers. It's embarrassing. I hope you don't think I was out of line here."

"I've tried to talk with him about sex and all, but he just 'Aw Moms' me and takes off. I'm glad he listened to you. Frankly, I don't trust the crap they teach kids in school. So, I think you did him a huge favor. I guess you know that boy has fallen in love with you. I can see it in his eyes."

"Yes. I'd say he made it rather evident this afternoon."

335

"It's a huge plus in your favor."

Flynn spoke the words he'd been thinking the entire afternoon, "I guess it is. But it always puts a huge burden on the loved one. In this case, me. I'm afraid Neil has already put me on a pedestal. That's scary. I don't belong up there—he doesn't know that yet. It hurts a lot when you fall off a pedestal. If I have learned anything about family life, it's that second marriages and stepkids are a mine field! I don't expect any jealousy from Monica. She might be a tad jealous of you for a while, but she has her own man now, and she can let go thinking she has to care for 'her old dad'. As much as you think Neil likes me now, there *will* be some rough patches. It won't be all peaches and cream. We need time together—all of us. Let's just take these next few days to really get to know each other."

Megan set her brandy glass aside. "What say we begin right now?" She slipped out of her robe and locked her arms around Flynn's neck. Her bare breasts were hot on his chest. "You know how wonderful that strong, hairy chest feels on my bare breasts?" she asked.

Flynn was having some pretty serious feelings of his own. "Never mind how it feels to you—you can *see* what this is doing to me!"

"Well, then, take that bikini off ."

Flynn felt giddy and concerned all at once. "You sure Neil won't catch us?"

"He sleeps like a rock," she said as she released Flynn from the confining bikini.

Their love making was exploratory and tender. Flynn knew deep in his being that this woman was sent from God just for him. A lone thought of Mary passed through his mind. That was followed just as quickly by the belief that she would be happy for him. That she would want him to spend the rest of his life with someone to love and to be loved by in return. Neil was a definite bonus.

They stroked and kissed–made passionate tender love for as long as the fire lasted. As the last embers glowed faintly, Megan took him by the hand and led her man to the bedroom.

A noise woke him. Blinking the sleep from his eyes, Flynn sat up and listened. There it was again! He thought he heard the squeak of a floor board on the outside porch. Quickly, he tossed aside the bed sheet and crept to the central hallway. Taking care to remain silent and not to hit his bare toes on some unseen object in the dark, he moved toward the living room in the front of the house. Moonlight filtered through the gauze like curtains at the windows. Unconsciously, he held his breath and watched. There! He saw a shadow flit quickly past one of the windows. The shape was moving toward the front door. Was it locked? He couldn't remember. Quickly, he stooped over and moved across the room to the door. The dead bolt was, indeed, in place. The door was secure. Flynn moved as silently and as quickly as he could back to the bedroom. Megan's beautiful, nude body was lit by the same moonlight. He would not allow anything to happen to this woman! He crept to the bed and gently shook her by her bare shoulder. She awoke and was about to speak when Flynn placed a finger to his lips indicating silence. He leaned over and whispered into her ear, "We're not alone. Listen."

She sat up–listening as commanded. Seconds later, they both heard the squeaking out on the porch. "Quick–go get Neil!" she said. Flynn grabbed up his shorts and took them with him to the boy's room. He opened the bedroom door and saw that the boy was still dead to the world asleep. He put his mouth close to Neil's ear– "Neil!" he said in a loud whisper. The boy started to mumble something as he was suddenly recalled from a deep sleep, his eyes still closed. Flynn gently placed his hand over the boy's mouth. Neil's eyes snapped open– focusing on Flynn.

"Quick. Come with me now–right now!" Flynn ordered in his stage whisper. The boy rolled his nude body out of the bed. "My clothes. I don't have my clothes!"

"Grab your shorts. We don't have time to get dressed." Having said that, Flynn realized he too was still naked. Quickly, he stepped into his own shorts. He waited while Neil pulled on his own shorts. Then taking the boy by the hand, he led him back into the hall. They were met by Megan, now dressed in a tee shirt and shorts. "Listen, we've got to get back to the boat!" she whispered loudly enough for both to hear, "All our weapons are still on the boat."

"Mom, what's going on?" Neil asked, his own voice a stage whisper.

"Bad guys out on the porch," Flynn answered. "Megan, how do we get out of here?"

Megan thought for a moment. "Through the hurricane shelter's outside door."

"The what?"

"There's a hurricane shelter under the cabin. Quickly now– both of you– follow me and stay *quiet!*" She led the way down the hallway. Nearing the kitchen, she stopped and tossed aside a large throw rug. Pointing to a pull ring set in a large trap door, she indicated to Flynn that he should lift the door. Flynn lifted the door, which revealed a set of wooden stairs. Megan led the way followed by Neil with Flynn last, bringing up the rear. He closed the trap door. The darkness was total. Flynn heard a match scratch against a match box, and a single light lit the room. Megan took a kerosene lamp off a shelf and lit the lamp. Flynn looked around. The room looked to be about thirty feet square with the walls and floor of poured concrete. The ceiling was constructed of wooden "I" beams and heavy planking. One entire wall was taken up by steel shelving. He looked closer. The shelves were laden with canned foods, bottled water, kerosene lamps, cans of kerosene, a portable radio, and flashlights of different sizes complete with plastic-wrapped spare batteries. He went to the last item he saw on the shelf, a Winchester, 12 gauge, pump-action shotgun. "Where are the shells for this?" he asked. Neil reached under the bottom shelf and handed Flynn a full box of double aught buck. Flynn began filling the gun with the deadly shot. Megan pointed to a steel door at the side of the room. "That's the way out."

"Okay, what's the plan?" Flynn asked, still speaking in whispers.

"Simple. We get the hell out of here and to the boat."

"What's beyond the door?"

"There's a set of concrete steps leading up to a set of steel doors."

"Where do we come out?"

"At the back of the house on the side away from the cove. Near a stand of pines."

"How far to the boat from there?"

"We'll have to get to the trees, go around, and make our way down the hill to the pier."

"In other words, we'll be in sight of anybody standing on the porch." Flynn thought for a minute. "Is there any doubt in your mind that this is Santini reaching out for us?"

"It's a safe bet. In any event right now, it doesn't matter who it is. We've just got to get our asses on that boat!"

"If this set up was your dad's idea, he has my admiration!"

"He was an old navy man, believed in being prepared–for anything."

"Megan, I've been thinking our chances would be better if we waited until we knew they were inside the house before we made a break for it."

"I don't hear anybody up there yet. Neil, go up those stairs very quietly, and listen for anybody moving around up there."

"Before he goes, is there a way to lock that trap door from down here?" Flynn asked.

Megan began to rummage through the shelves, speaking as she looked. "Pop had some sort of a home made gizmo he said was for the purpose– Ah! Here it is." She held up a very large "C" clamp. Flynn climbed the stair, listened for a moment, and then, very carefully secured the "C" clamp in place. That done, he motioned for Neil to take up his listening post. "Neil, come back down here when you hear anybody in the house," his mother ordered.

"I think it is time we got that back door opened and checked out the escape route," Flynn observed. He went to the door and tried the simple latch handle. The latch lifted easily enough, but the door would not budge! He gave it his best effort, pushing with all his might. Nothing! "By chance, is there a pry bar among your dad's tools?" Megan went to rummage through the wooden box of her father's tools. She returned with a very large screw driver. Flynn was about to insert the blade in between the door and the jam when Neil spoke up. "I can hear people walking around up there!" he said in a loud whisper.

"People? More than one?" Flynn prompted.

"They're talking too. I think there's two or three of 'em."

Megan stated what they each felt, "Jesus! We've got to get the hell out of here!"

Flynn began to work the big screw driver at the crack between the door and the door jam. It took several attempts before he had managed even a small crack. He handed the screw driver to Megan and began to push. Every muscle strained. Megan put the shotgun against the concrete wall to join in the push. With both pushing, the door began to give. Suddenly, with a with a loud, metalic screeching, the door opened. Neil came bounding down the stair. "They heard! They're running all over the place." Megan snatched up the lantern as Flynn herded Neil into the stairwell and at the same time, grabbing up the loaded shot gun. As they gathered for the final effort to get out, they could hear the men above attempting to get the trap door open. Flynn went to the top of the stair, and grabbing the handle which would unbolt the double steel doors, he attempted to twist it. It too was frozen in place by years of rust. The pounding gave way to gunfire as the intruders attempted to shoot their way in. Flynn considered the damage a shot of double aught would do to the frozen latch. He herded Megan and Neil to the entrance door, instructing them to remain behind the door and to cover their ears. He stood on the opposite side of the opening, and shielding his body by extending only the tip end of the barrel beyond the casement, he took aim at the latch. Breathing a silent prayer this would work, he pulled the trigger. The doors literally blew open. Some of the shot richiocheted back but missed all three. With his head ringing from the noise and sudden pressure, Flynn motioned his two charges to follow. He ran straight for the small stand of pines at the back of the house. On entering the tree line, Megan took the lead and led the way up over the small hill and around the cove toward the pier and their only means of escape, *The Lady Grace*. She stopped below the crest of the hill, and placing a finger to her lips, she signaled for silence. She then crept up the small hill to take a look at the pier and the situation there. Bright moonlight bathed the scene below. She could clearly see a single man at the head of the pier holding what looked like a military assault rifle, the familiar curved magazine in place. He was looking toward the house where gunfire continued. She dropped below the crest and motioned for her men to join her.

She gave her assessment. "There's a man up there at the head of the pier with an assault rifle." She began drawing a sand picture of the situation. "Look–here's the cove," she said, drawing a large "C" in the sand. "And this is the pier and this, the boat," she said drawing them in the center of the "C".

"Now, I think we can go on along this ridge and get to the bottom of the cove, which will put us within a short swim from the transom. That is out of the sight of the house or the guy with the rifle." Flynn and Neil both nodded their agreement. Megan led the way to the end of the small rise. She again made her instructions. "Now, this is very important. Swim underwater for as long as possible. If you come up for air, do it as silently as you can. Come up easy. Don't make any blowing sounds. Denny, head for the back of the boat. There's a swim deck there that will make it easy to get aboard. Get over the stern as silently as you can and head for the salon and the forward arms locker. I'm going to cut the stern line. Denny, I want you to grab any weapon you want. Ammo is in the bottom drawer. Your job is to kill the guy on the pier and cut the bow line. Neil, your job will be to stay with me and do whatever I tell you—understand?"

Neil nodded his agreement.

"What's the go signal?" Flynn asked.

"The sound of your shot killing the guard. Don't wait for me. As soon as you are aboard, do your thing!"

Flynn handed over the shotgun and slid on his belly toward the water. As he slid in, he was once more surprised at the water temperature—warm. As Megan had explained earlier, it was the warm Gulf Stream water mixed with the cooler Atlantic. Tonight, he was grateful for the warmth. Taking several deep breaths, he took a bearing on the back of the cruiser, which looked to be about seventy yards away, ducked beneath the surface and began swimming. Flynn swam for all he was worth. He opened his eyes and was shocked at the sting of the salt water. He couldn't see anything. When his lungs could stand no more, he surfaced, gulping in great heaves of air. When he could see, his heart fell—he had only traveled about thirty yards—not even half way. Again, he ducked beneath the surface and struck out for the back of that beautiful boat. He had to surface once more before his head bumped into the bottom of the boat. Fortunately, he didn't hit hard, but it took him by surprise none the less. He quickly reached for the swim stage, which was affixed to the transom just a few inches off the surface of the water. He pulled himself up on the stage and raised his head to look over the stern rail and to check out the lone guard. He was nowhere to be seen. Quickly, Flynn vaulted over the stern rail and scuttled on all fours to the stair leading to the salon. He moved through the salon and to the forward stateroom where he opened the arms locker, and after giving the matter some thought, he selected a pump-action shotgun, loaded it with double aught buck, chambered a round, and began thinking how he'd accomplish his mission. He'd have to cut the bow line to the pier. He searched for a knife of some description, finally locating a fish scaling knife in one of the bottom drawers. Remembering the jump seat on the forward deck and the entrance from below, he opened the small access door to the chain locker and the jump seat. Praying he'd be silent, he grasped the operating lever and let the floor board portion of the seat down. Standing on the coiled nylon line, which ended at the housed anchor, he slowly raised his head. He could now look out across the deck with only the top of his head visible. His target was now on the path leading to the house, just watching the house. Flynn raised himself into position and took aim. Praying God would forgive him, he pulled the trigger. The resounding blast and flash of light lit the early morning darkness. When Flynn could see, he saw that his target was literally blown to pieces from the waist up. He jumped out of the small cockpit and located the bow line. He began sawing on the line with a knife he fervently wished had been sharper. As he sawed, he heard and felt the twin Cummins diesels come to life. The boat began to back down putting a strain on the partially cut line. To Flynn's surprise, the line parted with a sound like a gunshot!

As the big cruiser backed out of the cove, Flynn jumped back into the jump seat cockpit, ducked down into the small space, and emerged in the forward stateroom. Through the elongated portholes, he saw three men running down the path toward the pier. As the boat picked up speed, he heard a shotgun report and watched the three men fall to the ground.

Flynn ran through the salon and climbed the ladder to the flying bridge to join Megan at the helm. As he reached the top, he saw the three men were now running back up the hill. Megan put the helm hard over and took the big engines out of reverse. Shifting the transmission into forward, she pushed both throttles full forward. The throaty growl of the diesels filled the air as the twin props bit into the water. Slowly, the forward thrust overcame the heavy cruiser's inertia, and she began to pick up speed on a south heading. Flynn looked around for Neil. He leaned close to Megan's ear, "Where's Neil?"

"I sent him down to the master stateroom. I told him to stay there." She looked at Flynn's near nakedness and suggested it would be a good idea if he joined Neil in the stateroom and to found something warm to wear. "But before you do that, please go back to the jump seat, and close the hatch. I expect things are about to get rough, and I don't want to ship a lot of water."

Flynn did as he was told, no bucking the skipper of the boat! With the hatch closed, he returned to the master stateroom where Neil was sprawled in the huge bed, a set of earphones clapped to his ears. When Flynn entered, the boy pulled the earphones from his ears and looked inquisitively at Flynn.

"Your mom thinks I'd better find something warm to wear. Where should I look?" In answer, Neil bounded out of the bed and opened one of the smaller built in closets. "There's some warm-up suits in here. Kinda one size fits all thing." Flynn, noting the boy's nakedness, asked if maybe he too ought to get into something suitable. "I will after I dry off and get warm." With that, the boy returned to the bed and bundled himself in the bedspread. Flynn located a warm up suit, which looked as if it would do. He stripped off the wet shorts and donned the warm-up suit. In the bottom of the closet, he found some slip-on deck shoes, which proved to be a near fit, good enough for the time being. He quickly returned to the flying bridge and took a position next to Megan.

"Where are we headed?" Flynn asked over the roar of the wind and engines.

"Key West. The navy and the coast guard are there. We may need them."

"How long till we get there?"

"At this speed—about two hours. Denny, I need you to go light off the radar for me."

"Light off? What does that mean?"

"Turn it on."

"Okay, what do I do?"

"Down on the lower helm station is the switch. Can't miss it. It's labeled RADAR. Just turn the arrow from standby to on."

Flynn dropped down the ladder, quickly located the switch, and turned the radar unit on. A voice spoke at his back.

"What's up?" It was Neil.

"Don't ask me. I'm just following orders." Flynn noticed the boy had chosen a warm-up suit almost identical to his own. "Anyway, let's get up there with your mom."

They had no sooner reached the flying bridge when Megan ordered Neil to get the night glasses. The glasses were quickly produced. After sending her son back to the safety of the master stateroom, Megan ordered Flynn to look back in their wake to check the island and their wake.

"What am I looking for?"

"Another boat chasing us—*them!*"

Flynn was momentarily embarrassed that he hadn't thought of pursuit. He lifted the large lensed binoculars to his eyes. The constant rhythmic pounding of the big cruiser made it all but impossible to hold the big glasses steady. After several moments of trying to see anything, he gave up.
"I can't see anything!" he said in frustration.

"Come here, and take the wheel," Megan shouted over the wind and noise. He did as ordered at the ship's helm. Megan relieved Flynn of the binoculars and instructed him to hold the present course while she scanned the sea behind them. After several minutes, she returned to the helm, setting the glasses in a slot in the dash, which appeared to have been tailor made for them.

"God damnit! I was afraid of that," she yelled.

"What?"

"We *are* being followed!"

Flynn turned to look into their wake. He couldn't see anything in the darkness surrounding their phosphorescent wake. "Where? I can't see anything."

Without looking away from the radar screen Megan shouted her answer, "Dead astern. Just cleared the island."

"Can they catch us?"

"Donno. Depends on what they've got under them. It will take a few more sweeps of the radar to see what the speed differential is."

"How fast can we go?"

"In a fair sea, running at flank speed, about twenty-eight knots. However, in this rough sea, we'd be doing well to average eighteen to twenty." She turned her full attention to the radar screen. "Of course with this pounding, the radar isn't all that accurate."

"Can you make a good guess?"

"Well, like I said, this is only a guess. I'd say they can catch us in maybe thirty to forty minutes."

"So—what do we do now?"

"Call out the cavalry!"

"What?"

"The navy, the coast guard—hell the army! Anybody! Follow me."

Flynn followed Megan down the ladder to the weather helm located on the starboard side of the main deck just behind the salon. It was protected from the weather and held radio and other bewildering navigation equipment. At the helm, Megan engaged the automatic pilot and went down into the salon. From the cabinet next to the stair, she selected a rolled up coastal navigation chart and unrolled it on the galley table. As she studied the chart, she asked Flynn to get Neil.

Flynn went down the three steps into the master's stateroom to summon the boy. Neil was seated on the bed, listening to his walkman CD player. He pulled off the ear phones and turned the CD off. "We're in trouble, aren't we?"

"Well, I really don't know enough about it to answer that."

"They're after us, aren't they?"

"Yes."

"Close?"

"Well, your mom is guessing it will take them about a half hour to catch us. She wanted me to come get you."

When they joined Megan in the main salon, she was replacing the microphone on the ship to shore radio. "The coast guard is dispatching a sea king."

"What the hell is a sea king?" Flynn asked.

"A very big helicopter capable of emergency operations at sea."

"How long until it gets here?"

"Not coming here. It'll meet us where I expect to be in thirty minutes."

"Do you really believe we can stay ahead of them that long?"

"Fellas, we don't have a choice! I'll keep a sharp eye on the radar." She bent over the flat screen of the radar unit to re-check things. After several sweeps of the radar, she turned to her men. "Bad news. I'm guessing they have about a five knot or so advantage on us. They're still slowly gaining."

"So, how long before they catch us?"

"Well, all things being equal, I'd say maybe twenty minutes."

"Look, what the hell is a knot?" Flynn blurted out.

"For our purposes, it means they are about six miles an hour faster than we are."

Flynn digested the explanation. "So, the coast guard will get here—or rather–*there* a good ten minutes too late."

"'Fraid so. We're going to be on our own for a while."

"Time to do some serious planning then."

Megan called the two to the galley table where she could consult the chart and make plans. She noted their position, which she got from her GPS unit, and in pencil, she made an "x" on the chart. She noted with an "o" the boat chasing them. She took up a rolling ruler, matched its edge against a compass rose on the chart, and rolled the ruler to the "x". Flynn watched, fascinated while she extended a line from the "x" along their course. She picked up a set of dividers, opened them to match a speed line for along the bottom of the chart, and began to march them along the course line. When she'd marked off thirty minutes of travel at their estimated speed, she made a very large "X" at that point on the course line. "That's where the coast guard will meet us." Without looking up, she did the same for the chase boat. Given the greater speed of the other boat, there was no doubt they'd catch up well before the helicopter would arrive.

Flynn summed it all up, "Well, it's up to us to defend ourselves until the cavalry arrives. So, let's get to it. Let's see what we've got to fight with."

Megan led the way to the forward stateroom and the weapons locker. She threw open the doors and stood back to consider the best weapons. Of hand guns, they had plenty. Longer range weapons were a problem. There was a single Winchester thirty aught six, lever-action rifle and two Remington, twelve-gage, pump-action shotguns. Their double aught shot was terribly devastating at fairly close range. There was plenty of ammunition.

"It looks like a looser to me unless we play it smart," Flynn offered.

"What are you thinking?" Megan asked.

"Well, first, I think you'd better get back on that horn and let the coast guard know our situation—goose 'em a bit. Then, we need to think of some way to lure the other boat in close enough, so we can make the best use of what we have without getting ourselves killed."

Neil picked up a flare pistol. "How about this? If they get in close, we could blind 'em with a flare!"

"That's not a bad idea at all!" Flynn said.

"Neil! I want you to stay down here where you'll be safe!" Megan was adamant.

"But I can shoot. You know that. You taught me. I can shoot any of these guns."

"Honey, you're deadly against bottles and cans—but they don't shoot back. You'll stay down here, and that's all there is to it!"

351

"Aww, Mom!"

"Megan, go call the coast guard," Flynn said as he drew the boy under his protective arm. "Neil, help me haul some of these guns up to the salon and load 'em."

They selected both shotguns and two SIG Saur automatics. Flynn stacked boxes of double aught buck shells and boxes of nine millimeter hollow points into the boys arms. He also grabbed up four extra clips for the hand guns. Together they went to the salon and began loading the guns and spare clips.

Megan returned to the radio and lifted the microphone from its holder on the bulkhead. She keyed the mike. "Coast guard, coast guard. This is *The Lady Grace*. Over."

Static hissed from the speaker. Megan repeated the call. This time the coast guard at Key West answered, "Motor vessel, *Lady Grace*, this is Key West Coast Guard. Over." The man's voice was calm and unhurried.

"Coast Guard, how you coming with that helicopter? Over."

"*Lady Grace,* this is coast guard. Please, give your present estimated position. Over."

Megan took a fast reading of the GPS display, "About three miles off Big Pine Key." She also gave their course and speed to the unseen voice.

"*Lady Grace*, this is coast guard. Roger your present position. Wait one while I contact the helo. Out"

They waited in silence for the radio to come back to life. After what seemed an eternity to Flynn, the speaker crackled to life. "*Lady Grace*, this is the coast guard. Pilot says he's about twenty minutes away. We've vectored him to intercept along your present course–two-two-zero about three miles off the coast. He'll be guarding the emergency frequency; one-two-one point five. Over."

"Do you think the guys in that other boat can hear all this?" Flynn asked.

"I doubt it. The coast guard give me this frequency earlier."

"What about the emergency frequency?"

"Who knows? It's a crap shoot. Why do you ask?"

"I was just hoping they'd be scared off if they knew a coast guard helicopter was on its way."

Megan picked up the microphone again. "Coast guard, this is *The Lady Grace*. Over."

"*Lady Grace*–coast guard. Over."

"Coast guard, I hope your helo is armed. Our drug runner is about five miles astern of me and closing fast. I estimate your helicopter will be about ten minutes too late. Over"

"*Lady Grace*, coast guard. Helo is armed. I will advise pilot of your situation. In the meantime, I would advise you to go dark and keep your radar lit. Over."

"Coast guard, *Lady Grace*. Wilco. Out"

She turned to the two most important men in her life. They all must live. "Okay guys, we're going to darken ship. Turn off *all* the lights. Look everywhere, and *be sure* every light is off."Flynn ran to the forward stateroom and began switching off every light he could find. He was surprised how many were lit. By the time he returned to the salon, the boat was dark. "How much time do we have?"

Megan consulted the radar once more. "I'd say ten minutes at the outside." Megan's voice was wavering, the strain clearly showing.

Flynn felt the quickening of his own heart. "Don't worry– we'll make it. Now, what's the plan?"

"I think one of us should get up on the flying bridge and operate from there. The other should work from the well of the main deck aft. That way, we'll have fire power from two levels. I don't imagine they think we're armed. Could work for us."

"In that case, I think I should take the flying bridge."

"Good, I was going to suggest it anyway."

Flynn picked up one of the shot guns, a box of shells, and a SIG Saur with two loaded spare clips. He gave into his impulse, leaned in, and kissed Megan. She took his face between her hands and gave him a long, tender kiss. Neil embraced them both. Flynn kissed the boy on the top of his head.

He climbed the ladder at the back of the salon bulkhead and took his place on the flying bridge. Wind whipped around his body, and the pounding of the big cruiser as she smashed into the waves and slid into the troughs, made it impossible to stand. He realized his aim would be literally hit or miss. He decided to lay prone on the deck of the flying bridge. Gradually, he realized his night vision was improving, or maybe, the sun was coming up. Checking his watch, he saw that sunrise was still hours away. The semi bright moonlight made it possible to see a little way beyond the cruiser's wake. Megan's voice broke his train of thought and concentration.

"What?" Flynn asked.

"I said the radar shows them about a mile behind us now. Can you make out any lights?'

Flynn concentrated and strained to see anything out there in the dark– nothing. "No, nothing yet."

"If they're running dark too, we won't see them until they're on top of us."

"Think they have radar?"

"Bet on it!"

Flynn leaned over the back edge of the flying bridge deck so he could see Megan at the cruiser's controls. She appeared to be upside down from his head down position, but he could see and communicate with her.

"Can you put it back on auto pilot so you can watch the radar?"

"Yes. Why?" she turned to face Flynn as she spoke.

"I was just thinking we ought to let the radar be our eyes. When you see they're getting in close, I think you ought to take up a position behind something. A place you can fire from hiding. I don't think they can see me until I fire this thing."

"Okay, what are you thinking?" she asked over the roar of the engines and wind.

"They're going to come up from behind. Right?"

"Most likely. Maybe a little off to one side or the other."

"Any chance they'll just blow this boat out of the water right away?"

"If I was in their shoes, I would."

"I'm willing to bet they don't have anything more than those M-16's or whatever. Can they hit any fuel tanks? the engines? Anything vital right off?"

"The fuel tanks and engines are below the water line."

"Where's Neil?"

"On the floor in the main salon."

"Good. Okay, here's what I was thinking. Put his thing on automatic, take your weapons, and hide behind that thing at the back."

"You mean the transom?" she asked, pointing.

"Yes. Let's let them come in close for a good look. They won't be able to see either of us. We've got to get them close enough for these shotguns to be effective. I should be able to see them as they come in close, and I can get off a few quick shots before they know what happened. When you hear me fire, you can raise up and get off several shots before they can even react. At least, it ought to work out that way."

Megan thought it over and finally agreed with the plan. She shouted down the stair to the salon and ordered Neil to stay put until she came for him. She engaged the auto pilot, turned off all the dash lighting, and closed the cover on the radar screen. The pilot house was now completely dark. She took up her weapons and took up her position at the transom. She chambered a shell in the shotgun and waited.

Flynn edged his way back from the edge of the overhang. His position about fifteen feet above the water should give him the high ground advantage—he hoped. Satisfied with his position, he began to concentrate even more intensely into the darkness beyond the boat's wake. If Megan were right, he ought to be able to see something any minute. *The Lady Grace* continued her headlong plunge into the night.

After what seemed to be an eternity, Flynn was able to pick out a dark shape slowly overtaking the boat on the port side. He let out a whistle to get Megan's attention. When he saw that she had heard his whistle, he simply pointed toward the dark object. He continued to observe it as it inched its way nearly abeam of the cruiser. Flynn raise his head a few inches to get a better look. He realized at once that the other boat was painted a flat black. Not a shimmer or a single shine gave it away in the dark of night. He strained to see any human forms– none. Then the black intruder began to inch ever closer to *The Lady Grace*. When they were about ten yards away, Flynn raised himself above the railing, bracing the shotgun's stock against his shoulder, and sighting along the grove sight, he selected a point that appeared to be the mid point of the boat's upper deck. He pulled the trigger, and even before there was an opportunity to check for damage, he chambered another shell and fired again. Just as he was about to pull the trigger for the third shot, Megan raised above the stern railing and got off her first shotgun round. Flynn saw her shot obliterate the boat just above the waterline. Flynn fired again as the boat slowed and began to turn away from *The Lady Grace*. Megan got off another shot at the stern of the fleeing boat. More debris flew into the air from her hit. As he was cautiously admiring their handy-work, he caught sight of a shadow moving on the deck at the rear of the pilothouse. The shadow came to the port railing and raised a hand toward the receding black boat. Suddenly, an intensely bright red rocket appeared overhead, arching directly at the boat. Flynn watched in speechless fascination as the rocket landed on the boat in a shower of red and white phosphorous sparks. Megan's voice rang out in the darkness– "Hit the deck!" she screamed. Suddenly, the sound of *The Lady Grace's* diesels was overwhelmed by an explosion. The night was suddenly lit by an intense light. Flynn closed his eyes and covered his head. After several seconds, he raised his head–there, about twenty-five yards away was the burning hulk of the other boat. He looked down to the pilot house. Neil was standing at the rail, a flare pistol in his right hand. Flynn climbed down to join Megan as together they surveyed the satisfactory ending to the pursuers' boat. Neil turned from the railing, a huge, self-satisfied grin on his face. Megan cut the engines to bare steerage way speed and turned on all the boat's navigation lights. Satisfied everything was in order, she went to Flynn's side and placed her arm about his waist, drawing him near. Flynn reached out his hand for Neil to turn over the flare pistol. There was a fleeting look of disappointment on the boy's face as he handed over his prize.

"Hell of a shot, my man!" Flynn said as he took the gun. "Really put the finishing touch on everything."

"Hey–what about my performance?" Megan asked brightly, the relief showing in her voice.

"Oh, I'd say it was adequate–just adequate," Flynn joked.

"I'll show you 'adequate'!" Megan said as she threw her arms around Flynn's neck and began to smother him in warm, tear-stained kisses. Flynn let the flare gun slip from his fingers to drop to the deck as he took Megan in his arms. As they kissed, Flynn could hear the sounds of a helicopter approaching in the distance.

About The Author

One time seminary student, naval aviator, police officer, advertising executive, political insider, successful radio talk show host, and author. Quite a background for a story teller.

This Jesuit-educated American of Irish heritage brings this multifaceted background to bear as he tells his riveting tales of murder, intrigue and suspense. Finneran enjoys that most sought after of all reader reviews. "I just couldn't put it down!" Indeed most readers say they find themselves "hooked" after just the first two or three pages of his books! His dialog wins praise for its "naturalness". His characters are believable and easy to visualize. "and it begins," as Finneran says, "as all good stories do with – What if...?"

Murder in Two Parts is Finneran's second published novel. His first, *Retribution!,* is still selling briskly across the Internet.

For more about this author and his work, look him up at www.patrickfinneran.com on the Internet.

Printed in the United States
798200001B